THE
BLOSSOM
TWINS

BOOKS BY CAROL WYER

THE BLOSSOM TWINS

CAROL WYER

bookouture

Published by Bookouture in 2019

An imprint of Storyfire Ltd.
Carmelite House
50 Victoria Embankment
London EC4Y 0DZ

www.bookouture.com

ISBN: 978-1-83888-160-3
eBook ISBN: 978-1-83888-159-7

PROLOGUE

Seventeen-year-old Kerry's heart beats a frantic rat-a-tat-tat. This is definitely where she left Isabella, on the large, grassy bank opposite Sunmore Hall, next to the triumphal arch. They'd arrived early to grab the spot and she'd been sitting on a jumper, a smile on her face.

'Isabella!' Kerry calls. Her shout is instantly suffocated by the crowd around her, which leaps to its collective feet with a mighty roar as the main attraction, the boy band Blasted, takes to the stage. Whoops, cat-calls, whistles and screams lift into the darkened evening sky, which only minutes before was filled with an enormous murmuration of starlings, swooping over the illuminated stage as the crowd waited, the air damp with expectation and perspiration.

She's clutching the cans of Pepsi purchased from the drinks tent only thirty metres away. Where the hell is Isabella? *Her head swings left and right, sweeping along the grassy bank in case her sister has moved to an even better vantage point, but she can't spot her. She pushes past an exuberant foursome – girls her own age, in matching T-shirts emblazoned with the group's logo – now leaping up and down and singing along to the opening bars of Blasted's latest hit. One of them is waving a glow stick like a frenzied conductor.*

Kerry grabs the girl's arm and pulls on it, attracting her attention. 'Have you seen my sister? She was sat here next to you!' she yells. The girl shakes her head and turns back to watch the act, who are now strutting up and down onstage, encouraging their fans to join in with the song.

Kerry moves in and out between sweaty bodies, all the while hunting for her fourteen-year-old sister, in a pink T-shirt and ripped jeans. She'd no idea so many people would attend the free concert at Sunmore Hall. Thousands of people have poured onto the manicured lawns behind the hall, most of them crammed directly in front of the elevated stage. It's impossible to spot anyone close to her in the crowds ahead. Still she moves forward, hands clenching what were icy-cold cans, but which have now warmed. There's no reason for Isabella to have left the spot where they were sitting. It isn't in her nature to suddenly take off. That's one of the things she loves about her sister – she's reliable and compliant, more so tonight because it's thanks to Kerry she's been able to come and watch her favourite band.

She spins around and tries the opposite direction. Thoughts like congested traffic jam up one behind the other: maybe her sister has gone to the toilet, moved closer to the stage or spotted a friend and joined them. Each suggestion is rejected. Isabella wouldn't do any of those things. What should she do next? Return to their original place and wait in case she turns up?

Another thought bumps the others from her mind: she'll ring her. Kerry places the cans down on the grass, reaches for her phone in her back pocket and then dials the number. She presses her phone hard to her ear and sticks a finger in the other, and is relieved to make out ringing. The relief is short-lived. Isabella doesn't pick up and Kerry berates herself for her own stupidity. Isabella probably can't hear Ed Sheeran's 'Shape of You' ringtone, not with everyone now joining in with Blasted and singing at the tops of their voices. Bodies merge with bodies so now all she sees is a giant, dark monster. Pick up, Isabella. *It's hopeless. Her sister will be engrossed like everyone else here. She'll be singing along. She loves this track.*

Isabella will return. She can't miss the massive stone archway modelled on some ancient historic archway in Greece or France or somewhere. Kerry doesn't care what it is; all she cares about is seeing Isabella standing in front of it again, like she had been throughout the warm-up act. She's about to ring off when a flashing in the thick-bladed grass only a few centimetres away to her right catches her eye.

The mobile phone lights up again and she shuffles forward, swooping on it before it can be damaged. She stands up, aware of bodies pressing against hers, bouncing along to the music as if together on a ginormous trampoline, trying to take her with them, and she resists, sticking elbows into their sides as she recognises the pink, spotted case and stares at the screensaver. It is the face of her kid sister, grinning goofily. Why is Isabella's mobile lying in the grass?

The lyrics sung by those around her assault her ears like some doomsday warning: 'You're gone. Gonna miss you forever.' Chilled blood washes through Kerry's veins. Something terrible has happened to her sister.

CHAPTER ONE

SATURDAY, 11 AUGUST – MORNING

DI Natalie Ward stretched fully. The bed in the spare room was not as comfortable as the double one she'd shared with David for the best part of two decades, but it would do for a while longer until one of them agreed to move out.

She swung her bare legs out over the edge and forced herself up. It was only seven o'clock on a Saturday morning, but she was due into work at eight, and with DS Murray Anderson on a well-deserved holiday in Australia, she was a man down. The ill-fitting blind was down on the VELUX, the only window in the converted attic space, but it didn't prevent light from spilling in and illuminating the corners of the shabby room. They'd had grand plans to convert it into extra accommodation for one of the children, but they'd had insufficient funds to carry out a full restoration and now the room was little more than a storage hole, containing a single bed and boxes of memorabilia.

She ducked as she stood up and kept her head lowered. It was tight for space up here, and even at its apex she couldn't stand upright. She eased herself towards the stepladder and clambered down it onto the landing. It was a nuisance sleeping in the loft space, but she was not going to climb into bed with David. She'd made her choice and she would have to lump it until they could make proper arrangements.

David was obviously still hoping for a reconciliation but Natalie was not going to be swayed. She'd stood by him the first time he'd admitted to a gambling addiction that had wiped out their savings, and tried again after his addiction had caused him to be in a betting shop when their daughter Leigh had gone missing, but the final straw had been when he'd turned to drink and neglected to notice their son Josh had been experimenting with drugs. She might even have forgiven him one last time if it hadn't been for the lies. Natalie couldn't bear being lied to. Her younger life had been blighted thanks to dishonesty and she wasn't having it ruin her adult one.

She entered the kitchen, where David had set up a cup for her and filled the kettle with water, but the gracious act wasn't enough to change anything. He'd lied again. In spite of everything, he'd lied again…

Natalie is exhausted. Work and anxiety over Josh's recent behaviour have taken their toll. Besides, she has other, greater concerns. Her feelings for David have diminished. In spite of all his efforts, she simply doesn't love him enough to make their relationship work. She needs to end it before they rip each other to shreds and ruin everything they've built up together. It's going to be hard and she's not sure when or even how to tell him.

She pulls out the bottle of wine from the fridge. It's a decent wine that David bought especially for her. She idly lifts the lid on the ceramic pot that contains the housekeeping money she leaves for David to use, anticipating it will require topping up, and is surprised to see it hasn't been touched. How has David paid for the wine? She recalls he took Leigh out to McDonald's and bought a DVD too, and he was drunk a few times. Where did he get money to pay for alcohol? She hunts in the glass recycling bin but only discovers one empty cheap bottle of whisky and two bottles of wine that she consumed, along with the usual jars and fruit juice bottles. That in itself wouldn't normally raise any suspicions had David not been completely drunk on more than one occasion this past week. The fortnightly collection is in two days' time. Why are there not more bottles here? The only conclusion she can come to is that David has hidden the amount he's been drinking.

She wanders into the sitting room, where David, pale-faced, is watching a drama. She asks him outright, 'The kitty money hasn't been touched. How did you pay for this wine and the DVD?'

'I did a translation for somebody,' he replies casually, eyes locked on the screen. 'For cash. I used that money rather than touch the kitty.'

She sits down on the chair near him and looks at him. 'Who?'

'Who what?'

'You're deflecting,' she replies. 'You know exactly what I mean and you're avoiding the question.'

'For fuck's sake,' he grumbles. 'Don't you ever switch off from work?'

'Tell me the truth, David.'

'Why do you always assume I'm lying?'

'You're doing it again. I only asked you to tell me who you did some work for. You ought to be able to reply without flying off the handle.'

He snaps off the television set and throws the control onto the coffee table. His chin juts out and he says, 'I translated a short document for Evans.'

Evans is a small legal practice in Castergate, where they live. She sips her wine. Suddenly it tastes bitter. She puts the glass down. No matter what he says, she knows he's lying. She knows him too well.

'If I asked to see this document, you could show it to me? Or if I mention it to Ralph Evans, he'll know what I'm talking about?'

'Yes. We done here?'

'No.'

'Are you accusing me of something, Natalie? Because if you are, I'd tread very carefully.'

'Tell me where the money really came from. Did you get it through gambling?'

A small muscle in his jaw flexes repeatedly. He's angry but also cornered. 'It was a fucking scratch card. One fucking card!'

'That's still gambling whichever way you look at it. You promised, David. You promised me again that you'd stop all this shit! How many more times are you going to break your promises?'

'I've been attending therapy sessions. I had a blip. It isn't easy but I've done no harm.'

'Yes, you have. You let me down. You let us down and you lied to me.'

'Fuck you, Natalie. You have no right to take any moral high ground with me. You keep secrets and tell lies too.'

Blood rushes to her ears. He's right in that she has something she intends telling him when the time is right but she's never lied to him. A voice in her head contradicts her with a, But you never told him the truth either.

She's about to back down when he comes at her again with, 'So, you want to tell me anything, Natalie?'

Maybe this is the right time to tell him they should separate. She stares at the wine glass for the longest minute then speaks quietly. 'Yes. There is.'

Natalie checked her phone but had no messages. She'd half hoped Mike would have texted her. She hadn't heard from him since he'd left for a five-day break to Scotland to visit his parents, with his daughter, Thea. He'd been due back the day before but there'd been no news. Even though they'd decided not to take their relationship to the next level until she and David had officially split up, they had been staying in touch with texts, and at work. David wasn't making matters easy. He'd refused to move out of the family home, and without any regular income, it was difficult to see what options he had.

Natalie paid the mortgage on the house, so she wasn't keen to move away either. They were at a stalemate until they could reach a resolution. At the moment, they were considering options, but from where Natalie stood, there weren't many to choose from. They'd also kept everything from the children, waiting for Leigh to finish school for the summer then for both children to return from a week's holiday in Devon with Eric, David's father, and his girlfriend, Pam. They were due back tomorrow and it would be time to come clean.

Natalie flicked through an estate agent's site, searching for cheap apartments to rent. She'd finally decided that as much as she wanted to live here with her children, she was the only person who could afford to leave. She'd have to keep up payments on the house as well as rent, but if David could earn enough to keep food on the table for the children, she might manage. That apart, the children needed a parent at home, and with her working chaotic hours, she couldn't always be there for them; it made sense for David to stay, even if he hadn't proved himself to be trustworthy in recent weeks.

A rustling alerted her to his arrival. 'I'm seeing Paul today,' he said. Paul was his sponsor, the guy helping him with his gambling addiction.

'That's good,' she replied, slipping her phone into her bag.

'Want me to make the tea while you grab a bath?'

'David, there's no need to do this. It only makes it harder.'

'I'm only offering to make you a cup of tea.'

His face was unshaven but the stubble couldn't hide his sunken cheeks. The last six weeks had taken their toll on both of them. It would be a miracle if the kids hadn't picked up on what was going on.

'I've been thinking. It's not ideal but I can probably find a flat near headquarters for a while. A couple have come up for rent. I'll look at them after work or during my lunch break. You stay here until you can sort yourself out and get some regular work, then we'll decide what to do with the house. We'll talk to the children tomorrow and explain what's happening.'

His eyes filled. 'Do we have to? Can't we give it another go? I've not had another setback since July. You know I haven't.'

'It's gone beyond the gambling.'

'You mean Mike?'

'No. I mean I don't have the energy. I'm tired of all of this – the work, holding everything together, not being a proper mother because I'm always on shifts and never knowing if I can trust you.'

'Without a shadow of a doubt you can trust me. I told you. I'm seeing Paul again today and I can change. I dropped into the local florist's yesterday and they're looking for a new van driver to start in a couple of weeks. It'll be nine to three thirty so I'll be able to collect the kids from school and sort them out as usual.'

Her stomach sank. Her brilliant husband, who used to translate documents for a top law firm, had become a shadow of the man she'd married, and yet she felt nothing but pity for him. She was disgusted by her own lack of emotion. 'Forget the tea. I'll grab something at work.'

'Natalie. Please!'

'Don't beg, David. Leave it. We've said everything we need to say. It's a question of being practical. We have to consider the children. It's about them now. We should talk to Eric and Pam. They'll want to help too.'

David shook his head. 'When did you become so cold and unfeeling, Nat?'

'After you let me and the children down yet again, and after everything, you still lied to me – about drinking and gambling,' she replied.

'People fib all the time. I've not done anything out of the ordinary. I only told a few white lies to cover up my actions, not to hurt anyone.'

'Lies always hurt those you love.'

'Don't be so melodramatic. I'm not Frances.'

She bit back a retort. David certainly wasn't her estranged sister and he hadn't treated her as badly, but his lies, like Frances's, had their consequences. She walked away before they could turn the discussion into a full-blown argument.

Natalie eased out of her car at Samford HQ, her mind on the conversation with David. It was going to be almost impossible to juggle her working life and being a part-time mother without some assistance. Her suggestion to involve Eric and his girlfriend had been sensible. If David was to find employment, he wouldn't be able to be there for the kids. It was a holy mess. She didn't hear DS Lucy Carmichael call her name and only turned when the woman was right upon her at the entrance to the building.

'Sorry, I was miles away,' she said.

'Not surprising with all that's going on,' replied Lucy, lifting a hand in greeting to the desk sergeant.

Natalie halted at the machine and rested her pass on the scanner to open the glass doors, wondering briefly how Lucy could have guessed what was happening in her private life.

Lucy continued, 'Did you catch Dan Tasker on the local news last night?'

Natalie blinked quickly. Lucy was talking about the arrival of the new superintendent who'd replaced Aileen Melody. He'd been stirring things up and some of the officers were suggesting he wasn't just a superintendent, that he was really a hatchet man for the top brass, checking crime stats and performance figures, and that jobs would be lost.

'I missed it.'

'It was pretty much the same thing he told us when he took over. About how we're cracking down on crime and putting more officers on the streets. He certainly has a good television manner. Looked very relaxed and personable.'

Superintendent Dan Tasker had a strong Welsh accent that went hand in hand with his muscular build; together with his Brad Pitt looks, he oozed plenty of charm, but he came with a formidable reputation. Anyone who thought Dan Tasker was going to go easy on them was in for a shock. Natalie was keeping her head down. She'd got along well with Aileen and was slightly concerned that Dan would not be as flexible as her previous boss. There was something disconcerting about a man who could smile winningly at you one day and bawl you out the next.

'There's a rumour he's going to be mixing up teams for better performance.'

'I wouldn't stand for that.'

'That's a relief. It took a lot of persuasion to keep Ian on board. He'd definitely pack it all in if he got moved to another team.' Lucy was referring to the junior member of the team, PC Ian Jarvis, in his mid-twenties. His ex-girlfriend, Scarlett, had left him because of his job and the dangers involved in it. She'd taken their baby, Ruby, with her and now Ian only saw them part-time. He'd seriously considered giving up his job to be with them but was, for now, staying where he was – the force was his first love.

'You heard from Murray?' Natalie asked as they climbed the stairs together, stepping aside to let a group of officers come bounding past them. Murray Anderson was her other DS, a loyal and dependable character who was also Lucy's best friend.

'We spoke on Snapchat last night. He and Yolande were at Bondi Beach and it was only about thirteen degrees. You'd think they'd have planned their trip better and gone when the weather's crap here and better there. Such a goofball!' Natalie knew Lucy didn't mean it. She and Murray were closer than siblings. So close, he had donated sperm for her and her partner Bethany, so they could have a baby – a baby that was due fairly soon.

'At least it's been quiet while he's been away and we haven't been stretched,' said Natalie as they turned onto their corridor and headed to the office, outside which stood a multicoloured seven-seater leather settee. Ordinarily it was empty but this morning it was occupied by a dirty-blond-haired figure who leapt to his feet and marched towards them.

'Good morning, DI Ward, DS Carmichael,' he said, giving them both a polite nod.

'Morning, sir,' Natalie replied.

'Apologies for ambushing you, but my office is currently being refurbished so I couldn't invite you upstairs. I've got a case for your team.'

Natalie refrained from comment. The building was relatively new, and she was certain none of the offices required any redecoration or refurbishment, but undoubtedly Superintendent Tasker had requested it as part of the deal that had seen him transferred to Samford. She swiped her card on the keypad to unlock the door, which he held open to allow her and Lucy to enter before following them into the room.

He rested a file on the first desk and, without any preamble, began explaining. 'Last night, a free open-air concert took place at Sunmore Hall. Approximately five thousand people attended, including Isabella Sharpe and her older sister, Kerry. Kerry left her sister sitting directly in front of the triumphal arch in the grounds soon after the support act left the stage at about nine. Kerry was gone only ten to fifteen minutes maximum, but when she returned, her sister had vanished. She hunted for Isabella but couldn't find her. She rang her parents at nine thirty, concerned for her sister's safety. Isabella had dropped her mobile phone and couldn't be contacted. The parents rang the police. Missing Persons was alerted and given the circumstances of Isabella's disappearance, and officers were brought in to search the 800-acre estate. At seven twenty this morning, officers discovered the girl's body hidden under bushes in what they call "the kitchen garden".'

He opened the file to reveal a photograph of a fresh-faced teenage girl with long dark hair and a straight fringe that hung below her eyebrows, partly shielding eyes the colour of caramel. 'This is fourteen-year-old Isabella Sharpe. According to her parents, she's an A-grade student who doesn't have a boyfriend and who is the model daughter. I want you to head the investigation. You have an exemplary success rate to date, and we require a quick result on this. It's important we gain the public's trust and confidence. We need to constantly prove we have the right officers, resources and expertise to fight crime in Staffordshire. The police in this area have been getting bad press recently and it's imperative we sway public opinion in our favour.' He gave a smile that didn't reach his eyes. There was no misunderstanding the subtext. This was about statistics. Aileen had tackled crime and demanded the best from her officers to make the county a safer, better place to live; Dan wanted results for a different reason – to further his career. Whatever his reasons for assigning her this case, she would do her utmost to get a result, but in her own time, not because her superintendent wanted answers yesterday. A child had died in suspicious circumstances and that warranted a thorough investigation.

'Any news on how she might have died?'

'Not had that information yet. Ben Hargreaves is the pathologist on this. I'm banking on you to keep me fully updated.'

'Yes, sir.'

'Good. I'll talk to you again when you have more details.'

As he pulled away towards the door, Ian approached. Dan looked the young man up and down before saying, 'I heard you were involved in a vicious stabbing earlier this year.'

'Yes, sir.'

'And that you came back to work only a few weeks later.'

Ian flushed and nodded.

'Then I hope your tardiness today isn't a sign your standards are slipping.'

'No, sir. I was delayed in traffic.'

'Might be an idea to leave home earlier then,' he replied and walked off.

Lucy winced. 'Ouch! I didn't see that coming. What happened to Mr Nice Guy?'

Natalie shot a look at Ian, whose face revealed nothing but whose fists had clenched unconsciously. 'We've been assigned to a case,' she said, distracting him from the moment. 'Isabella Sharpe. She was at a concert at Sunmore Hall last night.'

'The Blasted concert? I was there too.'

'Really?'

'Yeah. I was up front. It was packed.'

'I'm guessing you didn't see this girl,' said Natalie, passing over the photograph.

Ian shook his head. 'It would've been impossible to spot anyone.'

'We need to join Ben at the scene. Do you want to start with getting information on her and the family? Send it across to me as soon as you have it. The girls were watching the concert from the triumphal arch. Do you know what that is?'

'It's a large stone monument at the far end of the garden on an elevated grassy bank. It's quite prominent.'

'Okay. Once you've got all the information on the family, start looking at social media and see if she'd intended meeting anyone or if anyone took any photos of the event last night that might show her... You know the drill. Also, Isabella dropped her phone so see if Forensics have sent it back and if anyone can analyse it. Lucy, you and I will head to the crime scene and then on to the parents and sister.' She picked up the file and examined the photo again before making for the door.

Lucy turned to Ian. 'Don't let him get to you.'

'I can take it. I'm fine.'

'Sure you are. Like I said… don't let him get to you. He's new to this job and is flexing his muscles, that's all.'

Natalie hesitated by the door before adding, 'I know we're down a man but we're not going to rush this investigation. We do it by the book, thoroughly, as we usually do, understood?'

'Understood.'

CHAPTER TWO

A popular stately home, Sunmore Hall stood five miles out of Samford at the edge of Whitmore Stanton, an ancient village mentioned in the Domesday Book and once a settlement in a forest clearing before becoming part of the vast Sunmore Estate. With a population of less than a hundred, chocolate-box properties, a charming church complete with bell towers dating back to the fourteenth century, a thatched manor house that was once the school, and a duck pond, the village was popular with ramblers wishing to stop off at the Famous Grouse pub.

Natalie had never set foot in the place although she'd often driven past, and to be now passing between the two cubic lodges with Tuscan columns that flanked the main entrance, she realised it was far larger than she'd imagined. Parklands ran the length of the sweeping driveway to the country house, but she wasn't interested in the architectural magnificence of the building or the sculptured formal gardens, or the visitor signs pointing to various follies and walks around the estate – she was focused on locating the kitchen garden. Pulling up beside a line of police cars, her eyes fell straight on a familiar figure standing next to one of the forensic vehicles – Mike Sullivan, head of Forensics. He spotted her car and walked across to join her.

Natalie greeted him. 'Have a good break?'

'Really good, thanks.' His eyes crinkled warmly. The smile said more than his words, but both had agreed to keep their private lives separate from work and so Natalie didn't ask for any more details or tell him how much she'd missed him. They'd chat about it later when they were off duty.

'You seen the victim yet?'

'Yes. She's around the back in the kitchen garden. I'm surprised she was found as quickly as she was. The place is bloody enormous. It could have taken weeks to locate her. Follow me. I'll take you around.'

She and Lucy followed him, first crunching over gravel then passing through an opening in the wall leading directly into the kitchen garden, a cool haven of exquisite perfumes from pastel-coloured climbing roses in a variety of mauves, lilacs, creams, pinks and pale yellows; they were trained against the walls on wires and complemented the pastel-coloured herbaceous borders, stuffed with flowers and plants that Natalie could not name. Several wooden benches had been set out for visitors to sit and enjoy the quiet shade of the garden and admire the geometrically designed potagers connected by brick pathways. Her eyes flicked over the symmetrical planting and neat tripods of beans aligned perfectly in rows, the weeping cherry trees with ripening fruit on slender branches, the neatly clipped topiary bushes in the shapes of card suits, and finally rested on the officers beside a large greenhouse.

Ben Hargreaves had finished examining the young girl who was on her side, facing the wall, glassy eyes wide open under the soft curtain of black hair. Her face was alabaster-white as if all the blood had drained from her skin, and her parted lips, a light blue. Dark strands of hair that had come loose from a neat ponytail stuck to her cheeks like thin black threads, and Natalie wanted to brush them away. The girl was no more than a child, and something inside Natalie snapped. How could anyone take such a beautiful, young life? The girl's arms were bent at the elbows, and her fists slightly clenched. Pink love-heart earrings glittered in her earlobes, catching the light as it bounced off the glass panels of the house next to her.

'Was the gate to the kitchen garden open?' she asked Mike, her eyes resting on the girl's face.

'It's always closed each night but it's not locked. The head gardener shut it last night and police found it open this morning when they discovered her body.'

Isabella's body had been left under a wooden arbour swathed with scarlet roses, barely hidden from view. Several petals had tumbled from the flowers and scattered around her body like floral confetti. Natalie spoke up. 'There's eight hundred acres on this site and yet the perpetrator brought her here to a place where she would be certain to be discovered. These gardens are used daily. The produce grown here is used in the restaurant and café and for selling to the public. Somebody would have found her sooner rather than later. That tells me whoever killed her wasn't bothered about hiding her body. There must be numerous places they could have left her. There's an enormous pond, endless woodland… so why here?'

Lucy scratched her nose and cast about. It made little sense. 'Maybe she'd arranged to meet somebody here,' she offered.

It was a logical theory. Natalie acknowledged it with a nod and turned her attention to the pathologist, Ben Hargreaves, who had finished packing away his equipment and was ready to tell her what he'd established. He removed his glasses and polished them on a sleeve before speaking. Natalie had noticed him do this on other occasions and wondered if it was to give himself a chance to collect his thoughts. He'd changed his look in recent months. Gone were the ponytail and permanent stubble, replaced by a short, textured crop and hipster beard. The round spectacles had been replaced by dark, square-framed glasses. Lucy had quipped he was channelling his inner Clark Kent but agreed his new look suited him. What hadn't changed was his attention to detail and tendency to explain all he had uncovered in a quiet but determined fashion.

'There's sufficient evidence to determine cause of death prior to autopsy: petechiae in both eyes, commensurate with asphyxia, scrape marks caused by fingernails, presumably seeking to free herself from the grip, and cutaneous bruising and abrasions around her neck and throat that all suggest she was throttled, and with some considerable force. I fully expect to find the cricoid cartilage fractured, along with the hyoid bone and probably the trachea too.'

Natalie understood the medical terminology and was aware that the cricoid cartilage – a ring of cartilage that surrounded the windpipe – was almost always fractured during throttling.

Ben continued, 'I'll confirm that later in my report. There are visible indentation marks here,' he said, pointing to the darkened area to both sides of her throat immediately below the mandible, 'that suggest the assailant approached her from behind. The tissue above and below what we call the level of compression has engorged slightly.'

Natalie peered more closely but could not see the swollen skin tissue he was referring to – his eye was far more trained than hers in such matters. She could, however, see the broken capillaries, the red spots in the girl's eyes and on her face, as well as the bruising on her throat, and minuscule scratches that had come from her neatly painted nails, and she could picture the struggle that had ensued. The girl was slight-framed and would have been no match for her attacker.

'Any other bruises on her body?' Lucy asked.

'None at all. All the bruising is around the neck area as you can see.'

'Anything under her nails?' Natalie asked.

'Nothing obvious. We've swabbed them.'

'She might have scratched her assailant.'

'We'll definitely check for blood and skin cells,' said Ben. He bent back down, placed a hand on the girl's arm and patted it, a gentle gesture that endeared him further to Natalie.

'I'm ready to start on her when you are,' he said as he stood up again.

'Thanks, Ben.'

He lumbered away, head bowed, case in hand.

Natalie turned towards Mike. 'Any more thoughts?'

'Can't see any evidence of a struggle in this area. If she did try to fend them off, she didn't do it here.'

'She might have been killed elsewhere and dumped here then?' Lucy suggested.

'I think that should be considered. Her clothing doesn't show signs of a struggle either – no dirt, stains, or rips, other than the fashionable ones on her jeans. Nothing to suggest she had time to react.'

'Think the killer surprised her?'

'That seems the most likely explanation,' Mike replied. 'We'll search the entire kitchen garden but I'm not hopeful, Natalie.'

'Why put her here? Why not somewhere else?'

Mike shrugged. 'Can't help you out with that.'

'The killer could have carried her anywhere in this vast estate, but they chose to place her under a rose-covered arbour. There must be some reason for that.' The curled petals, soft as silk, were lying on the ground near the body. One had dropped onto the girl's hair and Natalie's eyes were drawn to it, icy fingers curling around her heart as she recalled a similar scenario: twin thirteen-year-old girls, side by side, plastic bags over their heads and blossom scattered over their bodies. It had been her first murder investigation and had changed her forever. She caught her breath and calmed herself down. This was a different situation altogether. This girl had been placed under an arbour. The petals had drifted down of their own accord, not been placed deliberately on her body, but she asked the question nevertheless.

'When she was first found, were there many rose petals on her?'

Mike called the crime scene photographer across and they went back through the pictures together, standing so close she could feel comforting warmth rising from his body as they examined each frame thoroughly. 'Shit! There are quite a lot of rose petals,' she said, guessing there were at least fifty scattered over the girl.

'She'd been here all night and the arbour is covered in roses. Quite a few have dropped since we arrived, and one rose can shed a load of petals.'

She chewed at her bottom lip. Mike was right. She was over-reacting, but the images of the four girls who had died during what became known as the Blossom Twins investigation wouldn't shift and she shook her head to dispel them. She'd seen enough.

'Any idea where the triumphal arch is?'

Mike shook his head. The photographer knew and gave them directions. She thanked them both and, together with Lucy, left the cool garden behind, striding back into the sunshine. Shielding her eyes from the dazzling morning sun, she looked across formal gardens, swirling beds that drew the eye to the huge fountain, complete with sculptured storks or herons or some such bird, that stood beside the water edge. Together, they crunched up the wide, gravelled path past stone planters filled with fuchsia blooms, towards clipped hedges that separated the gardens from the grounds; once there, standing in a wide opening between stone pillars, they looked out at endless green dotted with white-suited forensic officers, like giant white daisies, and towards the mound in the distance on which stood a large triumphal arch.

A semi-dismantled stage, taller than them both, where the band had performed only the night before, stood to their left. Natalie recalled a documentary about one of her favourite bands, Bon Jovi, and remembered that when equipment arrived at a venue, it was set up in a predetermined sequence: rigging, stage set, lighting. The band's equipment was the last to be brought and set up, arriving in custom-made cases, and after the show everything would be packed in reverse and taken away in trucks. The wooden structure that remained in situ was probably due for dismantling today, but all the lighting and audio equipment would have been taken out immediately after the show. She wondered what time the site had finally emptied of people – crowds, riggers, carpenters, roadies and ground staff – and made a mental note to ask.

Lucy cocked her head to one side, her heavy blue-black fringe swinging briefly away from her face. The sunlight made the smooth scar across the bridge of her nose glisten palely. 'I don't believe she was killed over there. That's quite a distance to carry a body. How far do you reckon that is?'

'Difficult to say without walking it. Got to be about two hundred metres. Come on.' Natalie checked her watch and strode ahead. It wasn't difficult walking but it still took them over two and a half minutes to reach the monument. 'Must be that – more if you add in the distance to the kitchen garden.' Turning around, she looked back towards the hall and tried to imagine what the whole area had looked like the night before, filled with Blasted fans glued to their idols performing onstage. It was possible that the assailant had snatched Isabella from here and taken her someplace else before carrying her to the kitchen garden, but that would have been a risky strategy. The place had been swarming with people. It would have been difficult to escape attention, even in the middle of a crowd of excitable fans. The idea that Isabella had gone to meet her attacker seemed the most likely at the moment; however, Natalie had long ago learnt that she should not jump to conclusions. The Blossom Twins investigation had driven that point home. A shiver crept up her spine. She and the team on that particular case had screwed up completely.

'Maybe social media will throw up something useful,' said Lucy.

'Let's hope so. A free event attracting thousands with no ticket entry! Trying to trace everyone who attended is going to be nigh on impossible,' grumbled Natalie. 'Okay, I've seen enough. We'd better break the bad news to her parents.'

They returned to the car park, where Natalie halted beside the squad car. 'Hang on a second. I want to check something,' she told Lucy and headed back to the kitchen garden.

Mike and his team were combing the area – suited officers were even in the greenhouse and hunting through vegetable beds. Mike caught sight of her standing on the pathway and walked across.

'What's up?' he asked.

'The rose petals,' she said. 'There seemed to be so many. Are there any other rose bushes like that here?'

'There are some trained up the wall, I think,' he replied, pointing right.

She moved towards them and stood in front of the wall. Petals had tumbled from the branches here too but nowhere near the number that had fallen under the arbour.

'Different plant, different location, less sunlight – I wouldn't read too much into the fact there are fewer petals here,' said Mike as if reading her thoughts.

Natalie had worked some tough cases in her time, but none had left their mark as much as the Blossom Twins. Natalie still felt responsible for the outcome of that particular investigation, and the guilt that accompanied it had never left her.

'The similarity struck me, that's all,' she said.

The corners of Mike's mouth pulled upwards as he spoke gently. 'They were twins, Nat. This is a lone girl who came to a concert with her sister. The Blossom Twins were snatched together and deliberately laid out facing each other as if holding hands, and covered in blossom. Isabella isn't.'

'She's in a similar position to them.'

'She's on her side, true, but there's no plastic bag over her head and it doesn't look as if anyone deliberately scattered blossom over her.'

'I'm reading too much into it then?'

'You're making sure you don't overlook anything,' he replied kindly.

'I don't know what I'd do if…' She didn't finish her sentence, nor did she need to. Mike knew all about her and what she'd been through.

He brushed the back of her hand lightly with his and brought her back to the here and now. 'You won't be faced with that scenario.'

She didn't reply. She'd been momentarily dragged into the past and a case she'd tried hard to bury at the back of her mind. Every time something triggered it, she'd have panicky moments as she recalled what had happened. She had to be stronger and turn her attention to the investigation she'd been given to resolve, not beat herself up over what she'd failed to do in the past. 'Yeah. Cheers.'

He nodded and ambled back to his fellow officers. As she turned to leave, a scarlet petal fluttered onto the ground beside the wall. She scurried off before she could become lost again in anxieties and recriminations. She had a job to do and the past was exactly that – the past: unchangeable but always with you.

CHAPTER THREE

'I was only gone a few minutes,' Kerry Sharpe wailed, her voice thick with emotion. She curled onto her mother's lap and Camilla Sharpe stroked her daughter's hair, all the while giving Natalie the thousand-yard stare she'd seen too often on the faces of deeply shocked victims' family members. The woman hadn't processed the fact her daughter was dead.

PC Tanya Granger, a liaison officer with twenty years of experience in handling such matters, was bustling about making tea. Her bright red hair, recently cut short and feathered, seemed at odds with her homely features and round face, but Tanya was all about compassion and she would soon step in and look after the family, helping them surmount the difficulties they were bound to face. Natalie looked over the heads of mother and daughter on the settee, through the window of the ordinary brick-built house, over to another that resembled it. Hawthorn Close was one of the streets that made up this area of Samford, known as Appleby Gardens – residences that stood on what had once been magnificent gardens belonging to a Tudor manor house, destroyed in a fire. The close consisted of several sturdy houses, all similar in shape and size and designed without much imagination – nothing like the grand residence that had once stood upon this land. A woman pulling on the lead of a beige and brown chihuahua paused by the squad car and cast a glance towards the property. Spotting Natalie, she lowered her head and scurried onwards, the little dog dancing behind her.

Camilla swallowed hard and tried to speak but no sound was forthcoming. Her husband, Ryan, hadn't moved from his position in front of the unlit gas fireplace since he'd been told the terrible news. His head was lowered and his eyes fixed firmly on his slippered feet.

Kerry was the only person in tears, and her anguished sobs filled the room. Her mother continued to caress her silken hair until the girl finally lifted her face again. 'I'm so sorry,' she whispered.

Camilla shook her head and found her voice. 'Nobody's blaming you, really they aren't.'

'But… I was… in charge…' The words came in between gulps of air and her face, covered in angry blotches through crying, screwed up again like a baby who needed urgent attention, but this time she controlled her sobs, muffling them and making soft snuffles.

Natalie waited until Tanya had reappeared with mugs of tea and then urged Ryan to sit down. He'd refused before but now he allowed Natalie to lead him to a chair. Lucy kept to the side of the room next to a bookcase filled with numerous paperbacks. The sitting room was only just large enough for them all, and no one wanted to crowd out the family or suffocate them with their presence.

'Can you go through exactly what happened once more for us?' Natalie asked Kerry.

The girl was willowy and had a pretty face with bow-shaped lips and dark eyebrows that sat in two groomed arches over chestnut eyes. She looked younger than seventeen and Natalie couldn't help but notice how much she resembled her dead sister. Kerry held onto the tissues Tanya had given her and tried to regain sufficient composure to tell them.

'Isabella said she was thirsty so I went to the drinks tent straight after Linear Smooth finished their act. There was already a queue so I had to wait – probably ten minutes, maybe fifteen. When I got back, she'd disappeared and then Blasted came onstage and everyone leapt about and yelled and shouted and I couldn't call her or find her. People kept moving about and I tried to look for her… She wasn't there. I thought about her phone so I rang it and then I saw it lying in the grass and I knew something had happened but I hoped it hadn't – that maybe she'd gone to the toilet and dropped her phone. Nobody would listen to me. They were all jumping about in time to the music. I found one of the security people but he said she'd probably moved closer to the stage to see the band, or gone to the toilet and not been able to make her way back because of all the crowds, and he told me not to worry. I didn't know what else to do. I went back to the arch in case she turned up and then I rang Mum.'

Natalie gave her a concerned smile. 'It must have been really worrying for you.'

She nodded. 'It was.'

'What did you say to Isabella before you left to get drinks?'

'I told her to stay put and I wouldn't be long.'

'Why didn't she go with you to the tent?'

'We didn't want to lose our place. We'd got a good spot and we could see the stage clearly from it. We put my jumper down and she sat on it to spread out.'

'Was your jumper still there when you got back?'

'No, it'd gone.'

'What sort of jumper is it?'

'A pale blue one with a big white star on the front.'

Lucy made a note of it. Natalie continued with her questions.

'What was Isabella doing when you last saw her?'

There was a pause. 'Smiling,' came the choked reply.

'Nobody standing near you saw her leave?'

'No. There was a group of girls right next to us but they thought she'd gone with me.' She tugged at the tissues and tears leaked from her eyes.

'It's okay… It's okay,' said Camilla.

'Mrs Sharpe, how did your daughter seem yesterday evening before she left for the concert?'

Camilla raised her head and said only one word: 'Excited.'

Ryan rubbed a hand over his face and snuffled before adding, 'She was looking forward to the concert. Not stopped talking about it for days. I dropped them both off. She actually bounced out of the car.' His face pulled into a mask of anguish.

'She was excited about seeing the band?'

'Oh, yes. She knows all their songs. Drives us mad some days singing them.' He stopped himself suddenly and corrected himself before continuing. 'She knew all their songs.' He released a groan like a low roar and covered his eyes with his palms. 'Oh, Lord! Not Isabella. This can't be happening! She was such a happy girl.'

Natalie pushed on. It was imperative she gather as much information as possible even though it was painful for the victim's family. 'I know this is difficult for you but I need to be clear about what happened. Did you have a row or fall-out that resulted in her going off, Kerry?'

Kerry shook her head vehemently from side to side. 'No, not at all. It was exactly as I told you. I went to the tent and left her sitting on my jumper.'

Natalie watched the girl's reaction and couldn't detect anything to suggest she was lying. She was clearly very upset by what had happened and was harbouring guilt, but nothing else was evident. 'Did she usually do what you asked?'

It was Ryan who spoke up. 'If Kerry told her to stay put, she would have. She thought the world of her sister. I don't know what happened but somebody managed to move her from where she was sitting – whether that was by force or with lies or manipulation

I don't know, but I can categorically say Isabella would not have moved from that spot.'

'That's true. She was such a good girl. Really.' Camilla's voice cracked.

In Natalie's opinion parents didn't always know the hidden truth about their children, especially teenagers. Her own kept secrets from her and David – they'd found out Josh had downloaded porn and taken drugs. Heaven knew what else he and Leigh got up to that she didn't know about. It was possible the Sharpes were either very naive about their daughter or only recalling the best in her because they were in shock. Natalie had to ascertain the reasons behind the girl's death and form her own judgement, so she needed to start digging.

'Did Isabella have a boyfriend?'

Ryan shook his head but Natalie looked to Kerry for an answer. Out of all of them, Kerry was most likely to know what her sister had been up to.

Kerry blew her reddened nose and stared miserably at Natalie. 'No. She wasn't interested in anyone. She never mentioned anyone to me.'

'And she'd have told you if she had been?'

'Most likely. We were very close.' The girl began to sniff again as more tears tumbled.

Natalie wasn't sure how close a seventeen-year-old and a fourteen-year-old were likely to be, but she wasn't going to argue with the distressed girl in front of her.

'It would help us if we could look in her room. Would that be possible?'

'Yes, I suppose so, if you think it will help,' said Ryan. His voice was little more than a mumble, his lips dragged down as if being tugged by an invisible force. He began to stand up but Camilla pushed herself to her feet.

'I'll take you,' she said.

Ryan shuffled towards the settee and put a hand on her shoulder, and an unspoken communication – a shared grief – passed between them. He gave a gentle squeeze before withdrawing and dropping beside Kerry, where he placed an arm around her shoulder and drew her to him.

Camilla led Natalie and Lucy into the hallway but as soon as she put a hand on the banister to mount the stairs, she halted. 'I can't…' Her body started to shudder and Natalie had to speak in comforting tones to get her to release her grip.

'We'll go alone. Come back into the sitting room.'

Camilla unclasped her hand and allowed herself to be ushered back in, where she collapsed onto the chair vacated by Ryan and flopped forward, hands covering her face.

'Mum?' Kerry's eyes widened in horror.

Tanya scooted across and squatted beside her. 'It's okay. Let it out,' she said.

'Why her? Why Isabella?' The room filled with Camilla's cries, and as Tanya soothed the woman, Natalie and Lucy moved off upstairs.

The sobs followed them to the top of the stairs and through a door bearing a large gold outline of a star, in the centre of which was the name Isabella. Natalie's heart sank at the normality of the small room: the hastily made bed with a large cream teddy bear lying on its back, the discarded outfits left on the duvet. Natalie could imagine her choosing the one she wanted to wear to the concert. The room was filled with colour: a flamingo-pink LED lightbox set up with 'Let It Shine', a happy sloth mug, a rainbow candle, a collection of multicoloured Beanie Babies, a Gryffindor scarf hanging on a chair, the entire collection of Harry Potter books on a shelf next to schoolbooks and brightly coloured boxes containing jewellery, a personalised sequinned make-up bag next to a pot holding pens and pencils, and a notebook covered with jolly panda heads. Natalie opened the book. Isabella had been writing poetry.

Lonely, scared deep inside,
Terrified you'll recognise
The fake person that's really me…
My personal anxiety

Turn my back on all my friends,
Even those so dear to me.
I have to face this all alone…
My personal tragedy

Natalie read out the words, brow furrowed, then added, 'Think she was depressed?'

'Maybe, but these are lyrics from one of Blasted's songs,' Lucy replied, moving in to look over her shoulder.

Natalie flicked through the other pages.

'I think they're all Blasted songs. She's copied out the lyrics. Must have been a big fan,' said Lucy.

'She was,' said a voice at the door. It was Kerry, clutching the doorframe and staring at the room with large eyes as if seeing it for the first time.

'Hey,' said Lucy. 'Are you a fan too?'

Kerry shook her head. 'Not really. Isabella was more into them than me. I like some of their music but some are a bit heavy for me.'

'Like this one,' said Natalie, reading the title, '"Disenchanted".'

'Yeah. It's a bit depressing.'

'Isabella was a happy girl, though, wasn't she?' said Natalie, studying Kerry's reaction.

'Some of the time. She had worries like we all do.'

'Like what?'

Kerry blinked a couple of times then said quietly, 'School, pressure, friends.'

'Was she finding school difficult?'

'No. She was really clever, much cleverer than me. She found it hard to live up to everyone's expectations.'

'What was the problem?'

'One or two of her friends were only hanging about with her because she helped them with their work, and she was getting fed up with being taken for granted.'

'She tell you this?'

'Yes.' Kerry nodded but also rubbed her lips together as if there was more.

Natalie eased closer to her and spoke in a lowered voice. 'Was that all? Or was there more to it than that – was she being bullied?'

Kerry swallowed hard. 'Not bullied exactly, but a couple of lads asked her to do their coursework assignments for them. They wouldn't leave her alone until she agreed.'

'Did she say who they were?'

'No, only that she was glad it was the school holidays and she didn't have to face them any more.'

'Why didn't she talk to anyone about this?'

'She said it was easier to help them out so they'd stop pestering her.'

'She should have spoken to her teacher about it,' said Lucy.

'And what? Get beaten up or victimised?'

Lucy didn't reply. Kerry was looking upset again. Natalie took up the line of questioning. If these boys had threatened Isabella, there was reason to talk to them.

'Kerry, we must speak to everyone who knew Isabella. It might not seem important to you, but if you could give us some idea of who these boys are, it could help us find out what happened to her.'

'I really don't know their names.'

'Who might know?'

'Maybe her friend Minnie Corbett.'

'Can you give us any contact details?'

Kerry nodded and disappeared to write them down for Natalie.

'We need to get onto this sharpish,' said Natalie.

'I'll talk to Minnie if you want to stay here,' said Lucy.

'There's not much more we can glean here. We'll leave it with Tanya now and see if we can track down these boys.' Natalie turned one last time around the room, getting a feel for the girl who'd been murdered at her favourite group's concert. Her heart was leaden. Death was cruel but the death of a young person was such a tragedy.

With Minnie's address written down in neat handwriting, Lucy and Natalie departed and headed towards Tapleworth, a large market town some thirty minutes south of Samford and the police headquarters. Tapleworth was famous for its castle, dating back over nine hundred years to Anglo-Saxon times, which overlooked the wide River Taple, after which the town was named. The castle was a regular haunt for visitors, offering a variety of attractions throughout the year. Natalie and her family had come to watch the medieval jousting competition the year before, and had climbed the two hundred winding steps to the old bell tower to look at the spectacular 360-degree view over the castle grounds. Leigh had grumbled all the way up but had stopped complaining the second she'd looked out over the church and towards the town itself, declaring it to be 'seriously awesome'.

Minnie's house was a plain, end-of-terrace property on a busy street towards the centre of town. Natalie perched on the edge of the stool that had been brought into the cramped sitting room and sat opposite Minnie Corbett, sandwiched between her parents on the settee. On the floor directly in front of them, acting as a buffer between them and Natalie, was a large, curly-coated dog whose sad eyes reflected the heavy mood in the room. Minnie's mother, a scrawny-faced woman with bright pink hair, in shorts and T-shirt, held Minnie's hand tightly in her own. The girl had sat open-mouthed at the news of her friend's death and only now, thanks to her mother's cajoling, was able to answer Natalie's questions.

'You'd be helping us a great deal if you could tell us who these boys are who were hassling her to do their coursework,' Natalie said gently.

Minnie seemed to come out of a trance, her dark brows drew together and she shook her head. 'She wasn't being hassled.'

'Her sister seems to think she was under pressure to complete the boys' assignments.'

'That's not how it was. Isabella got paid to do them.'

Natalie tried to keep the surprise out of her voice. 'She charged people to help them with their work?'

'Uh-huh. Everyone knew how clever she was. She always got top marks in every subject. This year we started our GCSEs and began to get coursework assignments. Some of them were really hard so she sent a message out to everyone in our class that if they needed help, she'd give it to them – homework, coursework, anything like that. She charged ten pounds for homework and twenty for coursework help, depending on how difficult the assignment was.'

'How many people took her up on it?'

'She never really said how many had paid her, but I know she'd meet them in the library or go around to their houses to help them. She was saving up for a new phone cos her parents couldn't afford to get her a nice one.'

'Can you think of anyone who she might have helped?' Natalie urged.

'I saw her talking to Tim Dorridge and Fred Sheldon outside school a couple of times, so maybe she helped them. But I don't know who else.'

Lucy, who was sitting on another stool opposite the family, wrote down the names.

'Did Isabella get on with everyone?'

'Yes. Everyone liked her. Some of the boys were even a bit in love with her cos she was so clever and pretty, but she wasn't interested in them.'

'She wasn't interested in any boys at all?'

'She liked boys but she wasn't into them, if you know what I mean. She was more into having fun with us girls than getting into a serious relationship.'

Natalie was forming a picture of an astute, bright girl – one who almost sounded too good to be true, apart from the fact she'd been using her abilities to help others cheat.

'You didn't go to the concert at Sunmore Hall last night, did you?'

Minnie's father spoke up. 'She's a big fan but we were at my mum's sixtieth birthday party. It was a big family affair so she couldn't go.'

'Isabella invited me to go with her and Kerry,' said Minnie, her bottom lip beginning to quiver. Her mother squeezed her hand again but tears welled in the girl's eyes and she lowered her head.

'You've been really helpful, Minnie. Thank you,' said Natalie. She handed her card to the family in case Minnie could think of anything else that might help them, and then she and Lucy took their leave.

As they got into the car, parked directly in front of the house, Lucy said, 'Isabella sounds almost too perfect.'

'Doesn't she? Well, apart from helping her classmates get through their coursework.'

'We've all been there and helped out our mates though, haven't we?' said Lucy.

'Not for cash,' Natalie replied as she slid into the passenger seat. 'We ought to have her room checked again to see if we can find any money. Quite the entrepreneur, wasn't she?'

'Can't knock her for that.'

'Got those names of her classmates? I'll get addresses for them and we'll pay them a visit.' Natalie rang Ian for the information, and as she waited, she wondered if schoolchildren would be behind the girl's murder. It had to be checked out, but to her mind, this was the work of somebody more grown up. Somebody like the Blossom Twins killer.

CHAPTER FOUR

It had started off according to plan – the black T-shirt with 'Blasted Tour' written on it, along with a great deal of false sincerity, enough to cajole her to join him. Isabella had been sitting on the grassy bank, a grin on her face like she knew a joke she wasn't sharing, when he'd approached her…

'Hi. You Isabella Sharpe?'

'Yeah…' The voice is hesitant.

He leans towards her so the nearby group of chattering girls can't hear him speak. They're not especially paying any attention to him but he doesn't want them to hear all the same.

'Kerry sent me. She bumped into Callum Vincetti in the drinks tent and wanted me to fetch you to meet him too.'

'Callum? You're kidding me.'

The girl's face lights up like all her Christmases have arrived at once and she scrambles to her feet. She's so keen to meet the lead singer of the group that she doesn't even ask his name, trotting excitedly by his side like a puppy.

They edge through the crowd, him leading the way. The atmosphere is heavy with expectation and laughter. Some members of the crowd have brought in their own refreshments and are chugging bottles of beer or drinking wine as they wait for the star attraction to hit the stage. No one pays any attention to the man with his head bowed, making his way through them, or the girl following.

They emerge from the mob and skirt around the masses towards the stage in front of Sunmore Hall. He has to be careful here because the real crew are hanging about and so he dives off towards the side of the hall, avoiding the stage and the roped-off area where questions would be asked. They move away now, in the direction of the car park. Behind them is a collective hum of voices, like the biggest bee swarm in the universe, punctuated by high laughs or whistles as an invisible energy sweeps over the crowd, keenly anticipating the group. Lights on the stage flash on and off again, and a cheer goes up only to die away when it is realised it's just the lighting managers preparing for Blasted's arrival. The band is still inside the hall, preening themselves, practising, psyching themselves up, ready to strut and swagger and bound about the stage in front of their adoring fans. They'll be on very soon but there's still time to do this. Outdoor concerts are one of the best venues to steal children away without being spotted – no CCTV cameras, no one aware of what is going on under their noses.

'In here,' he says, passing through the open gate into the kitchen garden. There are no cameras here or any visitors – it is the perfect spot. He stops to check she's still buying his story and she draws to a halt, cheeks flushed in anticipation.

She reaches into her back pocket and her grin disappears. 'I've lost my phone,' she says.

That's a bastard. He's been banking on using her phone to draw Kerry to him, and now he can't. He'll have to return to the spot where he found Isabella and either look for her sister there or find the phone, and that could seriously screw up his plans. Shit! He wanted two girls not one! He tries not to show his disappointment and says, 'I'll go back and look for it. Don't worry. It'll turn up. People are always losing stuff at these gigs. I'll get a few of the crew to search for it.'

'I wanted to take a selfie with Callum.'

'I think Kerry's got her phone. She'll take the photo for you,' he says.

The girl's face relaxes again and her eyes dart about, looking for her sister. 'Where is she?'

'Behind the greenhouse. Callum didn't want everyone to spot him. Follow me.' He strides away.

Isabella, pursuing him, is keen to see her idol but becoming increasingly wary. Her voice is tight now. 'I can't see anyone here.'

'Hi, Callum, Kerry,' he calls, lifting a hand as if signalling to somebody. 'I found Isabella.'

The girl is still behind him. He turns, blocking the path, and smiles. 'I'll leave you to have a quick chat and go search for your phone.'

She is disarmed and as he moves away and slips on a pair of gloves, she wanders forward a few paces, looking past the greenhouse in search of her sister and the lead singer.

'Hello,' she calls in a halting voice but gets no response. She's about to spin around but it's too late. Her reactions are too slow and it takes seconds to clamp his hands around her throat. She goes limp quickly and he is instantly filled with the sense of euphoria that accompanies the act.

He raises his head to the darkened skies and smiles at the inky, infinite space. Blood courses through his veins like liquid gold and provides a magnificent surge of power. He is invincible. How he loves this feeling! The broken girl lies weightlessly in his arms. He knows exactly where he's going to leave her. He grits his teeth in annoyance. This isn't really the way he wanted to be remembered. There ought to be two bodies not one, but it'll be too risky to go in search of Kerry. He can't afford to be identified. He'll have to make do with one girl. He curses under his breath, then as he approaches the rose-covered arbour, he smiles. One girl will do for now.

CHAPTER FIVE

Tim Dorridge and Fred Sheldon, who had paid Isabella to do their coursework, only lived ten minutes out of Samford town centre in the same block of flats, overlooking an Aldi supermarket. Natalie had been pleased to find both boys at the Dorridge's ground-floor flat. Tim's father, Steve, a burly man, showed Natalie and Lucy in and settled them in the sitting room before calling the boys.

Tim was the first to slope in. He was pale and gangly with bad acne and a droopy mouth that seemed to stay perpetually open. Fred was the polar opposite: dark-skinned, short and slightly stocky but with a quizzical air. Steve planted his feet wide in the doorway, like a nightclub bouncer, and urged everyone to sit down.

'What have these two been up to?' he asked, narrowing his eyes at them both.

'Nothing,' said Tim, folding onto a narrow settee and sitting uncomfortably. His eyes flicked towards Fred, who merely shrugged.

'We'd like to talk to you about Isabella Sharpe. We were told she helped you with your coursework,' said Natalie. She couldn't be sure if the boys already knew Isabella was dead, but judging by their reactions, they were certainly concerned about something.

It was now Fred's turn to look at Tim, who shook his head slightly as if to warn him to stay quiet. Natalie caught the movement.

'There's no point in denying it. We know she helped you and you paid her.'

'What?' growled Tim's father. 'How much did you pay her? And where did you get the money?'

Natalie noted the man wasn't so much horrified that his son had been cheating but rather annoyed by the fact he'd paid somebody to assist him.

Tim's lips curled up in a sneer. 'It was my money to do what I liked with,' he snapped.

'You're a bloody idiot.'

'Yes, I'm an idiot, and that's why I got Isabella to help me with my coursework. I was never gonna pass, was I?' The sneer had intensified. 'Is that what this is about? Cos I paid Isabella to do some crappy coursework?'

'Sort of. Did you get a good grade for it?' Natalie asked.

'I got a C.'

'Not an A?' Natalie kept her tone light and was met with head-shaking.

'I didn't want an A. I'm not that fucking stupid. Teacher would've known straight away I hadn't done it myself if it was that good. C's a pass. I only wanted a pass.' He crossed his arms and scowled.

Natalie nodded in the direction of the boy's friend. 'Fred?'

'Same. I got a C. It was what I wanted. I asked Isabella not to make it too obvious that it wasn't my work.'

Lucy, who'd been making notes, asked, 'What coursework was it?'

Tim let out a derisory snort. 'English poetry. We had to analyse some fuck-awful poems.'

'Watch your mouth, Tim,' growled his father.

Tim glared at him defiantly. 'Poncy poetry isn't going to get me a job, is it, Dad?'

'That's not the point. Watch your mouth.'

Tim snorted again but didn't swear any more.

Natalie continued with, 'Would I be right in assuming then that you were both happy with those grades?'

'Yes,' said Tim.

'And did she help you in any other subjects?' Lucy asked.

'It was only that one time. I just don't understand the point of poetry! I'm not the only one who went to Isabella for help.'

Lucy kept her eyes on the boy. 'Do you know who else did?'

'No, but I'm pretty sure others did. It was a dead hard assignment and none of us, apart from Isabella, really got what we were supposed to do. Isabella finds everything really easy.'

Natalie noted that he was still talking about her as if she were alive. 'Did the teacher not suspect either of you of cheating?'

Fred suddenly looked at his trainers. Tim's arms tightened around his body. She'd hit a nerve.

'Well?'

Tim cleared his throat. 'Mr Nubuck saw me about mine. He was surprised I'd done so well.'

His father shook his head in despair.

'And what happened?' Natalie asked.

'He couldn't prove anything.'

'But he had a good idea you'd had help with it?'

'Yeah. She was supposed to make it sound more like I'd written it. That was part of the deal, but she didn't and there were some fancy words I didn't know in it. Mr Nubuck was going to fail me, but I told him I'd googled the words and he couldn't mark me down for effort. In the end, he said he'd pass me but he'd be keeping an eye on me.' His chin lowered as he spoke. He was disappointed to have been caught out, but to Natalie that seemed little reason to attack and kill Isabella.

'What about you, Fred? Did you get challenged over your coursework?'

'No, he said it was well-written and was pleased I was getting to grips with poetry.'

'You both like Isabella?'

Fred's cheeks turned crimson instantly and Natalie had her answer. He was clearly one of the boys who fancied her. He nodded.

Tim spoke less enthusiastically, his words and tone not quite as one. 'Yeah. She's okay.'

Natalie waited a second before asking, 'Where were you last night?'

Tim's father took a step closer to Natalie. 'Wait a minute. What's this about? Not about schoolwork, is it? Has something happened to her?'

'Could the boys answer my question, please?' Natalie said.

'We went to a concert at Sunmore Hall,' said Tim.

'That's right. I dropped them off at six and picked them up afterwards,' said his father.

'Whereabouts were you standing during the concert?'

'Middle-ish. In front of the stage,' Fred answered.

'Did you see Isabella or her sister, Kerry?'

Tim shook his head slowly. 'No.'

'Were they there too?' Fred asked.

'Yes. By the arch. Do you know where I mean?'

'The stone archway on the hill?' Tim's eyebrows drew together.

'That's it. Did either of you see them there?'

Fred shrugged. 'No.'

'Tim?'

He shook his head again.

His father intervened. 'Has something happened to this girl?'

'I'm afraid so. I'm sorry to inform you that Isabella was killed last night.'

The man stared hard at her. 'You're joking!'

'We found her body this morning in the grounds.'

'What happened to her?'

'I can't divulge that, sir.'

'You can't imagine for a second these boys are involved in any way, can you?' His face contorted with confusion.

'I'm unable to discuss the investigation with you, but I am obliged to question the boys,' Natalie replied, keeping her gaze on them.

Fred looked like he was going to be sick. Tim's mouth opened further. They'd clearly had no idea that Isabella was dead.

'Did you take any photos of the concert last night?' She directed her question at Tim, who nodded dumbly. He reached into the pocket on his jeans and extracted a mobile.

'Would you mind if DS Carmichael takes a look through them?' Lucy put her notepad away in her pocket and stepped forwards to collect the boy's mobile.

'Hang on a sec. What's going on here?' Tim's father had moved closer still and was now standing between Lucy and both boys, his large frame blocking her view of Tim.

'We're trying to establish your son's movements last night,' said Natalie.

The man spoke again. 'We already told you – they were both at the concert.'

'I mean while the concert was taking place.'

'We were just watching the bands,' said Fred.

'What about during the break before Blasted came onstage?'

'I went to the toilet,' Fred replied.

'Where was that?'

'Not far away, was it, Tim? Near the drinks tent.'

'Tim?' Natalie asked, waiting for confirmation.

'That's right. I stayed where I was. I didn't go anywhere.'

'Can you hand over your phones to DS Carmichael, please? I'd like to take a DNA swab too.'

'Whoa! You can't do that,' said Tim's father.

'It would be wise to let us, sir. Isabella was killed at that concert, probably about the time the boys were separated. I suggest you let us do our job.'

'We didn't kill her!' Fred squealed.

'Maybe not but you'd like us to prove that, wouldn't you?'

Tim's eyes grew large. 'What happens if you can't?'

'I don't think you need to be concerned about that, not unless you actually had contact with Isabella?'

'No. I didn't,' said Tim, who lowered his head again. His whole face was ashen and Natalie couldn't determine if it was because of the shocking news about Isabella or if he had something to hide. If it was the latter, she'd make sure she extracted it from him.

Natalie and Lucy were back at HQ, having finished with the boys. The DNA samples had been sent for analysis, and a call to Tanya had resulted in the retrieval of seventy pounds hidden in a sock in Isabella's drawer. The boys had confessed to paying her twenty pounds each so that meant there were other pupils who'd bought her services.

Natalie started with those in Isabella's class who seemed the most logical place to begin, but with the school holidays under way, trying to locate all the children was a logistical nightmare. Having only found four, all of whom denied having any assistance from Isabella, they were thwarted. Natalie was unhappy about wasting time hunting down fourteen-year-olds who, to her mind, were unlikely to be the perpetrators, yet she had to pursue the line of enquiry. She was pinning more hope on Ian, who'd been examining social media uploads and photos of the concert but not yet found any of Kerry or Isabella.

'There were hundreds of selfie-obsessed people there. This process is taking forever and I'm sick of grinning people,' he complained.

'Given your grumpy attitude lately, that's no surprise, but you're going to have to suck it up, Mr Chuckle,' said Lucy, staring at her own computer screen.

'You standing in for Murray? That's the sort of comment he makes.'

'You got it. His last instructions to me were to make sure you're kept in order, so I'm doing my duty.'

'When you speak to him next, tell him I hope it's snowing… no, make that hailing, in Australia.'

Lucy grinned.

Natalie, who'd been on the phone during their exchange, wandered across. 'That was Mike. Forensics have found Kerry's blue jumper.'

Lucy looked up. 'Where was it?'

'Draped across the car park sign.'

'Some kind citizen found it and left it there for its owner?' Lucy suggested.

'That'd be my take, unless the killer deliberately put it there to taunt us.'

'Is there any CCTV on the car park?' asked Ian.

'Don't know. Can you check to see?'

'Will do. It'll give me a break from the endless bloody selfies.'

'Jumper's being examined,' said Natalie, returning to her desk and studying the plan of Sunmore Hall. 'I wonder where she lost it?'

'Her phone was near where she was sitting. Maybe someone picked up the jumper from the same place,' suggested Lucy.

Natalie screwed up her eyes and tried to imagine how Isabella might have got from where she'd been watching the concert to where she had died. It was extremely unlikely she was killed on the very spot she'd chosen to observe the band. The area behind the archway had been filled with people, and behind that was more open field. A killer forcing a girl in that direction would surely have been noticed, although all attention would have been directed towards the stage not behind. She put her finger on where the drinks tent and the temporary chemical toilet block had been erected. How had the killer managed to swoop in on Isabella at that moment and get her away? It was a conundrum.

Ian spoke up. 'There's one camera overlooking the car park but it faces the entrance towards the hall.'

'It doesn't overlook the car park sign then?'

'No, 'fraid not.'

Natalie heaved a sigh. They couldn't get any leverage and that bugged her. It was coming up to five and she still had to go and view the flat for rent. There wasn't much more they could do until reports came in so she called it a day.

'And of course, it has an ample-sized kitchen with a view over the garden,' said the pleasant-faced woman, who twiddled with the front door keys nervously. She'd explained the apartment had belonged to her recently deceased mother, who'd left it to her two children. It had recently been painted and furnished functionally for letting, and to Natalie's eye, it wasn't as utilitarian as she'd feared. She suspected the cupboard doors in the kitchen had been replaced, and the monochrome black-and-white scheme used throughout the flat gave it a simplistic but artistic feel – not at all what Natalie was accustomed to. It might be stylish but not homely.

Their house in Castergate was a mishmash of décor and furniture – to some it might even seem chaotic, but it oozed family life. A band tightened around her chest. This was harder than she'd imagined. She drew a deep breath and clenched her fists briefly. She could get by here. Enlarged and framed photos of the children on the walls and a few knick-knacks and houseplants would transform the place. Cushions and furnishings would help too. Part of her didn't care. It was simply somewhere to stay until she and David could move on to something more permanent, once the family home had been sold. The thought was depressing, and for a brief second, she wondered if she had the mettle to see it all through. The heartache was only just beginning.

'So, do you like it?' the woman asked.

Natalie nodded and with that movement sealed the decision. 'It's very nice.'

'I expect you have others you'd like to look at but this is very convenient for the shops and there's a personal parking space that goes with the flat.' She turned the keys around and around the heart-shaped key ring.

The amount being asked was reasonable for a place in this area, and Natalie would save money on fuel. She made a quick mental calculation and spoke before she could change her mind.

'I'll take it.'

The woman gave her a smile that crinkled the corners of her eyes. 'That's great. Shall I let the lettings agency know, or will you?'

'I'll sort it out but I would like to move in soon.'

'Sure. It's vacant. That won't be a problem.'

Natalie skimmed over the room, pausing at the two-person round plastic table. A black vase and artificial flowers had been placed on it to add appeal to any potential renter. It was not her taste at all, yet what choice did she have? Stay with David or insist he leave the family home? This was a step she had to take, and even though she felt sick to the pit of her stomach, she shook hands with the woman. She was committed. Her life had just changed forever.

CHAPTER SIX

SATURDAY, 11 AUGUST – NIGHT

Erin and Ivy Westmore giggled loudly at the sound. Ivy rolled her eyes at her sister and said, 'That's not an owl.'

The tent zip unfastened and the grinning face of their father appeared. 'It was an owl. I frightened it off.'

Erin pushed herself up onto her elbows, the rest of her body hidden inside the quilted sleeping bag, giving her the appearance of a mermaid with a fat tail. 'That was so not an owl, Dad. There aren't any owls on our street.'

He remained on all fours, only his face visible through the flap. He grinned. 'Sure there are. Great big white ones that sit in the hedges between the houses, looking out for new masters or mistresses, although I'm not sure they'll be interested in a couple of muggles like you.'

'We're not into Harry Potter any more,' said Ivy, the thinner-faced of the two girls who shared many features: snub noses, electric blue eyes, ebony hair cut in identical long bobs that fell forward over their pale-pink cheeks.

Chris Westmore gave a smile and cocked his head. 'Really?'

'Really,' insisted Ivy.

'Fair enough. Listen, Mum sent me to see if there was anything you wanted. We'll leave the back door unlocked in case you change your minds and want to come in.'

'Da-ad! We're not little kids,' Ivy said.

In this sombre light he had to agree they both looked older than thirteen, and they were beginning to resemble his wife, Judith, more and more each day, but they were still his little girls and always would be. He adopted a more serious expression. 'I know you're not but if the temperature drops or you suddenly get anxious or need the toilet, you have a choice.'

Erin thrust out her chin. 'We won't, will we, Ivy?'

'Nope.'

He caught the determined looks on the girls' faces and held up his hands. 'Okay. Don't shoot me. I'm only the messenger. Mum was concerned. You know how she gets. I'll leave you to it. Sleep well, girls, and watch out for those owls. They might try and carry you off to Hogwarts.'

Erin released a soft guffaw as he retreated. Ivy smiled in spite of herself and watched as the tent zip slid upwards with a determined buzz, then she said loudly, 'Night, Dad.'

An owl hooted back and the girls sniggered. 'It's still a rubbish impression,' called Ivy. The owl hoots faded as he retreated and the girls threw each other a knowing look before snuggling further into their sleeping bags.

*

He sank back into his armchair with a sigh. Tonight had been a good night – a very good night. This time there had been no mistakes and now two new victims were awaiting discovery, entwined and together for eternity. Such sweet girls.

He smiled to himself. He was never going to get caught. The reason serial killers got captured was because they had no patience or couldn't resist killing – driven by a bloodlust, or simply because they became far too arrogant and made mistakes. He wouldn't fall into those traps. He wasn't going to get found out. He'd already bucked the trend by leaving a four-year gap since taking the lives of the Blossom Twins, and although the temptation to quench the murderous desire had always been there, he'd refused to give in to it – until now.

He rubbed his hands up and down the arm of the chair. It was soft and cool like the girls' flesh. He recalled his previous victims: sisters Sharon and Karen Hill and twins Avril and Faye Moore – with their unblemished faces and wide, innocent eyes. He had covered his tracks brilliantly, and for the last four years, he'd been able to bide his time until the right moment.

That time had come. He clenched his fist momentarily as thoughts turned to Kerry. She should have died alongside Isabella. They were to be the first pair – his announcement. He was still annoyed that his careful scheming had gone awry but what was done was done and there'd be no more errors. He flexed the tension from his hands – strong hands that had done their work tonight – and savoured the memory.

He relaxed once more, picked up the wallet resting on his lap and extracted the photo he'd kept in it all these years. He traced a finger over it – his girls. He stared at it and listened to the slow, methodical thudding of his heart. He was strong. He was untraceable. The police would never work out who was responsible because he was intelligent and cunning and he had used his time wisely since the Blossom Twins to plot the perfect murders.

CHAPTER SEVEN

SUNDAY, 12 AUGUST – MORNING

Natalie's neck ached and cracked as she turned her head. She let out a lengthy sigh. She'd have to furnish her new place, and beds were expensive. It would be so much easier not to make the move and stay here in a house she knew and loved, but that was the coward's way out and she'd made up her mind to move on. The children would be back home today and she and David would have to break the news to them. She really wasn't relishing the prospect but she reasoned that many children suffered family break-ups and came through them relatively unscathed. It would be down to how she and David presented and handled it. She wasn't leaving her kids, for goodness' sake, only their father. She'd be open about everything and assure them they would still have both parents' love and support.

She swung her legs out of bed and stared at her bare feet. Who was she kidding? It was going to be messy and painful and she wasn't sure she had the strength to go through with it. She rubbed her neck and tried to ease the tension out of her shoulders. What a way to start the day! Why was she putting herself and her family through all this? The answer came back sharply: she had to. She couldn't put up with David's lying or gambling addiction any more, and moreover, she had feelings for Mike, feelings she wanted to explore, but not until she'd done the right thing by David. Was she being selfish? The small voice in her head said she was but the other, calmer voice that had guided her throughout her life whispered, *You don't love David. It's better to break up now and give both of you a chance to make fresh starts. You'll only hurt each other if you stay.*

Shit, this was so hard! She shoved her feet into her slippers and decided to concentrate on other matters: the investigation. Rising carefully to avoid hitting her head on the ceiling, she navigated her way to the steps and back onto the landing. The door to their bedroom was firmly shut. David had been drunk and uncommunicative when she'd returned home so she'd left him to the television and his glass of Scotch whisky and gone for a bath then to bed, for a disturbed night full of doubts and concerns that seemed amplified in the dark.

She dressed in the bathroom, where she'd left her clothes the night before, and headed downstairs. Looking inside the cupboard for the teabags, her eyes alighted on a box of cereal – Leigh's favourite – and her throat constricted. All this normality would disappear once she moved to that flat. Was she really up to this? She shut the cupboard door and headed out to the hallway. She couldn't face being in the house any longer. She'd grab a tea on her way to work.

Ian was peering at his computer screen when Natalie arrived, takeaway cup of tea in one hand along with a bag containing a muffin that she didn't really fancy eating.

'Hey, you're in early,' she said.

'Couldn't sleep. Guy above me decided to play the drums at about three.'

'Nice of him.'

'Wasn't it? I was going to bang on the ceiling and tell him to cut it out but I figured he wouldn't hear me. Besides, he's built like a brick shithouse. In the end, I decided not to confront him. I value my good looks too much,' he quipped.

Natalie hoped she wouldn't have inconsiderate neighbours like that in her new building and placed her tea on her desk with an ominous sinking in her stomach.

Ian kept talking. 'I've found something interesting on these uploads. I've been scrutinising these pictures and I'm pretty certain I've spotted Tim Dorridge and Fred Sheldon, and if I'm not mistaken, they're very close to that stone archway where Kerry and Isabella were sitting. Let me just magnify it some more. Look.'

Natalie squinted at the screen and could make out a smiling boy. He had his thumbs up and was pulling a face. Behind him she could make out Fred and Tim, who were talking to each other, unaware they'd been captured in a photo, and behind them, the tall stone side of the archway.

Ian pulled up a second picture of the archway and zoomed in on it until they could compare the two photos and confirm where the boys would have been standing. 'That's definitely it, isn't it?'

'It certainly is and the little shits said they were nowhere near it. What time was that taken?'

'No timestamp on it, so I can't tell you. It was uploaded to the Blasted Facebook fan page, but I can't tell you any more than that.'

Natalie pursed her lips in annoyance. 'Lies. Why lie to us?'

'In my experience people lie when they're hiding something,' said Lucy, who'd arrived silently and caught the tail end of the conversation.

'Me too,' agreed Natalie. 'Right, we'll have to talk to them again.'

'Ben's report is in for Isabella,' Ian said.

'And?'

'She was throttled. Significant damage to neck and throat structures. The mean son of a bitch throttled her to death.'

'Poor kid.' She moved towards her desk and picked up her tea, sipping it slowly. It was too sweet and milky but it was still warm enough to drink, and as she did so, she caught sight of Mike approaching. He waved a file at her before entering the office.

'Morning,' she said, trying to keep the pleasure out of her voice.

'Special delivery – hot off the press,' he replied.

'What is it?' asked Lucy.

'This, DS Carmichael, is proof that one of your suspects had contact with Isabella Sharpe.'

Lucy spun off her seat and made for Mike, who gave her a warm grin. His good mood was infectious and lifted Natalie's spirits. Mike opened the file and pointed at the results.

'The lying toerag!' said Lucy.

Natalie read more slowly and shook her head. DNA on the back of Isabella's T-shirt matched Tim's and yet the boy had denied seeing the girl. Natalie seethed quietly then recalled the boy's tentative question about what would happen if DNA was found on her body. He knew it would be and yet he'd still allowed them to swab him. He must have known it would be traced back to him. 'That's it! We're going to talk to him immediately. In fact, we're going to talk to both of them and, if need be, bring them in.'

'Want me to continue searching through these photos?' Ian asked.

'Yes, in case any of Kerry or Isabella show up.'

Mike shut the file up and handed it to her.

'Thanks for getting this sorted in record time,' she said.

'Not my doing. You happened upon a quiet period, so we were able to get it processed quickly. We're examining Kerry's jumper at the moment.'

'Great, thanks.' She thought she should say more but Mike gave another small smile and turned away. Like her, he played by the rules – and when he was working, nothing interfered with it, especially personal life. Their relationship, such as it was, would have to wait until out of hours and until she'd moved out of the family home. The thought soured her mood again so she changed focus. Two potential suspects had lied to her. Could she potentially be close to solving this investigation?

*

A dog barked several doors down from the Dorridges' flat – the mournful, repetitive sound of an animal abandoned for the day. Curtains were drawn in most of the windows, including those at the flat where they were knocking. Natalie hammered again, for the third time, and stood back as a chain was drawn from the other side of the door. A pasty-faced woman wearing a shapeless nightdress and with pale hair that seemed to erupt from her head like tiny corkscrews emerged.

'What do you—' she began aggressively, halting the second she spotted the ID cards being held up.

'We'd like to talk to Tim, please.'

She withdrew into the house and eyed them cautiously. 'Why?'

Natalie didn't get a chance to respond because the dark shadow that was Tim's father appeared and moved his wife to one side, behind the door, with a large hand. He lowered his head and spoke quietly. 'My boy had nothing to do with that girl's death.' A vein throbbed in his bull neck.

Natalie wasn't going to be intimidated by this man. 'Could we come in, please?'

'No, you can't.' He kept a meaty hand on the door, ready to shut it in an instant.

'I don't want this to become awkward. We need to ask your son some more questions. Fresh evidence has come to light.'

'What evidence?' He glowered darkly at her.

'I'm not prepared to discuss that on your doorstep. Now, if you don't want us to come in, we'll have to take Tim to the station for questioning.'

There was a yelp from behind the door. 'No. He hasn't done anything.' The woman pushed her face past her husband to talk to Natalie. 'You can't believe he has.'

'We need to clarify a few things. Your son lied to us.'

'Let them in,' said the woman, speaking to her husband. 'We have to sort this out.'

His nostrils flared but he acquiesced and moved aside to let Natalie and Lucy in. Tim's mother had disappeared down the hallway, presumably to fetch her son. In the half-light, the flat was dingy, everything looking colourless. This time they weren't invited into the sitting room but were kept waiting in the narrow hallway, watched by Tim's father, who didn't speak.

It was a few minutes before the woman reappeared. She'd put on a dressing gown and slippers and waddled towards them.

'He's coming. Steve, why didn't you take them into the sitting room?'

The man shrugged and she scowled at him. 'Sorry. This way,' she said to Natalie and Lucy. 'Do you want any tea or coffee?'

'No, thank you,' said Natalie. Lucy also declined with a shake of her head.

'They're not here for a social visit,' snapped Steve Dorridge. He received an icy look.

'Politeness costs nothing,' she retorted.

The conversation was interrupted by the arrival of his son, head already lowered.

'Hello, Tim.'

The boy didn't answer but gave a small nod of acknowledgement. Natalie spoke to him.

'I have to talk to you again about Isabella. I asked you yesterday if you'd seen her at the concert and you told us you hadn't. I'm asking you again if you saw her.'

The boy's head seemed to sag further but he didn't respond.

Both parents stared at the boy and Steve stepped closer to him, putting a hand on his shoulder. 'It's okay, son. Just tell them the truth and they'll leave us alone.'

Natalie tried again. 'Tim, we know you saw Isabella. There's no point in denying it.'

'Don't put words into his mouth!' said Steve defensively.

'Tim, tell me what happened.'

The boy swallowed hard. 'I didn't see her.'

'Now you know that's not true,' Natalie answered.

'If he says he didn't see her, then he didn't!' Steve's eyes narrowed as he spoke.

'I appreciate you want to protect your son but I'm afraid he's lying. We have a photograph that puts him and his friend, Fred, by the archway where Isabella and her sister were watching the concert, and we've discovered DNA on Isabella's T-shirt that matches your son's DNA. He not only saw her, he was in direct contact with her.'

His mother put her fist to her mouth and sucked in breaths. 'No. Tim. Is this true?'

The reply was so quiet, Natalie had to strain to hear it. 'Yes.'

His father shook his head. 'Tim, mate, you said you didn't see her. Now you're saying you did. Which is it?'

'Okay. I saw her but not by the archway. I was there with Fred but that was before the concert began. We were looking for the best place to stand and decided to go closer to the stage. I swear I didn't see her then. It was later, when Fred went to the toilet. She brushed past me in a hurry. I didn't realise it was her to start with, and by the time I did, she was almost gone.'

'Where was she headed?'

'I don't know. She was pushing past people and heading in the direction of the toilets. She knocked into me and I said something like, "Watch it!" but then she was gone.'

'Was she alone?' Lucy asked. Tim looked up at her as if noticing her for the first time.

'I think so. I was on Snapchat with some mates at the time. I had my head down until she knocked into me. That must be how my DNA got onto her T-shirt.'

There was more. Natalie could tell by the boy's face. 'It's unlikely, Tim. You said she brushed past lots of people and if she had, we'd have multiple samples on her clothing, but we haven't – only yours.' She left her words hanging in the air and finally Tim's face crumpled.

'Okay. I did see her. She appeared out of the blue while Fred was in the toilets. I caught sight of her ahead of me, weaving between some people. I was still feeling pissed off with her about that coursework. She almost landed me in the shit big time with Mr Nubuck, and she'd been avoiding me since that happened. I called out to her. I was going to have a go at her about it, maybe get the money back, but she either didn't hear me or was ignoring me, so I pushed forward and reached out for her. I grabbed the back of her T-shirt and yanked on it to stop her, and she saw it was me and said, "Not now. Later," and raced off. That's the truth.' He looked from Natalie to Lucy and back again. His eyes were damp and his forehead creased with worry. He looked earnestly at Natalie who spoke.

'You're telling us you had no more than a couple of words with her?'

'Yes. She rushed off and I didn't see her again.'

'How did she seem?'

He shrugged. 'In a hurry. I wasn't paying attention. I was hacked off with her and wanted to tell her that she'd almost screwed up but she just smiled… really nicely at me… and dashed off.' His voice expressed his surprise at Isabella's reaction.

'You say she'd been avoiding you since the incident with your teacher?' said Lucy.

'That's right.'

'But you could have spoken to her on social media or rung her?'

'She unfriended me on Facebook and I don't have her number.'

Lucy asked, 'Why did she unfriend you?'

'I don't know. She just did.'

'We can check that out,' Natalie warned, hoping to make him divulge more, but he shook his head.

'I only ever spoke to her at school.'

'Did you know where she lived?'

'Not really. Somewhere on one of the big housing estates, I think.' His shoulders slumped and his face was a picture of misery.

'What about Fred? Was he not in touch with her?'

'Yes, but Fred really liked Isabella. That's the reason he asked her to help him with the coursework. He didn't really need any help but he thought it would be a way in for him, and he asked me to do the same so it didn't look weird. I didn't really care if I passed or failed. I hate poetry and English. I didn't especially want to cheat but he didn't want to ask Isabella on his own. He paid for us both. I didn't give Isabella the money. He did.' He looked at his father, who put a hand on his shoulder for moral support. The boy had shrunk, all bravado evaporated, to leave behind a scared teenager in a Superman T-shirt and pyjama shorts, and Natalie judged he was, at last, telling the truth. An interview with Fred would confirm his story.

'You said you thought she was alone when you saw her. You don't remember seeing anyone at all nearby who might have been following her, do you?' asked Lucy.

'Nobody.'

'Not even her sister?' Lucy held up the photo of Kerry to jog his memory but he shook his head.

'No one. She was on her own when I spoke to her.'

'And she didn't look frightened or worried?'

'No. She looked… happy.' The boy rubbed at his face.

Natalie decided to end the questioning and speak to Fred. This was looking like a dead end.

*

Dew sparkled like minuscule crystals among the blades of grass as Judith Westmore picked her way across the lawn in her fur-topped mules. The dampness seeped through to her bare feet but the

morning sun warmed her face. It was going to be another beautiful day. She'd slept like a log and hoped the girls had too. It was
already ten o'clock, and they were certainly having a good lie-in,
so maybe they'd been awake most of the night and were catching
up on their sleep.

She edged closer to the high leylandii trees that separated one
side of their garden from their neighbours', treading on flattened
earth rather than the grass. Ahead of her, a blackbird tugged at a
worm then scuttled away before she could reach it, its breakfast
in its beak. Beyond, tucked into the corner of the garden next to
her husband's shed, stood the bright orange tent that they'd dug
out of the attic for the girls, who'd decided they wanted to try out
camping the easy way: at home. She smiled at the thought. Her
girls weren't terribly adventurous, not like she'd been at their age.
She and her parents would often go camping or caravanning during
the school holidays. Erin and Ivy much preferred to be indoors on
their smartphones or play together in their bedroom rather than
go outside, so it'd been a pleasant surprise when they'd asked if
they could pitch the tent at the bottom of the long, narrow strip
of garden and try a night under the stars. Maybe they'd enjoyed it
enough to consider going on a proper camping holiday with her
and Chris.

Chris had mowed the grass the day before and now, as she
moved towards the tent, small clumps of it stuck to the soles of her
mules. She ought to have put on proper shoes. Still, these would
wipe off and dry out in the morning sun.

There was no sound from the tent. The girls were obviously still
fast asleep. She hovered outside, deliberating whether or not to
wake them, then decided she would and unzipped the flap quietly.
She peeped in then drew the zip down fully and dropped to her
haunches. 'Ivy? Erin?'

She edged inside the tent and patted the nearest sleeping bag. It
had been padded out with something. She felt inside it and with-

drew a peach-coloured dressing gown and floral pyjamas belonging to Erin. She tried the other sleeping bag and discovered Ivy's nightclothes inside it. Neither girl was there. Confusion distorted her features. The girls had gone to the tent dressed in these very clothes the night before, intending to come back to the house to dress the following morning. What was going on? Why had they removed their clothes and stuffed them into their sleeping bags? Where were her daughters? She backed out of the tent and stood up, turning a full 360 degrees.

'Erin! Ivy!'

There was no reply other than an angry chirrup from the blackbird, startled by her shouting.

The girls had disappeared.

CHAPTER EIGHT

SUNDAY, 12 AUGUST – MORNING

A saucer on the table was filled with cigarette ends. Mrs Sheldon had opened a window to clear the air when Natalie and Lucy had arrived, but the stale stench of nicotine permeated the whole apartment: the yellowed walls, the carpets and even the chair Natalie sat on. Fred Sheldon confirmed what they now knew: it had been his idea to approach Isabella for help with the coursework and he'd paid her forty pounds – the total cost for both boys – taken from his savings account. He sat on a kitchen chair with his mother beside him in a flat similar in shape and size to the Dorridge's, but three storeys above theirs. His mother, a woman with sallow skin, a heavily wrinkled brow and feathery lines around her lips that Natalie thought had come from smoking heavily, seemed completely overwhelmed by the revelation that her son had been cheating.

'Why?' she'd exclaimed. 'You've been getting good grades. Why on earth did you dig into your savings to pay somebody else to do your coursework? What were you thinking of?'

The boy hadn't responded, merely hung his acne-ridden face in shame while she'd ranted further until Natalie had stepped in. She knew why he'd asked Isabella to help with his work. Tim had already told her – the boy had wanted Isabella to notice him and that had been the only way he'd been able to get her to do so.

Natalie addressed Fred again. 'Tim admitted he saw Isabella when you were in the toilet. Did he tell you?'

'Yes. He said she'd gone by but hadn't stopped to talk.'

'Did you see her?'

'No, I didn't.'

'Tim told us you liked her a lot. Is that true?'

His cheeks flushed. 'Yes. I did.'

'And you followed her on social media?'

He nodded.

'Do you know where she lived?'

Another slow shake of the head. Samford was vast and sprawling, spreading into nearby towns and villages, and it was conceivable that the boys would not know Isabella's home address unless they'd asked about and tracked her down. Natalie lifted the photo of Kerry and showed it to him.

'Did you spot Isabella or her sister, Kerry, when you and Tim were standing near the stone archway?'

'If I had, I'd have probably gone over and talked to her, but no, she wasn't there.'

'Why didn't you stay by the arch to watch the concert? You'd have got a better overall view from there.'

'It was too far away from the stage for us. We wanted to be closer to the group.'

Fred had pretty much confirmed Tim's version of events, and although Natalie was fairly certain neither boy was hiding anything this time, she was maintaining an open mind. What she needed was more evidence – something tangible that would lead them to Isabella's killer. Currently, she had nothing much and would have to hope Ian found something in the uploaded photos or somebody came forward. They'd have to make a public appeal. She looked across at Lucy, who'd been taking notes throughout the interview, but Lucy gave a small shake of her head to indicate she had no ques-

tions to ask. Natalie wound up the interview, leaving a crestfallen
Fred to deal with his mother's wrath over the coursework.

Back again at headquarters, Ian hadn't made any headway with
the photographs.

'Not spotted the girls in any of these pictures,' he grumbled.

Natalie understood how huge the task ahead of them was.
'I'll talk to Superintendent Tasker about making a public appeal.
There are too many people to track down and question, so we need
somebody to come forward. Who was operating the drinks tent?'

'A company called DrinkQuick. They attend a lot of outdoor
events and are based in Wayfield.' Ten miles east of Samford, and
only a short drive from Sunmore Hall, the village was known for
its extremely large common, a popular recreation spot for the local
people and site for many travelling fairs.

'Contact them. Long shot but they might remember seeing Kerry.'

'You don't think she had something to do with her sister's death,
do you?' asked Ian.

'Got to cover all possibilities and check she was telling the truth,'
Natalie replied. That was how she operated. Everyone was a suspect
in her book until proven otherwise. She'd seen what happened when
investigations were rushed or suspects overlooked. Mistakes were
made, and that wasn't going to happen while she was running an
investigation.

She left her team looking into the family's background and
checking Isabella's social media accounts in the hope they'd flush
out some useful information, and headed upstairs to talk to her
superior. He wasn't there so she headed to reception to see if he
was in, only to be told he'd been called out.

'Any idea how long he'll be?'

The desk sergeant shook her head. 'All hell broke loose about an
hour ago. Couple of girls disappeared overnight from their garden,

where they were camping. Family's worried they've been kidnapped. He was headed across to liaise with MisPers.'

There were so many missing children. She hoped they found these two. She only had to think back to earlier in the year when Leigh had run off to recall the sinking terror that had filled every vessel in her body when she'd thought her daughter was in danger. Her heart went out to the parents.

She was at the bottom of the stairs when she heard the desk sergeant call out, 'He's back. Just driven into the car park.'

Natalie wandered back to reception and waited for him there. It wasn't long before an athletic figure strode purposefully towards the building and the automatic doors opened.

He caught sight of her immediately. 'You waiting for me, DI Ward?'

'Yes, sir, I need to talk to you about making a public appeal for anyone at the free concert Friday night,' she said in a hushed tone, matching his strides towards the stairs.

He halted and with a, 'Follow me,' turned on his heel, pacing down the corridor that housed the interview and briefing rooms. He stopped in front of the first interview room and, ensuring the green light was visible, showing the room to be empty, he opened the door and indicated Natalie should follow him. It was a room she'd used on many occasions, with a wide desk in the middle and four chairs placed around it. Against the far wall stood another desk, on which was the recording device. He stopped in front of the desk in the middle of the small room and, leaning against it, faced her, his eyes fixed on her face.

'I'm afraid I can't authorise that just yet. I've just heard that two sisters disappeared overnight from their back garden and we're planning to launch a television appeal in a few hours. It's imperative we bring the girls home safely. I don't want to run a second appeal before or immediately after it because we might panic the public if they assume there's a correlation between the two cases. I'm sorry, but Isabella is dead, and while I agree we must do everything in our power to bring her killer to justice, I have to prioritise the girls who are possibly still alive and well. If an appeal brings them home unharmed, it'll be a positive result, and then we'll consider asking for witnesses to the moments leading up to Isabella's death.'

Natalie screwed up her face. 'It's important we gather information as quickly as possible, sir. You must understand that. Her killer could get away if we don't.'

He crossed one foot over the other and sighed heavily. 'I fully appreciate your concerns but you'll have to consider other options and ways of tracking down people who might have seen what happened to Isabella. The twins' uncle works for the local BBC station and the parents have already reached out to him. They're convinced the girls have been abducted, and although we've yet to fully understand what happened, I am powerless to prevent them from contacting the media. I can only reiterate what I told you: we can't run a public appeal about missing children alongside one about a murdered child. People will be quick to jump to conclusions and we could have a PR nightmare on our hands if we don't manage it carefully.'

That was the real reason for his refusal: image. He was more concerned about HQ's reputation. She'd have become angry had it not been for one word. Natalie blinked several times quickly. 'Twins?'

'Yes, Erin and Ivy Westmore.'

Natalie's heart hammered a staccato beat. It was seeing the rose petals on Isabella's body that had brought back the memories of the Blossom Twins. 'Sir, how old are the twins?'

'Thirteen. Why do you ask?'

She didn't want to appear to be dramatic so she kept her voice even and her face impassive. 'Just that we had a case a few years ago when I was in Manchester – twin girls, also thirteen years old, were kidnapped from their front garden and murdered. I wonder if there's a possibility of a copycat killer.'

He maintained a steady gaze. 'MisPers are looking into it and trying to establish if the girls ran away. You know the stats as well as I do. Most children who run away turn up again within twenty-four hours. Let's not get ahead of ourselves on this, shall we?'

Natalie didn't appreciate his tone but answered with a quiet, 'Yes, sir.'

He uncrossed his ankles and pushed himself away from the desk. 'I'm sure a DI with your formidable reputation will be able to use other resources to help find Isabella's murder.'

'Sir.'

He headed for the door and left the room, his efficient footsteps ringing out along the corridor as he marched back towards the stairs. Natalie inhaled deeply then followed him upstairs, stopping at the first floor then pausing to think. It wouldn't be likely that a copycat murderer had snatched the twins, would it? The thought of the Blossom Twins investigation raised gooseflesh on her forearms. It had been a disaster. Whilst investigating the case, involving sisters Karen and Sharon Hill, they'd allowed the killer to strike again, this time murdering twins Avril and Faye Moore, before they could catch him. They hadn't acted in time and even to this day, she wished they'd made the right decisions that would have saved the girls' lives. She'd have a word with DI Graham Kilburn, one of the detectives who worked with MisPers and who had helped find Leigh. Although it wasn't her investigation or even her business to interfere, she had to check there were no similarities, if only to push aside the nagging thought that now dogged her. She had her own case to work and needed to concentrate on that.

Upstairs, her team were still hunting through information, heads down. She quickly dialled Graham's number and heard a gruff, 'DI Kilburn.'

'Graham, it's Natalie Ward. Are you involved in the investigation into the disappearance of the Westmore twins?'

'I am.'

She could picture the serious man in his sixties, with his world-weary look and balding head. The last time they'd spoken was soon after he'd brought home her own daughter. Since then, their paths hadn't crossed. 'Can I ask you for a quick rundown of what happened? There was a case I was involved in a few years ago. I don't know… I wondered if there were any similarities.'

'We're still checking it out so I can't give you much. They were camping in their back garden and disappeared sometime between 10 p.m. and 10 a.m. The only way in or out of the garden is via a tall wooden gate locked from the inside. This morning it was unlocked and we've found prints on the bolt and key that match Erin's fingerprints, so we assume the twins let themselves out.'

'There's no way somebody could have climbed over to get to them and walked them out of the gate?'

'They'd need to be one heck of a gymnast and silent. Nobody disturbed a pair of Rottweilers that live outside, two doors down from the house. Let's say it's unlikely. All signs seem to point to the girls letting themselves out. They left behind their pyjamas, and their mother's hunted through their wardrobes and thinks they're wearing matching jeans and orange-and-yellow striped tops and trainers.'

'Any reason for them to run away?'

'None that Mr and Mrs Westmore can think of. You can never tell with children. They can be very secretive. We're checking social media and their friends now.'

'No ransom?'

'Nothing.'

Natalie rubbed her lips together in thought. On the surface it appeared as if the twins had run away, but that's exactly what they'd believed about April and Faye Moore. *The rose petals are to blame for this sudden concern. They've rekindled bad memories.*

Graham spoke again. 'Sound familiar?'

'Sort of. In our case the twins were playing in an enclosed front garden. The mother wasn't sure if she'd bolted the gate at the time and we never worked that out. All we knew was that in the time it took the mother to clean upstairs, the girls had vanished.'

'Well, if there are any developments, would you like me to run them past you?'

'Would you? If only for my peace of mind. I'm probably being melodramatic.'

'Not at all. You're a mother. It's natural you'd be concerned.'

'I'll let you get on.'

'Thanks. We've deployed search parties. The parents want to make an appeal to the public so I need to brief them for that.'

'Good luck.'

She ended the call. There was nothing she could do. If anyone could find the twins, it would be Graham and his team. She had confidence in them. The small voice in her head whispered, *But what if it's already too late?* She blinked hard until it stopped. She had work of her own to do.

Lucy had contacted the DrinkQuick owner, Brent Harding, who was at home in Wayfield and willing to talk to her about the concert.

'You okay dealing with the background stuff, Ian?' Natalie asked.

'Sure. I'm going through social media at the moment. I printed out all the useful information I've found so far on the family. Kerry's a hair and nail technician at Sally's Bar. Sally's home address is in there too.' He indicated the folder on her desk.

'Cheers. I'll take a look at it in the car. Lucy, I'll come along too. We'll try and get hold of Sally while we're out,' Natalie said. Half an hour out of the station might help calm her anxieties, and she wanted a look at Sunmore Hall again to see if it threw any light on what had happened. Tim had said Isabella had been picking her way through the crowd. Natalie had got him to pinpoint approximately where he'd been standing on a rough plan she'd drawn and wondered if Isabella had been making her way to the kitchen garden. She collected the folder and joined her colleague, who was waiting by the door.

'Let me know if you spot anything at all,' she said to Ian. 'Anything at all.'

Without a public appeal for witnesses, she had a mountain to climb to track down the person responsible for Isabella's death.

CHAPTER NINE

It was almost midday when Lucy and Natalie drew level with Wayfield's large common, bordered by the main road and flanked to the rear by dense woodland. The car park was rammed with vehicles: caravans, cars of all makes and models, and a line of gleaming motorbikes whose owners, dressed in leathers, were gathered close to an ice-cream van, enjoying refreshing ice lollies. Little grass was visible, covered mostly by people in various stages of undress who were sprawled out, basking in the sunshine. A group of some fifteen children were attempting to play football in the only unoccupied area, while adults and youngsters alike sat in groups or lay out on towels, some under makeshift sun shades, as if on the beach.

Lucy let out a lengthy sigh. 'Hottest day of the year,' she commented.

Natalie mumbled a reply. She didn't care much for sunshine. Her skin usually turned red rather than an enviable shade of golden brown. She preferred bright days of spring when the air felt arctic fresh in the morning and gently warming by noon.

Wayfield was a small village of about 150 houses, and originally part of the Sunmore Estate. Most of the houses lined the route but Lucy branched off right down a winding road, past fields and character cottages, before arriving at Brent Harding's bungalow, discreetly located up a private drive. The property was a modest red-brick building with freshly painted grey frames and front door, and an adjacent two-bay garage with a matching grey up-and-over door. A life-sized sculpture of a bronze peacock stood on the neatly mown lawn, and borders under the windows were filled to overflowing with yellow and orange marigolds.

Brent Harding, dressed in khaki shorts and a white T-shirt, had spotted their arrival and opened the door, a hand firmly on the collar of an eager golden retriever. Lucy made the introductions and, after patting the animal, followed the man into a light kitchen with French windows that opened out onto a large garden. He opened the door to let out the dog, now straining to be released. 'Go on. Off you go.'

The animal tore off, leaving them in peace. Brent offered each woman a seat and dropped onto a cherry-red chair beside the round white table that overlooked the garden. The kitchen was fairly minimal and an aroma of burnt toast hung in the air. He dragged a hand through long, floppy, dark hair and said, 'How can I help you?'

Lucy conducted the interview. 'Well, as you know, we're investigating the murder of a young girl sometime during or after the Blasted concert on Friday evening. First of all, we'd like to know if you saw her?' She showed him Isabella's photograph.

His nose wrinkled and he shook his head slowly. 'Sorry, I don't remember seeing her at all.'

'She was wearing a pink T-shirt and ripped jeans and pink trainers. She had pink love-heart-shaped earrings,' she added in case Brent had seen Isabella close up.

'No. None of that rings any bells. The tent got really busy during the interval. If she'd come in beforehand, I might have stood a better chance of noticing her.'

'How big is the tent?'

'It's really two six-by-three-metre canopy tents that fit together to make one long one.'

'So how many people can you fit inside it?'

'Well, maximum is probably sixty, but with staff, folding tables, fridges and so on, I guess about forty or so would be queuing inside at any one time.'

'Do many people stay inside to drink?'

'No. It's not like a pub or hospitality tent. It's more like a shop. Once they purchase drinks they go back outside.'

'Did you serve alcohol?'

'No, it was a soft-drinks-only event. We were selling mostly bottled water and fizzy drinks. The venue doesn't have an alcohol licence. It was easier for us too.'

'How many of you were serving?'

'Five. There should have been six of us but one was off sick.'

'I'd appreciate names and contact details of the others, please.'

'Of course. I'll sort that—'

The rustling of bags caused him to pause mid-sentence and announced the arrival of a woman. Brent leapt to his feet. 'You should have called me. I'd have helped carry them in. You know you're supposed to be taking it easy.'

'I saw the police car on the drive,' she said, handing over the plastic carrier bags. 'I didn't want to interrupt.'

Brent stacked them on the floor by the fridge. 'This is my wife, Sophia.'

The woman came across and greeted Natalie and Lucy. 'You here about the girl who died at the concert?'

'That's right.'

'Terrible. Just terrible.' She tucked her shoulder-length auburn hair behind her ears and plopped down on the chair her husband had vacated. The dog had appeared by the glass doors and was waiting to be let in, tail wagging. She ignored its whines. 'That her?' she asked, nodding in the direction of the photograph Lucy had shown Brent.

'Yes.' She passed it to Sophia, who gazed at it sadly.

'She's about the same age as our daughter.'

'Isabella was fourteen.'

'Shit! So young. Alex is coming up sixteen. She's on holiday in Devon with her best friend's family at the moment. I miss her every day. Those poor parents. I can't imagine what they're going through.' She handed the photograph back to Lucy and shook her head sorrowfully.

'Were you at the concert?' Lucy asked.

'Yes, I was there. I didn't spot that girl though.' She glanced at Natalie, who was silently observing the interview.

Lucy kept up her gentle questioning. 'You might have seen her sister. She came into the drinks tent to buy two cans of Coca-Cola after the support act finished and before Blasted went onstage.' Lucy lifted a second photo, this time of Kerry.

Sophia shook her head but Brent's eyes narrowed. 'It was hellishly busy then… I'm not sure but I might have seen this girl.'

'She was in a blue sleeveless top and white pleated short skirt.'

'I think I saw her… Yes, I did!' His voice rose as he recalled the situation. 'I didn't serve her though. She was in my queue but just before she reached me, she changed her mind and wandered off. I saw her again a few minutes later. She'd joined the line waiting to be served by Fergus.'

'Fergus…?' Lucy waited for a surname.

'Doherty. He lives in Samford. He's working with us temporarily over the summer. He's off to college in September. Oh, you asked me for contact details, didn't you? I'll get them for you.' He stood up in one movement and headed over to the worktop, where he detached his mobile from the charging lead, scrolled through it and jotted down details on a scrap of paper.

'Any idea what time you spotted Kerry?' Lucy asked after he'd returned and handed over the information.

'Sorry, I can't help you there.'

'I don't suppose you noticed anything suspicious, maybe when you were packing up – anyone walking about alone, or anything at all that struck you as odd?'

He rubbed a hand across his jaw thoughtfully before replying. 'Nothing. Once Blasted took to the stage, we didn't get many more takers for drinks, so we called it a day and cleared up about fifteen to twenty minutes before the concert ended. My mind was on packing away and getting home. The band was playing. The crowd was singing along. It was an ordinary concert. Nobody strayed into the tent or past it that I noticed.'

'Sophia?' Lucy said.

'I didn't see anything strange. I waited in one of the vans for Brent to finish up. I was messaging our daughter, Alex.'

'Where was the van parked?'

'Directly behind the tent.'

'Could you show me whereabouts you were set up on this plan?' Natalie asked, breaking her silence and extracting the sketch from her folder.

Brent stubbed a finger at a point to the left of the stone archway.

'There. Off to the side,' he said. 'That's usually where we set up when we're at an event there.'

'And in which direction were the vans pointing?'

'Towards the hall and car park. We're allowed to drive along a cordoned-off strip of grass and into the car park, here,' he said, again indicating a spot near the car park.

Natalie thanked him and nodded as Lucy again started asking questions.

'You didn't spot anyone headed to or from the hall or car park, Sophia?'

'No. There were loads of people watching the concert. You couldn't identify individuals – it was like one giant mass. There were a few security people – men and women in black, standing around the perimeter – but nobody else I noticed.'

'Who drove the other van?' Lucy directed her question to Brent.

'Fergus.'

'And you all left about the same time?'

'Pretty much, yes. Fergus was last to leave.'

Lucy read through the names Brent had noted down, to ensure she had all the information she needed to track down these potential witnesses. She paused when she got to Fergus's address and asked, 'Was Fergus in the tent with you all evening?'

Sophia spoke up. 'Not all the time. He and Evie popped out to watch both groups for a while. One of the perks of the job. It's often quiet while the bands are playing so we let the staff go off.'

'But he was there throughout the interval.'

'Ye-es…' Sophia paused and her brow furrowed. 'Apart from when he went off to the van to get some more bottles of water. We were running low, or so he thought. There were actually plenty under one of the tables, but he'd overlooked them. He was only gone a few minutes. Do you think he might have seen something?'

'It's definitely worth asking him the question,' said Lucy.

Armed with addresses for the other members of staff, she and Natalie thanked the Hardings and left. Once outside, Lucy handed over the contact details to Natalie. 'Fergus's address,' she said. 'It's Appleby Gardens, the same estate where Isabella Sharpe lived. That's why I asked about him.'

'Okay. Better talk to him first. He might have seen her if he was watching the band from close to the tent. Kerry and Isabella weren't standing too far away from him. Before we question him though, I want to take another look at Sunmore Hall.'

*

Forensic officers were still combing the area at Sunmore Hall for evidence, and crime scene tape cordoned off the kitchen garden. Natalie got out of the squad car and tried to envisage the area filled with concert-goers. Ten toilet cubicles were still in situ in the car park closest to the field where visitors would have trudged to get into position for the event. She wandered past the toilets to the pathways. One way was signposted 'Chinese Pagoda' and led in front of the still erected stage and beyond into a more densely wooded area. The other, 'Triumphal Arch', took them along a path that would have passed the drinks tents and ended by the grassy mound and stone structure. The cordon designating the public standing area was still in place, attached to low stakes hammered into the ground and wafting in the breeze. It could easily be stepped over and served only as a marker for the crowds. Natalie imagined several staff manning either side of the arena or field ensuring the concert-goers didn't stray too far.

'How many security staff were there?' she asked Lucy.

'Thirty.'

'That's not a lot for a crowd of five thousand.'

'I spoke earlier to Vince Day, the head of operations, and he explained that the biggest threat to security is when you can't get people out of a venue. This was an open concert with stacks of ways to escape and no alcohol, so they put on the minimum number of staff. They expected three to four thousand people to turn up and worked on one member of staff per one hundred and fifty people. The band had additional security surrounding the stage to prevent fans from getting too close.'

'I assume they were all watching the crowds like they're supposed to – facing inwards and keeping an eye out for anything suspicious – and yet none of them spotted anything strange? Nobody noticed a fourteen-year-old girl slipping away or being taken against her will?' Natalie could barely keep the frustration out of her voice.

'It seems that way. I've requested details so we can speak to them individually but Vince says the first they knew Isabella was missing was when Kerry asked for help in finding her.'

'Bloody hell! Well, I want all the security people questioned. Make it happen.' Natalie marched back to where the tent had been and faced the hall, head lifted to see if the kitchen garden was visible from this point. It wasn't. The toilet blocks obscured the view. Even if Isabella had walked to the kitchen garden with somebody while Fergus was outside, he'd have seen nothing. She sighed with exasperation.

Appleby Gardens actually consisted of six streets that, from an aerial view, twisted and wound around a green park after which the area was named. While the Sharpe family lived closest to the centre in Hawthorn Close, Fergus Doherty lived in Gate Street, one of the streets furthest from the centre, which linked directly to the main road and was about five minutes on foot from the Sharpes' house.

Fergus had a sparse goatee and sandy-blond hair, loose-fitting clothes and glasses that reminded Natalie of Shaggy Rogers from the cartoon *Scooby-Doo*. Unlike that character, he was not laid-back – in fact, quite the opposite, articulate and eager to please, inviting the officers into his parents' house and taking them into the sitting room. He perched on the edge of an armchair, hands in his lap, and listened to what Natalie had to say.

'Brent thinks you might have served this girl, Kerry Sharpe.' She gave him the photograph to study.

His head bounced up and down immediately and he said, 'I know Kerry. We were at school together. I was in the year above her. She lives around here somewhere.'

'You don't know where?'

'No. I've seen her walking to the bus stop though, so I guess it's not far away. Yes, I served her.'

'Did she chat to you?'

'There was no time to chat. There were loads of people to serve. I can't even remember what she bought – two cans, I think.'

'You didn't spot her sister anywhere?'

'She wasn't with Kerry.'

'You know Isabella?'

'I've seen her around – with Kerry. I've not spoken to her though. Was she the girl who was killed?'

'Yes.'

He didn't reply, just gave a solemn nod of the head.

'You popped out a couple of times to watch the bands, didn't you?'

'Yeah, that's right. I sat on the van's bonnet and watched from there. It was as good a spot as any, better actually.'

'You didn't notice anything odd while you were there, did you?'

'No, I didn't.'

'How about later, after you'd packed away?'

'Nothing I can think of.' He lifted clear eyes and shook his head. His hands remained relaxed and in his lap.

'You left the tent during the interval to fetch some more bottled water. Is that right?'

He frowned for a second then nodded. 'Yeah. I thought we were running low. I went to the van to get some more. Found loads afterwards, under the table!'

'Again, you didn't see any unusual activity when you were outside at that time?'

He gave an apologetic smile. 'Oh, apart from when I was driving off. I saw Kerry with two security guys over near the toilets by the car park. She was crying.' His brow furrowed. 'Maybe I should have stopped.'

'You weren't to know what had happened.'

'No. But I feel rotten now. I didn't think it was anything important. I was tired and wanted to get home, and I still had to take the van back to the barn where it's stored and pick my car up from there.'

'At Brent's house?'

'No. He rents a barn from a farmer down the road from his house and keeps all the gear locked away there. Shit! I should have stopped, shouldn't I?'

'The police had been alerted by then. There wasn't anything you could have done.'

He blew his cheeks out. 'Wish I'd stopped though.'

It was only when she and Lucy were back in the car, on their way to speak to the other members of the bar staff, that it struck her that Fergus had seemed a little too helpful and certainly not dismayed by what had happened to Isabella. She voiced her thoughts to Lucy.

'What did you think of him?'

'He seemed pretty keen to assist but told us nothing helpful. Natalie,' Lucy cocked her head before continuing, 'I'm only voicing thoughts – probably crazy ones – but you don't think he could have somehow coaxed Isabella into the van and then killed her later, do you? Or is that too crazy an idea?'

Natalie's nostrils widened as she inhaled. Was it possible? 'Not too crazy. Fergus went missing for a while during the interval and he lives near the Sharpes. We'll look into his background to see if we can find anything else that links him to the family. Although, he'd have had to have been really quick off the mark, waiting until Kerry was in the tent, then disappearing, grabbing Isabella, getting her into the van, returning and serving Kerry.'

'Nah, you're right. Now you say it, it sounds too far-fetched. Like I said, I was chucking it out there.'

'Always worth bouncing ideas around. We don't have anything else to go on at the moment.' Natalie fell silent again. Had she detected anything while talking to Fergus that made her suspect him in any way? The answer was no but that didn't mean Lucy was wrong, and Natalie was more than happy to explore every avenue if it led them to the killer.

CHAPTER TEN

SUNDAY, 12 AUGUST – LATE AFTERNOON

Evie, the final member of the DrinkQuick team who'd been working in the drinks tent, had noticed nothing unusual and didn't recognise the photos of either Isabella or Kerry. With that, Natalie and Lucy returned to Samford for their final interview.

Sunlight poured through the glass of the hairdressing salon where they'd arranged to meet the owner, Sally Downs. It was a modern shop, set up in what had once been an old pub, and consisted of two rooms. Sally had tried to preserve some of its history by keeping a lot of the original features: a large fireplace in the front room and black timbered beams that ran across the ceiling as well as four uprights that served to separate the rooms. Opposite the fireplace was a black two-seater settee, and identical black padded chairs were lined up in front of four round mirrors. Fairy lights filled the hearth of the fireplace to give the impression of twinkling flames, and photographs of stylish young men and women hung above it.

Sally's keys rattled as she dropped them onto the counter beside her bag. Natalie had read her file and knew she was close to her own age – mid-forties – although with her expert make-up and lengthy blonde hair extensions, Sally could pass for younger.

'It's good of you to meet us,' Natalie said.

'I had to come in to sort out some stuff for tomorrow anyway.'

'I take it you've heard about Isabella Sharpe?'

Sally looked downwards. 'Yes. Kerry's dad rang me earlier to say she wouldn't be in work this week. I really feel for the kid – for all of them.'

'Did you know Isabella?'

'Sort of. She dropped in a couple of times to say hi to Kerry.'

'They got on well, then?'

'Oh goodness, yes. The way Kerry talked about her, you'd sometimes think they were twins, not sisters. They seemed to hang out together in spite of the age difference.'

Natalie felt an invisible hand squeezing her heart at the mention of twins and her thoughts flashed back to Graham. She hoped he'd found the Westmore girls by now.

'Did Kerry tell you about the concert?'

Her face became even more serious. 'She did. She was so looking forward to it. What a tragedy. I don't know how she'll get over this.' Her eyes filled and she held up a hand to indicate she couldn't speak for the moment. After several sniffs, she tried again. 'I hope you catch the monster who's done this.'

Natalie fully intended to but she couldn't make promises. They needed evidence and lucky breaks if they were going to nail the bastard who'd murdered Isabella. She feared there wasn't much Sally could tell them but went through the motions and asked her what she knew about Kerry and Isabella.

'Like I said, they were very close. There was no doubt Kerry admired her. Kerry left school with a couple of GCSEs but Isabella was smarter and Kerry was really proud of her little sister.'

'You don't think there was any animosity between them?'

'Gosh, far from it. I used to hear her chatting animatedly about her sister to clients. I can't imagine what it'll be like for her now Isabella's gone.'

Lucy cleared her throat before speaking. 'Kerry hasn't seemed distracted or worried recently, has she?'

'No more than usual. She's a bit scatty at times. Lovely girl but she forgets things.'

'Like what?'

'To take a client out from under a hairdryer, where she's put her scissors – only little things. She's in a world of her own at times. Keen to learn though. She's studying a part-time diploma course in colour to become a hair technician.' Sally gave Lucy a sad smile and turned her attention to Natalie who had a question for her.

'How long has she worked for you?'

'Eight months. She came from Eddie Ford's salon. They didn't get along. His loss. I don't have any issues with her work.'

Natalie knew Eddie. He was the stylist who cut Leigh's hair. Leigh had insisted on changing from the hairdressing salon in Castergate, where they lived, to Eddie's more modern one on Greenhill Road in Samford because her friend Zoe went there. He'd styled Natalie's hair a couple of times too and done a great job, but nowadays she rarely had enough time or money for salon appointments, and used a home dye to colour the flecks of grey that had been appearing more and more frequently. Leigh liked Eddie, who fussed over her like a princess. Natalie had never seen Kerry there though. She'd ask him why they hadn't got along. The more information they could gather about the family, the better.

'You know Mr and Mrs Sharpe at all?'

'No. I've never actually met them.'

'Did Isabella and Kerry seem happy enough at home?' Lucy asked. 'I mean, did Kerry ever say anything to make you think there were any problems there?'

'She never bad-mouthed them, if that's what you mean, and I didn't get the impression there were any issues although Kerry did moan now and again about them giving her harsh curfews and not letting her stay out late like some of her mates.'

It seemed all was well at home, or at least Kerry had given that impression. Could there be anyone else who wished Kerry and Isabella any harm? Natalie thought of another possibility – a boyfriend or ex-boyfriend. 'Has Kerry got a boyfriend that you know of?'

'No. She went out with a lad last year for a few weeks but it fizzled out.'

'Do you know his name?'

'She didn't mention his name, only that he'd become a paramedic and moved away to London. That poor girl. The family must all be shell-shocked and Kerry is going to be so lost without her sister.' Sally pulled a tissue out from the bag and blew her nose. Natalie had no more questions for the woman and drew the interview to a finish. They still hadn't established a great deal other than the girls were close and they had no idea who would murder Isabella. Natalie stomped towards the squad car, determined now to interview every member of security, even if it took her all day and night. They needed answers. Someone must have seen something. She threw the door open and flung herself into the passenger seat. Who was responsible for destroying this family's happiness?

It was very quiet back at headquarters. The team spread out in the office with cups of takeaway coffee and sandwiches and trawled through the background information on Fergus and all of Isabella's family members, but they couldn't find anything that raised any red flags.

Having received contact details from the head of security for the event, Natalie decided they'd make a start on talking to the security staff present at the concert. Glancing at her watch, she realised her children would probably have returned home. She'd fully intended talking to them today about her and David, and about them splitting up. She rubbed at her head. It wasn't a good time. However, when was it ever a good time to tell your kids that their parents were going to split? She excused herself and headed for the roof terrace, where two officers were grabbing a few minutes' sunshine and a cigarette. She nodded in their direction, took herself to the far side of the terrace where they'd be less likely to overhear her conversation and rang David.

He sounded irritated. 'I thought you'd be home by now.'

'That was my intention but you know how it is. Are the kids home?' She didn't want to argue.

'Yes. Got back half an hour ago. They've both gone to their rooms. Dad's left. Natalie, this isn't right. I can't stand here one minute with a grin on my face and my arms open wide to greet them when I know I'm going to destroy their lives. You were supposed to be back before them. That was the plan. That was your idea.'

She understood his frustration but she couldn't stroll away from such an important investigation. 'I know and I'm sorry. Maybe we should wait until tomorrow.'

'And then what? You'll be too busy and it'll wait until the next day! This is purgatory,' he hissed. 'I can't act like everything is okay when it isn't, even if you can. I'm going to tell them, whether you're here or not.'

'No! Don't do that!'

'Then make a choice, Natalie, and come home.'

'For fuck's sake!' She kicked at the wall and one of the officers glanced at her before quickly averting his gaze. She lowered her head and dropped her voice again. 'Don't hold me to ransom like this. They need us both there to do this properly. Don't be such a shit.'

'I'm not the one who wants to break up our family. You are, so don't call *me* names.' His voice was icy and menacing – a side of David she didn't see very often.

Is that what happens when one partner feels betrayed? Do they turn on the other? She was momentarily bewildered. She'd stupidly believed she could end their relationship amicably; after all, they had decades of love behind them. Surely they could behave in an adult fashion? Her inner voice reminded her that this was exactly how adults acted, especially those who were hurting emotionally. She made the decision – the only one she could make.

'I'll come home.'

There was silence at the other end then, 'Right.'

'We'll talk to them together. I'll be back soon.'

'Okay.' He ended the call.

Below her the evening traffic was building up, cars filled with families who'd spent the day together, and Natalie swallowed the hard lump forming in her throat. She couldn't back down now. This was going to be the most difficult thing she'd ever done but she still had to go through with it. She'd leave the investigation in Lucy's and Ian's hands and return to Castergate to face her children and break the news as gently as possible.

The police officers were still in position with their backs to the wall, the late sun on their faces. She didn't look at them as she plodded towards the stairs, each footstep ponderous and heavy as if gravity was sucking at her boots. As she descended, her phone rang and the screen lit up – Mike. She thought twice before answering.

He sounded anxious. 'Nat, I'm at Blithbury Marsh. You need to come and see this.'

'What is it?'

'It's not good. The Westmore twins.'

Her lips went numb and for a second the world seemed to spin around her. 'Mike—'

'Just get over here and see what you think.'

She could tell from his words – or rather from what he wasn't telling her – this was going to be really bad.

CHAPTER ELEVEN

SUNDAY, 12 AUGUST – LATE AFTERNOON

Blithbury Marsh was a scenic wetlands reserve of approximately 110 hectares, close to the centre of Samford. The flat-surfaced pathways that covered most of the wild moorlands made it ideal for strolling, dog walking and birdwatching.

Natalie and Lucy pulled into the supermarket car park next to two ambulances and several police vehicles. From here, they could easily reach one of the reserve's entrances, now guarded by police officers. Bystanders of all ages had gathered in the car park to find out what was going on and Natalie recognised the familiar face of Bev Gardiner from the *Hatfield Herald*, a reporter who'd hounded Natalie in the past and almost put her daughter at risk. There was no way she was going to speak to that woman. Fortunately, officers were keeping the crowd at bay, and she and Lucy approached the entrance and Mike, who was waiting, his face contorted as if in pain. At the sight of it, Natalie could hardly control the hammering in her chest. She already knew what to expect and dreaded being right. Suiting up quickly, she and Lucy marched silently forwards, and once their names were noted in the log, they followed him, wordlessly.

Natalie had visited the area before with her own children when they'd been younger, taken them along the circular trail around the centre of the reserve to search for the numbered posts with rubbing plaques of some of the wildlife that lived there, and gone pond-dipping with them. The lump in her throat had returned, rendering her speechless. This was a place for families and couples – filled with birdsong, nature and life – not a place for death. A cloud of black-tailed godwits rose as one from the mirrored surface of the water, disturbed by officers searching for evidence in the long grasses. Lapwings tumbled above their heads emitting loud *pee-wits* before finally disappearing into the bulrushes. The obstruction in her throat grew in size as golden grasses swayed in the gentle breeze, beckoning her ever closer to the water's edge.

'This way.' Mike guided them to the water and stopped beside a large patch of bright pink flowers. His head dropped and Natalie followed his gaze. Erin and Ivy Westmore lay side by side, knees bent, facing each other. Natalie blinked several times and swallowed. They were fully dressed, in matching orange-and-yellow striped tops and jeans, and appeared to be holding hands, but their faces were obscured by the transparent plastic bags used to suffocate them, their features distorted. Natalie opened her mouth to speak and closed it again. Mike asked, 'You okay?'

She answered with a weak, 'Yes.' The effort of speaking galvanised her into action. She moved closer to take in every detail and stared at the bodies, sprinkled with deep pink petals from beautiful lacy flowers that appeared to hang in the air like a mist but were attached to clumps of tall dark green stems scattered in abundance around the marshy area. 'The plastic bags... the positioning of the bodies... it's identical.' Her voice was hoarse. The niggling feeling was intensifying as she took in the terrible sight in front of her eyes. 'It can't be him; he died in prison.' *But what if this was a copycat? What if there had been more than one killer at the time?*

'Are we looking at a copycat murderer then?' said Lucy, who was by Natalie's side. Natalie had briefed her loosely on the Blossom Twins case on the way over so she was up to speed.

'It appears that way but...' Natalie looked at Mike, who had been watching her keenly.

'It can't be Hoskins, Nat. It has to be a copycat.'

Neil Hoskins, a forty-year-old single man, had been picked up for jumping a red light only two streets away from the cemetery where they'd found Avril and Faye Moore. He'd been piano tutor to both girls and to the sisters, Sharon and Karen Hill, who'd been murdered before them. The twins' DNA was found in his car. Although he had claimed he'd given them a lift to the shops, he'd had no alibi to confirm his whereabouts, and child porn found on his laptop had given them enough evidence to question him. After intense interrogation, he'd broken down and confessed to murdering all four girls and been sentenced to life, only to commit suicide three months into his sentence.

'I know it can't be him. It's just we didn't release all the details. We didn't tell anyone about the twins holding hands and facing each other. Somebody else knew.'

'Someone leaked it or spoke to Hoskins before he died,' Mike reasoned.

'Or we got the wrong person,' she replied quietly.

'No, Nat, that's not likely. He confessed,' Mike said.

Lucy cast about and commented, 'There are a lot of petals. They've been deliberately scattered on the bodies.'

Mike nodded. 'They've been picked from flowers nearby. You can see where the stems have been stripped.' He pointed out bare stems where flower heads had been removed.

'Must have taken an age to pull off all those petals. What flower is it?'

'The person who found them is one of the volunteers here. He told me it's called ragged robin, because the petals look frayed or tatty.'

'Any reason the killer chose that particular flower?' asked Lucy, brow furrowed.

Natalie answered, 'Presumably because they're in abundance here. I don't think there's any hidden message in the flower choice.

Sharon and Karen Hill were left in a field and strewn with daisies that grew there. The bodies of Avril and Faye Moore were covered in cherry blossom.' She choked on her response, recalling the little girls holding hands in the cemetery under the cherry tree, and cleared her throat. The girls still haunted her dreams from time to time – forever young, forever together. She'd been part of the team responsible for their deaths. They'd chased after the wrong person, allowing the real killer to act. Avril and Faye ought to be alive today. She shoved such thoughts to the back of her mind and continued. 'It's some sort of ritual. When we were handling the investigation, we couldn't come up with anything to help understand why the killer left blossom on the bodies. We thought it was associated with funeral flowers or some sort of "in sympathy" message. Who found them, Mike?' she asked, dragging her eyes from the girls and pushing aside the memories.

'One of the volunteers here. He was checking the bird hides at the time he stumbled over them. He's at the wildlife centre along with other volunteers and staff members. They've been asked to give statements. DI Graham Kilburn is over there too. Superintendent Tasker is on his way. As you can see, I'm one of the first here. I rang you as soon as I saw the girls. I had a feeling…' He didn't finish his sentence.

Natalie winced and then let out a sigh. 'We can't take this on. I'll speak to Superintendent Tasker. Besides, we're investigating another murder.' Even as she spoke, a voice in the back of her head sent her brain whirling. When she'd seen Isabella, she'd been struck by the positioning of the girl, similar to that of Avril Moore and Sharon Hill. Although Isabella did not have a bag over her head, the deaths could all be the work of one killer. Her mind somersaulted. *Were all the deaths the work of one person?* Kerry and Isabella weren't twins but they looked alike in many ways. Sharon and Karen Hill had also looked alike, with the same long ginger hair, sandy eyelashes and pale amber eyes. Had the person responsible for Isabella's death intended murdering Kerry too and laying her out with her sister? It was possible, yet Kerry was older than any of the other victims. Sharon Hill had been a year older than her fourteen-year-old sister, Karen, and the Moore twins had been thirteen. Kerry was much older at seventeen. There was a pattern but it wasn't clear enough to Natalie.

She pressed a pressure point between her brows to ease the sudden pain in her head. She'd hoped to never see anything like this again. They'd found the person responsible for the murder of the Hill sisters and the Moore twins. Neil Hoskins had been convicted and sent to prison, where he'd suddenly claimed his innocence and slit his wrists with a razor blade smuggled out of the shower block. The pain intensified – needles into the backs of her eyeballs. It was no good. She had to talk to Dan Tasker and ensure he assigned somebody else to the case. She couldn't take charge of it.

As she withdrew from the bodies, she spotted the pathologist, Ben Hargreaves, picking his way towards them. Alongside him was the superintendent. She moved towards them, acknowledging them. Ben returned her greeting with a tight-lipped nod. Cases involving children were always difficult, especially for those who, like him, had a young family. Natalie had respect for the young man who had worked on a few cases with her and who could be relied on to be thorough and efficient.

Dan drew to a halt so he and Natalie could speak alone. 'What are your initial thoughts, DI Ward?'

'There are striking similarities in the way these girls have been murdered and positioned to those of a case we investigated in Manchester in 2014. We found sisters Sharon and Karen Hill, and twins Avril and Faye Moore, in almost identical positions with plastic bags over their heads, although we later established they'd been strangled and the bags added after they were dead. Their bodies were strewn with petals or blossom, hence the name for the investigation.'

'The Blossom Twins. Did you establish why they were killed?'

'No. Neil Hoskins, who was charged with their murders, never explained himself to us.'

'What was the significance of the blossom?'

'He claimed it was his way of apologising.'

Dan inhaled deeply then called across to the pathologist, who was bending down beside the twins. 'Ben, can you tell if they died through suffocation or whether they were strangled first?'

'Sorry, I won't be able to give you a definite answer until I've performed the autopsy,' Ben replied, his Brummie accent making his words almost musical.

'Okay, but make this a priority.'

Natalie continued in a low voice, 'I believe somebody knows details about that case that were never revealed to the public and has replicated the killing. It could be somebody who admired Neil Hoskins' work or somebody who knew him. Maybe even one of the investigating team leaked details. I simply can't say.'

Dan's light eyebrows drew together. 'This was the same case you spoke to me about earlier? The girls who disappeared from their front garden?'

'Yes, sir.'

He pursed his lips then asked, 'How certain are you that there is a connection?'

'The fact they're twin girls, the plastic bags, the positioning of the bodies, the petals sprinkled over them… I'd say almost 100 per cent certain.'

'Then I'm going to have to assign you to this investigation.'

'Sir, we're already looking into Isabella Sharpe's death. We can't put that aside.' Her heart smacked against her ribs. She had her suspicions but she didn't want Isabella's death to be linked to this case and she didn't want to be responsible for finding the bastard who'd done this to the twins. She couldn't face another Blossom Twins investigation.

'I understand your reluctance but you were involved in that investigation and are the best person to lead this one. Three children murdered within forty-eight hours of each other…' He paused to drive home his point.

Natalie didn't need him to finish his sentence.

Dan's clipped speech drew her back to the present. 'In the first instance, I'd like you to determine if there's any connection between these deaths. If not, I'll reassign the Isabella Sharpe case to another DI.'

'That's quite a load—' she began but he silenced her by raising one finger.

'I'll ensure you have assistance – today.'

'Sir.' As much as she wanted to distance herself from this investigation, she couldn't. She was already involved. The Blossom Twins murder enquiry had drained her emotionally and physically and had caused such horrific nightmares she'd had to seek medical assistance from a psychiatrist – help she'd relied on for years afterwards. Was she strong enough to face such trauma again, especially with her home life in tatters?

He sucked in his cheeks. 'I don't need to remind you how sensitive this is. Three children murdered in such a short space of time is going to set alarm bells ringing all over Staffordshire. We need to keep as tight a lid on things as we can. I'll speak to the press office and see if we can do a damage limitation exercise so as not to panic people. If you could give me information that would allow me to explain the cases are unrelated, that would be helpful.' His face remained impassive and his cool gaze rested on her. Dan Tasker was all about image – his and the police force's; that mattered more to him than the victims. It meant more than the actual lives of the two sweet children lying in the grass, and that fact alone helped her to make up her mind there and then: she'd unearth whoever was responsible for all of these girls' deaths, no matter what cost to her health or sanity. She'd come a long way since the Blossom Twins investigation. She had a good team to support her. She could do this. She lifted her chin.

'Yes, sir.'

'Good. I'll let you get started.'

'Have the parents been informed yet?'

'Yes, and they've been asked not to talk to any press. There are two liaison offers with them at the moment. Tanya Granger is one of them, I believe.'

'I'll head over and talk to them once I've spoken to the staff here.'

She made to move and was halted by a quiet, 'DI Ward.'

'Yes, sir.'

'Pull out the stops on this. We can't let this get out of hand. I'm relying on you.'

'Sir.'

A quick tilt of his head was all she received in acknowledgement. He walked away, back towards the entrance, leaving Natalie seething. His manner was brusque and callous. Three children were dead and the only reason he wanted their killer found quickly was so he wouldn't lose face.

Lucy tentatively approached as if she could tell their interaction hadn't been a positive one. 'You look like thunder,' she commented.

'I'm okay. Got to get my head around this.'

'Are we on the case?'

'Yes. We're handling both investigations.'

'You're kidding! How are we supposed to manage that?'

'We're getting help – more officers.'

Lucy released a derogatory snort. 'Great! Outsiders. Could do with Murray coming home instead.'

'We can't haul him back from Australia. We'll have to make do. Can you head to the centre to talk to the witness? I've got to make a call.'

'Sure. Shall I get hold of Ian?'

'Yes. Let him know what's happened but tell him I want him to stick to what he's doing for the moment.'

She moved away and made the call to David.

'Where are you?'

'David, I can't come home yet.'

'Why the fuck not?'

'You remember the Blossom Twins case?'

'Of course I do. Why?'

'I'm at a new crime scene… it's…' She wasn't allowed to discuss any investigation, not even with her husband, so she left it for him to put two and two together. 'I can't get away. I'm sorry. I'll be home as soon as I can. Can we leave this… talk… until later? Please.'

There was a pregnant pause during which she could hear the television in the background and then a resigned, 'Yes, sure. I'll talk to you later.'

'Thank you. I'm really sorry.'

'I know you are.'

'See you later.'

'Yes. Okay.'

She shoved the mobile in her pocket and returned to the spot where Erin and Ivy Westmore lay. Ben had removed the plastic bags and was gently examining their throats. Natalie was struck by the contrast in the dark silken locks of hair tumbling across pure white cheeks. Both girls looked like versions of a fairy-tale Snow White. Ben, on his knees, was engrossed in his work, noting ligatures, checking eyes for signs of suffocation. Mike watched on in silence.

'Superintendent Tasker's given me the investigation,' she said eventually.

Mike cocked his head to one side. 'And you took it?'

She nodded. 'Yes. I changed my mind. I want to nail this fucker.'

He gave a slight smile. 'Then I'd better find some evidence to help you do that.'

'Ben, can you give me any idea of how they died?'

'There's no sign of bruising around the mouth, on the chin or nose. There's no bruising on the inner surface of the mouth, which would usually be caused by compression from lips or teeth if the victims were suffocated. I can't confirm it yet but I suspect both girls died from strangulation rather than suffocation. Is that what you expected to hear?'

'Yes.'

'That's completely off the record. I might discover something else when I examine them.'

'I understand,' said Natalie. It was enough to get started. She was more convinced than ever that this case was a throwback to the Blossom Twins murders and that she had to steel herself for what was to come.

CHAPTER TWELVE

THEN

'Jennifer, you can't do this to me!' he wails.

She turns narrowed eyes onto him from the passenger seat. The seatbelt sits across the swell of her belly and her hands are protectively covering it, as if shielding his babies from their father. She's being unreasonable. Beyond unreasonable.

'Maybe if you hadn't been so narcissistic or unable to keep your dick inside your trousers, it wouldn't have come to this.'

'For fuck's sake. I've apologised. I've said it won't happen again.'

'Too right it won't. I'm not giving you the chance for it to happen again. You want to shag other women, go ahead. I don't give a fuck any more. I'm not shedding another tear over you. You don't deserve my love but these babies do. They're mine and I'm going to look after them, love them and bring them up… without you.'

'I have rights, you know?'

'Yes, and I won't stop you from seeing them, but we're not pretending to play happy families. We're through.' She sighs and leans back against the headrest.

He doesn't know what he expected – maybe a last-minute reconciliation or at least to go their separate ways without so much animosity hanging in the air. He's made errors but that doesn't mean he doesn't love Jennifer. He'd be a good father. He knows he would. His girls would look up to him and admire him. He needs another chance. The journey to Cornwall has been long and fractious, filled with uncomfortable silences, but he wasn't going to let her drive herself, not in her condition – there are only two months before the babies' due date. Besides, he needs this six-hour journey to convince her he can change and be the man she wants him to be.

'Look, why don't you think about it at least? I can transfer to this area. We can bring the girls up together here, by the sea, and we'll get a house near your parents. You won't need to go back to work. Solicitors work long hours as you know. You can be there for them all the time not just after work. They'll need you.'

She shuts her eyes and speaks in a monotonous tone. 'We've been through this a million times. I'm sick and tired of discussing it. I'm going to rent somewhere close to Mum and Dad so they can help out, and when the babies are old enough to go to nursery, I'll be taking up my old position at work, and that is that. There's no more to be said. I've organised it all. The local nursery is fabulous with one-on-one care for babies and they won't want for anything. They'll have Mum and Dad on hand and my sister, Louise, so drop it, will you? I'm not going to reconsider.' She opens her eyes again and looks at him coldly.

His hands tighten on the steering wheel. He's been trying so hard. For the last six hours, he's been truly nice to her, listened to her gripes, apologised for all the hurt he's caused, made promises he's not sure he can keep and begged. His knuckles turn white and he grits his teeth. Jennifer is taking his girls away and he can't do a fucking thing about it because she's their mother, a woman with better qualifications than he has and a well-paid job at her father's law firm lined up; a woman who can look after his babies without his assistance, and all she's willing to offer him is visiting and holiday rights. He turns to look at her and tries not to be drawn in by her maternal beauty, the glowing skin and the bloom of her cheeks. She's carrying their children and he wants to make amends, to start over again. He's about to speak when he sees a look of horror on her face. Her mouth opens but no sound emerges, and in the blink of an eye, he spots the car hurtling towards them and yanks *on the steering wheel to guide them back to their lane but overshoots and hears a screaming that pierces his ears and drills into his brain as his BMW flips onto its side and rolls over and over and over, and as he loses consciousness, he understands the screaming has stopped and his wife's eyes have shut.*

CHAPTER THIRTEEN

SUNDAY, 12 AUGUST – EVENING

Chris and Judith Westmore sat side by side on a large blue settee, their thighs pressed together, fingers entwined. Judith's eyes were bloodshot and her face covered in red blotches while Chris looked grey, his cheeks sunken and face lengthened by grief. Tanya's voice was calming as she encouraged Judith to assist Natalie, who was perched on a chair close to them. A second liaison officer, a man in his late twenties, silently stood close to the door.

'I can't go through this again,' said Judith, weakly.

'DI Ward needs to know everything, Judith,' said Tanya. 'Anything you can tell her could help.'

'All I know is they were gone. My babies. They weren't in the tent and I don't know why not.' Judith shook her head continually as she spoke. The tears fell again.

Chris squeezed her hand then rubbed his face with his free hand before speaking. His voice was thick. 'Judith went out at about ten to wake the girls up. We thought they'd been up until late and were having a lie-in. When she got there, the tent was empty. She came back into the house to see if they'd come back in overnight. I was in the kitchen getting breakfast. She said, "They're not there?" Then she went upstairs and checked their room but they weren't there either. We called out then I went into the garden. I shouted their names and then I discovered the back gate was unlocked. I ran up and down the road but couldn't see them anywhere. Meanwhile, Judith rang the police. That's all I can tell you. We told DI Kilburn everything. Surely you can ask him. We need… time.' Tears spilt over his eyelashes and he squeezed his wife's hand once more.

Natalie leant forward and spoke. 'I understand this is dreadfully hard for you, but as Tanya said, everything you tell me might help. Any details you can recall will help me build up a picture of what happened. Can you talk me through the evening before?'

Chris released his wife's hand and rubbed at his face again as if scrubbing off the skin. He sniffed back the tears before explaining. 'The twins had tea and went to their room. They came down at nine wearing their nightclothes and said they were ready for bed. They kissed us both goodnight and disappeared into the garden. I checked on them before turning in and they were both perfectly happy.' He swallowed the last word and a lone tear trickled down his face, catching in his stubble.

'Were they in sleeping bags when you checked on them?'

'Yes.'

'Did you notice any other clothes in the tent?'

'Only their dressing gowns and slippers. The girls were dressed in pyjamas and inside their sleeping bags, but those were left behind in the tent along with the dressing gowns and slippers. We were asked not to remove them.' He choked on his response and Judith reached for his hand again. He caught his breath several times before being able to answer Natalie's next question.

'You didn't know they had a change of clothes with them?'

'No.'

'Did they take a bag with them into the tent?'

He couldn't answer. Tears cascaded now. It was Judith who took over. 'They took a backpack – I thought it had books and games in it. I didn't ask what was in it.'

'Is the backpack still there?'

'Yes, but it's empty.'

'This may sound awful but I don't mean it to. I only want to understand why they might have gone off. Were the twins happy?'

'Very,' said Judith.

'You can't think of any reason why they might have left?'

'None. We're a very happy family.' Her lips quivered as she corrected herself. 'We *were* a very happy family. We got on so well – laughed, joked. There were no tantrums and the girls were inseparable. Really good friends. I don't understand…'

Looking towards Chris again, Natalie asked, 'Chris, the gate was unlocked when you checked this morning. Are you sure it was locked when you went to bed last night?'

'Definitely. I made sure it was. Nobody could have got into the garden unless they somehow opened it or climbed over and opened it. They couldn't have got in via neighbours' gardens. It's impossible. I don't understand what's happened. Please find whoever has done this. Find this sick bastard who did this to our girls.'

'We'll do whatever we can.' Natalie knew she couldn't make any promises. They might never find out what had really occurred but she would try. She'd put every ounce of effort she could into this investigation to give this couple the answers they sought.

*

Lucy joined DI Graham Kilburn, head of MisPers, in the visitors' centre at Blithbury Marsh. With his hanging jowls and sunken cheeks, Graham looked like the life had been sucked from him. The last time they'd been together had been earlier that year when Natalie's daughter had gone missing, but he'd lost weight since then and it had aged him.

Graham was in conversation with a rubicund man in camouflage jacket and olive-green trousers when Lucy arrived, but he spotted her and called her over. She edged past boards showing maps of the marshlands and photographs of the resident wildlife to join them. To Lucy, the room resembled a large classroom with tables laid out much like the desks had been at her school. It even had a faint aroma of marker pens.

'DS Carmichael,' said Graham. 'Am I to assume DI Ward is taking over the investigation?'

'Yes, sir. She asked me to talk to you and to the gentleman who found the bodies.'

'That would be me,' said the man, lowering his head in deference to reveal a large balding spot covered in freckles.

'I'd like you to run back over it with me, if you don't mind, Mr…?'

'Porter. Doug Porter.'

'Mr Porter, could you tell me when and how you came across the bodies?'

'I came in mid-afternoon as usual on a Sunday. I chatted to the others about the latest bird activity and left about five o'clock to check the hides and to see if anyone had recorded any fresh sightings of a pair of European bee-eaters that were here a couple of days ago – they're rare, you see. I checked both the hides, spoke to a few of the regular birdwatchers and was on my way back to the centre when I thought there was some unusual bird activity near the water's edge – they were agitated so I went to investigate in case there was a predator that was upsetting the birds… and I found them.' His eyebrows lifted upwards as he spoke and he opened his palms. 'They were lying there. I knew instantly they were dead… the bags… I rang the police on my mobile and then came straight back here and told the others. We cleared the hides and the circuits of people and put up closed signs to keep others away. That was the right thing to do, wasn't it?'

'Yes, it was. Were there many people here at the time?'

'Fortunately not. Only a dozen at most. It was getting end-of-the-dayish. Most people leave after five on Sundays. We tried to keep everyone away from the immediate area or crime scene as I understand you call it.'

He flashed a small smile, eager like a teacher's pet. Lucy wrote down his responses, slightly put off by his enthusiasm to assist.

'You didn't touch the bodies at all?' she asked.

His eyes grew wide. 'No… no, not at all. I didn't want to contaminate the scene.'

This was clearly a man who watched crime shows. He wrung his hands together and waited for more questions.

'You didn't recognise the girls… from their clothing? I mean, you hadn't seen them earlier?' she added quickly, aware the twins' heads had been covered with bags that had distorted their faces.

'I'm afraid not.'

'Did anyone spot the girls?' she asked Graham, who shook his head.

'They've all made statements but nobody noticed anything out of the ordinary or saw the bodies before Doug found them. I was called to the scene immediately and identified the bodies based on distinguishing features – Erin has a large freckle on the top of her left thigh and Ivy has a star-shaped scar on her right knee. There was little doubt it was them.'

He shifted uncomfortably and Lucy suspected he was feeling the full weight of the investigation. MisPers had a good record of finding teenage runaways, but over the course of the last year some of those had resulted in deaths and subsequent murder enquiries. Lucy wound up her questions with the man who'd found the bodies then asked to speak to Graham alone.

'What can you tell us that might help us?' she asked him quietly.

'Not much. When we were called to the twins' disappearance this morning, I was sure they'd run away. It seemed well-planned: they'd insisted on camping last night, which apparently was out of character for both girls; they'd changed into nightclothes and got into sleeping bags to convince their father they were ready to go to sleep but taken outfits to change into. We couldn't find anything on social media or from their friends to indicate what they'd planned but there was no way anyone could have got into their garden and snatched them. The back gate had been unlocked from the inside when we checked it, and Erin's and her father's fingerprints were on the lock and key. We tried tracking the twins' mobile phones but they weren't transmitting and we haven't found them yet. I maintain the twins deliberately slipped away, yet neither parent could think of a single reason why they'd do that. We checked with the twins' closest friends and extended family and got the same response – the twins loved their parents and hadn't fallen out with them. It makes no sense why they upped and left.' He dragged a hand over his cheeks, pulling the sagging skin down further so his face looked like it was melting. 'I'll hand it over to you then, Sergeant. I'll write up my report immediately for DI Ward and have it sent across. Anything else I can help with?'

'No, sir.'

'Okay, I'll leave you to it. Good luck.' He trudged off, shoulders stooped, a man broken by the horrors of life.

Lucy arrived back at headquarters at the same time as Natalie, who stopped off downstairs to use the toilets. It was late in the day now, coming up eight, but Ian was still at his desk.

'I was looking through CCTV footage in and around the Westmores' house on Emerson Lane,' he said. 'There's a surveillance camera outside the furniture warehouse bang opposite where they live, but it's been vandalised. The staff at the warehouse think it happened sometime between Friday night and Saturday morning when somebody sprayed the lens with red paint. It's the only camera in the area that's been vandalised. Given it only happened a day ago, and that the camera covers the road opposite, I thought it was a bit suspicious.'

Lucy nodded. 'Can't be a coincidence, can it?'

'I asked for the footage on the off-chance it recorded something beforehand.' His fingers raced across the keyboard as he rewound dates and times, searching for the moment the camera had gone out of action.

'Sounds sensible to me, if not a long shot.'

A rap at the door made them both look around. A dark-haired man with serious brown eyes and a brown leather jacket casually thrown over one shoulder stood in the doorway.

'Hi. I'm DS John Briggs. I've had orders to assist you. Apologies for the dress code. I was on a date when I got the call. Had to leave the lady hanging.' He swept his hand downwards over a white shirt and tight-fitting jeans.

'Oh, right. You got here quickly,' said Lucy, striding forward and shaking his hand.

'Apparently, there's a sense of urgency attributed to this investigation. I was told to drop everything, including my lovely partner.'

'Ah,' said Lucy with a shrug. 'That's police work for you. We all have to make sacrifices.'

John continued, 'I understand the case is being led by DI Ward.'

'That's right. She should be here soon. This is PC Ian Jarvis,' she said.

Ian nodded in the man's direction.

'Where are you so far with this? Got any ideas?' He followed Lucy into the room, tossing his jacket onto the back of the nearest chair at a desk that Natalie had been occupying. Lucy frowned. It was obvious the desk was in use – a bottle of water, a coffee cup and paperwork suggested it was occupied – but he paid no attention to that, casting about the office to get an idea of where he'd be working. He strode to the floor-to-ceiling windows and gave a low whistle. 'Nice view!'

Lucy threw him a look but he ignored it. 'Probably best if I let Natalie bring you up to speed. Help yourself to a free desk. That one's being used.'

He smiled a response but didn't move to lift his jacket. Instead he closed in on Ian and leant over him to look at the computer screen. 'It's blank.'

'The CCTV camera's out of action. Apparently, somebody has spray-painted the lens.'

'Why you looking at it then?'

'Thought there might be something on the footage before it went off – maybe a clue as to who vandalised it or movements close by. It's the only camera to have been damaged in the area so I wondered why.'

'Who gives a fuck why? If a camera is out of action, it's no good to the investigation. You're wasting your time on that, mate,' said John.

Ian shot a look at Lucy, who disagreed. 'We have to examine every possibility. That camera was situated opposite the Westmores' house on Emerson Lane. We'd be stupid not to check it out.'

John gave a light snort. 'Most likely it was a random act of vandalism and you'll find a bunch of little hoodlums responsible. You should be concentrating on other cameras in the vicinity, looking for any suspicious activity on them instead.'

He'd no sooner made the comment than Natalie appeared. Catching sight of the man, she drew to a sudden halt. He gave a smile that didn't reach the corners of his eyes.

'Good to see you again, Natalie,' he said.

She hesitated before saying, 'I guess you've been seconded to the team.'

'Superintendent Tasker thought it would be useful for you to have me here.'

She gave a brief nod and spoke to the others. 'In case you haven't had the chance to properly introduce yourselves, this is DS John Briggs. He and I worked together on the Blossom Twins investigation.'

He tilted his head slightly in acknowledgement. Natalie wiped the palms of her hands on her trousers. *Fuck! Of all people!* John

Briggs was as arrogant an arsehole as she'd ever met and had been hoping for the promotion she had got. He was difficult to manage, opinionated and the last person she wanted assisting her. There was also a more personal reason she disliked the man. During their time working on the Blossom Twins case, he had come on to her inappropriately. He'd invited her out for a drink, knowing she was married with children, and she'd refused, only to have him call her a cold bitch for doing so and accusing her of one minute leading him on and the next dropping him. None of it was true, and a younger, less confident and slightly confused Natalie had kept quiet about the incident. He hadn't asked her out again but she'd been wary of him thereafter. What was Dan thinking of? She knew the answer to that – to get the case closed as quickly as possible, and John was the man for that. She rubbed her sweaty palms again. This had suddenly made the investigation even more onerous; however, she owed it to the families to get answers, and for the time being, she'd have to get along with the man. She squared her shoulders and hoped to goodness she'd be able to keep him under control. She couldn't afford for him to send them spiralling in the wrong direction, not like he had done in the Blossom Twins case.

CHAPTER FOURTEEN

ERIN AND IVY

Erin unzips the tent quietly and pokes her head outside. The air seems cool after the warmth of the tent. It's been really tricky to get dressed in such a tiny space and they've giggled and bumped into each other several times as they've pulled on their matching outfits and done each other's make-up with only the torch app on their mobiles to light the tent. They're pleased with the result though. They could actually pass for sixteen.

The garden is silent and Erin creeps from the tent and stands facing the house, which is in complete darkness. 'Okay,' she whispers.

Ivy emerges, and after zipping the tent back up she shadows her to the gate. They don't speak as Erin turns the key and opens the gate, checks the road is empty and eases through. Ivy is directly behind her and watches the road as Erin pulls the gate to. They cross the road immediately to the furniture warehouse, away from the houses where people might spot them walking under the streetlamps that line the road. At the bottom of the road they turn left and walk arm in arm along the quieter road to the destination they've been given.

'You sure you know where the party is?' says Ivy.

'Course I do. I put the address in Google Maps. It's not far.'

'Isn't it amazing!' Ivy's face is pink with excitement.

'It's incredible.'

'Tell me again what Tom said. Go on. Word for word,' urges Ivy.

'You were there. You know exactly what he told us.'

'I know, but tell me again.' Ivy's enthusiasm is infectious.

Erin smiles then says, 'That Blasted are throwing a private party before they go on tour in Europe and Tom has got us invites to it—'

'—and Callum is going to be there and wants to meet us too!' Ivy finishes off the sentence and squeezes her sister's arm. 'It is going to be so cool. We're going to meet Callum Vincetti! Everyone we know is going to be so envious.'

'We have to be careful who we tell. Mum and Dad can't know about this.'

'I know but we can still tell Ashra. Are you going to tell Noah?' Ivy asks.

'No. We're through. He wants to go to the next level but I don't fancy him enough for that.'

Ivy nods at her sister's wise words.

'It's along this road,' says Erin, searching for the house numbers.

'Twelve. It's that one,' Ivy says, pointing at the next house along the road. She almost bounces in excitement.

The house is detached and ordinary to look at. Coloured disco lights are strobing behind the curtains, which haven't been fully drawn. Erin lets out a small squeal of excitement. 'That's it.'

They check each other over and walk past the house, pausing to look through the gap in the curtains. The room changes from deep blue to vibrant pink and Erin gasps as she says, 'I think I can see Callum.'

Ivy strains to see and makes out the shape of a young man facing the window. The light changes to bright yellow.

'It's him. I recognise his hair.'

'Come on. We don't want him to see us staring in.'

They hurry up the path to the front door. Music is coming from inside and there is the rise of occasional laughter. Erin looks at her sister and gives her an enthusiastic grin. The door opens and a man in a military-style jacket and jeans stands in front of them. He's holding a bottle of beer. Before they can say anything, he points the beer in their direction and says, 'You're the twins – Erin and... Ivy. That's right, isn't it? Tom said you were going to come. Glad you could make it. I'm the band's manager. Come in. What can I get you to drink... beer, wine, champagne?' He steps backwards and the girls enter the house. There's music playing in the room to their right – one of Blasted's tracks – and lots of chatter.

'OJ is fine,' says Erin.

'OJ it is. Tom's in the kitchen – I'll go tell him you're here.' He points at the door to the next room and says, 'Go on in and say hi to the guys. Callum's looking forward to meeting you both.' He meanders down the hall towards another room, calling, 'Tom, your friends are here.'

Erin's face pulls into a wide smile. 'Come on,' she says to Ivy. She pushes the door handle down and enters the room. Colours stream over the carpet – pink, blue, green – and the music is loud. Her eyes adjust and she looks about in confusion. The room is just a room – a sitting room with a settee and wall units and a television set. Blasted's music is being pumped out of a speaker, and the bizarre laughter and chattering is coming from another speaker attached to a laptop, which is open on a desk. There's nobody in the room and the person facing the window isn't a person at all – it's a full-sized cardboard cut-out. Something is wrong. Something is terribly wrong. They have to get out. Erin spins on her heel, mouth open, ready to urge Ivy to run, to get out of this place, but she is struck immobile by the sight in front of her. The man is holding onto her sister tightly. And he's not smiling any more.

CHAPTER FIFTEEN

SUNDAY, 12 AUGUST – LATE EVENING

After the update from Natalie, DS John Briggs made himself at home, got a cup of tea from the vending machine downstairs and was now reading through the case notes, occasionally resting his chin thoughtfully in his hand and looking into the distance. Natalie was going through information on Isabella and her sister, Kerry, while Lucy had her head bowed over her laptop, looking at anyone connected with the Westmore twins. Ian interrupted the silence by scraping back his chair and saying, 'Got something, Natalie.'

She rose to her feet only to discover John was ahead of her, leaning towards the screen. He moved away quickly but she spotted the tiny smile of satisfaction tugging at the corners of his mouth as he apologised for blocking her view.

A male figure in a hooded top was marching down Greenfield Road in the direction of Emerson Lane, the street where the Westmore family lived.

Natalie couldn't see the timestamp on the frame. 'What time was this taken?'

'Twenty past one on Saturday morning. The twins disappeared much later the same day, but this man's definitely acting suspiciously. He keeps stopping.' Ian ran the footage and indeed the man seemed to turn and check around himself on several occasions before moving on.

'Can we get a clearer look at him?'

Ian zoomed in on the image, and with his fingers grazing the keyboard, he succeeded in altering it.

Natalie asked, 'What time did the CCTV camera opposite the Westmores' house get vandalised?'

'Half past one, Saturday morning,' Ian said.

'That's some coincidence then, isn't it? I want to know who this bloke is and what the fuck he was up to.'

'Probably need to send it to the tech lab so they can run it through facial recognition technology,' John suggested.

'I was going to do that,' Ian replied.

'Sure.' John gave a nod and returned to his desk.

'It's pretty late and we need to be alert tomorrow, so I propose we leave this now and start again tomorrow at seven,' said Natalie.

'I'm happy to hang back and wait in case the techies can identify this character,' said John.

'I'll make sure they notify me as soon as they get a name and then I'll decide whether or not we act on it,' Natalie retorted.

John stared at her for a second. 'Of course.'

Natalie wasn't sure if he was deliberately needling everyone or was simply keen to get leverage on the investigation. There was no room on her team for office politics, and with Dan Tasker breathing down her neck for results, she had little choice but to try and get on with him. She dismissed Lucy and Ian and asked John to stay behind. He waited at his desk, and as soon as the others had left he said to Natalie, 'I never did congratulate you on your promotion to HQ. Well done.'

His eyes didn't crinkle when he smiled. Natalie rested her hands on the desk in front of her. 'I know this is going to seem a bit strange for you but we're after the same goal. We want to find out who was responsible for these deaths and as quickly as possible, but let me make this clear – I'm leading this investigation and I give the orders.'

'Fine. That it?'

Irritated by his insolence, she maintained her stance of arms in front of her and hands on the table and stared him down. 'No. The past is the past and I don't want any grievances or issues brought into this office. Superintendent Tasker has seconded you to us for a reason. He obviously thinks you'll be a help and that's what we need, so if you have anything you want to say, anything you wish to air, please do it now and then we can get on with hunting down whoever murdered these children.'

'I don't have any issue with you being in charge, Natalie. Do you have any concerns about me being part of the team?'

She looked him in the eye. 'No.'

'Good.'

'Play by the rules though, John.'

'I always do.'

'I don't want you to act on anything without going through me first. Understood?'

'Understood.' He got to his feet and lifted his jacket, putting it on before facing her. 'I'm not to blame for what happened, you know? It wasn't me who decided to pursue the wrong person.'

'You gave the DI that information, and as I recall you were keen to chase it up even though we had other suspects on the table.'

'I was enthusiastic, that's all. I didn't make the judgement call.'

Natalie drew a breath before saying, 'I know. I just don't want any slip-ups.'

'With all due respect, wasting time searching for people who graffitied a CCTV camera is not the way forward.'

'It might not be in your book, but in mine it's called being thorough.'

'We should be putting pressure on everyone who knew the girls, including their families and friends,' he continued undeterred.

'And we shall but this is the way I want it done. First, we do our homework.'

'I guess I'll have to toe the line. After all, you're the one who got promoted, not me.'

As Natalie pulled onto her drive, her stomach lurched. She was looking forward to seeing the children again but knowing she was about to turn their lives upside down was horrible. Every muscle in her body had tensed and a familiar throbbing had begun in her head – a tension headache was brewing, brought on by stress of the investigation, seeing John Briggs again and now this.

She remained in her car, willing herself to move but unable to do so. *Sodding, argumentative John Briggs.* They'd never rubbed along together. It hadn't been for want of trying on her part but John had always been the more competitive of them, the sergeant who was first with the answers and suggestions, constantly trying to impress his seniors, while Natalie had taken orders and followed up each and every strand of evidence. His failure during the Blossom Twins case had cost him the promotion he'd been desperately seeking. Natalie had received it instead, and it seemed he still hadn't managed to make that step up the ladder in the few years since she'd left Manchester. She was surprised at Dan Tasker's decision to bring the man across to join the investigation, but without challenging the superintendent face to face, she'd not know what had made him choose John Briggs. Moreover, she was annoyed she hadn't been informed of the decision and that the first she'd learnt of it had been when she'd found John in her office.

Her legs felt heavy and she had to force herself to open the car door. She ought to put all this to one side. She wasn't DI Ward here. Here, she was Mum.

The house smelt of warm Italian herbs, the assertive aroma of garlic and oregano that she always associated with David's home-made lasagne – his signature dish with wavy, velvety-smooth sheets of pasta covered in a creamy béchamel sauce and browned on top to perfection. David didn't enjoy cooking but he was good at it. Her stomach rumbled in appreciation.

Clapping and cheering came from the sitting room – some show on the television. She slid off her shoes and padded along the thinning hall carpet in stockinged feet in the direction of the noise.

'Mum!' Her daughter was halfway down the stairs and Natalie's mouth pulled into a natural smile at the sight. Leigh's hair had been neatly braided in cornrows, and together with a white vest and cut-off denim shorts over which she wore a floral kimono, she looked, in Natalie's mind, very trendy and grown up. The girl bounced down the stairs and gave a twirl.

'Very nice,' said Natalie approvingly.

'Grandad bought it for me. Pam helped me choose it. Isn't it cute?'

Although in her late fifties and with an adult son as her only child, Pam appeared to have quite an eye for dressing a teenage girl.

'Fabulous.'

'I got a green one with pale blue flowers too. Want to see it?'

'Of course.'

The girl bounded up the stairs again like an exuberant puppy. Natalie stuck her head into the sitting room where her son, Josh, was hunched over in a chair, thumbing his mobile, oblivious to the crowd on the television set who were cheering on a performing dog.

'Hi, Josh.'

He looked up and gave a nod. 'Hey, Mum.'

'You have a good holiday?'

'Yeah. It was awesome.'

'He met *somebody*.' Leigh was back, a pastel-green top in her hands. 'She's called Pippa.' She grinned wickedly and her eyes sparkled. Josh growled at her but she didn't stop. 'She's the same age as him and rich.'

'She isn't. You're talking rubbish.'

'She lives in a mansion with stables and is very posh.'

'Shut up! She isn't posh. She's normal like us.' Josh scowled at his sister.

Natalie took the kimono from Leigh's hands, held it up against the girl and nodded approvingly. It showed off the girl's peachy complexion and green eyes. She'd look gorgeous in it. 'Love it. I like your hair too.'

'Thanks. Zoe showed me how to do it.' Zoe was Leigh's closest friend. 'Rita Ora used to wear her hair like this.' Leigh's musical taste was forever changing and Natalie could never keep up with who she was into.

'Are you messaging Pippa?' Leigh said mischievously to Josh, who'd lowered his head again. 'Honest, Mum, she's dead posh.'

'Shut up!' Josh snapped.

'Okay, that'll do. Josh will tell me about Pippa if he wants to, and you should take this beautiful top back upstairs before it gets stuck down the back of the settee or something. You know what you're like with clothes. Where's Dad?'

'I'm here. I was setting up the patio heater.' David was behind her, standing awkwardly. 'You've timed it just right. We were about to eat. Thought we'd go outside for some supper.'

'Great, I'll set the table.' She caught the pained look in his eyes at her fake enthusiasm.

'All done apart from a place for you but we can soon fix that. Leigh, fetch a knife and fork for your mum.'

'We're having lasagne and garlic bread,' said Leigh, walking up to David and pecking him on the cheek affectionately as she made her way to the kitchen.

'That's certainly put her in a good mood,' said Natalie, knowing David's home-made lasagne was one of their daughter's favourite meals.

'She's been like that ever since she got home. I think she was spoilt rotten last week.' He rolled his eyes.

'She was. It was all, "Grandad, can I have this? Grandad, can you get me that?"' grumbled Josh.

'And you felt left out?' said David.

'Well, not really, but you know what she's like, always trying it on. She does it with you too.'

Warmth flooded Natalie's body at such perception. Ordinarily, Josh paid no attention to what was going on around him, but her son had changed in a short space of time. Not only was he suntanned from his trip but he'd assumed a layer of confidence. She casually wondered if it was on account of his new relationship. 'Got any photos, then?' she asked.

'Yeah, one or two.'

'I'll go check the lasagne,' said David. 'It should be ready.' He left them to it.

'Shove up. Let's take a look at them,' she said, balancing on the wide arm of the chair to look at Josh's screen.

He didn't protest and flicked through some pictures of beaches, the perfect whitewashed house that Eric and Pam had rented, some of the pair of them with Leigh standing on a cobbled street with bunting hanging above them, and one of a petite girl with a heart-shaped face, delicate features, heavily made-up eyes in a rainbow of blue, purple and pink, and black hair in a braided ponytail. Her smile lit up her entire face. 'This must be Pippa. Pretty girl.'

'Yeah, she's cool.'

'But not posh,' Natalie said with a grin.

Josh returned it, making her heart lift. He was so handsome when he smiled. If this girl could make him smile more, she already liked her.

'Leigh talks crap some days. They lived in Uptown in a rented flat until her mum got the job of live-in caretaker at a large house in Derby. The real owners are away a lot. They stay in a smaller house in the grounds.'

'Derby's not too far away.'

'No, it isn't.' He didn't continue but Natalie guessed he had plans to keep seeing Pippa.

Leigh reappeared and announced, 'Dad says it's ready and to go outside.'

Natalie got to her feet. Josh slipped the phone into the pocket of his jeans and stood up. For a moment, with both her children close to her and the atmosphere convivial, she wondered if she was doing the right thing. She was stringing them along, pretending all was normal, and soon she'd bring it all crashing down on them. She ought to wait. Give it more time. It wasn't fair to them. As they made their way to the back door that led from the kitchen to their small garden, she caught David's eye and her heart sank. What she was doing was terribly wrong. She shouldn't be putting off telling them about her and David. There would never be a 'right' time. She would have to face this head on and soon – very soon.

After the children had eaten and headed up to their respective rooms, David and Natalie remained in the garden, talking in low voices. The two glasses of red wine she'd consumed had mellowed her slightly, and when David said he was sorry to hear about the investigation, she heaved a deep sigh.

'It's all such a fucking mess. I should have been clear from the off, refused to head the investigation and taken time off to deal with all of this – us, the kids, and yet…'

David stared at his wine glass and gently swished the contents. 'You wouldn't be you if you'd walked away, especially if it's linked to the Blossom Twins. I'm only going to say this because I care about you, but watch it, Natalie. You know what happened after that case. I wouldn't want you to go through that again.'

'Thanks.' His words touched her. He'd been by her side when she'd suffered horrendous nightmares that had woken her scream-ing, and during her lowest moments, he'd driven her to her therapy sessions and waited outside, then, asking no questions, had taken her back home, where he'd made her cups of tea and held her when she'd cried. There'd been so much love and tenderness between them and yet it had petered out to leave two people who were on the cusp of destroying each other. The sadness sat like a lump of lead in her chest.

He cleared his throat. 'I've been thinking about… us. If you want to wait a while until you get somewhere with this investigation before we tell the children, I'll play along, but I don't know if they'll pick up on any tension or work it out. Just saying.'

'I know. They're bright kids. We have to tell them. The investigation could take months. Give me a few days.'

'You still want to go through with it?'

She looked at him and said softly, 'Yes.'

He drained his glass in one gulp.

'I found a flat yesterday. I agreed to take it on. It's near work. I'll help out with mortgage payments until you can get on your feet and we decide what to do about the house.'

His eyes narrowed. 'Oh, I see. You have thought this through, haven't you?'

She winced at his sudden icy tone and all feelings of relaxation vanished. 'I was being practical. I thought I was helping.'

He picked up his empty glass and stood to leave.

'Don't go off like that,' she said.

'Like what?'

'Angry.'

'How do you expect me to behave? Smile and say, "Yes, Natalie. No, Natalie. Great idea, Natalie?" It doesn't matter what I say or do any more. You've made up your mind. You want to go and live in a flat, then go ahead. The kids are staying put, here at home in our house, with me. You want to leave everyone who cares about you and who loves you, then do so. I'm not stopping you. I've tried. Heaven knows I've tried everything to prove I'm sorry, to reason with you, to make amends, but it's not enough for you. So, guess what? I'm done with trying. When you're ready to sit down and break the news to Josh and Leigh, let me know. And I suggest if you don't want them to find out sooner, you try not to make too much noise in the attic bedroom.' He disappeared through the kitchen door and she shivered.

This was turning into an impossible situation. Had she got the courage and temerity to see it through? She'd be breaking the hearts of those she loved most. She shut her eyes and thought back to why she was leaving: David. She cried out to her innermost soul for the answer and it came back like an echo – she didn't trust or love him enough to stay. There was no going back. The decision had been made. A tear trickled down her face. This was, without a doubt, the hardest thing she'd ever done.

CHAPTER SIXTEEN

MONDAY, 13 AUGUST – MORNING

It was not until after the morning briefing that Natalie received information from the technical team regarding the identification of the man who'd been walking along Greenfield Road. Natalie took John with her to speak to the man, a thirty-year-old unemployed graffiti artist known to the police as Sludge.

'Why's he called Sludge?' asked John as they drove towards the house in Dovedale Avenue.

'It's his tag – his signature. His real name's Rowan Stevenson. He was charged back in 2016 and served three months for criminal damage. Not reoffended since,' Natalie replied, turning into a road and slowing down to locate number 119.

John turned his head this way and that, then pointed to his left. 'A bit further along. That was 115. We need the next house along.'

Natalie drew up behind a VW Beetle from the 1960s with faded purple paint and a flat tyre. John glanced at the shabby semi-detached building with heavy curtains drawn at all the windows and declared, 'Think we've found the right place. What a dump!' He threw open the passenger door and eased out onto the pavement, waiting for Natalie where once there had been a gate and a pathway to the front door, now overgrown with moss and weed. A broken light hung from the open arched porch and the bell didn't work. Natalie knocked loudly. A muted wailing came from somewhere inside the building but no one answered. She banged again and stepped back to look for movement. The downstairs curtain moved and a face appeared at the window. Natalie held up her ID card and motioned for the person to open up.

'Want me to go around the back?' asked John.

'Give it a second,' she replied. Sure enough, the door opened and a young woman answered. Behind her was a dark hallway, wallpaper peeled away to reveal bare, dirty walls. There was a smell of rotting onions and Natalie tried not to wrinkle her nose at the off-putting stench. 'We'd like to talk to Rowan Stevenson,' she said, showing her ID card again.

The woman, who could be no older than twenty, was gaunt-faced. She rubbed her fingers under her nose and sniffed. 'Dunno if he's here.'

'Then go and find out,' said John, eyes flashing. 'Or we'll come in and look for ourselves.'

His words had an effect. The woman backed off and shut the door with a bang. He swore under his breath.

Natalie, irked he'd interfered, banged on the door again. 'Open up. We need to talk to Rowan. It's important,' she called.

'I'll try the back door,' said John and he marched off to the side entrance. The gate was locked and he rattled the handle in vain. 'The fuckers,' he grumbled.

'Someone's coming,' said Natalie. The door opened again and this time a man with a long hipster beard, waxed moustache and hair pulled into a man bun stood in front of them. It was Sludge.

'Rowan Stevenson?'

'Yes.'

'I'm DI Ward and this is DS Briggs from Samford HQ. We're investigating the murder of two young girls and we believe you were in the vicinity of their home in the early hours of Saturday morning at about the time a CCTV camera on the street where they lived was vandalised. Could we come in and discuss this matter with you?'

He shook his head. 'No one comes in. I'll talk to you here.'

'We might have to do this at the station then.'

'Whatever,' he replied.

'Can you account for your whereabouts on Saturday morning at one twenty?'

'I was out and about.'

'Were you on Greenfield Road?'

'I don't know if I was or wasn't.'

'What do you mean by that?'

'I wasn't aware of my surroundings.'

'Were you drunk?'

'No comment.'

Natalie resisted the urge to sigh. 'You're not in custody. What do you mean? Were you high?'

'Maybe,' he replied.

'Had you been taking drugs?'

'I don't remember where I went.'

'Let me refresh your memory for you. A CCTV camera picked you up on Greenfield Road at one twenty. Where did you go after that?'

'Can't remember.'

'Okay, I'm not going to piss about. Get in the car. We'll do this properly.'

Sludge shrugged nonchalantly and shut the door firmly before slouching towards the squad car. John opened the back door and, putting a firm hand on the man's head, pushed him into the car.

'Careful. Don't want me to go to the press and complain about police brutality,' said Sludge.

'Shut up and get in,' growled John.

Natalie threw him a look but he deflected it and climbed into the passenger seat. She was going to have to try harder to control the man. He was like a disobedient Rottweiler.

*

Sludge had demanded a lawyer be present during his interview, so while they waited for the duty lawyer to appear, Natalie rang Eddie Ford, the hairdresser who cut and styled Leigh's hair, and who had employed Isabella's sister, Kerry, for a while.

She could make out the hum of hairdryers in the background with the occasional raised voice and easily imagined the warm smell of hair products that seemed to be permanently present in the salon. Eddie's Scottish accent broke through the background noise.

'Hi, Natalie, do you want to make an appointment for you or Leigh?'

'Neither at the moment, thanks, Eddie, although I suspect Leigh will want to come in soon. She was complaining about split ends last night.'

'She's such a diva. Love her to bits though. Okay, I'm listening.'

'It's official business. It's about Kerry Sharpe.'

'Ok-ay. What about her?'

'I understand she worked for you for a short while.'

'Three weeks and one day to be exact.'

'Why did you fire her?'

'Erm, because she was crap at her job, spent every spare minute on her phone and left one of my clients sitting under a hairdryer until she almost melted. And she had a lousy attitude.'

Judging by his tense tone, he found Kerry frustrating. 'I don't suppose I could drop by and chat to you about her, could I?'

'What's this about?'

'Have you not heard about her sister?'

'No. What about her?'

'She was killed on Friday night.'

'Oh my! I'm sorry to hear that. I didn't know her but all the same… What time were you thinking of calling by?'

'Lunchtime? Unless you could come here to the station.'

'Sure, I can do that. Let me check my appointments.' There was sudden silence as the hairdryer stopped whirring and then he said, 'Actually, I've just had a cancellation. I could nip by in about half an hour if that suits you.'

'Yes, it would.'

'Okay. See you then.'

She ended the call and looked at Eddie's details in front of her on the screen. His salon was on Greenfield Road, a street that led to Emerson Lane, where the Westmore family lived, and the same street where a man, who they believed to be Sludge, had been caught on CCTV. She tapped her pen against her front teeth. How great a coincidence was that? Looking at his photograph, she could detect distinct similarities between him and Sludge. Both were about thirty and both had facial hair – although if her memory served her correctly, Eddie's beard was shorter and neater than the man's beard in the photo, and he wore glasses. The man in the photo wasn't wearing any. She chewed over this information. She needed to talk to both men – something wasn't sitting right for her.

Lucy and John had left the office to interview security staff who'd been on duty at Sunmore Hall on Friday evening. Ian had uncovered the identity of one of the concert-goers who'd been standing close to Kerry and Isabella at Sunmore Hall and was interviewing her downstairs. With no one to share her thoughts with, she rang Mike.

'Morning!' His voice lifted her spirits.

'Hi. How are you getting on?'

'Still full-on here at Blithbury Marsh. No sign of the girls' mobiles.'

'I have a question for you. How accurate is automated facial recognition technology?'

She heard a slight sucking in of breath. 'Hmm. I'd stand by the technology – it supposedly has a ninety-seven per cent accuracy rate – but lighting and the distance of the subject from the camera play their part, and there have been reports to suggest it isn't always accurate, especially with some ethnic groups.'

'There could be an outside chance it's wrong, then?'

'Why do you ask?'

'I've got a suspect I'm about to interview who claims he can't remember where he was in the early hours of Saturday morning, but using CCTV footage which we ran through the lab, we've come up with his name. I have doubts. Especially as I'm also about to speak to somebody else who resembles the suspect. I just wanted to air my thoughts, that's all.' *And hear your voice.*

'I wouldn't let anything cloud your judgement,' he replied.

It was the right response. She couldn't pre-judge or jump to conclusions. There was only one way to do this – systematically and following all procedures.

'Cheers.'

'Anything else I can help with?'

'Find me some evidence,' she replied.

'Doing our best. Talk to you later.'

She detected the smile in his voice and felt better.

Her call to Mike was followed swiftly by Ian's return to let her know the duty solicitor was with Sludge.

'How did you get on with your witness – the girl at the concert?'

'Waste of time. The first time she registered Kerry was near her was when she asked the group of girls if they'd seen Isabella. She says none of them noticed anything unusual, but she has given me contact details for her friends, so I'll try them. I doubt they were any more observant.' He shook his head in disbelief.

'Try them later. I'd like you to interview Sludge with me.' She shuffled her notes into order and headed downstairs, Ian trotting by her side.

With the tape recorder set up, introductions made and the solicitor sitting quietly next to Sludge, Natalie tried to ascertain his whereabouts during the early hours of Saturday morning.

'Rowan, we'd like to know your movements from Friday evening to the early hours of Saturday morning.'

'Sludge.'

'Sorry?'

'Nobody calls me Rowan. I'm Sludge.'

'Would you answer the question, please?'

'I don't know my movements.'

'Why not?'

'I was off my tits,' he replied with a grin.

'Are you saying you were inebriated?'

'Inebriated, drunk, pissed, out of my tree… whatever you want to call it.'

'Can you talk me through what you do remember?'

'I went out about seven to the pub and met up with some lads I know from there. Another regular who I don't know very well came in with some of his mates. They were all pretty well pissed up and the next thing I knew we were all invited to a party at this bloke's place, somewhere in Samford. I had a great time… drank far too much. Things become a bit vague though and I think I might have dozed off for a while. Anyway, at some point I decided to leave but the others had already gone and I didn't have any money for a taxi back home, so I walked. I don't remember much after that at all – I might have taken a few wrong turnings. All I know is I woke up in some bushes near my house.' He smirked and Natalie tried hard not to snap at him.

'Who were these men you met at the pub?'

'Buzz… Garth… Robbie.'

'I need full names.'

'I don't know their full names. We meet up in the pub now and again and chat. Sometimes we play darts or cards.'

'Come on. You know more than that. Don't mess me about.'

'I don't know their names just like they don't know my real name.' He gave a loose-shouldered shrug and spoke to his solicitor. 'I don't know them, right? I want that made clear.'

'Can you describe these men? Where they live, what they do?' Natalie asked.

'Dunno where they live or much about them. Think Buzz has a girlfriend or wife but I'm not sure. Robbie works in a paint factory. That's about it. They were there on Friday evening, so ask them.'

Natalie sighed. 'Okay, which pub did you meet them in?'

'Bean and Whistle.'

Ian duly noted the name. Natalie stared at Sludge, who returned the look, his arms casually folded.

'I haven't done anything wrong,' he said, a smile playing at the corners of his mouth.

'I'm not suggesting you have. Can you tell me what you wore to the pub?'

He shrugged. 'Jeans, T-shirt, top.'

'Did you wear a hooded top?'

He cocked his head and answered with, 'Might have done.'

Natalie kept her voice even although she was becoming exasperated. 'Surely you know what clothes you were wearing.'

The solicitor whispered something to him and he nodded. 'Yes, I borrowed a sweatshirt that was lying about in the squat. I don't know who it belongs to. I think it was left behind by one of the guys who moved off last week. It might have had a hood. I didn't notice. It was dark blue, I think, or maybe even black. I didn't have it when I woke up so I can't be sure.'

Natalie pulled out the still taken from the CCTV camera and showed it to him. 'Is this you?'

He squinted at it. 'Hard to tell, isn't it?'

'Let's say for a moment that it is you. Can you explain why you were on Greenfield Road at one twenty Saturday morning?'

'Like I told you, I haven't a clue where I went that night. I wandered about and got lost. I woke up several houses from the squat.'

'And that would be on Dovedale Avenue?'

'Yes.'

'Where was this party you attended?'

He gave a noncommittal response.

'Sludge, where was the party?'

'Somewhere near the pub. I was a bit pissed by then and didn't pay much attention to where we were walking. I just followed the others up front.'

Natalie tried a different question to throw him off balance. 'Do you know Chris and Judith Westmore?'

'No.'

'Do you know their children, Erin and Ivy? They're thirteen-year-old twins.'

His forehead creased. 'No.'

Natalie showed him a photograph of the family but he shook his head.

'I've never seen them before.'

'What about these girls?' She passed him pictures of Kerry and Isabella, and once more he shook his head.

'Do you recognise this building?' She showed him a picture of the furniture warehouse opposite the Westmores' house.

'Yeah, I know that. Furniture store, isn't it?'

'The CCTV camera in front of the building was vandalised in the early hours of Saturday morning. Do you know anything about it?'

'No.'

'Somebody sprayed it with red paint.'

He maintained steady eye contact with her but remained silent.

'I understand you have been charged in the past for vandalising public areas, walls and buildings.'

'I served my time for that.'

'I have been reliably informed that you invariably used red paint when defacing property.'

He shifted in his chair but kept his eyes on Natalie. 'I haven't graffitied anything since I got released.'

'Mr Stevenson isn't here to discuss past misdemeanours, DI Ward. I suggest you keep your questions relevant,' said the solicitor.

'Mr Stevenson can't remember what he did that night and a CCTV camera was put out of action thanks to somebody spraying it with red paint. We have footage of a man who, using facial recognition technology, has been identified as a match to Mr Stevenson.'

The solicitor gave a small smile. 'I'm afraid that isn't foolproof. It was dark. The person captured on CCTV bears similarities to Mr Stevenson, I grant you, but I'm sure there are plenty of other men of similar size and height, with similar facial hair, who could pass for Mr Stevenson.'

Natalie's fists clenched. The wretched man was right. She'd hoped that Sludge would be more cooperative than he was being and that this revelation would get him to open up. It didn't. It only served to make him smirk some more. She was fighting a losing battle. She'd have to locate these so-called friends of his and find out his exact whereabouts. It was all time-wasting.

She appealed to Sludge. 'We're investigating the abduction and murder of three children – two of whom lived opposite the building where the camera was vandalised. It would help us hugely if you could at least give us reason to eliminate you from our enquiries and even provide some proof as to your whereabouts.' For a split second, she thought she spotted something in his face, but the smirk was back in a flash and he shook his head.

'I can't help you,' he said.

Natalie paced the corridor. She had no time to waste, and chasing about after Sludge was exactly what she'd hoped to avoid. She'd sent Ian upstairs to uncover more about Sludge's whereabouts and requested Sludge and his solicitor wait a while to assist them further with their enquiries.

The duty sergeant at the far end of the corridor called out to her and she headed his way. 'You have a visitor. He says you're expecting him – Eddie Ford. Owns a hair salon,' he said.

'Yes, thanks, I am. I'll come and fetch him.' She strode into reception and spotted the man, who stood up as soon as he saw her and walked towards her. She hadn't seen him for at least a month and his beard had grown. He resembled the man that the CCTV camera on Greenfield Road had captured more strongly than she'd first imagined. Could the tech team have got it wrong?

CHAPTER SEVENTEEN

MONDAY, 13 AUGUST – LATE MORNING

Eddie sat with his legs crossed, eyebrows drawn down. 'Kerry was a right madam. I was under the impression it was all such a drag for her. She'd sometimes answer back too, and that cheesed me off. She was only a junior. I expected more respect from her.'

'You obviously gave her warnings before firing her.'

'Oh sure, but she didn't seem to care. I used to wonder why she'd asked for a job in the first place.'

This sounded quite unlike the same girl currently employed at Sally Downs' salon.

'Did you ever meet her sister, Isabella?'

'No.'

'Her parents?'

'Once. I met her father. He dropped her off at work and came in. He took me to task, the cheeky sod, and said I'd upset Kerry. I put him straight.'

'You hadn't upset her?'

'Maybe I did. I caught her texting on her damn phone instead of dealing with a client, and I warned her another mistake like that and she was out. Her father said her version of events was quite different and that I hadn't instructed her to remove the client from under a hairdryer but had stormed into the back and yelled at her for no good reason. It was lies. The other stylists were happy to back me up but he didn't call in again. Kerry's behaviour didn't improve much. I had to ask her to leave in the end, what with texting and boys hanging outside the shop, waiting to talk to her.'

'Boys?'

'A couple of loutish sorts. I got the impression she was seeing one or both of them but she never actually said anything about them. She'd nip out in her breaks and have a giggle with them then come back inside looking smug.'

Again, this was at odds with what Sally had told her. According to Kerry's current employer, she hadn't been involved with anyone since the lad who became a paramedic and moved away. What was really going on? Only Kerry could tell her that, and she'd be next on her list to interview. It was important to exhaust all potential avenues however obscure or unlikely they appeared to be. *If only they'd been more thorough during the Blossom Twins case.*

'Eddie, do you know Chris and Judith Westmore?'

'The names ring a bell.'

'They have twin girls – Erin and Ivy.'

'I know who you mean. The twins came to the salon about a month ago. They were going to a party and wanted their hair interwoven with flowers.'

'Did you know they live on Emerson Lane? That's close to the salon, isn't it?'

'Yes, it's the street at the bottom of Greenhill Road, but no, I didn't know they lived there.'

'You never saw them around?'

'The first time I saw them was when they came into my salon.'

'Would you mind telling me your whereabouts on Friday evening?'

'I locked up the salon at 6 p.m., took a quick stroll into town to deposit the takings at the ATM and got back about half an hour later. I didn't go out after that.'

'Not at all?'

'No. I had a glass or two of wine, chucked a ready-made meal in the oven and watched television.'

'Can anybody vouch for you?'

'No.'

'What about Saturday night?'

'Pretty much the same. I dropped off the day's takings at the ATM after I closed up. I spent the night catching up on *Game of Thrones*. I've only recently got into that show. There's such a buzz surrounding it and I don't want to get too far behind. The clients invariably talk about it.'

'You don't live alone, do you?' She already knew the answer to the question but it gave her the chance to see how he reacted.

His forehead wrinkled in confusion. 'No, I live with my wife, Nia. We've got a four-year-old daughter, Pixie, but they're both in Blackpool for a long weekend, with friends. Nia isn't keen on *Game of Thrones*, so I used the time she was away to chill and catch up with it. Can I ask what this is about?'

'The twins disappeared Saturday night and the CCTV camera facing their house was defaced. The surveillance camera on Greenfield Road picked up a man walking towards Emerson Lane about ten minutes before the camera was vandalised. Eddie, was that person you?'

He shook his head. 'Absolutely not! I was inside all night.'

'You didn't go out for a walk in the early hours?'

'No, I was asleep then. I went to bed around eleven. I thought you asked me here to talk about Kerry, not the twins. I wanted to help you.'

'And you have. Thank you.' Natalie eased off. She wasn't gaining anything by alienating him.

'Have you found them – the girls?' He sounded anxious and she couldn't be sure if he was playing her or not.

'They were discovered yesterday.' Her face said more than her words and he picked up on it.

'Were they dead?'

She nodded quickly.

His jaw dropped dramatically and he lifted a hand to his mouth. 'No!'

'I'm afraid that's true, so you can see why I'm keen to talk to whoever was walking along Greenfield Road at that time. That person might have spotted the person responsible for damaging the camera.'

'It wasn't me. I didn't leave the flat above the salon. I can't help you. Sorry.'

She examined the still taken from the CCTV camera. The person in it wasn't wearing square-framed glasses and neither was Eddie. 'I've just worked out what's different about you,' she said lightly. 'You're not wearing your glasses. Have you had laser surgery?'

'I'm wearing contact lenses.'

'I didn't know you wore contacts.'

'I tend not to wear them when I'm working. My eyes get dry and sore, so I stick to the specs.'

She nodded and gave a small smile then asked, 'You categorically deny leaving the flat and walking down your street in the early hours of Saturday morning?'

'Yes. Whoever that person is, it isn't me.'

There was little else she could do. Eddie denied leaving his flat above the shop and she couldn't prove otherwise at the moment. She was, however, becoming increasingly convinced that whoever had put the CCTV camera opposite the Westmores' house out of action had done so deliberately. There had to be a way of proving who it was. For now, she was going to let Eddie go.

Her mobile buzzed and she took the call in the corridor. John and Lucy hadn't uncovered anything from the security staff who'd been on duty at the open-air concert.

'No one saw a thing,' said Lucy, her voice barely able to hide the frustration she was experiencing. 'Not one of them spotted Isabella slipping through the crowds or going to the kitchen garden. Can you believe it?'

Natalie could. The whole area had been crowded. The staff had been looking out for potential troublemakers not an innocent-looking teenage girl. Nevertheless, the investigation was stalling and that knowledge filled her with dread. She had to track down the perpetrator before they decided to strike again because a small voice in her head warned her they would.

As she walked from reception, having shown Eddie out, she was pleased to see Ian waiting for her. He'd been hunting down information on Sludge while she'd been talking to Eddie, and judging by his expression, he'd found some.

'According to the landlord of the Bean and Whistle pub, Sludge and the others he mentioned were there until about 10 p.m. He says the pub CCTV footage proves that and is sending it across for me to look at. He also reckons he knows about the party, which took place in High Bank. Looking at the map, there is no way Sludge would walk down Greenfield Road to get back to the squat. It's in completely the wrong direction.'

'But if he was drunk or high or both, as he suggested, he might have headed off in the opposite direction by mistake.'

Ian showed her a map of the area on his iPad. 'Even if he went wrong, he'd have headed down Market Street and arrived at the underpass under Samford bypass. Even blind drunk, he'd surely have realised he was way off course.'

'It's something to go on but it's not concrete enough. Get the full names of those men he mentioned – Buzz, Garth and Robbie – and talk to them. Find out what actually happened that night. Tell Sludge he's free to go for now but we'll want to interview him again.'

'On it.'

She walked towards the stairs, halting in her stride when a voice called her and the desk sergeant caught up with her.

'Letter for you. I put it in the postal tray but seeing as you are down here…' The post was usually collected downstairs and distributed to the various offices and departments when somebody was free to do so.

'Thanks, Malcolm.' The letter had been sent first class on Saturday morning, postmarked Samford and addressed for her personal attention. She ripped it open absent-mindedly, her mind on her next move in the investigation. She had to work out if the cases were definitely linked. She pulled out the single sheet of white paper, unfolded it as she walked up the stairs and stopped dead. The note, typed out in large, bold font, was brief:

I'm back!

CHAPTER EIGHTEEN

MONDAY, 13 AUGUST – AFTERNOON

Natalie immediately took the note she'd received to Forensics and then ascended to the second floor to inform her superintendent. Dan, reclined in his chair, spun a silver fountain pen slowly between his fingers.

'Could be from a crank.'

'Sir, I think it might have come from the twins' killer.'

'That's illogical. How could the perpetrator of that crime even know you were heading the investigation into their death? The letter was postmarked Saturday, suggesting it was posted sometime after the last collection on Friday and the first on Saturday. At that time, the twins were alive and at home. You're jumping to conclusions. I understand your concerns, given the similarities between this case and the one you handled in 2014, but I think you're allowing that to cloud your judgement. It's my understanding that the person responsible for the Blossom Twins murders, Neil Hoskins, was brought to justice and has since died. We are looking at a copycat killing here and I need you to remember that. It might be an idea for you to talk the old case through with DS Briggs to bring clarity to the situation.'

She held her breath. Was he suggesting that John Briggs had a more level-headed approach to the Blossom Twins investigation?

'About that, sir. It would have been the decent thing to do to have informed me before assigning DS Briggs to my team.'

'As I recall, I advised you that you would be receiving assistance.'

'You did but it would have been helpful to have known who you had in mind.'

He stopped twirling the pen and leant forward. 'Is there a problem here, DI Ward?'

'No, sir...'

'Good. It was my decision to request DS Briggs join the investigation. He also has first-hand knowledge of the Blossom Twins investigation and will prove a valuable asset. Now, have you ascertained any connection between Isabella Sharpe's and the twins' murders yet?'

'Not yet, sir.'

'Then I suggest you return to your team and find out if there is any.'

'Sir.'

She spun on her heel, fuming at his attitude. He'd made her feel like an incompetent junior and hadn't taken her concerns on board. How bloody dare he! Aileen Melody would have listened to her and understood her anxieties. *But Aileen has gone and you're on your own here.* She clomped back to her office, angry at her superior's attitude but furious with herself for rushing to him without first having had the note properly examined.

The team were working as one and the office was an efficient hive of activity. Lucy and John had returned and were at their respective desks, heads bowed over laptops, phones clamped between shoulders and chins. She sat at her desk, the muscles in her neck and shoulders bunched. Turning on her laptop, she stared at the screen with unseeing eyes. What was she missing? Was Isabella's death linked in some way? The Blossom Twins murderer had only ever killed in pairs, so if this perpetrator was emulating Neil Hoskins, it wouldn't make sense for them to only kill one girl. There would be two.

She pulled up the photograph of Isabella and set it side by side with the photograph of the twins. Isabella and Erin had been placed in similar positions but where Erin faced her sister, Ivy, Isabella faced a wall. Natalie's eyes were drawn to the rose petals. Had they been scattered onto the body and blown off? She scrutinised the photo again before enlarging it. Mike had claimed the petals had tumbled naturally onto Isabella's body, but examining the crime scene pictures in greater detail, there appeared to be more petals on her body and the ground immediately around her than elsewhere under the arbour. Isabella was alone but positioned almost identically to Erin. This had to be the work of the same killer yet there was no plastic bag placed over Isabella's head and no second body – that of a sister. Lost in thought, she hadn't noticed Lucy cross to her desk.

'Natalie, we've received footage from the Bean and Whistle pub that backs up Sludge's account of events on Friday night. He was definitely at the bar with three men, identified as Barry "Buzz" Woodsman, Garth Langford and Robert Moss, known to his friends as Robbie. Sludge was standing beside the bar for most of the evening and left at about ten along with three other men who came in for half an hour at nine thirty and mostly chatted to Robbie while Sludge and Garth played darts.'

'Any idea who the other men are?'

'Ian's spoken to the landlord again, and he's identified one of them – Simon Vaughn – and confirmed he invited everyone back to his house for a party. He's a self-made scrap merchant who's suddenly done really well for himself. He used to live in a terraced cottage nearby but now he's got a big property in High Bank. He's still one of the pub's regulars though. I'm going to talk to him about Sludge now.'

Natalie leant one arm on the table and thought before saying, 'See if you can pinpoint his movements after he left the party. I don't believe his memory is that much of a blank. I think he's hiding something. Take Ian with you. He's familiar with the roads and routes around there.'

As soon as Lucy and Ian disappeared, she strolled towards John and stood in front of his desk. He glanced at her before saying, 'Couldn't get anything helpful out of the security staff at Sunmore Hall, so I've been trying to contact both bands' personal security teams. The support act left as soon as they'd performed, so no joy there, and Blasted are in Germany at the moment, so it's tricky getting hold of anyone to assist.'

'John, I want to run something past you. You've had a chance to examine the crime scene photos at Sunmore Hall now. Does it strike you that the way Isabella's body was arranged is strikingly similar to the way Erin Westmore was placed, and for that matter, Sharon Hill and Avril Moore back in 2014?'

He pushed back from the desk and folded his arms. 'Yeah, my thoughts ran along similar lines. The positioning is identical, never mind similar. Isabella was deliberately left like that.'

Natalie nodded, hoping he'd arrive at the same conclusion as her, which he had.

'What's missing, of course, is another girl – a sister – lying opposite her, and, of course, the plastic bags. There's one other thing that doesn't fit the scenario too; Kerry's older than all the other victims. The other girls were all thirteen or fourteen.'

'I agree about the age difference, but this has made me wonder if the cases are linked. What do you think?' she asked.

His head bobbed from side to side as he tried to decide on a definite answer. 'I think it's possible but we haven't established any connections between Isabella and the twins, so we're pissing in the wind at the moment. Neil Hoskins was our link between the Moore twins and the Hill sisters. He knew all four victims.'

Natalie agreed. The only person she could think of who knew both the Westmore twins and Kerry and Isabella was Eddie Ford. Although he had no apparent motive to kill the girls, there was nobody who could support his claims that he'd been at home at the time, and that set alarm bells ringing in the back of her mind.

They'd been pursuing Sludge in the hope he had vandalised the CCTV camera opposite the Westmores' house, or could shed light on whoever had done so. They'd thought the camera had been deliberately sabotaged in order for somebody to snatch the twins. It was purely assumption, and whichever way she looked at it, it was no more than a shot in the dark, but with little else to go on what choice did they have?

Natalie needed to up her game. She debated telling John about the note she'd received, but after her dressing-down from Dan, she decided it was wiser to wait until Forensics had examined it before sharing that particular nugget of information with anyone else. However, John was the only other person who knew the details of the Blossom Twins case as well as she did, and who had as much of a personal stake as her in catching this perpetrator. After all, he'd played his part in allowing Neil to slip through their fingers and murder Avril and Faye. He probably shouldered more guilt than anyone. She'd have to give him his chance to prove himself.

*

Lucy and Ian arrived at Simon Vaughn's house, a semi-renovated farmhouse with a small stable block. A woman in jeans was grooming a horse beside the gate and waited for them to approach, identity cards lifted.

Lucy spoke. 'DS Lucy Carmichael and PC Ian Jarvis. We've come to talk to Simon Vaughn about the party on Friday night. Is he in?'

'Yes, he's working from home. Oh, here he is! Si… police for you.'

A ruddy-faced man in an open short-sleeved shirt, shorts, flip-flops and sunglasses was striding towards them with all the sureness of a self-made man. He drew to a halt and held out a hand. His voice betrayed his working-class roots and he spoke in a gravelly baritone. 'Afternoon! How can I help you?'

'Mr Vaughn, we're here about your party on Friday night.'

He gave a grin. 'We didn't upset the snooty neighbours again, did we? I don't know – us lowering the tone of the neighbourhood, eh, Mandy?' He winked at the woman.

'I wouldn't know about that, sir. We're here to talk to you about Rowan Stevenson,' Lucy replied.

'Who the heck's that?'

'You might know him as Sludge.'

'I don't know anyone by that name.'

The woman patted the horse, which stood placidly. 'I do. He was a ratty little man with a beard and a man bun. He sort of gate-crashed the party. Si went to the local pub for a drink with a couple of friends before the party kicked off and came back with half the pub in tow.'

Simon gave a half-hearted, sheepish grin. 'I'm a regular at the Bean and Whistle. I nipped into the pub before the party started. I'd already had a few bevvies with my mates and was feeling... let's say "generous-natured", so I invited a few of the guys there back to the party. I don't remember the bloke you're talking about though.'

Mandy continued, 'I spoke to him for a while but he didn't have a lot to say for himself. He kept checking his phone like he was expecting a call. He was a bit different to everyone else. I wondered why he stayed cos he looked pretty uncomfortable.'

'I remember him now! Yes, he tagged along with Robbie. I don't know why he came either cos he turned out to be a right party pooper. I offered him drink after drink, but he stuck to fruit juice! Fruit juice, I ask you!'

'You're saying he didn't have any alcohol?'

'I didn't give him any, did you?' Simon asked Mandy.

She rubbed the horse's nose. 'No. I took the wine bottle around a few times but he refused.'

'I don't suppose you noticed what time he left?'

'You're joking. It was my birthday. I was having a great time. Mandy? You any idea?'

The woman's nose wrinkled but her forehead remained immobile and smooth. 'I can't be sure but I spoke to him around midnight. He was on the landing looking for the toilet. I told him where it was. And I remember Robbie leaving around one o'clock – we were winding up about then and I told him not to forget to take Sludge home with him. He laughed and said no worries cos he'd already left.'

'When you saw Sludge on the landing, how did he seem?'

'Bored. Distant. Not the best party guest,' Mandy replied.

'What did he talk to you about earlier that evening?'

'I did most of the talking. He mumbled a lot. You can tell when people aren't really listening to you. Well, that was him.'

'Neither of you saw him leave, then?'

'No.'

'Can either of you remember what he was wearing?'

Mandy answered, 'Jeans and a dark blue sweatshirt. I remember because he was so scruffy. Not that I give a stuff about what people wear, but he stood out.'

'Did this sweatshirt have a hood?'

'Yes. It did.'

With notes taken and the interview at an end, Lucy and Ian rang Natalie to pass on the information. Although it appeared Sludge's alibi held up until about midnight, neither host saw him after that, and one thing was for certain: he had not been drunk or high and would certainly have known where he was headed. Natalie requested they bring the man back to the station for further questioning and asked John to search through further CCTV footage on the route Sludge would have taken, to help pinpoint his movements for when they next interviewed him.

She left him to it and headed off to talk to Kerry Sharpe again. Since speaking to Eddie about the girl, she was confused about what had really happened at Eddie's salon. Sally Downs, the girl's current employer, spoke well of the girl, yet Eddie had not. He'd also mentioned that Kerry had been talking to boys outside the shop while Sally had said Kerry hadn't been involved with anyone since the lad who'd left the area. Natalie had two different pictures of Isabella's sister in her head and wanted to clear matters up; after all, Kerry was the last person they knew of to see her sister alive.

CHAPTER NINETEEN

MONDAY, 13 AUGUST – AFTERNOON

Natalie pulled up on the road outside the Sharpes' house. From the outside, it looked a perfectly ordinary house yet behind its brick exterior was a world of pain. Three reporters stood on the pavement, faces turned in her direction, eyes hungry for details. Natalie spotted Tanya Granger's car parked three spaces down from her own and was pleased the liaison officer was with the family. Tanya managed to steer families through these awful times with patience and empathy, and Natalie admired her ability to be a friend and advisor to all who needed her.

She answered the questions fired at her with a quiet, 'No comment', rang the bell and waited for somebody to open the door. A face appeared at the window of the house next door, a neighbour, and vanished again when the person caught sight of Natalie looking back. She rang again and after a long minute the door was opened and Ryan Sharpe faced them. He shuffled backwards a few paces to allow her entry. He'd not shaved since she'd last seen him and stubble clung to his face, the colour of putty, in irregular patches on his chin and cheeks.

'Have you any news?' he asked.

'Sorry, no, I've come to ask Kerry a few more questions, if I may.'

'Oh. Sure. She's upstairs. Shall I get her?'

'If you wouldn't mind.'

He lumbered away, like a man twice his age. Natalie could hear Tanya talking in a soothing tone to Camilla in the kitchen and edged towards the open door to say hello. Camilla was bent over the kitchen table, head in hands. Natalie tapped lightly and Camilla lifted her head.

'Sorry to disturb you. I've come to talk to Kerry.'

'Fine. Tanya's been helping us. I want to see my daughter. I want to see Isabella and I want her brought out of that place so we can say goodbye to her... properly.'

Natalie had met other parents in similar situations. It was natural to want closure, and for many that would only come when their loved one's body was released from custody.

Tanya spoke. 'I'm arranging for Camilla and Ryan to see Isabella.'

Natalie nodded. This wasn't her department. This was Tanya's. Natalie had to break the terrible news and Tanya and her colleagues helped the families pick up the pieces of their shattered lives immediately afterwards, rallying around them until they could cope again.

There was a movement behind her and she turned. Ryan had an arm around Kerry's shoulders. Her eyes were red-rimmed and her cheeks sunken. Grief had eaten away at the girl, whose head was bowed. 'Hi,' she said softly.

'Hi, Kerry. Would it be okay if I talked to you again about Eddie Ford?'

Ryan's eyes widened slightly. 'Is Eddie involved?'

'We're interviewing everyone we believe had some relevant connection to Kerry and Isabella. I've also spoken to Sally Downs.'

'Oh. Okay.' His eyes dimmed again.

Natalie looked at Kerry. 'Do you want to go in the kitchen or sitting room?'

'Sitting room.'

'Want me to come too?' asked Ryan.

'No, it's okay,' said Kerry.

He removed his arm and stood back, allowing Natalie and Kerry to go into the room opposite. Natalie left the door open and sat down next to Kerry on the settee.

'I'm trying to find out what happened at Eddie's salon and why he fired you,' Natalie began. 'Why don't you tell me your version again.'

'There's not much to say. I cheesed him off no matter what I did. I couldn't do anything right. I was only a junior. It was my first job and I didn't know much, but every time I made a mistake, he'd go off on one at me. I told Dad and he got really upset about it and had a word with him. He didn't shout at me again after that for a couple of days and then he fired me.'

'What was the reason for that?'

'He said I deliberately left a client under a hot hairdryer but I didn't. He hadn't set the timer correctly and it didn't ping when it should have. I only take clients out from under the dryer when the timer rings. She got too much heat on her highlights and it dried out her hair. He had to put tons of conditioner on it afterwards to prevent the ends from breaking. He blamed me for it but it wasn't my fault. By then, I didn't care. I was glad to get out and I'd met Sally. She was happy to give me a job.'

'Isabella came to visit you at the salon a couple of times, didn't she?'

'Yes. The first time she stopped off, Eddie was all cheesy and nice to her. Then the second time, she came by during my lunch break to bring me some lunch and we were sat chatting in the back room when he came storming in and told her to leave cos she wasn't staff. He had a right go at me about that and said I had to keep my private life and work life separate.'

'Why was he so angry?'

'I don't know. Maybe he overheard something?'

'Like what?'

Kerry shifted slightly. 'I think Isabella made some comment about his stupid square glasses. Maybe he heard it.'

Kerry was still acting as the innocent but Eddie had accused her of being rude and answering back so maybe the comment had come from her not Isabella. There was also the matter of the boys who'd visited her outside the salon when she was supposedly working. 'Were you going out with anybody at the time you were working at Eddie's?'

Kerry's neat eyebrows arched in surprise. 'What do you mean?'

'Did you have a boyfriend?'

'What's that got to do with Isabella's death?' Ryan had appeared and was looking puzzled.

'I'm trying to find out why Eddie fired your daughter from his salon.'

'Because he was a bully,' Ryan replied. 'He picked on Kerry from the off. She'd come home in tears sometimes. I spoke to him about it but he denied it, of course. I even told Kerry to jack in the damn job but she stuck it out, credit to her, until he got rid of her.' He gave her a proud smile.

Natalie sensed a shift in Kerry's attitude. She lowered her head again and stared at her painted nails.

'What's Eddie been saying about Kerry?'

'Nothing to concern yourself over,' said Natalie.

'Why were you asking about boyfriends?'

'Eddie mentioned seeing a couple of lads waiting outside the salon for Kerry.'

'No, he was mistaken, wasn't he, Kerry?'

She nodded. 'He was wrong. I wasn't seeing anyone. I nipped outside once or twice to say hello to some boys I used to go to school with, but that was all. I split up with a boy, Curtis, a year ago.'

'I take it Curtis was the young man who became a paramedic?'

'Yes. He moved to London. I haven't seen him since he left.'

'I don't see what bearing this has on your investigation,' said Ryan, cautiously.

'I'm only getting the facts straight.'

'Is there anything else you want to tell me, Kerry?' Natalie asked.

The girl shook her head but Natalie couldn't help but feel there was something.

'If you can think of anything, give me a call, won't you?'

Kerry answered with a quiet, 'Yes.'

'Have you any idea who is behind this?' asked Ryan.

'We're doing our best to find out.'

'Please. Find them. Get justice for our girl.' His eyes brimmed again with tears as he spoke.

'We really are doing everything we can,' repeated Natalie in the full knowledge that whatever they did, it would never truly be enough to mend the broken hearts under this roof.

On her return to HQ, Natalie discovered Lucy and Ian had brought in Sludge, who was once again in the interview room. John had been busy too and had obtained valuable information that would assist them in the interview, so she took him in with her to speak to the graffiti artist.

'I told you everything I remember,' he bleated, looking towards his solicitor for guidance.

Natalie tutted. 'I'm sure you've guessed we have fresh evidence that suggests you were not drunk or high and that you left the party at the house in High Bank sometime between midnight and one o'clock. We've been through more surveillance footage since we last spoke to you and can pinpoint you at five to one in the morning, heading down Market Street in the direction of the underpass. From there, it's a ten-minute walk to Greenhill Road, where you were again picked up on a CCTV camera.'

He looked up at the ceiling and wouldn't meet Natalie's eyes. She had him. She pulled three photographs out of a folder and laid them out on the desk in front of him.

John spoke for the tape recorder. 'DI Ward is showing Rowan Stevenson three photographs: JB301, JB302 and JB303.'

Natalie said, 'I'd like you to confirm that the person in these three photographs is you.'

Sludge looked down at last and said wearily, 'Yes.'

'As you can see from the timestamp in the top right-hand corner, these photographs were taken at one-minute intervals: 12.55 a.m., 12.56 a.m. and 12.57 a.m. In the first photograph, JB301, you appear to be reaching into a waste bin positioned outside the Rocket Café on Market Street. In the second photograph, JB302, you are extracting an object, and in the third, JB303, the object you're holding can be seen quite clearly. What is that object, Rowan?'

'Sludge. Not Rowan.'

'*Sludge*, what did you fish out of the bin?'

He glanced at his solicitor and then back at Natalie before admitting the truth. 'It was a can of spray paint.'

'And what colour was the paint in the can?'

'Red.'

'How did you know it was in the bin?'

'I was told to collect it from there.'

'How did you receive that instruction – text message, phone call?'

Sludge pressed his lips together tightly.

'You don't want to go back to jail, do you? Defacing private property is an offence, you know? We could help if you speak to us.'

He looked again at his solicitor, who nodded and suggested he explain himself. Sludge drew a deep breath before confessing. 'A few days ago, there was a bloke hanging outside the squat. He promised me a hundred pounds if I sprayed the CCTV camera on Emerson Lane – half the money up front, the remainder afterwards. It was easy money. I wasn't doing any real harm.'

'You didn't ask this man why he wanted the camera vandalising?'

'Yes, sure I did. He said he used to be a night security guard at the warehouse but they'd fired him and put up the camera instead, so this was his way of getting back at them.'

'And you believed that? It's a public surveillance camera. It's not on private property.' Natalie was incredulous.

Sludge opened his palms. 'It didn't matter, did it? A hundred pounds for doing next to nothing! It was only a bit of paint. It'd have been cleaned off easily enough.'

'Why all the secrecy about leaving a spray can in a bin? Why didn't he just give you the can there and then, or even tell you to buy it?'

'He said he didn't want it to get traced back to me, or to him for that matter, so he'd use the bin as a drop zone like spies do when they want to pass on information. I thought he was nuts but I went along with it anyway.'

'Describe this man to us.'

'Good six foot tall. Even taller. He was wearing a military-style jacket with the collar turned up, sunglasses and a baseball cap pulled low over his forehead. I think he had long hair and a beard a bit like mine, and he spoke with a Scottish accent.'

Natalie gripped the edge of her file of notes. That description fitted Eddie Ford, who had a strong Scottish accent. She hunted for a photograph of the man and revealed it to Sludge. 'Did the man look like this?'

Sludge looked at it and pulled a face. 'Difficult to say.'

'Why did he choose the bin outside the Rocket Café on Market Street?'

'No idea. He told me to head that way at about quarter to one Saturday morning, collect the can, go to Emerson Lane and spray the camera by the furniture warehouse.'

'When did you collect the rest of your money?'

'Straight afterwards. It was in a bin by the underpass.' He looked down at the desk.

There was something about this sudden movement that made her say, 'Hang on. You went through the underpass on your way to the warehouse. You could have collected the money beforehand.

In fact, you could have taken the money and not sprayed the camera at all.'

He continued to study the desk. 'But I told him I would, so I did.'

Sludge didn't strike her as the honourable sort. 'Didn't you check the bin at the underpass before you went to the warehouse? In case the money had already been dropped there?'

'Yes… okay. I checked the bin, hoping he'd already left it there, but he hadn't.'

'But it was there later when you returned.'

'Yes, it was.'

'Am I right in saying that in the twenty minutes or so it took you to check the bin, vandalise the camera and then return to the underpass, the money appeared?'

'Yes. It was in an envelope.'

'Do you still have the envelope?'

'No. I threw it away.'

'Where?'

'I threw it back into the bin.'

It seemed the person who'd asked Sludge to vandalise the camera had been keeping an eye on him, but nobody else had shown up on CCTV footage at or around that time. They'd known to keep out of the way of the cameras. She made a mental note to have the bins on Market Street and by the underpass searched in case they hadn't yet been emptied.

'Did you see the man at any point?'

'No.'

'And what did you do with the empty paint can?'

'Threw it in the bin where the money had been left.'

'Had you ever seen the man before?'

'No.'

'Have you seen him since?'

'No.'

'Did he leave you any contact details?'

'No.'

'You're telling me you accepted fifty pounds from a complete stranger and trusted that same person to give you another fifty pounds for following a series of bizarre instructions and defacing public property?'

He shrugged half-heartedly. 'You're making it weirder than it was.'

'No… it is actually weird.'

'It might be but it's the truth.'

'What have you done with the money?'

'I spent it.'

'Already? On what?'

'I owed some of it to mates and I bought a couple of bottles of vodka and some food with the rest.'

Natalie sighed. 'Okay, tell me exactly what you bought and where you got it.' She'd have to confirm he was telling the truth because this was sounding increasingly bizarre.

He leant towards her, face serious. 'Everything's true,' he said. 'Really it is.'

Natalie had a feeling he was telling the truth. The person responsible had set up such an elaborate trail it was alarming. Natalie was now concerned she was dealing with somebody much cleverer than she'd first suspected.

Natalie exited the interview room with a determined stride. John trailed behind her and called after her, 'No need to thank me for finding that footage of Sludge outside the Rocket Café.'

She halted in her tracks and turned to him. 'If you expect thanks every time you do your fucking job, you're mistaken. We all take the credit on my team, so don't try and be the glory boy.'

'Ma'am,' he replied.

Natalie set off again, taking the stairs two at a time, marched into the office and barked instructions at Lucy and Ian. 'Check out Samford Grocery Store and make sure Sludge was in there earlier today, buying these items.' She slapped the list on a desk. 'See if the waste bins by the underpass and on Market Street have been emptied. I want to know if there is or ever was a night security guard at the furniture warehouse on Emerson Lane, and if so, who the fuck he is. In fact, find out about all the employees there. See if anyone has been fired recently… and I want everything you can get on Eddie Ford, who runs Eddie's Hair Salon. You've exactly no time to do this.'

CHAPTER TWENTY

THEN

Jennifer's chest lifts and lowers, accompanied by hissing and wheezing, the sort of sound made by a foot pump – a pump that would inflate an air mattress. He shuts his eyes. His little girls are running down a sandy beach, their tiny hands clenched protectively in his large ones as they race towards the waves together, squealing in excitement. One of them is holding a blue bucket covered in gaily coloured fish in her free hand, the other has a small inflatable lilo in bright pink that he's pumped up so they can all ride the waves, and their shining eyes are bright with happiness.

'Yay!' yells one as they charge into the sea and the cold water takes their breath away. They stand in a line and allow the waves to curl around their feet, and as they recede the sand sucks at their feet The girls giggle. He holds onto their hands so they don't fall over. The girls beam up at him, and in that one moment, his heart swells with pride. He is a good father.

The machine keeping his wife alive clunks again and brings him back to the moment. He opens his eyes and studies her, unrecognisable with blackened, swollen eyes and bandaged head. He can't make out where one tube enters and another leaves her body, there are so many, carrying fluids to and from her broken body. The mask covering her nose and mouth carries the oxygen she and the babies need, and the machine that whirs and clunks with regular monotony is keeping her lungs working. The blinking lights of the heart monitor show she is alive, although how one defines alive is debatable. She has little to no brain function and is unlikely to regain consciousness. She could not exist without this life support, and were it not for the babies, they would have pulled the plug on her. His little girls aren't ready to be born yet. He reaches for her hand and squeezes it oh so gently. 'Hang on,' he whispers. 'Hang on for the girls' sake. They need you.'

He glances up at the window and watches white-uniformed nurses race past in the corridor outside. He and his wife are cocooned in this world, this clinically white room, filled with technology. She'll never leave it. She'll never return to practising law. She will never take his girls away now. He releases her hand and sits back in the armchair that the nurse with wide grey eyes gave him, all the while treating him with concern and sympathy, her sorrow oozing from every pore, her warm hand on his as he wept crocodile tears. He permits himself a smile. He is certain the pretty nurse will be happy to offer him consolation should he need it. Maybe in time, but for now, he only needs his wife to stay alive for a while longer.

Oh yes, he's going to make a great father.

CHAPTER TWENTY-ONE

MONDAY, 13 AUGUST – LATE AFTERNOON

'Hello, Natalie,' Eddie said from his stooped position, trimming a woman's shoulder-length hair, clipping in swift, expert movements. He rose, placed a hand on her shoulder and said, 'Excuse me for a minute.'

The woman, who'd been engrossed in a magazine, gave a smile and returned to her article. Eddie kept hold of his scissors and moved towards Lucy and Natalie.

'We need you to answer some more questions, Eddie,' Natalie said.

'Can we do it here?'

'I'd rather do it at the station.'

Eddie pleaded with his eyes. 'I'm halfway through doing a client's hair,' he whispered. 'Can't we do this out the back?'

Natalie reluctantly agreed and followed him into a small kitchen set up behind the salon. He placed his scissors on the chipped Formica tabletop and faced Natalie. The staff room was in sharp contrast to the flashy salon that clients saw, with unwashed mugs and boxes of hair products piled on shelves under a sink and a fridge, slightly yellowed with age and use, in one corner.

'I told you everything I could about Kerry,' Eddie hissed.

'This is about you, not Kerry. I need to go through a few things with you. I understand you were born in Glasgow.'

'Yes.'

'But you left Scotland in 2012.'

'Yes. I moved to Manchester.'

'Any special reason why?'

'Felt like a change. I was bored with Glasgow.'

'You trained at the Toni and Guy hair academy in Manchester between 2013 and 2014.'

'That's right.'

'And then you moved to Samford in December 2014.'

'Yes. I worked at the Toni and Guy salon here for a year before setting up this place.'

'When you worked in Manchester, did you ever come across the names Karen and Sharon Hill or Avril and Faye Moore?'

His brows knitted together and he hesitated before asking, 'Weren't they in the papers – the Blossom Twins case?'

'That's correct.'

'Definitely not. Besides, I only worked on older models – men and women.'

Natalie waited for a second, nodded and then said, 'I have to ask you again about the other night. You claimed to be indoors on Friday night.'

'That's right. I was.'

'You didn't leave the house at all?'

'No.'

'Are you familiar with Market Street?'

'Who isn't around here?'

'Answer the question, please.'

'Yes. I'm familiar with Market Street.'

'Did you walk down Market Street on Friday evening?'

'Yes, I deposited the shop takings at the ATM.'

'What time would this have been?'

'After I shut the salon. Six-ish. I told you this when you spoke to me about Isabella.'

'Did you throw anything into the waste bin immediately outside the Rocket Café on Market Street?'

The frown between his eyes deepened and he scratched at his beard as he thought carefully about his response, actions noted carefully by Natalie, who was searching for clues as to whether or not he was lying. 'I bought a sandwich and chucked the wrapper outside in the bin. I'd missed lunch.'

'I thought you had a ready-made meal at home.'

'I had that later. I was feeling peckish when I went to the bank and bought a sandwich to tide me over.'

Natalie pulled out a photograph and pushed it towards him. It was of him throwing something indeterminate into the same bin where Sludge had pulled out a spray can several hours later. The still had been captured at ten past six Friday evening.

'Is this you, Eddie?'

His lips parted but no sound was forthcoming.

'Eddie?'

'Yes. It's me. What's going on? Why have you taken that picture?'

'It's come from a surveillance camera on Market Street. As you can see you appear to be dropping a package into the bin.'

'It's a sandwich wrapper – one of those cardboard box wrappers.'

'But where's the sandwich?'

'I ate it in the café.'

'So, you ate the sandwich while in the café but strolled outside with the wrapper and dropped it in the bin?'

'Exactly that. Can you please explain what is going on?'

'You're saying you dropped a sandwich wrapper into the bin outside the Rocket Café.'

'Yes. Why?'

Natalie explained, 'We have a witness who claims a man who bears a close resemblance to you paid him to vandalise the security camera on the furniture warehouse in Emerson Lane and left a can of spray paint in that very bin for him to collect. Do you have anything you'd like to say about that?'

His mouth flapped wide open and his eyes blinked repeatedly before he could utter, 'That's a lie. I did nothing of the sort.'

'The man they spoke to had a Scottish accent, long black hair and a beard, and wore a military-style jacket. Do you own a jacket like that?'

'No. I've never owned one.'

'You deny approaching anyone and paying them to deface a security camera?'

'Too right I do. Why would I do that?'

Natalie didn't give him a reply, merely continued, 'You told me you didn't know the twins or their parents, Judith and Chris Westmore until recently.'

'That's right. I hadn't met them until they came into the salon last month.'

'Have you ever had a client by the name of Amber Dunn?'

'Sorry, I don't know what you're getting at.'

'Amber Dunn is the twins' aunt and I believe she used your salon two weeks ago.'

'I still don't understand.'

On a nod from Natalie, Lucy pulled out her notepad and said, 'We contacted Amber Dunn and she told us, "Last month, I stayed with my sister, Judith, for a few days. I'd been going through a rough patch and decided to cheer myself up by treating myself to a new hair colour. I made an appointment for Friday, 27 July at Eddie Ford's salon to get my hair lightened from brown to blonde. I had a consultation with Eddie himself, and agreed to have my hair coloured honey-blonde. He put on a pre-lightener which turned my hair bright orange. I wasn't concerned at first, thinking it was part of the process, and I fully expected it to change to blonde once the dye had been put on, but when it was rinsed off, it was definitely still orange and I challenged him. He denied it and said it was a lovely shade of honey-blonde and that hair like mine with warm colours in it always turned this colour. He said I had natural strands of red in my brown hair that had affected the dye. This wasn't at all the colour I'd wanted or been shown in the samples and I hated it, so I refused to pay him. At this point he became very angry and said he'd done exactly what was asked of him. I was frightened by his attitude but left the salon without paying him. He chased me down the street and grabbed hold of my elbow. I told him to let me go or I'd involve my sister, Judith, who was a lawyer, and he let go of me, but I could see he was still furious and he said, 'This isn't over yet.' I was very shaken by his attitude. I went back to my sister's house and when she asked me if I was happy with my hair I told her I was. I thought Eddie Ford was a nasty piece of work and would cause her trouble if she became involved.'" Lucy looked up from her notes.

Eddie was rubbing his forehead and shaking his head. 'No. This is all wrong. I remember the woman now but I didn't know she was related to the twins. It's true, I was annoyed with her. I'd done exactly what she'd asked me to. She flew off the handle at the last minute, refusing to pay. Naturally, I was unhappy that she refused to pay her bill, and when she marched out of the shop, I tried to catch up with her to ask her to at least settle for half of it, but she was really defensive and I backed off. I had no idea…' He pressed the fingers of both hands against his forehead and groaned. 'I didn't know.'

'It's normal for hairdressers to chat to their clients and Amber was here for quite some time getting her hair dyed. I find it surprising she wouldn't tell you why she was in your salon – after all, she was a new customer – or mention she was visiting her sister, or even speak about the twins, who had been here at the beginning of the month, getting their hair braided for a party,' said Natalie.

'She didn't. If she said anything, I didn't register. I zone out sometimes when clients are talking. I'm concentrating on what I'm doing, not on what they're saying.'

'You didn't retaliate in any way?'

'No!'

'What did you mean by, "This isn't over"?'

'Nothing. I didn't mean anything. It was… words.' He tugged nervously at his beard. 'I was pissed off. I work hard to keep the salon afloat and she'd had an expensive treatment. It all costs money and I have to think about my profits and my reputation. The colour was fine. She should have paid her bill. I didn't carry out any threat. Honestly, I didn't.'

'I spoke to Kerry and she said you got angry with her too and on one occasion you threw Isabella out of the salon.'

'They were giggling and carrying on in here and making rude comments about the clients. I could hear them in the salon and was concerned that my clients could hear them too, so I told Isabella if she couldn't keep her voice down she'd have to leave, and she flounced off.'

'Have you anyone who can back you up?'

'I don't think so. I don't know.' He looked about then sighed. 'No. I think the other stylists were out at lunch at the time.'

'We need to firmly establish your whereabouts on Friday and Saturday nights – that's from the moment you shut the salon.'

'I told you. I stayed at home – upstairs. Alone.'

'Did you go online or talk to anybody?' Natalie suggested.

Eddie looked like he was going to be sick. His face had paled and his hands were now shaking. 'No. Yes! Wait. I spoke to my daughter, Pixie. She'd had a nightmare and couldn't get back to sleep. She wanted to hear my voice so Nia let her ring me.'

'What time would that have been?'

Eddie fumbled in his pocket and dragged out an iPhone, scrolling through the details of incoming calls, and looked at Natalie with relief on his face. 'It was at one fifty on Saturday morning. Nia apologised for waking me up but I didn't mind. I chatted to Pixie for a few minutes.'

Natalie would be able to establish if the telephone call had been received at or near the salon, but it wouldn't answer the question of whether or not he'd paid Sludge to deface the camera by the furniture warehouse, nor did it give him an alibi for the time the twins went missing. 'I'm going to need to take a DNA sample,' she said.

'But I haven't done anything wrong,' he replied.

'Are you refusing to give a sample?'

He shook his head and dragged his hands over his beard then sudden surprise widened his eyes fully. 'No. I'm not refusing but surely, you can't think—'

'We need to eliminate you from our enquiries.'

'Yes, of course you do.' He rubbed his beard again.

'We'll take that sample and then be off.'

While Lucy swabbed Eddie's mouth, Natalie messaged Ian and asked him to establish if any of the members of the Hill or Moore families had visited the Toni and Guy academy in 2014, but she had a feeling they'd get nowhere with this line of enquiry. Although some evidence pointed towards Eddie, she suspected the real killer wanted the police to chase after the hair salon owner. He regularly made the trip to the bank to deposit takings after hours. The killer would only have to follow the man to find that out. But who would know enough about Eddie to implicate him, and why?

Lucy bagged the sample, and Natalie spoke to the man. 'We might need to talk to you again.'

He lifted his scissors and said, 'I didn't do any of it. I swear.'

'Then we'll endeavour to prove that,' said Natalie.

Once outside again, she looked at Lucy. 'I don't think he's responsible.' She opened the car door, climbed inside, and slammed the door shut. 'Somebody is playing with us, Lucy. Somebody is being a clever bastard.'

CHAPTER TWENTY-TWO

Ian shook his head. 'Nobody at all has been fired from the warehouse and there's never even been a night watchman or security guard working there.'

'I figured as much,' Natalie replied. 'At least we now know for sure.'

Ian continued, 'All the bins in Market Street and those by the underpass were emptied first thing this morning, along with all the bins in central Samford, so there's no evidence of any spray can or envelope, and I spoke to the owner of Samford Grocery Store and he remembers Sludge. He's pretty certain Sludge bought vodka although he can't remember what else. Sludge most likely spent the money just like he said he did. Finally, we got nowhere with the Toni and Guy academy. They've kept records of their models and clients and they have no cards or records for anybody called Hill or Moore in 2014.'

'Eddie checks out too,' said Lucy. 'He deposits the salon's takings most evenings at the ATM. I spoke to the manageress of the Rocket Café and he is a regular there. He definitely bought a sandwich on Friday evening. She remembers because he told her he'd missed lunch and was starving.'

'He could still have dumped the spray can along with the sandwich wrapper. This could be one giant smokescreen,' said John, who was sitting with his legs apart and elbows balanced on his thighs. Natalie could almost feel the testosterone bouncing off him.

She tapped her pen against the desk in irritation. Her gut told her Eddie wasn't involved. She'd spoken to the man on a few occasions over the last couple of years. He'd cut Leigh's hair – and hers for that matter – chatting amiably to them both as he did so, and there'd been no giveaways or anything in his manner to suggest he was capable of such deception. Or was it that she didn't want to believe she'd misjudged the man? She prided herself on reading people.

'I think he was chosen deliberately,' she said.

'Okay. Why?' said John.

'For starters, his salon is a stone's throw away from where the Westmores live. He'd be likely to know them.'

'But other people on the street know them too.' John dismissed her argument with a wave of his hand. 'Sorry, but that's crap. Let's face it: no killer's going to spend ages hunting for potential fall guys.'

'No, it's possible,' said Ian. 'The perpetrator might have known about Kerry working for Eddie as well.'

'For crying out loud. I bet lots of people knew that fact: her mates, his staff, customers, parents, his friends, social media contacts – list's bloody endless, mate,' said John. 'He's got no fucking alibi for either night. So what if people saw him regularly on Market Street? It's far more likely he'd be deliberately setting up some sort of pattern so when he dropped a can of paint into a bin, nobody would suspect him… and what about his wife who just happened to be away the whole weekend? The same weekend Isabella, Erin and Ivy all got murdered. The bastard's lying.' John snarled the words.

Natalie still wasn't going to be pushed on the matter. John had done that before, in Manchester, convincing the DI at the time of one person's guilt when it had been another's. She didn't disagree with what he was suggesting; however, she wanted to keep other avenues open. 'Okay, we'll come back to that. What about other suspects?' she asked.

'What about that bloke who disappeared to get more bottles of water at that concert – Fergus? Does he have any connection to the twins or their parents?' John asked flatly.

'None I could establish,' Ian replied.

'Has he got an alibi for Friday night into Saturday morning, or Saturday night into Sunday morning, when the Westmore twins were killed?' John persisted.

'He parked the DrinkQuick van at the barn in Wayfield, then drove home to Samford and went to bed. Didn't get up until mid-morning Saturday, and Saturday night into Sunday morning, he was at home.'

'Anyone vouch for him?'

'He was online in his room, but he says his mother was around and could vouch he was at home.'

'Any fresh DNA evidence on the bodies?' John wasn't giving up.

'Nothing.'

John grunted. 'Looks like we're royally fucked then or we *actually* go after Eddie Ford.'

Natalie bristled at the comment. It was far from over and she wasn't going to focus energies on one man. 'No, we go back to the beginning. Isabella was charging schoolmates for coursework. I know some of her classmates are currently abroad or away on school holidays, but track them down and talk to them. One of them might know something. Similarly, we talk to the twins' friends. It seems they let themselves out of the gate that night, presumably to meet somebody. There is a connection – we just need to find it.'

'Any chance of a break first?' John asked. 'I could do with some food.'

Natalie looked at the clock on the office wall. It was coming up six and she hadn't noticed the time slipping away. Ordinarily her team didn't request breaks when on such an important case. They were used to grabbing snacks from the machine or a quick takeaway when out on the road. John wasn't accustomed to team life so she decided to make allowances. 'That's fine. Go ahead.'

'Cheers.' He scraped back his chair and ambled off.

Natalie addressed the others. 'You've been working non-stop. Take some time off too, both of you.'

'I'm fine, thanks,' Ian replied.

'He's a machine,' said Lucy with a grin. 'A non-stop working machine.'

'Some fucker is murdering children. I'll take time out to eat when we have an idea who it might be,' said Ian, his face scrunching up as he spoke.

'Incoming from Ben Hargreaves,' called Lucy, clicking on the email and downloading the attachments. There was a collective silence as she skimmed through the pathology report. Natalie felt herself holding her breath until Lucy said, 'Substantial bruising and severe damage to the neck structures and fracture of the hyoid bone in both children, indicative of considerable force. No ligature marks but abrasions, markings and internal damage are all consistent with throttling.' She looked up.

'Same as Isabella.' Natalie tilted her head back and sighed. 'Fuck. We know these cases are connected. We need to work out how. I'm going to let the superintendent know where we are on this. You try and contact as many of the girls' friends as possible.'

She made her way upstairs only to bump into John bounding back down. 'Thought you were getting some food?'

'I was. Went on the roof to eat it and have a quick vape. By the way, the superintendent just asked me where we were on the investigation and I told him we were still looking at Eddie Ford.'

'What gave you the right to discuss the investigation with him?'

'He asked me. What was I supposed to say? I don't know what we're doing, sir?' He squared his shoulders but she wasn't intimidated by his aggressive stance.

She jabbed a finger at him and said, 'You should have referred him to the leading investigating officer, which happens to be *me*.'

His lips curled for a second but he managed to catch himself in time and his mouth pulled into a smile. 'I'll be sure to remember that next time.'

'Make sure you do. We don't have time for office politics. Do I need to remind you there's a murderer out there who's killed three girls and who, in all likelihood, will strike again?'

'You think he will?'

'Yes, I fucking well do. Now get down there and help out.'

She continued upstairs although now she had little reason to brief Dan. She needed air and threw open the door to the roof terrace, crossed to the far side and kicked the wall once, sharply. Pain rose up her shin. *Fuck!* The man was impossible. She exhaled a couple of times, drawing deep breaths until she was more in control. Her mobile rang – it was the letting agency – and she took the call.

'Detective Ward? It's Mary Dubrovnik from Samford Lettings. I'm just checking to see if you are happy with our terms and conditions we sent across to your email today.'

'Sorry, I haven't had a chance to look at it yet.'

'Well, when you do, please download and sign the agreement and we'll be good to go. And may I remind you, we require two months' rent up front, as per the agreement.'

'Two months?' she repeated absent-mindedly. She hadn't really thought about that in her haste to agree to move in. That was quite a sum to find.

'Yes, up front.'

She'd have to take out a payday loan. No. That wouldn't be enough money – shit! Where was she going to get the deposit money? Her mind couldn't process it all at the moment. She had more important matters to attend to.

'I'll read the email as soon as I can. I'm up to my neck at the moment.'

The voice was smooth. 'Of course. I just thought I should let you know we'd emailed you the agreement.'

'I'll get back to you as soon as I can.' Natalie wanted the woman to go. She couldn't handle this on top of everything else.

'Of course.'

She jammed the mobile into her pocket. This was crazy. Everything was building up around her and she didn't have time to deal with it all. A vision of John's sneering face sent her hurtling back inside. This was her investigation and she'd not let it get sidetracked by that arrogant sod.

By nine they'd spoken to as many of the youngsters' friends as possible but had found nothing useful. They still had lists of others to contact the following day. Natalie had sent an update via email to the superintendent with the information regarding the pathology reports and was, like the members of her team, in need of rest.

'Time to bugger off home. We're done today.'

John gave a full-body stretch, arms above his head. 'I could do with a drink. Anyone want to join me?'

'Bethany's expecting me,' said Lucy apologetically as she gathered up her bits and pieces and headed off.

'Sorry. Another time,' said Ian, scooting after her.

'What about you, Natalie?' he asked.

'Not me. Ought to catch up with the family,' she replied, mindful of the smirk playing on his lips. She was sure he was recalling the last time he'd invited her out.

He pushed back his chair and strolled past her, pausing briefly to speak in a quiet voice. 'If you change your mind, you know how to contact me.'

'I won't.'

He just smiled and meandered away, a slight swagger to his athletic gait. She counted to twenty and then followed him out of the building.

Natalie had been relieved to discover her family was out when she got home. A note scrawled in biro and signed by Leigh informed her they'd all gone out to Nando's and then on to the bowling alley, along with Zoe and Josh's friend Toby. She wondered idly what David was doing while the kids were bowling then decided she wasn't bothered and checked the fridge for something to eat, settling on some cheese and biscuits and a glass of wine, as she had no inclination or energy to cook.

She flopped in front of the television and thumbed through endless channels of faces and scenes she couldn't focus on, and in the end, she headed for the attic and bed. She didn't hear the children and David return. She was lost in nightmares where John Briggs was her superintendent and she was being tried in court for gross misconduct.

CHAPTER TWENTY-THREE

'Update on Eddie Ford,' said Natalie, catching the attention of both Lucy and Ian. 'His mobile didn't leave the house on Friday or Saturday night and he received a call at one fifty Saturday morning from his partner, Nia, that lasted almost six minutes. No DNA matching his sample has been detected on the twins' bodies or clothing, or on Isabella Sharpe's. At the moment, we simply don't have enough evidence against him to consider charging him. I'd like you to interview Nia. She came back from Blackpool last night.'

Her eyes were drawn to the corridor and John, who was fast approaching with a disposable coffee cup in his hand. He strode in, head high, a superior look in his eyes.

'Morning, John. I was saying that Eddie's phone appears not to have moved Friday or Saturday night.'

John remained standing. 'About Eddie. I went to the Rocket Café first thing and spoke to the manageress.'

Natalie bristled. He'd not spoken to her about this and she'd not given him authority to do so. He anticipated her annoyance. 'I understand I probably should have mentioned it to you, but I was only working off a hunch. I didn't think it would hurt to use my initiative.'

Ordinarily she encouraged her team to do exactly that but this was John Briggs – a man she didn't completely trust. She suppressed her feelings – she couldn't bawl him out in front of Lucy and Ian. 'And what did you find out?'

'Eddie told us he visited the café regularly. It struck me that given the proximity of the café to Emerson Lane, the twins might also have visited the café and it appears I was right. They often went in with their friends after school and on some Saturday afternoons. The manageress went so far as to say Eddie had been in on several occasions at the same time as the girls and, although she couldn't be certain, he had exchanged words with them.'

Natalie felt her throat tighten. Another red flag had been raised. Eddie had lied when he'd said he'd never seen the twins until they'd come into the salon. John had been right to pursue this. 'He certainly denied knowing the twins and this indicates he's been lying. We'll follow it up and talk to Nia.'

'We should ask her about their time in Manchester too. Find out if she was involved with him then.'

'Agreed. However, I still find all of this evidence pointing in his direction a little too *convenient*.'

'Convenient?' John asked.

'Yes. The fact he fired Kerry from his salon, that he lives and works close to the Westmore twins, and that he even had an argument with the twins' aunt. Everything, including the fact he was filmed on CCTV throwing something that we can't identify into the same rubbish bin used as a drop zone for the spray can used by Sludge. It's all too tidy. What we don't have is a clear motive as to why he would murder any of the girls. I don't want us to become blinkered and read too much into it. We do our jobs thoroughly and get the right results.'

John's face was determined and she questioned whether or not she was being deliberately reluctant to chase after Eddie purely because John was insisting they did. She couldn't let personal matters cloud her judgement. She nodded in his direction and said, 'Okay. You can follow it up and talk to Nia. Lucy and I will talk to the twins' friends and see if we can get any further leverage in this.'

John acknowledged her with a small salute and sat down opposite her, placing the cup on the desk. The logo showed it had come from the Rocket Café and Natalie wondered if he'd deliberately positioned it so she could see the logo, then dismissed the thought as petty. Catching the small smirk on his face, she decided it had been deliberate. He was point-scoring and he'd won this round.

'As I was saying, I want us to continue talking to the victims' friends. See if any of them know what Erin and Ivy had planned to do the night they disappeared. They changed from nightwear to clothes to meet somebody. We need to find out who. There must be another suspect or suspects we haven't yet identified. We also need to establish links between Erin and Ivy Westmore and Isabella Sharpe. And… we need to work quickly.'

'How about checking with the twins' head teacher? See what they were like at school. Often parents don't know the half of it. Maybe they were a bit rebellious,' suggested Lucy.

'You reckon?' John's face scrunched up.

'I was at that age, so why not?' Lucy replied, not put off.

'Yeah. Why not?' He lifted his coffee and drank it, eyes back on Natalie.

Ian spoke. 'I've been through all CCTV footage in and around Emerson Lane where the twins lived and there's no sign of them on any cameras. That includes any private cameras and surveillance equipment.'

'No sign at all of them? Maybe they got picked up by a vehicle?' Natalie suggested.

Ian responded with a shake of his head. 'If they were picked up, it'll be difficult to trace it. There's a high volume of traffic in the area. Emerson Lane is not only close to the bypass but to other arterial routes and an A-road which passes straight through the centre of town.'

The only other area they could look at was near Blithbury Marsh, where the twins' bodies had been uncovered, but it would take a huge amount of technical data and time to narrow down any possible vehicles spotted at Blithbury Marsh and near Emerson Lane, and it could all be to no avail. Nevertheless, she ought to ask the question of the department. 'I'll talk to the technical team and see if it's possible to identify and match vehicles spotted by both Blithbury Marsh and Emerson Lane. Somebody had to park fairly close to the marsh to drop off the twins' bodies.'

'Nearest place is the car park next to the marsh and the cameras on it are dummies,' said Ian.

'Crap. I'll ask all the same.'

'Should we arrange for Sludge to try and identify Eddie?' John was like a dog with a bone. It was getting on Natalie's nerves. She'd agreed he could check up on the man and made it perfectly clear they were going to concentrate on other possible avenues.

'We'll consider that if any fresh evidence comes to light, but until then, we're going to pursue other lines of enquiry,' Natalie said firmly, staring directly at John. His nostrils flared but he didn't persist. 'We'll continue interviewing the twins' and Isabella's friends. Everyone clear?'

She was met with affirmations from Lucy and Ian, and tapping her papers into a tidy pile, she slid them into her folder and was the first to head off. She had three classmates to interview. She preferred to be as involved as her officers in the case rather than delegate, especially when the case was as important as this one. She glanced over at John now hunched over his desk, back turned to her. The man was a thorn in her side. She could do with him helping them look for other suspects and not be hell-bent on pursuing Eddie. However, she couldn't ignore facts and everything had to be followed up. Eddie had omitted to tell them about his encounter with the twins in the café and John was right to look into it. Her thoughts turned to the interviews and she headed downstairs where she was surprised and pleased to see Mike in reception.

'You going out?' he asked.

'Yes.'

'I'll walk you to your car. Mine's just up here.'

'Mine's right at the end, under the oak tree.'

They headed out into the warm sunshine. They didn't hurry. Mike threw her a smile. 'You okay?

'Bearing up. You?'

'You know. I had hoped we'd find some time to… well… chat.'

'Bloody impossible at the moment. I wanted to talk to the kids this weekend but with this investigation full on…' Her eyebrows lifted in apology.

'I understand. No pressure from me. You have your hands full. How you getting on with John Briggs?'

She sighed. 'He's flexing his muscles, trying to prove his worth. He's not as easy to get on with as Murray, but I can't fault his enthusiasm.'

'You know he and Dan are mates, don't you?'

'Mates?' She drew to a halt.

'Well… acquainted. John's been on undercover operations the last year, in Frone.'

Frone was a market town, standing in the valley of the River Trent, and once a principal stopping-off point for stagecoaches travelling on one of the roads turnpiked during the eighteenth century. Today, several pubs and hotels bore testament to that important past, and the town, which still boasted a lively weekly market, was only twelve miles north of Samford.

Mike continued in a low voice. 'He and Dan worked together before that. Rumour has it that John Briggs is his golden boy and Dan has been keen to get him into HQ alongside him. Apparently, Briggs is destined for promotion and a permanent position here at Samford HQ.'

'That explains a lot,' she said with a huff. 'The fucker went behind my back to update Dan on the case. I thought he was being keen, but the shit is only looking out for himself. He's trying to get ahead. I'll have to watch out and make sure I don't slip up.'

'You won't slip up. Besides, forewarned is forearmed.'

'Thanks for the heads up.'

'Any time. Thought you should know. Look, if you get a moment, text me and we'll grab five minutes together.'

'You know that's going to be impossible for a while. Especially now John Briggs is toadying to Dan.'

'It'd be nice to have a proper chat – tell you about my trip with Thea… shoot the breeze.'

She smiled at his sudden American drawl. 'Yeah, sure. I'd like that… a lot.'

'Great. I have to go. I was on my way back to Blithbury Marsh.'

'Nothing new to report?'

'I wish. You'll be the first to know if there are any developments. Oh, wait, that note you took into the lab – there are some partial fingerprints on the envelope which don't match any in our database, and the note itself is spotless. Whoever sent it was careful to leave no trace. The paper used is HP white copier paper that you can purchase pretty much anywhere they sell stationery items or online. It's a standard font but sized slightly larger at sixteen point rather than the usual twelve. That's all we can tell you at the moment.'

'Nothing to go on, then?'

'Not much. Sorry.' He stopped beside a BMW and blipped his key fob at it to unlock the doors. 'Catch you later.'

She continued walking to her own car, not looking back. If anyone was watching from an upstairs window, she didn't want them to see anything other than two colleagues quickly discussing a case they were both working. Tongues wagged. Her heart was thumping against her ribcage. John Bloody Briggs. She knew he was trouble. He'd better not mess up her investigation or her career. How she hated all the sodding politics. It made it all the more difficult to do her job, and now she was aware that Dan and John were friends, it meant she'd have to really watch her back. She unlocked her door and got into the car. Lucy was exiting the building and heading for the squad car. She waited for John to emerge but he didn't appear, so after a minute, she started her engine and drew away. *Focus on the investigation*, she told herself. It was the only way forward.

It took her five minutes by car to reach Swift Terrace, a narrow street of terraced houses, once inhabited by workers who'd toiled at one of the three flour mills that had been important back in the 1800s before the canals had ensured flour was imported and the mills had been knocked down. Now all that remained of that particular history was a pub, aptly named the Mill. The dwellings had been replaced by modern versions, offering the conveniences of modern-day living: heating, lighting and plumbing. These residences weren't glamorous but they were a far cry from what had once stood here – tiny buildings with outside toilets and cramped living quarters.

She rang the doorbell at number 23 and waited for a response. The door opened and a small round face with large brown eyes appeared. The child, who was about three, was immediately scooped up by a wary woman in loose-fitting trousers and a long, flowing top. 'You know you mustn't answer the door to strangers without me being with you,' she chastised, her voice belying the fondness she felt for the child.

'Mrs Khatri, I'm DI Natalie Ward – I rang earlier. I'd like to have a quick chat to Ashra if I may.' She held her ID high so the woman could check it and was beckoned inside.

The television in the sitting room was on and in front of it lay discarded plastic figurines, a brown toy dog in a striped jumper, a book with a colourful cover and various other toys belonging to the toddler. Catching sight of Peppa Pig on the screen, the child wriggled like an eel from her mother's arms and wandered immediately across to the set, where she stood in front of the screen, absorbed in the magical world in front of her. On seeing Natalie, Ashra, who'd been curled up in a chair with an iPad, stood up.

'Hi, Ashra, I'm Natalie.'

'Hi.'

'Is it okay to talk to you about Erin and Ivy?'

'Yes.'

'Do you want to stay here or would you prefer the kitchen?' Mrs Khatri asked. The toddler giggled loudly at the television set and dropped to the floor, crossing her legs to watch the programme. 'Maybe the kitchen would be quieter,' she said.

'It's fine here,' said Natalie, not wanting to make the already nervous girl feel intimidated. Having her little sister in the same room would help.

'If you're sure.'

Natalie gave her a smile and was offered a seat. She began her questions. 'You know why I'm here, don't you?'

'Ivy and Erin were killed.' The girl whispered the words.

'That's right. You were in the same class as them, weren't you?' Her eyes filled with tears. 'Yes.'

'Were you good friends with them?'

'Yes.'

'Did you see them outside school too?'

'Sometimes.'

'Here?'

'Yes.'

'At their house?'

'Yes.'

'Did you ever go along with them to the Rocket Café in town?' The girl nodded. 'We went there a lot.'

'Did you ever see this man in the café?' She pulled out the photograph of Eddie and showed it to the girl, who nodded once more. 'Did he ever talk to you?'

Ashra frowned as she pondered her answer. 'Yes, he told the twins they had lovely hair and should visit his salon sometime – that he was always looking for hair models to practise on.'

'He actually said those words?'

'Yes. The twins thought he was weird but then they found out he really did have a hair salon and talked about actually doing it. They'd get cool new hairstyles and even get to go to shows and stuff if they did it.'

'Did they go and see him about being hair models?'

'Erin didn't want to do it, so in the end, Ivy didn't either.'

'They went to the salon in July, didn't they?'

'Oh, yes. I'd forgotten about that. They had flowers put in their hair for a party. They looked really pretty.'

'They didn't mention the hair modelling again?'

'No. I don't think they talked to him about it.'

'Did you ever see this man again in the café?'

'No. I didn't see him. If he was there I didn't notice. I was just hanging out with my friends.' Her eyes were damp but she didn't break down.

Natalie gave her another smile of encouragement and said gently, 'You're doing really well.'

Her mother responded with a, 'Yes. Very well, Ashra.'

Natalie continued, 'I don't suppose you know exactly when this man approached the twins about being models, do you?'

'Not really. It was ages ago… not the Easter holidays…' She struggled to think. 'It was sometime during the half-term holidays after that.'

The school holidays had fallen at the end of May to coincide with Whitsun. That narrowed it down to the last week of May.

'That's very helpful, Ashra.'

The girl blinked back tears.

'Did the twins share any secrets with you?'

'A few.'

'Did they tell you what they were planning to do on Saturday night?'

'No.'

'Did they mention spending the night in a tent?'

'No.' She shook her head as she spoke.

'They said nothing to you at all?'

'No. Why were they in a tent?' Confusion clouded the girl's face. 'I thought they were at home. We were on Snapchat for ages and they said they were at home in their bedroom. They didn't say anything about a tent.'

'Did you chat to them online a lot?'

'All the time.' The words were pained. Ashra had lost two close friends and the enormity hadn't quite hit home.

Natalie kept talking in case emotion overtook the girl and she became unable to assist. 'Can you think of anybody the twins might have gone to meet?' When no answer was forthcoming she tried with, 'Somebody they'd maybe talked about? Somebody they liked? Somebody they hadn't told their parents about?'

Ashra swallowed. 'There are two boys... not from our school... from Samford Academy...'

'Go on, Ashra,' said her mother. The child in front of the set chuckled heartily at the antics of the pink pig, oblivious to the conversation going on.

'They're older than us. The twins had been hanging with them recently.'

'Can you give me their names?'

'Harry Brown and Noah Powers.'

Judging by the way she said their names, she didn't like the boys much.

'Do you know where they live?'

'I think one of them lives in Appleby Gardens.'

Natalie wrote down the names and noted the address – Fergus Doherty, who'd served Kerry at the concert, and the Sharpe family also lived in that same area.

'Do you happen to know Isabella Sharpe?'

Ashra looked blankly at her. 'No. I don't know her.'

'She went to your school. She might have been in the year above you?'

The girl shook her head. Cheery music signalled the end of the television programme and the child scrambled to her feet and rushed across to Ashra, jumping up onto the chair and squeezing in beside her to stare at Natalie. Ashra put an arm around her little sister and Natalie was taken by the natural gesture. A vision of a photograph of her and her sister Frances flashed before her eyes. Once upon a time, they'd been as close as this, sharing chairs and with arms around each other. The memory threatened to distract her so she blinked it away.

'Why is the lady asking questions?' asked the child.

'To help find the bad person who hurt Ashra's friends,' said her mother.

'Oh!' The girl's eyes grew larger still, and she snuggled even closer to her sister.

Natalie continued, 'Did anyone else from your class go with you, Erin and Ivy to the Rocket Café?'

'It was usually only the three of us. We live the closest to the café and it was sort of our place to go. Everyone else prefers Costa but we liked it in the café.' She wiped at her eyes and her sister spotted the movement.

'Ashra's sad,' said her little sister.

'That's because she's upset about Erin and Ivy,' said Mrs Khatri, giving Natalie a quick look.

'Yes, and you're going to find out who hurt them,' said the child, looking at Natalie.

'I'm going to try to,' Natalie replied. 'I'm definitely going to do everything I can.'

CHAPTER TWENTY-FOUR

TUESDAY, 14 AUGUST – AFTERNOON

After leaving Ashra and her family, Natalie headed directly to the Rocket Café. It was a huge concern that Eddie had lied again. He'd denied knowing the twins before they'd come into the salon in July, and yet he'd spoken to them in the café in May. Once again, evidence pointed towards him.

The Rocket Café stood on the main street with two small orange tables and chairs outside on the pavement, both occupied. Natalie pushed open the door and discovered the trendy interior stretched further back than she'd imagined, beyond the serving counter into a darker interior with booths to one side and tall tables and high stools to the other. She was greeted by a woman with short brown hair and a wide smile.

'I'm DI Ward,' said Natalie quietly, flashing her ID card. 'I'd like to ask you a few questions, please.'

'I spoke to one of your colleagues this morning,' the woman replied.

'DS John Briggs?'

'Yes. That was his name.'

'I need to follow up on that conversation.'

The woman nodded and called through the doorway to the kitchen behind, saying, 'Jamie, can you look after the counter for a couple of minutes?'

'Sure,' came the reply.

'This way,' she said to Natalie. They passed the tables and booths and exited through the rear door into a small back garden, clean and tidy with an orange table, much like the two outside the front of the café. She sat down on one of the chairs. Natalie joined her.

'I'm Tina by the way. Is this about Eddie again?'

'I'm checking some facts.'

'He definitely came in on Friday. I told DS Briggs so.'

'Yes, thank you for that. I'm actually here to ask about Erin and Ivy.'

'The twins?'

'Yes. I expect you've heard the bad news.'

'I have and it's absolutely evil what's happened to them. Can't believe it.'

'Did they come in here often?'

'At least once a week. They used to like to sit at the table in the window – the big round one.'

'One of their friends said Eddie spoke to them about becoming hair models.'

'Did he? I wouldn't know.'

'But he comes in regularly too, doesn't he?'

'He comes in a lot of days – picks up lunch or a coffee. DS Briggs was asking me the same sort of questions, trying to find out if Eddie knew the girls.'

'And did he?'

'I'll tell you what I told DS Briggs: I think so. There might have been a couple of times when he came in late in the day to buy a sandwich and the girls were already sitting at their usual table, but I can't be completely sure. Loads of customers pile in once schools finish for the day, and I'm usually too busy to notice what people are up to.' John had been economical with the truth – Tina hadn't been as sure about seeing Eddie talk to the girls as he'd suggested.

'Did you know the twins well?'

'I barely knew them at all. They weren't chatty. I served them milkshakes or whatever they asked for but I don't know anything about them.'

'They used to come in with another girl?'

'Quiet little thing. Yes. She always sat with them.'

'You don't know her name?'

'No.'

'Did they ever come in with two boys?'

'Funny you should say that. They did, only last week – Wednesday morning. The place was quiet and I was cleaning the tables when they trooped in.'

'All of them came in together?'

'No, I mean the twins came in with the boys. The other girl wasn't with them.'

'Can you describe the boys?'

Tina's eyebrows lifted. 'Now you're asking me. Erm… one was quite tall – taller than me, with one of those in vogue haircuts. Jamie's hair's the same style – a sort of curly perm with shaved back and sides. I didn't get a good look at the other boy but he was dark-eyed and had a bit of an attitude.'

'What do you mean?'

'Just attitude – you know… bit surly.'

'Were they rude to you?'

'Not to me. The twins bought the boys soft drinks and sat with them. One of the customers complained that she'd overheard them swearing and I was going to have a go at them about it but they cleared off before I had the chance.'

'Were the twins ever rude to you?'

'No. They were fine. All three girls were generally quiet, which was why I didn't mind them taking up my table even though they didn't spend much.'

'You don't happen to know this girl, do you?' She showed Tina a picture of Isabella Sharpe. Tina peered closely at it but returned it with a shake of her head.

'Sorry, I don't recall seeing her and I have a good memory for faces.'

'Would you say you know a lot of your customers well?'

'Only some of them well. Some people only come in to get a takeaway drink or grab a bite to eat. There are regulars who want to talk more than others.'

'What about Eddie? Is he talkative?'

'He's actually my hairdresser, so I usually have a couple of words with him.'

'I guess you know his wife too.'

'Not as well as I know Eddie. She's only been in a couple of times with their little girl – Pixie. I believe she works somewhere in Birmingham, so I don't see her very often.'

'How many people work for you?'

'Only Jamie, but he doesn't serve customers. He works in the kitchen at lunchtimes. He's normally left by now,' she said, glancing at her watch.

With little more to glean from Tina, Natalie took the gesture as her cue to leave. She'd told John he could follow up on Eddie, so she didn't make her way to the salon. Instead, she returned to the station to try and get some information regarding the two boys Ashra had mentioned.

*

Lucy and Ian had also learnt about Noah Powers and Harry Brown. They were talking to the twins' class teacher, Alan Huntsman, who had driven back from a family holiday in Wales to help them out with their enquiries.

'The twins were inseparable,' he said. 'They were in the same class for every subject. Performed the same too – both good at

English but poor at maths; both good at athletics but bad at team sports. They were almost identical in every way. They were lovely girls with really nice dispositions. Such a sad loss.'

'You hadn't noticed any change in behaviour in them recently, had you?' asked Lucy.

'Funnily enough, I had. I caught them in the corridor one lunchtime. Kids aren't supposed to be inside during recreation times and it was most unlike them. They were usually really well-behaved but that day they were hanging around the student lockers with a couple of fifteen-year-old lads in Samford Academy uniforms. The girls said they were only showing them around the school. I told them all to scoot and got some lip back from one of the lads. I rang a colleague at Samford Academy and described the boys. He was pretty certain he knew who they were: Noah Powers and Harry Brown. Apparently, they were known troublemakers so I warned everyone on our staff to keep an eye out for them in case they were up to no good, but I don't think they returned. Anyway, I don't know if it was because of that incident, but Erin and Ivy weren't the same after that day. They'd ignore me when I spoke to them or give me dark looks – only little differences and not significant on their own, but yes, I did think the girls' attitudes changed.'

'Did you see them again with Harry and Noah?'

'I spotted them outside Samford library a few days after that incident.'

'Can you recall when you saw them all by the lockers?'

'Couple of weeks before term ended. I remember thinking it was a good thing the summer holidays were almost on us and hoped the twins would forget about that pair. They were nice girls – really sweet. It's absolutely dreadful what's happened. Who could commit such an atrocious act?'

'That's exactly what we hope to find out,' replied Lucy.

*

Natalie had succeeded in getting details for Noah Powers and Harry Brown, both of whom had poor school attendance records. She'd established Noah and his father, Glenn, had moved to rented accommodation on Gate Street – the same street where Fergus Doherty lived. She was preparing to ring the father when John entered the office, his face stern.

'We have to consider bringing in Eddie,' he said.

'Have you found out something?'

'No. His partner, Nia, had fuck all to tell me other than what a great guy he is, but I'm not buying that and I'm sure he's hiding something.' He tossed his jacket onto the chair and rolled up his shirtsleeves as he spoke.

Natalie watched him for a moment before speaking. She wanted to gauge his reaction to her next comment. 'I visited Tina, the manageress at the Rocket Café.'

'Oh, yes.'

'And she wasn't completely certain Eddie had spoken to the twins. That's not what you told us.'

He looked blankly at her. 'She told me otherwise. She was sure he had.'

Natalie shook her head. 'Don't piss me about, John. You didn't report what she actually said. You twisted it to suit you. You've been determined to go after Eddie and only Eddie.'

'That's bollocks! Tina told me she thought he'd spoken to the twins. Eddie's a liar and we need to nail the bastard. Tell me I'm wrong if you think so.'

She shook her head. She didn't approve of his methods but he was right to be suspicious of Eddie. 'Okay, I'll accept you're telling the truth, but when I spoke to Tina, she was not sure at all. I'm not going to turn this into a big issue but we must follow procedure. We can't afford for mistakes to be made.'

'That won't happen.'

'Good. As it happens, one of the girls' friends claims Eddie spoke to the twins and suggested they become models at his salon.'

'Models?'

'Hair models. Salons often advertise for models. It's a way for trainees to practise and sometimes they use models to show off what they can do at big events.'

'I was bang on then, wasn't I? The bastard *is* lying through his teeth.'

'He is, but hold your horses. I don't want you running away with this. Something else has cropped up – a couple of lads from Samford Academy recently started hanging about with the twins. Both have reputations for being rebellious and disruptive, and one of them, Noah Powers, was expelled from his last school in Manchester. He came to Samford in March this year and… he's living in Gate Street in Appleby Gardens.'

'Isn't that the same street as that bloke who served Kerry Sharpe at the concert?'

'Yes – and only a short walk from the Sharpes' home.'

He rested a finger against his lips before saying, 'Okay, that all sounds very interesting, but when I wanted to check out Eddie because all the evidence pointed towards him, you tore a strip off me and said everything that linked to Eddie was too *convenient*. Doesn't the same apply to this boy – this Noah – knowing the twins, living near Isabella?' He looked at her coolly.

'I agree, but as with Eddie, we'll investigate thoroughly.'

He screwed up his eyes and emitted a *pfft* sound. 'Hang on, a few minutes ago you confirmed Eddie is a lying piece of shit, and now you want to waste time talking to a pair of juveniles.'

'None of this is a waste of time,' she replied.

'From where I'm standing, it is. I think we should talk to Eddie.'

'We will, but I want to check out these boys first. They might know something – maybe even where the twins were headed on Saturday night.'

John pursed his lips and said, 'I think we should put it to the superintendent and let him decide.'

'Absolutely not. I'm in charge of this investigation and I say we talk to these teenagers first.' The ringing of her mobile prevented her from arguing with John. Lucy was calling in with an update. Natalie listened intently, responding with, 'I've just been looking at that pair. Yes. Follow it up.'

She ended the call and said, 'Lucy and Ian have spoken to the twins' class teacher, who was concerned that they were hanging out with a couple of troublemakers from another school – Noah Powers and Harry Brown. They're going to interview the boys. We're going to speak to the Westmores again.'

John threw her a look but moved across to his desk without saying a word and picked up his jacket.

CHAPTER TWENTY-FIVE

The squad car pulled up outside 62 Gate Street, and Ian and Lucy got out. A chest-high brick wall hid the weed-riddled front garden and the wheelie bins propped up under the window from view. The house was quite some way down from Fergus Doherty's but looked identical with its red brick and white, plastic-framed windows and front door.

Glenn Powers, in khaki shorts and matching T-shirt bearing a logistics company logo, answered the door and showed them into the kitchen where his son, Noah, was perched on a stool, a toasted sandwich in his hand. He nodded in their direction and mumbled, 'All right?' as a greeting before taking a large bite. Tomato ketchup oozed from it to plop onto the plate.

'Sorry to disturb you but we need to ask Noah some questions about Erin and Ivy Westmore,' said Lucy, acknowledging the boy.

The man's eyes narrowed and he asked, 'Why?'

'Are you aware the twins were found dead on Sunday afternoon?'

'Yes. Noah told me about it. His friends told him.'

'You knew the girls well, didn't you?' Lucy directed her question to the teenager.

Noah swallowed his mouthful. 'Not exactly.'

'How well did you know them?'

'What do you mean?' he asked casually.

'Well, enough to go to the Rocket Café with them last Wednesday.'

He deliberated before answering. 'Yeah. That's right. We had a drink with them.'

'And?'

'That's all. They went home.'

Ian looked up from his notepad. 'You meet up any other times?'

'A few.'

'You saw them regularly?' Ian asked.

'We hung out a bit.'

Ian nodded. 'We? Do you mean you and Harry Brown?'

'Yeah.'

Ian made a note of the name and allowed Lucy to continue. 'When was the last time you saw the twins?'

'Wednesday. We met them outside the library and then we all went to the café.' He inspected his sandwich rather than look at Lucy, and she wondered if he was telling the truth.

'Is that all you did... hang out with the girls?'

'Dunno what you mean,' he replied. He cast a furtive look in his father's direction.

Lucy picked up on it. 'Were you going out with them?' she asked.

'Going out?' He sneered at the suggestion. 'That sounds dead serious and grown up.'

'You know what I mean.'

'You mean did we get off with each other?' He shook his head with a semi-smirk on his face as if Lucy had suggested something amusing. When she didn't answer he replied with, 'No.'

'You were seen with the twins on more than one occasion – one of those was during a school lunchtime when you were inside their school building, which I understand is against the rules. What were you doing by the lockers?'

'We only went to have a look around their school. They suggested it. We were talking when one of their teachers told us to clear off.'

'What were you talking about?'

'Can't remember.'

'You can't remember?'

'No. It was ages ago.' He shrugged and pulled a piece of sandwich off, popped it into his mouth and chewed with his mouth open.

Lucy tried again. 'We're trying to find out why the twins left their house on Saturday night. It would help us hugely if you could tell us what you know. Did they talk to you about going off somewhere on Saturday night?'

He shook his head, lips pursed.

'Did they plan to meet you?'

'No.'

Ian joined in again. 'What about your friend, Harry? Did they arrange to meet him?'

'No.'

Lucy stared at the boy. 'Noah, where were you Saturday night?'

'Here. With Harry. We were playing video games.'

She looked at Glenn Powers, who nodded. 'I went out. They were both here when I left.'

'What time did you get back?' she asked Glenn.

'About midnight. They were still here when I came in.'

'Where did you go?'

'What? Am I a suspect now?'

'Only getting my facts straight, sir.'

Glenn rolled his eyes and spoke to Ian, ignoring Lucy. 'I went to Derby to meet a *friend*.'

'And this friend will confirm that, will they?' Lucy said.

'If needs be, then yes, she will. I thought you wanted to talk to Noah, not me. Anyway, I don't see what more he can tell you.

He's already told you he didn't see the twins on Saturday night and doesn't know where they were going or why.'

His chin jutted in defiance but Lucy maintained eye contact with him and said, 'We're trying to establish what happened to the twins on Saturday night. Your son and his friend have been seen hanging about with Erin and Ivy, so it's only normal to try and find out what sort of relationship they had with the twins, and whether or not the twins divulged their intentions to either of them.'

'Did they?' Glenn asked his son. 'Did those girls tell you what they planned on doing?'

Noah scoffed. 'No, course not.'

Glenn looked back at Lucy. 'There, you have your answer. Now, would you mind leaving us to finish our meal?'

Lucy wasn't going to be pushed out. She hadn't finished yet. 'Noah, did Erin and Ivy ever mention a man called Eddie?'

'Don't think so.'

'What about running away from home?'

He snorted. 'No. They never said anything about running away.'

'Did you talk to them online?'

'Now and again.'

'Snapchat?'

'No. That's for girls.'

'WhatsApp?'

'Yes.'

'And you hung out with them now and again?'

'I already told you that, didn't I?'

'Okay. Thank you. Do you know Fergus Doherty?'

His face screwed up in confusion. 'No, who's he?'

Lucy sidestepped the question. 'Do you know him, Mr Powers?' she asked.

'Never heard of him. You finished now?'

'Thank you, yes. Did you know the twins, Mr Powers?'

'No, I didn't.' He marched off and opened the front door, where he waited for Lucy and Ian to leave. As soon as they did, the door shut with a bang.

'Slightly aggressive,' said Ian.

'Maybe that's because they've got something to hide,' Lucy suggested.

*

A fluffy grey cat was asleep full length on the back of the settee where Judith and Chris Westmore sat, holding hands, fingers entwined. Natalie had edged forward on her armchair and was trying not to sink into the over-soft cushion. John was on a dining chair that had been brought into the room specifically, and he was sitting quietly while Natalie asked the questions.

'Had you noticed any difference in the twins' behaviour over the last month?'

Judith shook her head, tear-stained cheeks glistening. 'No,' she whispered.

'They weren't a bit stand-offish, rebellious, argumentative?'

'No. They weren't stroppy at all. Not like some of our friends' children. We always said we were very lucky,' said Chris, sadly.

'Did they talk to you about their friends?'

'Not really. They mentioned names, said the odd thing about so-and-so doing this in class, or that. Apart from Ashra, they didn't have any close friends. They were each other's best friend.' Judith looked to Chris for confirmation and he agreed.

'They were self-contained. Always close,' he said.

'Do either of you know Eddie Ford?'

'Eddie the hairdresser?' Judith asked.

'Yes.'

'He did my sister's hair, and the twins' once.'

'You don't use him regularly?' Natalie asked.

'No, we usually go to one of the bigger salons in town. I took the twins to Eddie's a few weeks ago because it was more convenient and our usual hairdresser couldn't fit them in. They wanted their hair done for a party and his place is only up the road.'

'Your sister told us she wasn't happy with what he did to her hair,' Natalie said.

'She never complained to me about it. I even asked her if she was pleased with it because she'd wanted it bleached blonde but came back with it a sort of orange colour. She said she preferred that colour to blonde. Why did she lie?'

'She didn't want to get you involved.'

'Why not?'

'I don't know other than she didn't want a fuss made or you to get involved.'

'She should have told me. I'd have gone and seen Eddie with her and got it sorted.'

'But you knew nothing about it?'

'No.'

'Did Erin or Ivy mention Eddie asking them to be hair models?'

'Really? They didn't say anything to me about that.' Judith's face was blank with confusion.

Natalie could sense John fidgeting on his seat and heard him ask, 'Did you get along okay with Eddie?'

'I didn't know the man.'

'But you avoided his salon,' John persisted. 'Even though it's closer than going into town.'

'His place didn't appeal to me. That's all. I've only spoken a couple of words to him, and that was when I took the twins in to get their hair done.'

'Yet your sister went there rather than use the salon you frequent.'

'What is this? Why are you asking about Amber? She was going through a break-up. She wanted a new look to cheer herself up.

She made the decision to get her hair done on a whim, and given the salon is not far away, she went there. She didn't mention she was unhappy with the result. I don't see what this has to do with my children being murdered.'

Natalie sensed Judith's sudden tension and butted in with, 'We're simply following up a few details. I'd like to ask if you know anyone by the name of Powers?' She noticed Chris's neck muscles tighten and continued. 'Noah Powers.'

A look passed between him and his wife. Natalie had touched a nerve. Chris answered her question. 'A couple of months ago, Judith spotted the twins in town with two boys who were clearly older than them. One of the boys, a lad called Noah, had his arm around Erin's shoulders. Well, obviously, we talked to the girls about the fact they were only thirteen and maybe a little young to get into relationships yet. We didn't force the issue but we voiced our concerns and the twins seemed to take it on board. Ivy even giggled about the idea of them being romantically involved with the boys and said it wasn't going to happen. They'd met the pair at Samford Shopping Centre and made friends with them.

'We trusted our girls and we let it drop but the boys began to appear in the street quite regularly, walking past the house, backwards and forwards, or halting outside and staring up at the twins' bedroom window. After a few times of this happening, I decided to challenge them. The next time they strolled past, I went outside to have a quiet word and got nothing but verbal abuse in return. The twins denied encouraging the boys and so when I saw them hanging about outside on the pavement a few days later, I threatened I'd report them to the police for harassment. They were foul-mouthed and I actually thought Noah was going to hit me, or worse. He marched right up to me with such a menacing look in his eyes that for a split second, I thought he might have a knife or weapon. His mate pulled him back. I lost my rag and said I was going to call the police.

'The following day, Noah's father appeared on our doorstep, demanding to know what right I had to threaten his son. He told me Noah and Erin were seeing each other and I'd have to get used to it. I disputed that fact and he laughed in my face, told me I ought to keep a closer eye on my daughters – that they weren't innocent at all, and that they'd been around to his house on plenty of occasions.

'We argued about it and he prodded me in the chest and told me if I was going to bully his son, I'd have him to contend with. I hadn't bullied him! That man was worse than his son – shouting and swearing and telling me my daughters were little tarts. Of course, I challenged the twins about going to Noah's house and they admitted they'd been around there, but only to play online games together. They denied any involvement with the boys. Erin was in tears about the accusations. She'd never so much as kissed a boy.'

'And you believed the girls?' Natalie asked.

He looked her in the eye. 'DI Ward, you never knew my daughters. They were good girls. They weren't angels but they were honest, good girls, and if they said they'd only been to Noah's house to play online games, then that's exactly what happened. Those two shits, however – I wouldn't trust them as far as I could throw them.'

'Did the twins stop seeing the boys after that?'

'Yes. They steered clear of them.'

'Are you sure about that?'

'Definitely. They were very trustworthy,' said Chris.

Natalie didn't want to upset the parents any more than they already were by telling them that their daughters had lied and had not only been WhatsApping the boys but had been seen in the Rocket Café with Noah and Harry on Wednesday. However, John waded in with, 'We believe the twins were with these boys last Wednesday morning.'

Judith sat up straighter. 'That's not possible. They were at Ashra's house. They went there, didn't they, Chris? They wouldn't lie to us.'

'We'll talk to Ashra,' said Natalie smoothly, silencing John with an icy look.

'These boys…' said Judith. 'Did they kill Erin and Ivy?'

'We're still looking for the person or persons responsible and establishing facts at this stage.'

Chris ran his hand over his chin, his bristles rasping as he did so. 'They couldn't have slipped out to meet up with them, could they?'

'That's one of the things we're trying to determine,' Natalie replied.

Chris's face drained of any remaining colour and he groaned, releasing his wife's hand as he did so. 'What have we done?'

'Chris, what do you mean?' Natalie said.

'I told Noah's father if his boy or friend showed up again, I'd take matters into my own hands.'

'You threatened him?'

'He accused my daughters of sleeping about! I didn't threaten *him*. I told him if his son and friend went anywhere near my daughters, I'd make sure they didn't go near any other girls again. I was furious. It was nothing but hot air. That's all it was, but what… what if… he and his son retaliated because of it? What if this is my fault?'

'I think you're reading too much into it. People don't usually attack children because of an argument,' said Natalie calmly. She ignored the look on John's face, which said exactly the opposite. It was true: people killed for all sorts of reasons, and Glenn Powers and his son might be behind the twins' deaths. If they were, what on earth was their connection to Isabella? The investigation was becoming even more complex, and all the while she was mindful that the killer could strike again.

*

The powder shot up his nostrils, flared in anticipation of the rush. He sniffed a couple of times to make sure it had been properly inhaled, then wiped his nose with the back of his hand and cleared away the evidence from the toilet cistern where he'd laid it out. He tilted his head back and stared at the ceiling, letting his synapses ping wildly like pistol fire. A smile glued itself to his lips, stretching them widely. The plan was now going so well he ought to be high as a kite without any drugs, but the fact was, he needed the blow to keep up the intensity of what he'd put into place.

A small voice in his head reminded him he'd been taking the coke regularly, at least twice a week. 'Recreational usage,' he growled back at the voice.

What about the amphetamines? *the voice reminded him.*

'Bugger off!' he snapped. He shut his eyes and waited.

The drug acted quickly and positivity soon coursed through his body. The smile returned, tugging at the corners of his mouth as he pondered his next move. He was so far ahead of the team investigating the murders that he almost felt like leaving clues to help them out, but that might trip him up. Some killers got too cocky and made that very mistake, and it usually resulted in their downfall. He didn't need to prove he was more intelligent than the police chasing after him – he knew he was.

His conscience made one last attempt to warn him that he was overusing, but he silenced it and reminded himself he was intelligent and would never move on to harder drugs like his weak-willed mother had. She'd got into all sorts of shit that messed her up big time, even though she had a kid to look after – bitch!

He was fully aware of the short- and long-term effects of what he was taking: gregariousness, the illusion of self-confidence, the feeling of being bloody fantastic! Which, of course, he was. The dumb lot in charge of finding him didn't know their arse from their elbow. Of course, he was fucking superior. He didn't need a good snort to know that.

CHAPTER TWENTY-SIX

TUESDAY, 14 AUGUST – EVENING

Harry Brown was shorter than his friend and had dark, brooding looks. He glared fiercely at Lucy and Ian when they arrived, but when questioned about the twins he showed a little more remorse than Noah. Lucy wasn't sure if it was the presence of his mother that made him responsive to her questions, or if he was just less aggressive than his friend, but he sat down on a well-used kitchen chair and tried to be helpful.

'They were mates,' he said in answer to Lucy's questions.

'Weren't they a bit young to be your mates?'

Harry stroked the Staffordshire bull terrier sitting on his lap. His mother stood by the kitchen sink, arms folded, listening to the conversation.

'We didn't know how old they were when we first met them. They didn't act young.'

Ian was ready with his notepad and had a few questions to ask. 'How often did you meet up with them?'

The boy shifted his gaze from Lucy to Ian. 'A few times a week after lessons ended. Sometimes we went to the shopping centre, other times the library.'

'Did they ever come back here?'

'No.'

'What about Noah's house?'

'Yeah, sometimes. His dad is nearly always out and they have a wicked TV screen. Really good for playing video games.'

'And that's what you did?'

'Yeah.'

'Nothing else?'

The boy blinked a few times before saying, 'Not much else.'

Picking up on his reaction, Lucy stepped in with, 'Were you more than friends?'

'No, we messed about, that's all.' He kept his hand on his dog, whose eyes were half shut, watching Lucy.

'Can you explain what you mean by *messed about*?'

'Uh…'

'You kissed?'

The boy rubbed the dog's head and avoided Lucy's steady gaze. 'We didn't go further than first base though.'

Lucy wasn't sure she believed him but put aside that subject. 'Did you meet up with their friend Ashra?'

'She tried to join in but the twins didn't want her around with us. She got her knickers in a twist when Noah told her to get lost. Told him he was a prick and stomped off.'

'So, it was usually you, Noah and the twins?'

'That's right.'

'Did you go to the Rocket Café last Wednesday with them?' Ian asked.

'Yeah, but it was dead boring in there so we didn't stay long.'

'Where did you go afterwards?'

'Noah's,' came the mumbled reply.

Lucy took over the questioning. 'Were the girls unhappy at home?'

'I don't think so. They complained about being treated like little kids but never said they were unhappy.'

'Were you friends with either of them on social media?'

'Only on WhatsApp.'

'Did they tell you where they were going on Saturday night?'

The dog let out a sigh of contentment and the boy looked up at Lucy and said, 'They didn't say anything about going out.'

'You were with Noah that night, weren't you?'

'Yeah. At his house.'

'What did you do all night?'

'Played games. I came home at ten, didn't I, Mum?'

'That's right. He was home by ten,' said his mother.

'I have to ask you this and please think very carefully before you answer. Did you arrange to meet the twins Saturday night?' Lucy asked.

'No. They said they were busy.'

'You did invite them, then?'

'Yeah, we asked if they wanted to come over and chill with us.'

'And what was their exact response? This is important, Harry, so please tell us what you can remember.'

'They couldn't come cos they were busy,' he repeated.

'Did they say why they were busy?'

'No.'

'Didn't you ask them?'

'No. We weren't that bothered.'

Ian frowned in concentration. 'When was the last time you spoke to them?'

'Wednesday. We all went to Noah's after the café, but they left after about ten minutes. They didn't contact us after that.'

'Wasn't that unusual?' Ian asked.

'Yeah. I think they'd kind of lost interest in us. Noah said Erin wasn't putting out any more and Ivy was acting weird with me. We figured they were ghosting us. And now they're dead.' His mouth turned down and his bottom lip quivered. He stroked the dog again, as if to distract himself.

Lucy noticed the movement. 'Did the twins ever mention a man called Eddie?'

'No.' It was the same reaction as Noah's. Then, 'Maybe. Ivy said something about a bloke called Eddie who asked them to be models. Sounded weird to me. You don't go up to girls and ask that, do you?'

'Did they take him up on his offer?'

'I dunno. They never said.'

'Can you think of anywhere they might have been going that night?'

His hand rested on the dog's head and he replied, 'No. No idea.'

*

Natalie returned to Ashra Khatri's house, this time with John, and was once again asking her questions. 'We won't keep you. We need to tidy up a few loose ends,' said Natalie.

Mrs Khatri bustled them into the sitting room and fetched her daughter, who stood awkwardly in front of the officers, her fingers rubbing at a sparkly bangle on her wrist. There was no sign of the toddler who'd been there earlier, and Natalie assumed the child was asleep.

'Ashra, we've spoken to Mr and Mrs Westmore and they said the twins were here last Wednesday, but they weren't, were they?'

'They were.'

'We know they were with Noah and Harry so you don't need to cover for them.'

'I'm not. They did come over… about half past two.'

That was after they'd been to the café with the boys. Natalie was glad she didn't have to tell the grieving parents their daughters had been lying.

'Did you know that they'd told their parents they were with you?'

'No… well… I suppose so.'

'You aren't in any trouble. We only need to find out what Erin and Ivy were up to. Did they ever ask you to cover for them – say they were here when they weren't?'

'Yes. But nobody asked me about them.' Her eyes grew large and she looked to her mother. 'I didn't lie for them.'

'Why did they need you to cover for them?'

'So that they could meet Noah and Harry. Their mum and dad didn't want them to see them. They said they were too young to have boyfriends.'

'And is that what Noah and Harry were – boyfriends?'

'Kind of.'

'Did the twins ask you to cover for them regularly?'

'About five or six times. Mostly since the school holidays started. I didn't want to do it but they asked me to and we were friends.' Her eyes became dewy again and her fingers edged slowly around the bangle, turning it around and around.

'It must have been difficult. Didn't they invite you to go with them to meet Noah and Harry?'

'No.'

'I expect you felt quite left out.'

'I didn't like them – the boys – they were horrible to me. I don't know why Erin and Ivy liked them so much. Erin was really into Noah. I told her to stay away but she really liked him, and Ivy fancied Harry. I wasn't… I wasn't welcome.' A tear escaped and trickled down her face.

'You'd been friends for a long time, hadn't you?' Natalie said.

Ashra continued to spin the bracelet, more quickly now. 'Yes.'

'When did you last see them?'

'When they came by on Wednesday, after they'd been out with Noah and Harry. They said they'd dumped them. We were going to go out together this week – just us girls again.'

'They'd dumped the boys?'

'That's what they told me.'

'They didn't intend meeting them on Saturday?'

'I don't think so. They said they weren't going to hang with them any more.'

'That's really helpful. Thank you.'

'Is that all the questions?' Mrs Khatri asked.

'I think so. I'm really sorry about your friends, Ashra,' said Natalie as she made to leave.

The girl's eyes filled with tears and she nodded a response.

'She was a very good friend to them,' said her mother.

'Yes, I'm sure she was.' Natalie gave them both a gentle smile and turned to leave.

John added his thanks and joined her. 'If it wasn't that pair, who the fuck were they planning on meeting?' he said as they walked to the car.

'Beats me but we'll have to get to the bottom of it.'

'Could have been Eddie. Something to do with that modelling session.' John threw himself into the driver's seat.

Natalie slammed her door shut. 'I'm not going to discount that possibility.'

He started up the engine, and as they pulled away, Lucy's voice came over the communications unit. 'Got an update for you, Natalie. Noah was definitely shifty but his father saw us out before we could probe any further. Harry was more open and says they haven't seen the twins since last Wednesday.'

'That tallies with what we've established. The twins told their best friend, Ashra, they weren't going to see the boys again after Wednesday. Glenn showed you out? Interesting. He had a run-in with Chris Westmore a few weeks ago over the twins.'

The comms unit crackled noisily then Lucy said, 'Glenn was out Saturday night. Claims he went to Derby to meet a *friend*.'

'Do we know who this friend was?'

'No. He was very cagey about it.'

'It might be an idea to bring him in for further questioning. Would you do that?'

'Roger that,' said Lucy.

The unit fell silent and Natalie looked across at John, whose forehead was creased in thought. 'We need to check out Glenn's alibi,' she said.

'What about Eddie? We haven't finished with him yet, have we?'

'No, but I want to see where this leads us.'

John drummed a beat against the steering wheel. 'Glenn Powers has no link to Isabella Sharpe.'

'None that we know of *yet*, apart from the fact he lives close to the family in Appleby Gardens. That's something we need to investigate.'

'Why are you so keen to ignore Eddie?'

'I'm not. I'm conducting the investigation as I see fit. We should follow this up.'

'You're in charge.'

His words bugged her, then she decided they were meant to do so. She gave a brisk nod and said, 'Let's see what we can establish before Glenn turns up for his interview.'

It was an hour later when Natalie and Lucy began interviewing Noah's father, Glenn Powers. He sprawled in the chair, legs apart, and scowled.

'I don't see why you've brought me here,' he said to Natalie. 'They've no right to do this, have they?'

The duty solicitor assured him it was perfectly legal.

'Mr Powers, we'd like you to confirm where you were on Saturday evening.'

'I went for a drink in Derby with a friend.'

'And this friend's name?'

'Sheila Newport.'

'Were you with Sheila all evening?'

'Yes. We met in the Queen's Head pub on Union Street at seven thirty.'

'What time did you leave the pub?'

'Nine-ish. I went to her place for a while and then came home about midnight.'

'And Noah and Harry were up when you got back?'

'Noah was in his bedroom.'

'You told my colleague that both the boys were up when you got back. Is that correct?'

'I meant they were both there when I left, and Noah was there when I returned.'

'But what you actually said was, "They were still here when I came in." Is that not so?'

He blew his cheeks out in an exaggerated fashion. 'I didn't want her to think they'd done anything wrong. They hadn't.'

'By her, do you mean DS Carmichael?' Natalie asked, poker-faced.

'Yes. DS Carmichael. I'm sorry but she and the other officer were suspicious of the boys. I waded in to help them out.'

'By telling a lie.'

'It wasn't a lie as such. Noah *was* in his bedroom. Harry had gone back home. Where's the harm?'

'The harm is in not telling us exactly what happened when we're investigating a murder enquiry. What else are you keeping from us, Mr Powers?'

'Nothing!' He held up his arms in a submissive gesture.

'The twins visited your house on several occasions.'

'So what? The twins visited the boys. That doesn't mean anything. My boy didn't kill them. I didn't kill them!'

'It would have been helpful if you'd told us that. You withheld information.'

'I didn't want you to jump to any wrong conclusions about Noah or his friend.'

'You told DS Carmichael you didn't know the twins but they went to your home on several occasions to play PC games with Noah and Harry.'

'I didn't know them! I only saw them to say hello to when I came in from work.'

Natalie bit back an acerbic retort. 'We will need to talk to Sheila Newport to confirm what you have told us. Could we have her contact details, please?'

'I only have her phone number.' He reached into his pocket and drew out a Nokia, scrolled through it and read out the number for Lucy to write down. Lucy excused herself.

Natalie continued with her questions. 'I'd also like to know your whereabouts on Friday evening.'

'I was at home.'

'Alone?'

'Yes.'

'Where was your son?'

'Out.'

'Any idea where he was?'

'No.' He folded his arms and tapped a forefinger against his bicep, an impatient gesture that Natalie did not miss.

'You seem irritated.'

'I am. What is this all about? I haven't done anything wrong.'

'We spoke to Mr Westmore and he told us that you two had an argument a few weeks ago.'

The irritated tapping stopped in a flash. 'It was an outburst.'

'An outburst during which you accused his daughters of being tarts and threatened the man. Can you explain yourself?'

'Noah told me the snobby bastard had threatened to set the police on him if he went around to the twins' house again. I wasn't very impressed, especially as his daughters had been to our place quite a few times, and whenever I saw them, they were all over Noah and Harry. In fact, I was fucking furious. Westmore's a stuck-up git who thinks he's better than the likes of me, so I went around to his house to set him straight.'

'You threatened him,' repeated Natalie.

He lifted his face to the ceiling and let out a heavy sigh. 'I'd been drinking. I was pissed off with him and my mouth ran away from me. I didn't hurt him or properly threaten him.'

'Mr Westmore says differently.'

The head lowered and his nostrils flared. 'Then he is a fucking liar. He gave as good as he got and then said he'd set the police on me. Tosser!'

'You kept valuable information from us, Mr Powers.'

'I didn't think it was important.'

'Who the hell are you to decide what is and isn't important? Two thirteen-year-olds are dead!' snapped Natalie.

Glenn looked down at the table. 'I didn't kill them nor did my boy.'

'Then you'd better start talking because any more lies and so help me, I'll have you put in the cells.'

Upstairs in the office, Lucy was talking to Sheila Newport on the telephone.

'Yes, Glenn was with me on Saturday night. Is he in any trouble?'

'He's helping us with our enquiries at the moment. Could you be specific about times?'

'I met him in the Queen's Head pub in Union Street, Derby, at around seven thirty. We had a few drinks and then he came back to my place, which is near the pub.'

'And what time did he leave your house?'

There was a pause followed by, 'No later than ten.'

'Have you known him long?'

'That was our second date.'

'How did you meet him?'

'A dating app. The first time we met was during the day at a coffee shop. We got on well so we arranged another date…'

Lucy could tell by the hesitation that there was more so she waited and was rewarded for her patience.

'It was going okay Saturday night but once we got back to my place, I realised he wasn't for me.'

'Why was that?'

'He was full on and I wasn't ready for that. I told him I needed to get to know him better but he was insistent. I told him to shove off.'

'Full on?'

'Wanting to have sex.'

'Did he become aggressive?'

'No, but he was majorly annoyed that I'd led him on.'

'Had you?'

'We'd been sending flirty messages – nothing unusual – for a couple of weeks and I really liked him. It was only after we got back to my place on Saturday night that I realised I didn't fancy him enough and I didn't want to have sex with him. He was put out about it.'

'Could you confirm that you asked him to leave at about ten?'

'That's right.'

'And he left without any fuss?'

'He called me a cow then grabbed his jacket and stormed out.'

'He hasn't contacted you since?'

'No.'

The door to the interview room opened and Lucy returned with a sheet of paper. She passed it to Natalie, who read it then spoke again. 'Let's go back to Saturday evening. You went to Derby for a drink with Sheila at the Queen's Head pub.'

'Yes.'

'You said you left around nine o'clock and went back to her place, then got home around midnight.'

'That's right.'

'According to Sheila you left her house around ten o'clock.'

His lips pressed together and a dark shadow flitted across his features.

'What were you doing between ten and midnight?'

'I was in my car.'

'For two hours?'

'I'd been drinking! I was over the limit. I hadn't expected to be driving home so soon. I'm a lorry driver. I can't afford to lose my licence. As soon as I'd left Sheila's place, I realised it was stupid to drive, so I pulled over. I didn't want to get stopped by a copper.' His face oozed indignation.

'What did you and Sheila argue about?'

'You probably already know if you've spoken to her.'

'Answer the question, please.'

'Sex. It was going well, then she went cold on me and chucked me out. Happy now?'

'Would you agree that you felt sexually frustrated and angry when you left her house?'

His eyes screwed up so tightly, Natalie could barely see the pupils. 'I don't have to answer that. It's none of your business.'

'It's my business when two girls who you accused of being "tarts" went missing at about the same time as you were driving about frustrated and angry.'

'Yes, I was angry. I thought we were on the same wavelength but it turned out we weren't. She'd been leading me on.'

'Where exactly did you go when you left Sheila's house? This is very important.'

'I stopped off in a layby and listened to the radio.'

'Which layby?'

'I don't know? I was pissed off at the time. It was just a layby.'

'How far away from her house?'

'I can't be sure. I was angry. I didn't pay any attention to where I was.'

'That's not really a good enough excuse. We can track your vehicle for that night or you can make life easier for us. Which is it to be?'

His lip curled and he growled, 'I don't remember.'

Natalie could sense his anger as it built up, but undeterred she said, 'I need you to be more cooperative. This is, as I have explained, a murder investigation. That same night, two girls left their home and were found dead the next day – two girls who were involved with your son and his friend. Now, we could trace your car using surveillance cameras and waste an enormous amount of resources and time in doing so, or you could help us out by telling us your movements on Saturday night. For the last time, where were you on Saturday night between ten and midnight?'

Glenn shut his eyes and inhaled deeply before saying, 'No comment.'

The hands on the office clock showed it was 9.42 p.m. and the overhead lights illuminated the now dark office. Outside, the clear sky had turned navy and the first stars had appeared. Natalie had been in the office five minutes and was still fuming. She smashed her desk with her fist. 'Why the fuck is Glenn holding out on us?'

'Because he has something to hide,' said John.

Natalie could only agree, but what was the man hiding, and was it relevant to the case? Her head continued to throb in spite of the paracetamol she'd taken earlier.

'I've contacted the tech team. They're searching through camera footage for his vehicle,' said Ian.

Natalie replied with, 'The bastard's wasting precious time. Sod him. He's not leaving here until we know exactly where he went after he left Sheila's place. We'll keep him in a holding cell overnight and see if that helps him become more cooperative. Ian, do social services know about Noah?'

'Yes, they'll arrange for him to be looked after tonight.'

'Good. In that case, we'll let Glenn stew here and tackle him again first thing tomorrow, and we'll speak to Eddie again,' she said, looking pointedly at John, who acknowledged her with a nod. 'Okay, clear off, everyone. Day's over.'

Ian cleared his desk quickly and was first to leave.

Lucy took longer and lifted an envelope from her desk. 'I almost forgot. There's a letter marked for your attention,' she said, placing it in front of Natalie before making for the door.

Natalie glimpsed the Samford postmark and the typewritten address and froze. 'When did it arrive?'

'I don't know. It was on my desk when I came in earlier. See you tomorrow.' She strode off down the hall.

'Shit!' Natalie said quietly.

'You okay?' John asked.

'Hang back a sec, will you?'

'Sure.' He leant against the table and observed her as she pulled on a pair of plastic gloves before opening the envelope. Holding her breath, she dragged out the piece of paper inside. Like the first note she'd received, this one was in bold typed font. There were only two words:

Remember me?

CHAPTER TWENTY-SEVEN

THEN

Clunk… whir… wheeze.

The familiarity of the noise is almost friendly, like a tune to welcome him as he breezes in and catches himself in time. The fetching nurse, Pearl, with the wide grey eyes, is hovering over his wife, Jennifer, and he has only a split second to adopt the practised look of concern before she greets him.

'How is she?'

He always asks the same question in the same hopeful tone, as if there's an outside chance of improvement, and when the reply comes he feigns the resigned look that accompanies the words, 'Hanging on.'

'The girls?' he asks and relishes the warmth that radiates from Pearl's eyes. She is charmed by their resilience – his little fighters. She's a single mother with an eleven-year-old daughter of her own called Mikayla. He wonders idly what sort of stepmother she would make, then almost immediately dismisses the idea. He alone is going to be the centre of his daughters' universe. He is going to lavish them with all the love and attention that he never received as a child. He blinks away the memories of the woman he once knew, eyes wild, head thrown back, screaming for her fix. He's going to be there for his children, guide them and love them more than anyone could possibly love another human.

Clunk… whir… wheeze.

'How are you?' Pearl asks.

'Bearing up.' The truth is he's never been happier. He has nobody breathing down his neck, complaining when he isn't at home or going through his pockets and phone to see what he's been up to. The freedom is heady but not as heady as knowing he's soon going to be a father. Jennifer's parents and sister, Louise, have been here the last two days, hollow-eyed and grim-faced. It's been tough. They want to share the responsibility of bringing up their girls. Some shit about reminding them of Jennifer, and he nodded and agreed and kept up the front of the grateful son-in-law who wouldn't be able to cope without them. He'd squeezed tears out of almost dry eyes and promised the twins would stay with them even though it was never going to happen. Jennifer had tried to take the girls away and her parents had been party to that. They don't deserve the babies. Their part in this is over – once the babies are almost at full term, they'll be delivered by caesarean and then her life support will be switched off. His heart thuds like a beating drum at the prospect of finally meeting his daughters. He has chosen their names. Jennifer had wanted to call them Carly and Orla and would not heed his choice, but now it is entirely up to him, and he has chosen the perfect names for them.

Clunk… whir… wheeze.

Pearl bustles about the machines surrounding his wife's bed and although he hasn't flirted exactly, her cheeks flush charmingly when he tells her she smells nice.

'What are you thinking about?' she asks.

'Names for the twins.'

'Have you chosen any?'

'Yes, we picked them a while ago,' he replies. 'Lily and Rose.'

She nods approvingly. 'They're gorgeous names. I expect the girls will be every bit as pretty as those flowers.'

'They will be – delicate and beautiful, like their mother,' he says, trying hard not to smile at such an untrue statement.

She gives him a radiant smile and checks Jennifer's vital signs.

He watches in silence. He'll have all the support he needs from the hospital staff to bring his children into the world. They're fighters and *everyone here loves them. Afterwards, they'll turn off Jennifer's life support and her entire family will be there for that. Of course, he will shed a tear or two, but when it's all over, he and his children will bid them all adieu.*

Clunk…

He's about to speak when one of the machines emits a high-pitched noise that increases in intensity.

'She's arresting!' *yells Pearl.*

A white-coated doctor charges into the room and shouts for the cardiac arrest trolley. The monitors that display his wife's and children's heartbeats are flickering. The line representing his wife's heart is dropping, and the red numbers denoting blood pressure, changing rapidly… then flatlining.

'Arrested!' *yells the doctor.*

He can't drag his eyes from the monitor. Everything in the room is a blur apart from the two remaining lines that flicker and hold steady. 'Fight!' *he says under his breath.*

Suddenly the room is jam-packed with people clustering around his wife's bed. Pearl's fingers dig into his shoulder and she urges him yet again to leave the room as a trolley containing cardiac arrest equipment is raced in. He doesn't want to leave them. The doctor yells at him to get out. His eyes are glued to the monitor. Flicker… flicker. Then suddenly his babies' heartbeats lurch as one and plummet.

'The girls!' *he yells but he's pushed out into the corridor and the door is shut. He presses his face against the pane, palms flat to the glass. The bedsheet's been tugged from Jennifer's body and electrodes attached to her chest. The doctor accepts two handheld pads, instructs the nurses to move away and presses the pads onto his wife's body. Current rushes into her. His eyes are so damp with tears he can't see clearly.*

'Come away. You can't do anything.' *Pearl's voice is loud in his ear and she is tugging at his sleeve.*

He moves like a ghost along the corridor, unaware of his footsteps and Pearl's hand still on his shirtsleeve, breathing in her floral perfume as she opens a door and helps him to a seat. Hot tears roll down his cheeks. Pearl squats in front of him, her eyes mirroring his concern, trained on him. 'They'll do everything they can to save them,' she says, but his heart jackhammers in his chest – he can't lose his girls.

CHAPTER TWENTY-EIGHT

'I admit it does look suspicious, but we can't automatically assume this message is connected to the investigation. It could be a prank,' said John.

Natalie stood her ground. 'I believe it's connected and I think this killer is messing with us.'

'What makes you think that?'

'It's addressed to me and it's the second one I've received. The other one is in the lab in case there are any prints on it.'

'You didn't mention it.'

'I wasn't sure there was a connection but now I think there could well be.'

'What did the other one say?'

'It said, "I'm back." Think about it, John. First, I get a note saying, "I'm back," just after we discovered the twins, and now this one: "Remember me?"'

John paced the room before speaking. 'That suggests we didn't get the right person for the Blossom Twins murders in 2014 and that the actual killer is here and murdering again.'

He dragged a hand over his face, which was suddenly older and more careworn. 'If Neil Hoskins wasn't the killer, that screws everything up.'

'After he was charged and imprisoned, Neil claimed he wasn't the murderer.'

'But he admitted to killing the girls at the time.'

'Later, he said he was innocent. He tried to get his sentence overturned. He pleaded to be retried and then, when he got nowhere with his appeal, he committed suicide.'

John rubbed his eyes and sighed loudly. 'No. You can't be right. We were thorough, weren't we? Everything pointed to Neil. He was our man. This murderer can't be the same person who killed those girls in 2014. This has to be somebody else.'

'Okay, let's assume Neil was guilty and committed suicide because he hated prison or felt guilty or for whatever reason he took his life. Who are we dealing with now? This killer knows details that were never released. For one, the bodies are positioned exactly the same way as Sharon and Karen Hill and Avril and Faye Moore were. How could this perpetrator know that? Exactly the same way, John: face to face, holding hands. And then there's the blossom, sprinkled on their bodies.'

'We can't have gone wrong, Natalie. You were part of that investigation and you know how thorough we were.'

Natalie wanted to stand her ground but she also didn't want to argue with John. The fact was they hadn't been thorough enough, in her mind, and the senior investigating officer had been quick to accept Neil's confession. As much as she disliked John Briggs, he was the only other person who knew exactly how the investigation had panned out, and although he'd been one of those who'd been keen to accuse Neil Hoskins, he was also an officer who wanted justice. 'I'm just saying we should at least consider the possibility. In the meantime, I'm sending this note to Forensics.'

'Did they find anything on the other one?'

'Some partial fingerprints on the envelope but they've not been identified yet and I suppose they could belong to post office workers.'

'How come the notes were addressed to you? How does this person know you're heading this investigation?'

'Bev Gardiner, one of our local reporters, wrote about it in the *Hatfield Herald*. It wouldn't be difficult to find out who was leading officer on this.' She slid the note back into the envelope, ready to take it upstairs to Forensics.

'Natalie…' he said suddenly, his eyebrows drawn together. 'You don't think we screwed up on the Blossom Twins case, do you?'

'I really don't know but I can't think how else a killer would know those details unless they knew Neil and had been given that information.'

John rubbed at his chin, his head moving up and down slightly, small movements that accompanied his train of thought. 'There's a chance that's exactly what's happened. Maybe Neil wasn't working alone. I'm sure we got it right with Neil. That has to be the explanation. He had an accomplice or an associate who knew all his secrets.'

Natalie admitted it was a logical explanation. John seemed sideswiped by the note; all his usual bravado had vanished. She addressed him with, 'I'll take this to the lab now. We'll check out Glenn and Eddie tomorrow. If this isn't the same killer, it's a copycat and probably somebody who knew Neil. We'll tackle that angle. You happy with that?'

He cleared his throat and his words tumbled out. 'Yes. Look… I know I come across as a bit full on but I want the same result you do, and just between us… this is my big chance to prove myself. I've been working hard towards promotion, and getting on this investigation could open up that possibility, so of course I need it to go well and for us to get results… the right results.'

It seemed strange hearing the cocksure John speaking from the heart but she understood. However, sometimes being overzealous led to errors. John didn't need that particular sermon. The fact that there was a chance Neil had not killed the Blossom Twins had given him sufficient doubt to toe the line.

'Thanks for letting me know about this,' he said, indicating the envelope.

'See you tomorrow,' she replied.

'Yeah. Night, Natalie.'

The house was silent when Natalie got in. She felt like an intruder as she carefully navigated the stairs, assiduously avoiding those that she knew creaked. She didn't want to wake anyone. She didn't want to have to put on a false smile and pretend to be content in front of the kids. David had shut the bedroom door but Leigh's was open as usual. Her daughter still hated the dark and slept not only with the door ajar, but with fairy lights over her bed that made her room look like an enchanted cave. Natalie stood in the doorway. Leigh was fast asleep, her mobile phone on the floor by the bed where it had fallen. Natalie crept into the room and studied the girl's face, trying to take in every detail and commit it to memory. Both her children were growing into adults and she wanted to be able to recall every stage of their lives. Once she and David told them they were splitting up, things would change. Moments like this were precious. She dropped a kiss on her daughter's forehead and edged back out of the room onto the landing, almost colliding with her son.

'Oh, sorry!' said Josh, who was still dressed in jeans and a sweatshirt.

'It's okay. I didn't want to wake anybody.'

'I was up.'

'You online?'

'Yeah. Needed the toilet.'

'Go ahead.'

'You sure?'

He headed into the bathroom and she meandered to his room. The computer was illuminated and a game paused, a sniper with his gun aimed directly at her heart frozen on the screen. Josh's headset lay beside the keyboard and she thought back to Erin and Ivy, playing online with Noah and Harry. The world was a different place to when she was their age. Then there was no Internet and no online activities or virtual places where children could discuss anything and keep their lives hidden from their parents. When she was thirteen she'd played outside on her bike or board games with her sister – her sister who she no longer acknowledged. She shook her head to remove the memories of Frances. Josh returned and scurried back to his chair in front of the computer. He clipped his headset back on and she threw him a smile.

'Don't stay up too late,' she mouthed, knowing he'd be there as long as he wanted to be. He had no school the following day or a job to get up for. This was how so many teenagers spent their time nowadays, and for all her efforts to keep up with her children, it was a world she struggled to understand. She blew him a kiss and made her way to the bathroom. Her head still throbbed and her bones ached with weariness. As much as she wanted to keep pushing on, the case would have to wait. She needed sleep, and if she was to find the person responsible for murdering Isabella, Erin and Ivy, she needed sharp wits. She removed her contact lenses, peeled off her clothes and grabbed David's old shirt that she usually slept in from its hook behind the door. She paused before putting it on. She ought to buy a new nightshirt. This would be a reminder of the past and she needed to look to the future. For now, she had little option, so she did up the buttons and scrubbed her teeth. Tomorrow was another day. She hoped it wasn't going to be a bad one.

*

He eased back in his armchair and savoured the whisky, allowing the alcohol to wash around his mouth before the fiery liquid descended his throat.

Things were going just fine. He'd sent a second note and by now DI Natalie Ward would be wondering who she was dealing with. The answer was simple: she was dealing with somebody who could easily outwit her and her team. He was several steps ahead of her and would stay that way. With his free hand resting on the arm of the chair, he thumbed through the selection of photographs on his mobile, snapped at the shopping centre, where he'd collected pictures of his potential victims back in May. He'd been patient and now that patience would pay off. He hadn't struck again since the Westmore twins, yet DI Ward couldn't be sure of that fact. She'd be waiting and worrying that there would be two more victims hidden away. He swilled the amber liquid in his glass and wondered when he should act next. Putting the glass to his lips and sipping again, he decided it would be soon. He rather fancied the idea of DI Ward spinning like a top, unable to predict his next move.

He wasn't going to be predictable. That would be how he'd get away with it. Oh, dear! Natalie Ward was going to rue the day he'd shown up in Samford. He'd escaped her once before and he was going to do so again.

Eeny, meeny, miny... oh! This pair. They would be perfect.

CHAPTER TWENTY-NINE

Natalie had managed to leave the house again without seeing David or her children, and she grabbed a takeaway egg muffin and tea on her way to work. She wasn't, however, the first in the office. John was already at a desk, studying a computer screen. He looked up immediately.

'I was going back over what you said last night about the note and the Blossom Twins killer,' he began. 'I think we should try and establish a connection between those people we've interviewed and Neil Hoskins on the off-chance one of them knew him. I've contacted the prison and requested visiting and email records. If this is a copycat murderer or somebody who partnered him, that person must have been in touch with the man.'

'That's good,' said Natalie and she meant it. John had taken on board her concerns over the posted note. 'I thought we'd start with Eddie Ford, before he opens the salon this morning. See what he has to say about talking to the twins. You up for that?'

'I'm in. I was searching for possible links between him and Neil but I haven't come across anything.'

'We'll ask him outright. Come on.'

Eddie Ford leant against the full-sized fridge-freezer in his kitchen with his arms folded and his legs crossed at the ankles. His wife,

Nia, stood by the sink opposite, rubbing a cloth around a plate, apparently ignoring proceedings. It was the first time Natalie had met his wife and she found her somewhat detached. Nia was clearly a good ten to fifteen years older than Eddie, with light auburn hair scraped back from her stern, pale face and held in place with a sparkly pink barrette at odds with her washed-out black leggings and loose-fitting T-shirt.

Eddie was in a prickly mood. 'I honestly don't recall any conversation with the twins.'

'You were in the Rocket Café when you asked the twins if they'd like to be hair models. They were sitting in the window seats along with their friend Ashra.'

Eddie screwed up his face. 'Maybe I did but I honestly don't remember it.'

'People who keep repeating the word honestly are usually lying,' commented John.

'For crying out loud! I'm *not* lying. You keep hounding me at every opportunity and it's beginning to annoy me. If you're looking for a scapegoat, look elsewhere. I didn't have anything to do with their deaths.'

'Nia, you went away last weekend, to Blackpool, didn't you?' Natalie said.

Nia looked across, plate in one hand and cloth in the other. 'That's right.'

'Had the trip been planned for a long time?'

'About a month,' she replied. 'My friend's little girl is the same age as Pixie. We thought it would be nice to take them away together.'

'When did you tell Eddie that you were going away?'

'Same time I booked the hotel.'

'Have you ever seen the Westmore twins in the salon?'

'I don't usually go into the salon, only if I need to speak to Eddie.'

'What do you do?'

'I work three days a week in Birmingham as an administrator for a children's charity. Pixie goes to nursery those days. The other days, I'm a full-time mum.'

'Do you make lunch for Pixie when she's at home?'

'Yes, unless we go out with friends.' She ran the cloth around the plate and put it in the rack.

'Do you eat lunch with her?'

'Yes, if we're in.'

'But you don't usually make any lunch for Eddie.'

'Sometimes.'

'Eddie, why don't you pop upstairs for lunch instead of going out to get something to eat?'

He shrugged. 'I do now and again, but I can't be bothered to mess about making my own lunch when I can get something already prepared. The café's not far away and I get a proper break from the salon.'

'It seems odd that you are only downstairs working but you don't come up to see your wife or daughter during working hours. I'd have thought that would be one of the perks.'

Nia spoke sharply. 'He does if we're not out at swimming, with friends or at the park. We don't sit about cooped up all day, waiting for Eddie to take a break.'

'Eddie, did you ever cut this man's hair?'

John passed over a photograph of deceased Neil Hoskins.

'Who is he?' Eddie asked.

'His name was Neil Hoskins.'

Nia looked over her husband's shoulder at the picture. 'I know who you mean. He was the Blossom Twins murderer. It was all over the news at the time.'

'That's right.'

'I've never met him,' said Eddie.

'Me neither,' said Nia with a shudder.

John took the photo from Eddie and put it back in his folder.

'I'd like to go back to Erin and Ivy Westmore,' said Natalie. 'How many girls do you invite to be hair models?'

'I ask loads of people – old or young. I'm always on the lookout. There's a sign up in the window advertising for models. Some days, I ask total strangers in the streets. It's a way of drumming up business too. Some of those people might drop into the salon purely to see what we're about. There's so much competition in the town. I have to make my mark somehow. I don't remember asking the twins. Maybe I did. If I did, my mind was elsewhere at the time.'

'On what?'

'The salon, ordering products, doing the books – any number of things.'

'That's very convenient,' said John, darkly.

'But true,' Eddie replied.

Unable to make any headway with Eddie, and with nothing to link him to Neil Hoskins, Natalie and John returned to base to interview Glenn Powers, Noah's father, who'd spent the night in the holding cells. Lucy, tasked with trying to uncover links between him and Neil, had established Glenn had made several goods deliveries to the large electronics retail store where Neil had worked.

Lucy presented the facts and added, 'At the time, Neil Hoskins worked as a salesman in an open-plan office on the second floor.'

'I thought he was a piano tutor. He taught piano to his victims,' said Ian.

'He was a part-time piano tutor but he also worked in sales for Tindford Electronics.'

'So Glenn might have come across Neil when he was delivering goods there?' said Natalie.

'Unlikely. I was told sales people have nothing to do with deliveries at all. Health and safety rules state only warehouse operatives can be in the warehouse.'

Natalie wasn't convinced. 'That's still an important connection. Neil might have bumped into Glenn there. Just because it wasn't in his job description to meet deliveries doesn't mean he didn't come across Glenn or have any involvement with him. See if you can pursue that further, Lucy. Contact Neil's old colleagues and speak to them. Is Glenn's lawyer about?' she asked Lucy.

'Yes, he's in the interview room with Glenn. We've got some info at last on Glenn's whereabouts Saturday night. Tech team located his car just outside Derby on the main road travelling in the direction of Uptown at ten fifteen. It passed another camera at ten forty just outside Uptown on the same road and was next picked up on the same main road, heading into Samford at eleven forty-three. It was picked up one more time, close to his residence, at two minutes to midnight. It appears he stopped off somewhere between Uptown and Samford but the team couldn't trace his car on any of the roads leading off the main road.'

'He didn't stop off immediately after leaving Sheila Newport's house in Derby as he claimed. He carried on until he'd driven through Uptown. I think it's time to find out exactly where Glenn really stopped off and see if we can establish any connections between him and Neil.'

John accompanied Natalie down the corridor, talking all the while. 'I don't mean to push so hard but if Glenn Powers knew Neil Hoskins, that's a major step forward.'

'I understand and agree but we can't make this happen. You know as well as I do we require facts. Facts and evidence. We don't have either.'

'But if we could get him to confess he knew Neil—'

She stopped him with the shake of her head and said, 'That's how we nailed Neil. I want proof and facts this time.'

He clamped his mouth shut and they continued to the interview room to begin the questioning again.

'Morning, Glenn. How are you?' Natalie asked pleasantly as John set up the recording device.

'Tired.'

'You'll be able to return home and rest up once you've answered our questions.'

Glenn sank into his seat and shut his eyes briefly. 'Go on.'

'I appreciate your cooperation.' She waited until John was seated. 'Wednesday, August the fifteenth, eight forty-five, interview with Glenn Powers. Those present: DI Ward, DS Briggs, Mr Rupert Baker-Jones and Glenn Powers. Glenn, we asked you yesterday about your whereabouts last Saturday night between ten and midnight. Can you tell us where you were?'

'No comment.'

Natalie gave a tight smile before saying, 'You were lying to us when you told us you stopped off soon after leaving Sheila Newport's house on Saturday. What was it you said again?' She picked up her notes. 'Ah, yes: "I'd been drinking! I was over the limit. I hadn't expected to be driving home so soon. I'm a lorry driver. I can't afford to lose my licence. As soon as I'd left Sheila's place, I realised it was stupid to drive, so I pulled over. I didn't want to get stopped by a copper."'

She checked to make sure he understood where this was going. His face registered resignation.

'We have now traced your car and know for a fact that you drove from Derby to Uptown without stopping. The journey time from where the camera in Derby picked up your vehicle to where your car was next picked up in Uptown is fifteen minutes, which is exactly how long it took you to travel that distance. You didn't break the journey at any point during that stage. However, you did make a stop soon afterwards, one that took approximately an hour. I'd like you to explain yourself now, Glenn.'

Glenn sighed then said, 'I was parked in a layby.'

'Which layby would this be?'

'On the main road between Samford and Uptown, close to the McDonald's roundabout.'

'The layby that's also a well-known dogging site?'

'Yes.'

'Are you telling me you spent an hour watching people have sex?'

'No. I was one of the people others were watching.'

'Why didn't you come clean yesterday and save us all this bother?'

'Mr Powers was concerned he would be prosecuted under the Sexual Offences Act 2003 or under the common-law offence of outraging public decency,' said his solicitor. 'He was also worried that his name might appear on a sex offenders register.'

'Can you prove it?' John said to Glenn. 'Give us the name of the woman you were having sex with.'

His solicitor urged him to speak.

'I don't have her contact details and I have no idea where she lives. I can only tell you her first name – Goldie – and that she drives an Audi A2. We've met on a few occasions.'

'Do you know the number plate of the vehicle?' snapped John, picking up a pen. Natalie thought it was highly unlikely the man would remember such a detail but didn't say anything to John who was staring hard at Glenn. The man wet his lips.

'Not really. I think it's a 65 plate but I can't be sure.'

'You realise you could have helped our investigation by telling us your whereabouts sooner, don't you?' said Natalie.

'Yes.'

'You've wasted our valuable time,' said John, jabbing his finger in the man's direction. His chair scraped noisily as he stood to chase up the information he'd been given. 'DS Briggs leaving the room,' he said out loud, giving Glenn one last cold stare.

Once the door had shut, Natalie resumed the interview. 'How long have you lived in Samford?'

'Since March this year.'

'Before that you lived in Manchester. Is that right?'

'Yes.'

'I understand you worked for Javil Logistics.'

'That's correct.'

'What did that job entail?'

'I was a delivery driver.'

'What did you deliver?'

'White goods, in the main.'

'Did you deliver to Tindford Electronics?'

'Yes.'

'Did you meet anyone called Neil Hoskins there?'

'I don't think so. I met loads of people. It's difficult to remember names.'

'Who did you deal with at Tindford Electronics?'

'I remember that. It was an old guy called Ron, from Hungary. Ron wasn't his real name but he said nobody could pronounce it so everyone called him Ron. There were a couple of younger lads but I only ever said hi to them. It was always Ron who offloaded the goods and signed my ticket.'

'Have you ever heard of the name Neil Hoskins?'

His face and body language gave no indicators that he was lying when he said, 'No.'

'The last time we spoke, you told us Erin and Ivy Westmore had been to your house on several occasions.'

'That's right.'

'You spoke to them?'

'Only to say hello.'

'You also visited Mr Westmore at his house and threatened him.'

'I already explained that. I'd had a few drinks, and after Noah told me that the bloke had had a go at him, I visited him. I didn't mean any of what I said. I was just pissed off with him. Noah had already had a rough time at his last school and I'd hoped he'd have a better time here in Samford.'

'He was expelled from his last school, wasn't he?'

He inspected his nails briefly. 'Yes.'

'Why was he expelled?'

'Possession of a dangerous weapon – a knife. He threatened one of the kids with it. Charges weren't pressed. The school handled it. He only had the knife on him for protection. He'd been getting a lot of bother from the kids.'

'Over what?'

'In truth, I don't know. Noah wouldn't talk about it. All he said was they'd made racist remarks about his mother.' He picked some imaginary dirt out from under a thumbnail and spoke more quietly. 'She was from Ghana. She died a couple of years ago.' Pain flashed across his face and then he looked up. 'Noah's not a bad lad. He has trust issues but he found a friend in Harry. I thought he'd settled here okay and I didn't want anyone cocking things up for him. People like Chris Westmore are judgemental. They look at him and automatically assume he's going to be trouble but he isn't. He's been through a lot the last couple of years.'

'Remind me again what you were doing Friday evening?'

'I was at home. All night.'

'And where was Noah?'

'Out.'

'Where?'

'He didn't say.'

'Didn't you ask him?'

'No. He gets defensive when I pester him.'

'But he's your responsibility and a minor. Surely you worry about where he is and what he's doing? You clearly were angry when Chris Westmore threatened to report him to the police.'

He hung his head as he spoke. 'It's not always easy being a single parent. Noah puts up barriers and… it's hard enough without falling out over little things,' he added.

Natalie understood the difficulty of the situation. It was challenging to find common ground with her own children some days.

'You live in Gate Street, in Appleby Gardens, don't you?' Natalie said.

'That's right.'

'Have you ever met anyone by the name of Isabella Sharpe?' His house was only a few streets away from where the Sharpe family lived.

'No.'

'She hasn't been to your house?' Natalie passed him a photograph of Isabella. 'DI Ward is showing Glenn Powers a picture of Isabella Sharpe.'

'I've seen her. A girl came by the house to drop off some homework or something for Noah. It was about a month ago, but she didn't tell me her name. She didn't want to come in or speak to Noah. Just asked me to give him the folder, which I did.'

'Did you see her again?'

'No.'

The door opened and John announced his return. He showed Natalie a note which read, *Goldie contacted. Whereabouts confirmed.* She placed her palms on the table and spoke to the solicitor. 'Mr Baker-Jones, your client is free to go for the time being but I shall be talking to his son again.'

'Is that it?' said Glenn.

'Yes.'

'I spent all night here. Was that really necessary?'

'If you'd cooperated sooner, you could have avoided that,' she replied.

'And I can leave now?'

'Yes. We might need to talk to you again so don't leave the area.'

Glenn shuffled to his feet and mumbled, 'Fuck me. What a carry-on.'

John turned off the recorder and waited to show both Glenn and the solicitor out. Shutting the door behind them he asked, 'What now?'

'Check out a Hungarian man called Ron. He works in the warehouse at Tindford Electronics. See if he remembers Glenn delivering to the place, and ask him if Neil Hoskins ever came into the warehouse.'

'Even though Glenn was in the layby when the twins went missing?'

'Yes. I want to make sure. Goldie could be covering for him. And we talk to Noah again. He knew Isabella and we can't be certain of the boy's whereabouts Friday or Saturday.'

'Fair enough but let's face it: Noah doesn't fit the profile of the bloke who paid Sludge to graffiti the camera.'

'I realise that but the fact he knew Isabella needs following up, so find out where he is, will you?'

He shifted from one foot to the other before saying, 'I ought to point out that this is time-wasting and I think we're moving too slowly with this investigation. We need to ramp up proceedings. The killer could strike again. You know what happened in Manchester.'

Natalie knew only too well what had happened. While they were chasing after a potential suspect for the murders of Sharon and Karen Hill, the killer had snatched Avril and Faye Moore and killed them. It was a scenario she didn't want to face ever again. She lifted her chair so it made no sound as she repositioned it under the desk.

'I've noted your thoughts. Now, find out where Noah is.'

CHAPTER THIRTY

Once Natalie got word that Noah was staying at his friend Harry's house, she wasted no time. She donned her jacket and was ready to depart when John appeared at the door.

'I've tracked down and spoken to the Hungarian guy, Ron, who works at the warehouse at Tindford Electronics in Manchester. He remembers Neil Hoskins and the Blossom Twins case like it was yesterday. Said he never saw the man other than if they both happened to leave the staff car park at the same time. Neil certainly never came into the warehouse. Ron also said if Neil knew Glenn, it would be a surprise to Ron. Glenn was invariably late for his slot time, would offload as quickly as possible and head straight off to his next drop. Ron used to call him Galloping Glenn cos he was always racing off. I guess we can say it's unlikely Glenn knew Neil. You were right. It needed checking.'

Natalie merely nodded.

'And Goldie Broadchurch, Glenn's dogging partner, is in reception,' he said.

'Can you deal with it? Make sure she's 100 per cent certain Glenn was with her Saturday night.'

'Sure.' He spun on his heel and headed away.

'Lucy, come with me,' said Natalie.

'Ian checked with Isabella's friends and none of them were aware she knew Noah,' said Lucy, pausing as they greeted other police officers in the corridor. 'The Sharpe family didn't know Neil Hoskins, although they remember the news surrounding the case, trial and conviction. You still think there's a connection between the case in 2014 and this one?'

'Yes, I do. It's something I can't shake off.'

'Copper's instinct?'

'More than that.' Natalie wasn't going to desist from pursuing this angle, not until she was certain the cases were unrelated. *You can't change what happened.* The voice of her psychiatrist echoed in her mind. Some investigations tore officers apart, and that one had inflicted serious damage on her mental state. She couldn't change what had happened and four girls were dead; the deaths of two of them, Avril and Faye Moore, still weighed on her shoulders even though she wasn't to blame for the choices made. However, now she was in charge of this investigation, and what had happened in the past only served to drive her onwards.

Noah and Harry sat on the edge of Harry's bed. The room smelt of stale socks even though it was relatively tidy.

'You need to be straight,' said Natalie. 'Don't mess us about or we'll march you straight down the station and charge you with wasting police time.'

Harry's mother stood by the bedroom door. The boys kept their heads lowered.

'Do either of you know this girl?'

Natalie showed them a photo of Isabella. Noah opened his mouth to speak but received a subtle jab in the ribs from Harry's elbow. Harry said, 'No.'

'Okay, bring them in,' said Natalie. 'We'll do this the hard way down at the station.'

'Whoa!' said Harry's mother. 'You can't take them off like that.'

'Watch me,' Natalie said coldly. 'They're hiding something and I've no time to waste.'

Noah opened his mouth again, ignoring his friend's look. 'We knew Isabella even though she wasn't at our school. We weren't friends or anything but I heard from one of the kids in her class she was some kind of genius. She used to help out with coursework or homework or whatever, for a few pounds. My dad was on my back about my grades. He stressed big time after I got kicked out of my last school and gave me a ton of grief about not working hard enough. We had some shitty maths to do that I didn't understand. I asked Harry but he didn't get it either, so I waited for her at the bus stop where she caught her bus to school, and asked if she could help me. I paid her five pounds to do it for me. She didn't live far from me so she dropped it off on her way home.'

'Was that the only time you had contact with her?'

'Yes.'

'What did you do about other homework that you couldn't do?'

'Got friends to help me.'

She noticed Harry's cheeks redden and realised he was Noah's usual go-to for schoolwork.

'What were you doing on Friday evening?'

'Chilling.'

'Where?'

'We went into town for a while. Came back here. Played on the PS4,' said Noah. This could be verified using CCTV footage.

'What about Saturday evening?'

'We were at my house. Harry left about ten.' It was the same story she'd heard before.

'Tell me about Erin and Ivy. How often would you say you met up with them?'

'Saw them at school. Used to meet up sometimes afterwards at the shopping centre or the library. Now and again, they'd come back with us and chill at my place.'

'Remind me how you met the twins?'

'Met at Samford Shopping Centre at the beginning of May. They were getting their photo taken with a cardboard cut-out for a competition. They looked cute so we stopped and talked to them.'

Natalie looked sharply at Noah. 'What competition?'

'To meet the lead singer of Blasted and appear on the cover of their next album. They were searching for twins to enter, and the girls thought it would be a laugh.'

Natalie shot Lucy a look. This was the same group who'd performed the free concert where Isabella had been killed. 'Tell me more about this.'

Noah shrugged. 'There was a bloke with a camera and a big cardboard cut-out of Callum Vincetti. There was a sign saying something like, "Meet the lead singer and be the next cover models on Blasted's album."'

'What did this contest involve?'

'The bloke took a photo of the twins either side of the cut-out of the singer and then entered them for the contest.'

'Did he ask for any contact details?'

'Yeah, their email addresses and phone numbers. They were pretty made up cos they got an email from the publicity guy saying they'd been shortlisted.'

'Did you see that email?'

'Yeah. They were well excited about it. Wouldn't shut up about it for a while.'

'Do you remember the PR man's name?'

Noah looked at Harry, who said, 'Tom something.'

'Can you describe the man who took the photograph?' Lucy asked.

The boys looked blank. 'Not really. He had a beard,' said Noah.

Harry thought for a moment. 'He had a baseball cap.'

'What else can you tell us about him?' Lucy was writing quickly. They'd got a new lead and a promising one at that.

'He had an accent,' said Noah.

'What sort of accent?'

'Scottish.'

Natalie's pulse increased. The twins had been to Eddie's salon a month later. If this man had been Eddie, they'd surely have recognised him and besides, Eddie was known to quite a number of people in town and surely wouldn't have risked being seen at a local shopping centre doing this. It was further proof if not the clincher she needed to discount Eddie as a suspect. 'Did the twins mention meeting this man, Tom?'

Noah's face screwed up. 'No, but they told us on Wednesday that they'd spoken to him on the phone and it was obvious they wanted to tell us about it so we were like, "Oh yeah," and playing it cool. Then they got annoyed with us and said we were jealous, which is mad. We weren't. We didn't give a shit if they won the contest or not.'

'You think they might have won?'

'They seemed pretty pleased with themselves so maybe.'

'But they didn't tell you they'd won?'

Harry shook his head. 'No, but they were pretty made up about something.'

Given this new information, Natalie was keen to talk to Kerry again. If she and Isabella had also had their photo taken for the album cover, she might have made a monumental leap closer to finding the killer.

CHAPTER THIRTY-ONE

The house was silent apart from the noisy chirping of sparrows outside the kitchen window. Camilla Sharpe was hollow-eyed, her gaze fixed on the cows painted on the ceramic mug in front of her. Tanya Granger had been at the house when Lucy and Natalie had arrived and made tea for everyone. A copy of the *Hatfield Herald* lay on the table with its headline 'Police Hunt for Child Killer'. Natalie didn't read the article but she was aware of the photograph, an old one of her in her uniform, staring fiercely at the camera lens as if ready to exact punishment on the perpetrator.

'I wondered if we could talk about Isabella again. Are you okay to do that?' she asked Kerry. Again, she noted similarities between the girl and her dead sister: the dark hair, the bow lips and the same eyes. The more she studied the girl the more she convinced herself Kerry and Isabella had looked very alike – almost like twins.

'Yes.'

'Did you and Isabella enter a contest to meet Blasted's lead singer?'

Kerry's hand tightened around the tissue she was holding and she whispered, 'Yes. At Samford Shopping Centre. They were looking for twin sisters to photograph for a new album cover. I told the man we weren't twins but he said they were also photographing sisters, so we should enter. Isabella was really keen, so I agreed to it. We told Mum about it.'

Camilla nodded.

'When was this?'

'Ages ago. The beginning of May. Mum?'

'It was when your dad and I went to visit Gran. The second Saturday, I think. You took the day off work,' said Camilla.

'Oh, yes. Um… I think it *was* the second Saturday. Isabella and I went shopping together.'

'Where was it set up?'

'Just inside the main entrance to the centre by the doors.'

'Did the photographer have a name?'

'Nick somebody. He was wearing an official Blasted badge. He said he was part of the publicity team for the group.'

'Did Nick have an accent?'

'Scottish, I think.'

'Can you describe him?

'He had a beard and he was wearing a Blasted T-Shirt and a baseball cap.' Natalie knew for certain it couldn't be Eddie. Kerry knew the man and there was no way she'd mix this person up with her former employer. Eddie was innocent.

'What happened after you had your photo taken?'

'I gave him my email address.'

'Did you give him your phone number too?'

'Not at the time. I gave that to Tom, who contacted me to say we'd been shortlisted.'

'When was this?'

'About a month ago.'

'Who is this Tom?'

'Tom Perry. He's a junior member of the publicity team. He asked us to fill in details about ourselves – hobbies, jobs, likes, that sort of thing. We told Mum and Dad about it.'

'We checked through it and it all seemed above board to us,' said Camilla.

'Did you hear from Tom again?' Natalie asked.

'He rang to say we hadn't won. Mum and Dad were disappointed for us. Isabella was really upset. She'd been so hopeful. Especially with getting shortlisted.'

'Did you hear from Tom or anyone on the publicity team again?'

'Yes. Tom sent me an email to say how sorry he was that we'd not won and we exchanged a few more emails after that. He told me about Blasted's free concert.'

'Is that why you went to the concert, because he told you about it?'

'No. We knew all about it and Isabella had already asked me if I'd go with her cos she wasn't allowed to go on her own. I told Tom we were going along and he said he was going too. He suggested we meet up during the interval to say hello properly. I thought that would be cool. I got on really well with him and it was a chance to actually meet him.'

'And that's why you went to the DrinkQuick tent during the interval?'

Tears sprang to her eyes. 'Honest, I wasn't gone that long. I only waited for a short while but he didn't show up, so I got the drinks and left. I thought he'd forgotten or gone off the idea, or couldn't get away.'

'Have you spoken to him since the concert and found out why he didn't meet you?' Natalie asked.

'He emailed the next day to say sorry. He'd had to go abroad last minute to sort out the publicity for the overseas tour and he said he'd ring me when he got back. I told him about Isabella but he hasn't replied to that email.'

Natalie could almost feel the pieces of this jigsaw shunting into place. This person had duped the girls into giving out personal information and used it to contrive a complicated plot to kill them, one that would confuse the police. 'Did you tell Tom about your hairdressing job?'

Kerry bit her bottom lip and nodded. 'Yes, I put all my jobs on my form and he asked me why I'd left Eddie's. I told him about it and he was really annoyed at how Eddie had treated me. He said I should have taken him to court and accused him of unfair dismissal.'

Tom had won the girl over, taking her side and being outraged on her behalf. It was little wonder she'd liked him. This would also explain how the killer had known enough about Eddie to trick the police into believing Eddie was behind the murders.

'What did Tom tell you about himself?'

'He's twenty – his birthday's in September – and he lives in Manchester. His mum died when he was eight, which is why he and his sister, Astrid, are so close. She works at McDonald's at the moment but wants to be an actress. She shares a flat with two other girls and a cat called Archibald. He studied music at Manchester University and he's worked with some well-known groups and been to lots of music festivals and concerts. This year, he joined the publicity team for Blasted but he isn't really into their music and likes a lot of the same sort of stuff as I do…' She rubbed her lips together and said, 'It wasn't lies, was it?'

Natalie was saddened by such naivety. The girl had clearly been taken in by this person. 'Did you tell Isabella about meeting Tom?'

'No.'

'Why didn't you say anything to her?'

'I didn't want her to think I was using her to meet Tom.' Her lip trembled as she spoke.

Natalie edged her away from the guilt that was clearly mounting. 'What arrangements did you make with Tom?'

'That he'd hang by the entrance to the drinks tent during the interval and look out for me.'

'Did he describe himself to you?'

'Uh-huh. Six foot tall, green eyes, brown hair. He joked he looked a bit like Harry Styles when he had longer hair.'

'Talk me through where you waited, if you noticed anyone looking at you that you thought might be him, anything you can think of.'

'I went to the tent but didn't see him so I joined a queue for drinks. He said he'd be in black jeans and a Blasted T-shirt with "Staff" written on the back. I kept an eye out for him while I waited for drinks, and at one point, I thought I'd spotted him, so I stepped out of the queue and went over to the bloke, but it wasn't him. I'd lost my place in the queue though and had to join the back of another queue to get served.'

'Fergus Doherty served you, didn't he?'

'He did. I was going to ask him if he'd seen anyone waiting about but I chickened out. Fergus creeps me out and I didn't want to look like a loser who'd been stood up. I decided Tom wasn't going to show up and went back to Isabella, but she'd disappeared.'

Lucy, who'd been quiet all the while, asked, 'Why does Fergus creep you out?'

'It's the way he looks at me. He used to stand by the school gate when we were both at school and stare at me and my friends.'

'Has he ever asked you out?'

'Fergus? No way!'

'He lives nearby, doesn't he?'

'Yes.'

'Do you see him often?' Lucy continued.

'Now and again, but not to talk to.'

Natalie continued questioning the girl. 'Is there any chance Isabella could have talked to Tom alone?'

'No chance. I only gave out my email and phone number.'

'Do you still have the emails you got from Tom?'

'When we found out we hadn't won the contest, I deleted them all, so I only have some of them from last week when Tom was emailing me almost every day.'

'We'll need to take your phone to check them all.'

'That's fine.' She nodded at the mobile on the table and Natalie picked it up.

'Do you have a computer?' Natalie asked.

'No. I use my smartphone all the time.' The girl worried the tissue in her hand, her eyes darting left and right as she tried to make sense of what she was being asked.

Natalie gave her a small smile and said, 'I know this is really hard for you but can you recall seeing anyone behaving oddly, maybe looking at you or your sister, during the concert?'

'No. Nobody. Do you think Tom killed Isabella?' The girl's eyes grew larger.

'I don't want to jump to any conclusions at this stage.'

'But if he did… it really was my fault.' She turned to her mother.

'Don't even think that. You aren't to blame,' said Camilla. It wasn't enough. The girl suddenly hunched forwards and held her hands over her eyes, shoulders shaking as she cried. Her mother put an arm around her and tried to soothe her, to no avail.

Tanya looked at Natalie and an unspoken word passed between them. Natalie got to her feet. 'We'll leave it for now and come back to you as soon as we have some news,' she said to Camilla, who nodded while her daughter continued to sob quietly.

Lucy was first to speak as they took brisk steps back to the car, her voice urgent. 'Fergus Doherty was at the concert. He could actually be this Tom Perry. He disappeared for a while during the interval on a wild goose chase to get water that wasn't needed. He knew Kerry was in the tent and he knows Isabella.'

'I understand what you're saying but the timing wouldn't work out. Fergus got back to the tent in time to serve Kerry. Besides, Kerry didn't recognise Tom's voice when he rang her and she knows Fergus. Also, this goes against the theory that the killer is the same one who killed in Manchester in 2014. Fergus wasn't in Manchester at the time and if he was, he'd have been really young.'

'He might have heard about the killing or known Neil Hoskins somehow and be emulating him.'

'It's a long shot, Lucy. A really long one.'

'We're not far away from his house. At least let's talk to him, if only to eliminate him from this once and for all.'

'Okay, but first I want to see if there actually is a Tom Perry who is part of Blasted's publicity team, and I want to involve the technical team. We need to get Kerry's phone back to the lab. I don't understand much about it but I know things can be traced using IP addresses and they might be able to pinpoint where Tom's phone was when he rang Kerry.' She thumbed through Kerry's emails. She was right. Tom had contacted her every day the week before, and all the emails had been sent between four and five o'clock. It was strange he'd only sent them at that time of the day but nevertheless it was a starting point.

Natalie emailed the correspondence to HQ, dialled the office and spoke to John, explaining what they'd found out. 'I've forwarded the emails. Once you get them to the tech team, see if Samford Shopping Centre has any CCTV and if we can find out more about this photo shoot by the main entrance. We know it took place on Saturday, 12 May, but see if there were any other dates. I'll bring in Kerry's phone so they can try and resurrect deleted emails. How did you get on with Goldie?'

'Goldie was definitely with Glenn Powers on Saturday night. She's a married woman with a fetish for open-air sex. She doesn't want her husband to find out about her extramarital activities.'

'Any proof of this? Text messages between them, anything?'

'No, but if we go to the layby later today we'd probably come across some witnesses. I don't think it's worth it. Glenn was definitely with her. They've done this several times in recent weeks.'

'I agree. We're done with Glenn for the moment.'

'Okay. I'll let the techies know Kerry's phone is coming in too. You're sure Eddie isn't involved in the murders?'

'Kerry would definitely have recognised him as the man at the shopping centre. I believe the killer has tried to implicate Eddie rather cleverly to steer us off track.'

She waited for John to contradict her, but he didn't. Instead he said, 'I'll get onto this immediately then.'

Fergus's jaw dangled. 'What's up?'

'We have a few more questions if you wouldn't mind answering them,' Natalie replied.

'Okay…'

'Can we come in?'

He shifted from one foot to the other and then let them come in. The television screen was on in the sitting room and a PS4 was hooked up to it. Lucy looked at the video game boxes scattered on the floor by the television set; judging by the titles, they were nearly all war games.

'What were you doing last week?' said Natalie.

'All week?'

'Every afternoon, between four and five.'

The look of surprise melted away quickly. 'Erm. I don't really know. Monday I was here. I was out Tuesday, at my friend's house. I can't remember about Wednesday. Oh, yeah. I had to go to the Cash and Carry with Brent. Thursday I went to town, and Friday I was helping Brent get the tent up for the concert.'

'Were you online between four and five o'clock any of those days?'

'I don't think so.'

This wasn't getting them anywhere. If Brent confirmed the visit to the Cash and Carry, it would be unlikely Fergus was involved. She asked the last important question. 'Have you ever heard of Neil Hoskins?'

He looked vacantly at her. 'No.'

It was enough for her. This was a dead end. She thanked him for his time and marched away from the house.

Lucy pulled a face. 'I'll double-check with Brent to make sure Fergus is telling the truth. It was worth following up,' she said.

Natalie agreed. It was always best to follow up. That way, mistakes were less likely to be made.

CHAPTER THIRTY-TWO

WEDNESDAY, 15 AUGUST – LATE AFTERNOON

Leigh Ward lay back against her pillow and flicked through her mobile.

'I'm dead bored,' said Zoe, her best friend.

'Me too.'

'Want to go into town?'

'Got no money.' Leigh pulled a face. She'd hoped her dad would give her some but he was stuck in his office, tackling a translation, and when she'd tried to ask him earlier, he'd been in a bad mood and told her he had no spare cash. It wasn't fair. All her friends got more pocket money than she did.

'Yeah, I spent my allowance already,' said Zoe, holding up her screen and pouting for a selfie. She showed the result to Leigh, who gave her approval.

'Deffo put that one up on Insta. Try on the green top.'

Zoe picked through Leigh's clothes. She'd tried most of them on already along with every pose possible. She lifted the top then put it back down with a sigh. 'Let's go out somewhere.'

'Where?'

'The old rec.' The recreation ground was where most of the local teenagers met up when they had nothing to do.

'It's way too early. Nobody we know will be there at this time.'

'What do you suggest, then?'

'I dunno.' She snapped a picture of her friend with her mobile and added rabbit ears and a bow to it.

Zoe joined her on the bed and watched as she did it, then shook her head. 'Delete that. I look like crap.'

'No, you don't. You look cute.'

'Delete it anyway. I look about ten years old.'

Leigh got rid of the picture and tossed the mobile onto the duvet.

Zoe's phone pinged. 'Holy shit!' she said.

'What?'

'Tom's emailed me.'

Leigh perked up. 'What's he said?'

'Sorry again that we didn't get selected for the album cover shoot. He thought we were the best two girls even if we weren't actual sisters, but he has some good news.' Zoe's cheeks flushed pink as she read on.

'Go on. What?'

'You'll never guess?'

'What?'

Zoe's eyes shone. 'He might, just might, be able to get us on a guest list for a secret party to meet Blasted. He's going to ring me later to let me know.'

'You're shitting me!'

'No. Look for yourself.' She held out the phone.

Leigh read the email and then leapt to her feet and threw her arms around her friend, squeezing her tightly. 'This is mega!'

'I know.'

'Wait till I tell Mum and Dad.'

Zoe shook her head. 'No. You can't! You read the email. It's a secret party. You can't tell anyone. Not until we know we're on the list.'

'Okay, but then I'm telling them.'

'Yeah. Sure. Like you told them about the album cover contest.'

Leigh grimaced. 'Well, I didn't want my mum flipping. You know what she's like. She'd want to know everything about it and then tell me I couldn't do it.'

Zoe grinned at her. 'Us meeting Callum Vincetti. That's so frikkin' awesome.'

Leigh could only return the happy smile and agree. It was indeed awesome.

*

Ian gave Natalie an update as soon as she appeared. 'Blasted are currently touring Europe and I can't get hold of a soul to find out about the publicity team.'

'Keep trying,' she replied.

'Tom won't be his real name,' muttered John from behind his desk.

'No, I guess it won't be; however, we still have to follow it up.' Natalie chucked her bag on the floor by a desk and dropped onto the chair. John seemed to have reset himself to nitpicking mode. The man could be quite moody. She remembered he was exactly the same during the Blossom Twins investigation, constantly challenging the DI at the time.

'How did you get on with Samford Shopping Centre?'

'No CCTV footage dating back that far, and the centre staff knew nothing about any pop-up photo contest near the front entrance. The only thing left to do is try all the shops in the centre and see if anyone who works in them saw the guy, and that will take a fucking eternity.'

'What are you looking at?' she asked.

'I've got a mate who's into computers and all that technical shit. I'm trying to find out if we can track down Tom, or whoever they are.'

'I thought the technical team were handling it.'

He looked up. 'Doesn't hurt to get outside expert help, does it? This guy's a bloody genius – a techie wizard.'

Natalie said no more. This individual had to be traced quickly, whatever his real name was, and if John knew someone who could help them do so, then she'd accept that help. Feeling slightly irked that she had nothing else to go on for the time being, she stood up again and headed out to the coffee machine then up to the roof terrace, where she punched out a text message on her mobile.

It was only a matter of minutes before Mike appeared. 'Got your message. Everything okay?' he asked.

'I fancied a quick hello and to see your friendly face.' She passed him a coffee.

'How did you know I was gagging for a coffee?'

'I didn't. I was at the machine and got two so it would at least look like you were here for a reason other than meeting me.'

'Sneaky. I like it. Where's Boy Wonder? Is he helping the superintendent take down a villain in Gotham City?'

She smiled in spite of herself. 'He's getting involved. He's dragged in a mate to help uncover our perp's IP.'

'Thought the tech boys were onto that?'

'They are. He wants to speed things up. Part of me agrees with his approach and the other part feels uncomfortable about it. It's not the fact that's he's being proactive – I applaud that; it's that he isn't waiting for the technical department to produce results. I'm so bloody square that I think everything should go through correct channels. Maybe I should be more maverick myself.'

'I can't actually imagine that.' Lines creased winningly around his eyes as he squinted at her. 'No. Maverick you are not.'

'Then maybe it's a good thing we have him on the team.'

'Change of tune. That's interesting.'

'He's opened up about his promo and reason for pushing on with this case.'

Mike sipped his coffee. 'Started wearing his heart on his sleeve, has he? I still don't trust him. He's an expert at toadying.'

'I don't trust him either but he is trying to get a result.'

'That's good then. Bet you miss Murray though.'

'Murray somehow completes the team. John isn't fitting in the same. I keep noticing looks pass between Lucy and Ian every time he opens his mouth. I think they're missing Murray more than I am.' She lifted her cup to her lips.

'That might change once he gets assigned permanently to your team.'

'You are bloody kidding me, aren't you?' she said, almost choking on the last of her drink.

Mike gave a light shrug. 'Well, not if he gets promoted, obviously.'

'How do you know all this? We work in the same building and I never hear any gossip or rumours.'

'That's because you don't hang out in Forensics, where everyone comes along to catch up on the latest news and developments. My team know everything that goes on in this building.'

'Now I know you're joking.'

'Maybe. It made you smile though, didn't it?'

She screwed up her paper cup and threw it towards the bin. It landed slap bang in the middle and Mike applauded. 'Thanks, I feel better.'

'Then my work here is done.'

'No, it isn't. I wanted to tell you that I'm ready to commit. I'm going to talk to the children tonight or tomorrow at the latest. I can't put it off any longer. I'm creeping about the house like a stranger, trying to avoid everyone because I don't want to have to lie to them. It's crazy. I'm going to be renting an apartment nearby. Once I tell them, I'm going to move out.'

He watched her carefully then said, 'And you're sure you're ready for all of this? It's going to be heavy going for a while. I've had first-hand experience of the hell it creates – rows, fall-outs and even hatred. You prepared for all of that?'

'I am.'

'Then you won't be facing it alone,' he said. He was about to advance towards her when footsteps rang out on the staircase and Lucy emerged.

'Natalie, John's friend has discovered Tom Perry's IP address – it's the library in Samford.'

'Looks like he might be a valuable member of the team after all,' muttered Mike. 'Talk later.'

'Will do.' She hastened after Lucy, feeling more optimistic – not about her personal circumstances, although having spoken to Mike, she now felt less daunted by what she had to do. If they'd located the correct IP address, it might only be a few steps to actually tracking down the killer.

Samford library looked like an ordinary glass office block from the exterior, situated along a street of similar offices, but once inside the revolving door, it was a world apart from any library Natalie had ever visited.

The largely white interior, punctuated with splashes of red, was carpeted in rich blue-grey and had been cleverly designed to maximise the space to provide not only a place to choose books but for people to relax. The ground floor was broken up by curved white bookcases, each creating a private reading zone and containing a circular crimson sofa.

There appeared to be no one about so while Lucy headed towards a door marked 'Private', Natalie wandered towards the far end of the room in the hope of finding a member of staff.

Natalie hadn't visited a library since her children were young. She never had time to read except on holiday, and they hadn't taken one of those in a long time. The carpet under her feet was springy and new and there was nothing fusty or dated about this place. She reached the end and was surprised to discover a coffee machine and cups set up in a recess in the shelving, and modern red chairs spread out, facing a wall on which was a flat television screen, showing a flickering log fire. The overall impression was of intimacy and homeliness.

She looked back as Lucy called her over. A woman in a flowered blouse and skirt, with a large bag on her shoulder, stood beside her. She jangled her car keys.

'I'm sorry, we're shut for the day. I was in the back. I thought Bradley had locked up.' She cast about in search of the man. 'Bradley Foster's our security chap.'

'Security in the library!' Lucy's eyebrows lifted high as she spoke.

'You'd be surprised what goes on in a library, and this one has had a huge amount of money spent on it recently. We've got valuable computers upstairs for people to use. They've got security tags attached, which will trigger alarms if they're removed, but we need Bradley for all sorts of reasons.' Her head turned left and right as she searched for the man. 'I really have to leave. He should be here somewhere. He ought to have locked the door though.' She let out a sigh of relief as a man in his late fifties, of average height – but self-assured, with a shaved head and wearing a dark blue suit that stretched over a powerful frame – came through a door marked 'Toilets'.

'Everything okay, Val?' he asked.

'The police are here.' The woman toyed with the keys in her hand.

Natalie introduced herself and Lucy and explained why they were there. 'We're trying to work out who was in the library and might have used the computers on certain days.'

'I'm not sure how to go about that. I just work on the desk. You should maybe speak to my boss, Debbie Yarlet.'

'Could we examine the computers?'

'They're switched off and there's some sort of code you need to log in.'

'Could we at least look around?'

The woman looked at her watch. 'I'd really like to help you but I have to collect my kids from their childminder.'

'It's okay, Val. I can handle it,' said Bradley.

She shot him a grateful look. 'You sure?'

'Yes.'

The woman scurried off and Bradley headed to the doors and pressed a button to lock them. 'Don't want anyone wandering in off the street while we're upstairs,' he said.

They followed him to the second floor, which housed reference books. There were several private workstations equipped with two red designer chairs and plug points for visitors to charge their mobiles or laptops as they worked. Red and grey round stools like huge stepping stones could be moved at whim to suit visitors who wished to find a quiet nook in which to read, and hidden between the bookshelves were larger tables to accommodate groups of people.

Bradley led them behind more shelving towards the wall, along which were three computers. He pointed out the leads that locked into a subtle panel and said, 'Those belong to the library. They're all fitted with a device that screams if disconnected from the wall – the same sort of thing you find on some electronic goods in shops to stop them from being nicked. We've got CCTV here but I'm usually around to act as a deterrent in the afternoons, which is when we occasionally get trouble from schoolkids who just want to spoil it for everyone here.'

Natalie thought back to the twins who'd begun hanging about with troublemakers. She reached into her bag for a folder and pulled out a photograph of Erin and Ivy Westmore. 'Did these girls come in here often?'

'Oh, I know these two. They're twins. I had to ask them to cut out the swearing a few weeks ago. They were here with a couple of lads who were sprawling about, pulling books off the shelves and chucking them about the place. They seemed to think it was funny. They cleared off after I spoke to them.'

'Can you describe the boys?'

'Both had attitude, loads of swagger. One was about your height,' he said, looking at Natalie, 'with dark hair, shaved at the sides and curly on top. The other was shorter but equally rude.'

'I don't suppose they gave their names, did they?'

'I think one was called Harry but only because one of the twins called him that. Might not have been his real name.'

'Do you know the twins by name?'

'No, but the staff probably would. They check the books in and out. I just watch out for trouble and help move the furniture.'

Natalie put away the photograph and removed one of Isabella. 'Do you know this girl?'

He nodded. 'That's Isabella. She got killed, didn't she?'

'She did. On Friday.'

'Terrible. What a horrible world we live in, eh? She came in here a few times.' Bradley didn't seem to know the twins had also been found dead and was astonished when Natalie told him.

'Oh my! I had no idea. That's awful.'

'Their names have only recently been released.'

'I don't read newspapers. They're full of depressing news. That's why I like it here. I get time to read the books when it's quiet.' He tut-tutted as he thought about the twins.

Natalie wanted to know more about Isabella. Could it be more than coincidence all the victims had been in the library? 'What was Isabella like?'

'I don't want to speak ill of the dead, but she was a mouthy miss too.'

This came as a surprise to Natalie. 'Was she rude?'

'Cocky more than rude. She and her school chums would usually get drinks from the machine downstairs, take up residence at one of the larger tables up here and chat loudly. They treated it like a coffee house rather than a library. This area is for research and working, and she and her friends annoyed some of the regulars. I asked them to pipe down several times but I only got some lip back from them, and she was no better than the others. Then she started taking phone calls, which is against the rules, for obvious reasons. I asked her to turn off her mobile and she told me to get lost. Eventually, I had to ask her to leave but she refused and said I couldn't chuck her out, that I couldn't touch her or she'd accuse me of molestation.'

'And how did you react to that?'

'I got Val, who you just met, to accompany me to ensure I didn't molest the girl, took her by the top of the arm and marched her out of the building. She shouted a lot at me but I can take it. Some of these teenagers are a right handful.'

'Did she come back?'

'Not after that incident. If she had, I'd have only sent her packing again. It's still wicked what happened to her though.'

'Did any of these girls we've talked about have run-ins with other members of staff?'

'As it happens, yes. They gave Val a bit of grief, like I said, and Shaun had trouble with the twins a few weeks ago when I was off.'

'Shaun?'

'Shaun Castle. He was head librarian at Uptown but it's closing down and so he comes over here now and again. There's no head librarian at this branch. The authorities have piled money into refurbing the place but cut the staff down to a few part-timers. Mental, isn't it? Anyway, Shaun had trouble with those two boys a few weeks ago when I wasn't here and threw them out – them and the twins.'

'Did he say why?'

'One of the lads had deliberately scratched an obscene image into one of the workstation tops. It's had to be taken out and replaced – yet another waste of taxpayers' money,' he added.

'You said you are here most afternoons; would you be able to remember who was using these computers on specific days?'

'Sorry, I'm usually downstairs so I wouldn't have a clue what was going on up here.'

Natalie asked, 'Can people bring in their own laptops here?'

'Oh, sure. They can log on to the library's Wi-Fi but they have to book time to use their own devices, so there'll be a record of who has done exactly that on our main system. I can't access that but I can have the information sent over to you tomorrow.'

'Please.' She checked to see where the CCTV cameras were positioned and discovered one overlooking the computers. She'd only spotted one other camera downstairs close to the entrance. She'd request the footage all the same and see if they could spot anyone in the library at around the times Tom had been online.

Thanking Bradley, she and Lucy headed for the door. He unlocked it, wished them a good evening and disappeared from view. Natalie peered in the window, ignoring the large poster that advertised a forthcoming author book signing, and watched his retreating back. He lifted a mobile to his ear as he disappeared through the door marked 'Staff only'.

Lucy's voice rose from behind her. 'Three victims, all of them in trouble for being cheeky in the library, which also happens to be the place where Tom logged on. I know what I'm thinking.'

'Me too. Check out that security bloke for me, will you? I'll look into the head librarian, Shaun Castle. Something definitely doesn't smell right here.'

CHAPTER THIRTY-THREE

WEDNESDAY, 15 AUGUST – EVENING

Natalie found Ian still glued to his computer screen, clicking through images of faces – pictures taken at the Blasted concert at Sunmore Hall. He isolated a picture of a young woman with multicoloured hair, her arms outstretched around the shoulders of two older boys, standing close to the stone arch.

'I've identified somebody who might have been standing close to Kerry and Isabella the night of the concert,' Ian said.

'Who've you got?'

'According to her Instagram account, this is Merry Darcey. I've tracked down a nineteen-year-old Merry Darcey in Tapleworth. I doubt there are too many young women of the same name.'

'Great. Want to follow it up then?' she asked.

'Wanted to check with you before I did.'

'Go ahead.'

Lucy spoke up. 'I still need to confirm Fergus went to the Cash and Carry with Brent, the owner of DrinkQuick, last Wednesday.'

'Okay. John, you busy?' Natalie asked.

'Nothing that can't wait.'

'Find out whatever you can on Bradley Foster. He currently works at Samford library as a security guard.'

'No problem.' He logged into the police general database and started searching.

Natalie slid into position and began her own search. Shaun Castle, a forty-two-year-old librarian, had no criminal record and was, according to the national register, married with two girls, aged ten and three. She found a photograph of the man on the local authority website. With light brown, thinning hair and a long, pale face and glasses, he appeared to be a serious, inoffensive man. However, she was fully aware of how appearances could be deceiving and would question him.

Ian ended his phone call and interrupted her with news that Merry wasn't answering her phone, which appeared to be switched off. He'd then called her parents, who'd said it wasn't unusual as she was a dancer, currently in a musical production that didn't end until ten thirty.

'I left a message for her to contact us, or I could shoot across to Tapleworth and talk to her after the performance.'

'No, leave it until the morning,' said Natalie, aware Ian lived a good hour from Tapleworth, and even if the girl had spotted something, they couldn't act upon it until the following day. She needed her team to be fresh and alert, not drained and making mistakes.

John joined in with, 'I've got nothing on Bradley Foster. He's ex-army, married, grandfather of three. He's got a long-service and good-conduct medal and has been awarded a citizen award for helping the homeless.'

Natalie grunted. On the surface the man was squeaky-clean. 'All the same, follow it up.'

Lucy came off the phone and shook her head. 'Brent confirmed Fergus's whereabouts. We can strike him off our list of potential suspects.'

Natalie eased back in her chair and skimmed through the rest of the article on Shaun Castle as she spoke. 'I suggest you go home. It's been another long day and we still need to hear back from—' She stopped, her eyes glued to the words on the screen. 'Well, well,

well. Shaun Castle, the head librarian, has only been there since 2015. Before that he was at a branch in Manchester.'

John dropped his jacket back onto his chair and scooted over to read the article. 'That particular branch is close to where Avril and Faye Moore lived. I remember the area – Livingwell.'

Natalie was fully alert once more, her thoughts lining up. Livingwell was the area where all the victims at the time had lived. 'We can't do much now but first thing tomorrow, check the library's main computer and see if the times Tom was online correspond to the times Shaun was at the library.'

Lucy was quick to add, 'If it is this person, I doubt very much he'd use the actual computers at the library to email his victims.'

'My thoughts exactly. If he is involved, he'd be more likely to have taken in his own personal device and logged on using the library's IP. First things first, we have to establish the times he was at the library and if he had the opportunity to set up the photo shoot at the shopping centre. Lucy, make sure John has the dates and times we believe this character was online before you leave.'

She read through the rest of the article and flicked through some sites to try and get more information on the man but didn't turn up anything. He had no social media profiles at all. She vaguely acknowledged a couple of 'goodnights' but her mind was on Shaun Castle, the head librarian. Was he their killer?

'I'll call in as soon as I have the info,' said John. 'This sounds promising.'

'Can't afford to get too excited until we are sure,' she said, aware she sounded terribly cautious, before adding, 'However, it's the best lead we've had so far.'

He left with quick, efficient steps and she understood his eagerness. She was keen too although her enthusiasm was always peppered with the need to ensure she was following procedure and making all the right moves. If they cracked the case, John would probably get the promotion he was so desperate for, and it might even change him for the better. She gathered up her belongings and hesitated before leaving the office. Would she talk to her children tonight or leave it until tomorrow when they might have more of an idea as to who had killed Isabella, Erin and Ivy, and she could think more logically? She made the decision. It would be tomorrow. She couldn't face the drama tonight. She shut the office door and began walking, pausing only when Dan Tasker strode towards her.

'I hear you're making headway,' he said.

She felt her face set hard. John Briggs had been passing on information again. All generous thoughts about him evaporated.

'We have a lead, sir.'

'So, I understand – a librarian. You're sending John to check it out.'

Her jaw ached with tension but she said, 'That's correct. We need to ascertain if the individual in question was on the premises at the same time as our perp was online, and if that's the case, we'll seize his electronic devices and examine them.'

'You have a warrant in place?'

'I'll arrange one should it be necessary, sir.'

'That's okay then. Good work, DI Ward. Goodnight.' He took off again, brisk paces down the corridor, and she was struck by how much John emulated this man – the clipped speech, the way he looked directly at people when he quizzed them and the walk, the confident swagger of a man going places.

A moment of lucidity hit her. John Briggs wasn't trying to get a promotion – he'd already been promised it.

Back home, David was in the kitchen, pouring a glass of wine.

'Before you say anything, this is my first,' he said.

'I wasn't going to comment. Pour me one too, will you?'

He did so in silence. She was too tired to bicker and sat on a kitchen stool, reaching for the glass and taking a gulp. It was chilled and fruity and just what she needed after the last few days.

'Hi, Mum.' Leigh was at the door.

'Hey.'

Leigh headed for the fridge and rummaged around, pulling out a yoghurt. She scowled at it. 'Don't we have any strawberry ones left?'

'Not unless the magic shopping fairy's been while I was at work,' Natalie replied and earned a half-smile.

'The shopping fairy had work of their own to do,' came the reply by the sink.

'Translation?' she asked.

He nodded but remained standing, one hand in his jogging bottoms pocket, the other wrapped around the glass stem.

'Mum, Dad, can I go over to Zoe's tomorrow?'

'I don't see why not. What have you got planned?'

'Chilling.'

'You chilled here today,' said David.

'And tomorrow I want to go to her house. There's nothing to do here.'

'And what's so different about Zoe's house?' asked David.

'She lives nearer the shops, for one, and she doesn't have a brother who gets on her nerves.' She pulled the lid off the yoghurt and spooned a small fraction of it out into her mouth. 'It's the school holidays and we're not doing anything fun.'

The girl had a point. She'd had a good time away with her grandfather and his girlfriend and now she was kicking her heels at home. 'We'll go away for a couple of days soon,' Natalie offered.

Leigh carried on half-heartedly eating. She didn't seem convinced. David remained quiet, like he was half expecting Natalie to tell Leigh that her mother would soon be leaving home. It wasn't the right moment, not to blurt it out.

'But we won't. You'll be stuck on this case for ages and then the holidays will be over.' She stared at her mother, no animosity on her face, but Natalie had to admit it was possible. Even if they got leverage on this investigation, it could be a while before they brought the perpetrator to justice, and the way things were going at work, with John's likely promotion, she was beginning to wonder if she wouldn't lose her position. Dan obviously favoured John, and in her experience, those not in favour got moved on.

'No, we'll do something – weekend in Blackpool maybe.'

It seemed to do the trick. 'So, can I go to Zoe's tomorrow? Dad's busy and Josh is always playing games or going off with his mates.'

'Yes, you can go,' said David.

Natalie nodded her consent.

Leigh's face brightened. 'I'll go message her.' She left the yoghurt pot on the top, half-eaten.

'Hey, what about this? You haven't finished it,' called David.

'I don't like cherry. I only like the strawberry ones,' she shouted back.

David rolled his eyes.

'She'd have left it even if it had been strawberry. She only wanted to get us to agree to her going out.'

'Don't you think I know that?' he snapped.

'Just saying.'

'You don't need to be a detective to work it out.' He slugged his wine then said, 'So, you decided when you're leaving yet? You keep creeping about the house, avoiding us all, so you must be keen to go.'

'This weekend.' There, the decision had been made.

'Tell me, Natalie, would you leave if Mike wasn't on the scene?' He scrutinised the contents of his glass, as if afraid of the answer.

She gave it anyway. There was no point in protecting his feelings. They had to move onwards and the only way to do that was with brutal honesty. 'Yes, I would.'

'Because of the gambling?'

'No, David, because you lied to me, and after everything, when you promised you'd never lie to me again, you still did. It's all about trust and I can't trust you.'

'But you still have some love for me?' His eyes filled and her heart cracked to see him suffering.

'I care about you.'

'Now who's swerving the question?'

'I'm being honest. Love isn't one-size-fits-all. There are varying degrees of affection and love. We've been together for years and that sort of time and emotional involvement can't result in zero affection. I care a lot about you and I want you to sort yourself out. You're a great father and you've been a good husband over the years. Times and circumstances alter and I've changed as much as you have. It's time to move on. You're hurt about Mike, but I haven't been seeing him behind your back while this is going on. I promised you I wouldn't get involved with him, not until we'd told the children what was going on, and I've stuck to that.'

'You expect me to believe that?'

She resisted the urge to jump down his throat. She was trying to remain calm and open. The least he could do was try to do the same, yet at the same time, she understood he was hurting inside. She had to accommodate those emotions. 'Yes.'

'You've screwed up our marriage, not me,' he suddenly snapped, his face reddening. 'You and Mike. I saw you in the car the night you brought Josh home. You've been carrying on behind my back, far longer than you let on. You're so big on honesty and so hypercritical of my flaws yet you are no more than a hypocrite yourself. Admit it: you and Mike have been in a relationship for far longer than you've let on.'

She couldn't lie. She'd been challenged and she had to tell the truth; whether or not he liked it was not her problem. 'Okay. He and I had a one-night stand the first time I found out about your gambling – way back when you spent all our savings. It was only the once and we never repeated it. I was angry and hurt and believed, at the time, that I was going to leave you. I regretted it immediately and told Mike I wasn't going to repeat it.' Now it was all out in the open.

David looked at her with sad eyes. 'I knew it. I didn't stand a chance.'

He didn't get the pity he was clearly searching for. His pathetic look only served to strengthen her resolve. 'You had loads of chances. More chances than you bloody well deserved. I carried you, David. All the time you were seeking help for your addiction, I was struggling to keep this family together. I wanted the old David back. I couldn't have done any more than I did to help you, and just when I thought you were finally on the right track, you started gambling again. You had more than enough chances, David, and you tossed every single one of them away.' She stood up, glass in hand, and headed for the sitting room. She might only be here for a few more days but she wasn't going to be made to feel guilty.

She lifted her mobile phone and checked the bank account. There wasn't enough to pay the deposit on the flat and pay for everything here at home. Her children couldn't do without, not because of her and David's failings. She did some calculations and went onto a payday loan website, but the interest rate was shockingly high. She'd visit her bank and arrange a proper loan, do it correctly without ridiculous levels of repayment. That was the way forward. Whether things with Mike worked out or not, she'd still put her children first and she'd be beholden to nobody but herself.

CHAPTER THIRTY-FOUR

THEN

He holds his breath and stares at the incubators. The twins are side by side, swaddled under blankets and faces concealed by medical apparatus so only their tiny clenched fists are visible. His girls. Jennifer wasn't so lucky but thanks to the skill of the surgeon, his little fighters have made it.

A waft of floral perfume. Pearl is by his side.

'Can I touch them?' he asks.

'Not yet.' She sees the look of disappointment on his face and adds, 'Soon.'

He's going to chuck in his job. It's about time. He doesn't enjoy it anyway, and besides, he ought to find an occupation that will allow him to spend more time at home; after all, his girls will need him. There'll be care and support available but he wants to spend the maximum time he possibly can with them.

Pearl throws him a warm look. There's a spark there. They both know it. He returns his gaze to the girls.

'They're so little,' he says, unable once more to tear his eyes away from the two miracles in front of them.

'But strong,' Pearl says. 'Like their father.'

He permits a small smile. He's strong all right. Far stronger than Jennifer ever gave him credit for. She thought she held all the aces but she was wrong because look who was left standing – him.

'Have you no other family of your own?' Pearl asks. It seems strange to her that he's always alone. No one is ever here other than Jennifer's parents and sister, none of whom can look him in the eye. Was he really that bad a husband? Or is it guilt they feel for their part in helping to persuade Jennifer to leave him?

He shakes his head. His mother was a heroin addict who overdosed while he was in school. A memory flashes before his eyes that he can't blink away...

He's six years old and waiting on the wall in the playground, white socks around his ankles, kicking his legs and scuffing the backs of his shoes, not caring that he'll be in trouble for ruining them. His mother is late – later than usual. In his hand he's holding a picture he's drawn for her – a picture of them in a house with a large sun above the roof and a big red car outside. It's the house of their dreams, the one they'll move to one day when she has enough money to leave the flat they share with another mother and her baby who cries all the time. She'll love the picture and she'll hug him and put it up in their bedroom. He studies it, proud of the care he's taken to colour the whole sky blue – her favourite colour – and the trees and flowers he's added outside, in what will be their garden.

Most of the other kids have gone, a chattering, noisy mass whose voices gradually faded as they walked down the street away from the school, leaving only a few to be collected. He doesn't know the others who are waiting. They're older than him and standing in pairs or small groups, talking. His classmates have all left and so he sits alone, the drawing in his hands, his backpack over his shoulders. Time passes. Stray parents rush in, full of apologies and smiles, taking their children by the hand and beetling off to parked cars. He observes their departures as if watching a film, and he feels slightly disengaged, like he's not part of this real world. Miss Hastings is on duty and looks across at him. She's his form teacher and knows only too well that his mother is often late.

As she waves goodbye to the last child, she crosses the small playground and puts a hand on his shoulder.

'Come on inside. We'll wait there for her.' She takes him back into the classroom and offers him some biscuits from her drawer, then stands in the corridor, deep in muffled conversation with the headmistress.

He studies the biscuit, round and sprinkled with sugar with black bits in it. He picks one out with his fingernail and licks it off. It's a juicy raisin. He bites into the biscuit and lets the sugar dissolve on his tongue. He normally only gets plain biscuits so this is a treat. He eats the remainder and looks out of the window across the playground to the gate but there's no sign of his mother. He studies his drawing and traces the smile on his mother's face with his finger. She's going to be so happy with this. He pulls out his pencil case from his backpack and adds a big brown dog to the scene. He'd love a dog to play with. They'll have a dog when they move. He's so lost in his artwork, he doesn't hear the classroom door open. He looks up suddenly, expecting to see his mother, but instead a policewoman and a woman with a serious face and kind eyes stand by the door. Miss Hastings is crying and suddenly he understands… his mother isn't coming – not ever.

'No. I have no family now,' he says to Pearl. 'Just the girls.'

She takes his hand and squeezes it gently. Her skin is silky soft and her hand fits in his like a glove. Things are going to get better. The future is brighter. He has family now. Family he can truly call his own.

CHAPTER THIRTY-FIVE

Natalie swallowed the paracetamol and chugged the remainder of the bottle of water. Lack of food and sleep, and two further glasses of wine, had taken their toll. Her head was fuzzy but her determination still strong. She ate the bread she'd put in the toaster even though she wanted to be sick, and drank the tea. The house was quiet again and it felt odd. Mornings were always noisy with Josh sitting on the staircase, thumbing his phone, and David yelling at Leigh to get a move on. She wasn't used to this lack of activity. She plodded out into the hallway to collect her car keys and spotted Josh on the stairs, dressed in his pyjamas. He rubbed sleep from his eyes.

'Morning. What are you doing up?'

'I've got an interview this morning – kitchen crew at McDonald's. It's only washing up and stuff but it's money and I can do up to thirty-five hours a week.'

Her mouth flapped open in surprise. Josh had been loath to get a job so far this holiday in spite of his parents' attempts to cajole him into it. 'That's brilliant.'

'Should I wear a suit to the interview?'

'Maybe not a suit but smart trousers and a shirt,' she said.

'Cheers.'

'Does your dad know about this?'

'No. I only found out late last night. I'll tell him later.'

'What about getting to the interview? Don't you want a lift?'

'Nah. I'll catch the bus.'

She gave a smile. 'Where's Josh?'

He looked puzzled. 'What do you mean?'

'Come on. You're an alien, aren't you? Admit it. You've beamed down and taken over Josh's body.' She knew it was a bit of a lame joke but it made him smile all the same.

'Not funny, Mum. I want some money. All my mates are going out to places – the cinema, skating, away – and I never have enough to join them.'

Her face changed. 'I'm sorry.'

'It's not your fault. Some families are poorer than others.'

She stepped forward and gave him a warm hug, feeling his body stiffen slightly.

'Mu-um! It's only a rubbish job in a kitchen.'

'I'm proud of you.'

'I haven't even got it yet.'

'I know but I'm proud of you for acting responsibly.'

'Yeah. Okay.'

'Wear your black school trousers and a shirt and polish your shoes. Don't go to the interview in trainers and remember to take your CV along and… text me the minute you hear you got the job.'

His face broke into a smile. 'Yeah.'

She hurried out of the house feeling heartened. Her son was growing up fast, and having seen a glimmer of the man he was becoming, she was sure he'd turn out okay.

*

He'd definitely snorted too much coke and had been floating on cloud nine, right next to his dearly departed mother. He'd waved at an imaginary figure and shouted, 'Cooee, Mummy. I'm up here with you,' then rested his head against the chair and looked around the bare room until his mind began to focus again.

He'd disposed of the cardboard cut-out of lead singer Callum Vincetti, bought from the Blasted fan website. The sitting room appeared perfectly normal: television, bookcases, faded settee, a few ornaments and pictures picked up from car boot sales. There was nothing to give away who he really was or what he'd done.

He was fucking invincible!

He lifted the newspaper he picked up after his morning run. The headline read, 'Child Killer Still on the Loose'. That was him on the loose. He chuckled, and letting the newspaper fall to the floor, he gripped the hand-strengthening exerciser, squeezing it several more times. His hands were powerful. They were large, plain hands with fingers that could crush the life out of a teenage girl. He stared at them. Even when he was married he wore no wedding ring. What did a band of gold or platinum mean anyway? It didn't strengthen a marriage or relationship.

His thoughts turned to Pearl and Mikayla. He'd loved the girl so much at first. She'd taken to him quickly and would even run to greet him when he came home from work, flinging her arms around his waist and calling him 'Daddy'. He'd have done anything for her. She was such a sweet thing and a far cry from the sullen teenager she suddenly became, with a potty mouth and attitude. He clenched the gripper even more tightly. Mikayla, Isabella, Erin and Ivy. They were all like most girls today – so rude, so arrogant, so vulgar. His daughters wouldn't have been like that. Rose and Lily would have been a class apart. Thoughts of his daughters swam through his mind and he let them. His girls would have been perfect.

The euphoria caused by the cocaine was waning, leaving him focused and confident.

Enough of this nonsense. He needed to concentrate. He had a big day coming up. His victims were prepped and all too willing to meet him. He rubbed his hands together in glee. Tomorrow was going to be mega.

*

Ian had left a message on Natalie's desk to say Merry Darcey was downstairs in room 1C. She joined him in time to catch the tail end of the interview.

'I remember her,' said Merry, studying the photograph of Isabella. 'She was sat on the grass during the interval.'

'Did you speak to her?'

'No. She was sitting on a jumper and a security guard came up to her and said something. She jumped to her feet and raced off after him. I only noticed cos she had a really happy look on her face.'

'A security guard spoke to her?'

'Uh-huh. There were loads of them about all dressed the same in black T-shirts with "Blasted Tour" written on the back, and with those earpieces in like bodyguards wear, and ID around their necks. I don't know what he said but it wasn't bad news, not judging by her face. She scooped up the jumper she was sitting on and disappeared like a shot.'

'Could you describe this guard?'

'I only saw him for a brief second.'

'Try. Was he tall?'

'I don't remember.'

'What colour hair did he have?'

'Dark. Brown or black, I think. He definitely had a beard.'

Ian withdrew a photograph from the file and placed it in front of Merry. 'Is this the man you saw?'

'That looks a bit like him but I'm not entirely sure.'

'Did you see where he went?'

'No, sorry.'

'Did you see where Isabella went?'

'No. She slipped into the crowd and I didn't see her again. I didn't even know she'd gone missing.'

'Did you see her sister hunting for her?'

'Sorry. No.'

Natalie looked at the photograph. It was a photograph of Eddie Ford, the hairdresser, yet she knew Eddie was not behind the murders. The killer had somehow managed to look a little like Eddie and convince Isabella to follow him. Her mobile rang, and seeing John's name appear, she excused herself to take his call.

'There's no doubt Shaun was in the library on all the dates and times in question. The staff here at Samford library say he shut himself away in the office most afternoons and they have no idea what he was up to in there. He's taken a day off work so I'd like to head directly to his house, do a quick search and bring him in for questioning.'

'Absolutely. I'll ensure you have a warrant.' She tried not to sound needled. Dan might have been curt with her the evening before, and John was most likely going to be promoted and might even take over her team, but she was going to remain professional to the end. She couldn't be held accountable if she made no mistakes, and she would fight to maintain her position. Her track record would have to speak for itself. 'Lucy will join you at Shaun's home address.' She ended the call and raced upstairs to organise everything. Shaun Castle, the man with the serious face. Had he killed all those girls?

With Lucy dispatched with a warrant, Natalie joined Ian and Merry in the interview room once more. Merry had given Ian as much information as possible, including the names of her friends who were also at the free concert, and was about to leave. An officer was waiting to escort her to reception.

'Thank you for coming in,' said Ian, opening the door for Merry.

'It's okay. I hope you find the man.'

Natalie waited until he'd shut the door again before telling him what was happening with regards to Shaun Castle.

'Does that mean we've tracked him down at last, then, this Tom person?' Ian asked.

'We can't be certain of that yet. The more evidence we have against this person, the stronger our chances of convicting them. Oh, and we can discount Bradley Foster, the security guard at Samford library. He has alibis for both nights.'

'I'll talk to Merry's friends then and see if they spotted anything unusual at the concert?'

'Yes. We need everything we can to throw at this individual and quickly. I don't want any more girls to disappear.' The conversation was interrupted by the buzzing of her phone with a text message from her son. It was brief.

Got job.
Start tomorrow.
X

It brought a quick smile to her lips. At least one of her children wouldn't be bored over the summer holiday and he'd have some extra money for the things he needed. That left only Leigh at a loose end. She messaged him back.

Congrats. That's brill.
So proud of you. X

She settled back down to work. She'd try and get to the bank at some point during the day and ask about a loan. She needed to get her life in order and sort out the deposit on the flat. For now, though, her attention was on ensuring they got the right man. She pulled up all the information she could on Shaun Castle. If she could establish a link between him and Neil Hoskins, she would have even more reason to charge him.

CHAPTER THIRTY-SIX

THURSDAY, 16 AUGUST – LATE MORNING

'I have no idea where he is,' said Shaun Castle's wife for the third time. She stood beside the sink, a tea towel in her hands. The kitchen was in disarray with packets of cereal and bottles of milk on the worktop, unwashed breakfast bowls still on the table and a toddler with a runny nose sitting on a chair, spoon in her hand, staring up at Lucy. A spaniel ricocheted around the room, chasing after a ball until the object got stuck under the cooker, and the animal pressed its face as far as it could to retrieve it, paws scrabbling on the tiles until Kim Castle pushed it away and knelt down, feeling for the ball, all the while talking to Lucy.

'He's been under a lot of pressure recently, what with Uptown library closing and his job under scrutiny, and I don't work, not with this one still at home,' Kim said, nodding towards the child, who'd stopped staring and was spooning chocolate loops into her mouth.

Lucy cast about the room. It was what she called friendly chaos, with children's pictures stuck haphazardly to sections of wall that weren't taken up with appliances or cupboards. The fridge was covered in plastic letters that spelt out 'Daisy.'

'Is that your name? Daisy?' Lucy asked the toddler.

The girl nodded gravely, picked up a dropped chocolate loop with her chubby fingers and pressed it into her mouth with a snuffle.

'Here, poppet, let's blow that nose,' said Kim, drawing out a tissue from a box on the worktop. She moved towards her daughter with practised skill and helped the child clear her nose.

'Mrs Castle, was Shaun here last Friday evening?'

'No, he had to go to a meeting – a last-ditch attempt to rescue the library.'

'What time did he leave?'

'Six thirty.'

'And what time did he get home?'

'After one. I waited up for him to hear how it went.'

'That was a very long meeting.'

'Yes, it was ridiculously long. Shaun complained about the length of it too. He said the councillors were being deliberately difficult and they had to keep breaking to discuss proposals in private. Shaun kept me updated throughout so I wouldn't worry about him or what time he'd be in.'

'Where was the meeting?'

'Samford library.'

'And how did he seem when he got home?'

'Agitated. He wasn't very hopeful.'

'Were you both here Saturday night?'

'Shaun was. I went out at eight. It was my girls' night out. We go once a month, every month to the same place – the wine bar in Uptown. We have a meal and a few drinks. Shaun looked after the children.'

'Did you ring him while you were out?'

'No.'

'What time did you get home?'

'About one. I can't be sure.'

John said, 'We have a warrant to examine your husband's computer.'

'Why would you want to do that?'

'Where does he keep it?' John asked brusquely.

'In the spare room. He uses it as a home office.'

'Upstairs?'

'Yes, but why do you want it? What has he done?' The woman pleaded to no avail. John walked off. She looked at Lucy.

'We have to check it over as part of our investigation. He might have been in contact with three recent murder victims.'

'Shaun? No way! That doesn't make sense.'

'The victims were all young girls who used Samford library, and Shaun had a run-in with two of them – twins, Erin and Ivy Westmore. We're searching for somebody who logged into and used the library's IP address on certain days – days your husband was at the Samford branch,' she explained.

Daisy continued to eat her cereal, one piece at a time.

Kim rubbed her forehead, her eyebrows pulling towards each other as she picked her way through her thoughts. 'He told me about some teenagers mouthing off to him. There's no need for that behaviour. It's a library. I know he was put out about it but as for contacting them via the Internet, that's so not Shaun.'

'Was he angry about what happened?'

'More saddened. He's very old-school and he hates swearing.'

'Have you any idea where your husband was the second Saturday of May? It would have been the twelfth of May.'

'You are kidding, aren't you? I don't remember where either of us was last week, let alone that far back.'

'Does he work Saturdays?'

'No.'

'So you spend Saturdays together?'

'In the main. Sometimes he goes to one of the libraries to catch up for a few hours. Why are you asking me about that?'

'Just clearing up some details. Do you ever use Samford Shopping Centre?' The shopping centre wasn't far from the library.

'Only now and again.'

John bounded back into the kitchen. 'There's no laptop upstairs.'

'It's not down here,' she said.

'Where else might it be?'

'Nowhere that I can think of. He went out to clear his head. I'm sure he didn't have it with him, unless it was already in the car. Are you sure it's not upstairs?'

'It isn't. Would you try ringing him again?' asked John. She'd made one attempt soon after they'd arrived but Shaun hadn't picked up.

She did as he requested but held up the phone so he could hear the call going straight through to the messaging service.

'Tell me about how he's been acting recently. You said he's been under a lot of stress because of anxiety over his job,' said Lucy.

'There've been so many staff cuts in the sector in recent times, and they've shut library after library. Shaun's worked in this profession all his life, and although we knew his job was at risk, we had to wait to hear for certain. This morning he got the official letter to say there would be no openings for him.'

'I understand Uptown library actually shut its doors a month ago?' said Lucy.

'That's right but Shaun's still been working there, cataloguing the books to send to other libraries. He also goes to Samford library a few days a week, and to Trove. They haven't got a head librarian either.' Trove had once been part of the thriving pottery industry in the area, but it was now in decline and had high levels of unemployment and crime.

John was quick to say, 'You used to live in Manchester, didn't you?'

'Yes.'

'And Shaun was head librarian at the Livingwell branch?'

'Yes.'

'Why did you move?'

'He was given the opportunity to run the Uptown library. He came to look at it, loved it and took the job immediately.'

'Would I be right in saying you gave up your life in Manchester to move to Uptown?'

'Yes.'

'You leave any family there?' John's questions were quick, barely giving her a chance to pause between answers.

'My parents are there. Shaun's live in Wales.'

'You still visit your folks?'

'Of course. Why?'

'Tell me, do you recognise the name Neil Hoskins?'

'No.'

'Think carefully. Neil Hoskins.'

'No.'

'Does the Blossom Twins case ring any bells?' he said.

Her eyebrows arched in surprise. 'Oh, him, the man who… the little girls in Manchester,' she said quietly, then nodded at her child to try and convey the fact she didn't wish to discuss the matter in front of her daughter.

John picked up on the signal but continued regardless. 'Yes. Did you know Neil Hoskins?'

'No. Of course not.'

'Did Shaun mention him?'

'He didn't know him either.'

'Did he mention him?' he repeated.

'Only in passing, when the case was in the newspapers. What are you suggesting? Are you mad?' Her face turned red. 'If you have come here to hurl ridiculous accusations, you can leave immediately. I won't stand for that.'

'No, we definitely *aren't* accusing him of anything. Shaun can help us clear up a few matters,' said Lucy, jumping in before John could upset the woman any further with his curt attitude.

'Don't you think it's convenient that he's not here and his phone's switched off?'

'Are you suggesting he's deliberately avoiding you?'

'You said it, not me.' John stared hard at her but she didn't look away. 'We have a warrant to search the premises so I'm going to keep looking for his laptop,' he said, and without waiting for a reply, he left the room.

Kim looked across at Daisy, who was ignoring the adults and setting out her cereal pieces into a smiley face. 'He's been so distracted recently, he could easily have forgotten to charge his phone, what with all the pressures. He's been pretty upset about everything. He hates what's going on in the world – he blames the Internet for the demise of society. I'm not just talking about the fact fewer people are using libraries but the attitude of some of our youngsters. Those kids at the library a few weeks ago annoyed and upset him. For a grown man, he's very sensitive. The Internet is a real bugbear here. Shaun limits the time our eldest, Cara, is online, and flatly refuses to let her have a smartphone.'

'How old is Cara?'

'Ten. He reckons she's too young but all her friends have them. She's at a friend's house now.'

'I expect that causes a few arguments.'

'The occasional disagreement but Shaun's very mild-mannered and states his reasons why it isn't a good idea. He doesn't argue as such.'

'As such?'

'What I mean is he doesn't argue. If something annoys him, he takes it to heart and it eats away at him and that's what makes him so depressed.'

Daisy had finished her cereal face and clambered down from her chair. She headed to her mother and stood closely next to her, protectively. Lucy was touched by the act – the child watching out for her mother. In a month or so she and Bethany would be parents. Spud would undoubtedly become a cute toddler like Daisy. 'I don't like that shouty man,' Daisy said softly.

Lucy smiled at them both. 'He's an acquired taste. So, Daisy, what are you going to do today?'

'We're going to the park.'

Lucy felt a surge of warmth as she realised she'd soon be able to take her own child to the park. Being with Daisy had reminded her of what really mattered most in her life – Bethany and Spud. 'What's your favourite thing there?'

'The slide.'

'That's a good choice.'

The child didn't move, and her mother put a hand on her head, stroking it gently.

'This is all going to be all right, isn't it?' asked Kim.

Lucy gave Daisy one last smile and snapped back into professional mode. 'It would really help us if we could talk to Shaun. Any idea at all where he might be?'

'He might be at the library. He has to return his keys this week and clear his desk, so maybe he's gone there. It's a really special place to him. Uptown was his pet project and it's such a lovely, old-fashioned library – right up Shaun's street. He absolutely loved working there. He always said it was like going back in time to a better, nicer era. He was promised he'd be able to run it exactly how he wanted and he's invested so much time and energy promoting it, holding events there and getting the library on the map. That's what makes this all the harder. If he'd stayed at Livingwell, he'd probably still have a job.'

'I take it that in the eyes of the authorities, he failed to make it as successful as they hoped?'

'It was very successful, which is why we can't understand why the authorities suddenly decided to close it without any warning. Shaun believes it's because they overspent on the refurbishment at Samford and have to sell Uptown library to pay off the debt. They should have let him know but they've kept him in the dark and he can't do anything about it now.'

'And he hasn't been offered a position at Samford or Trove?'

'No, nothing except a letter to say thanks and goodbye.'

Lucy had an idea of why Shaun was upset but it didn't explain why he'd murder young girls.

'How would you describe Shaun?'

'Kind and gentle. He doesn't deserve to lose his job.' Tears shone in her eyes. 'I don't understand why you're looking for him. He won't have done anything wrong. He won't have been in contact with any girls. He's a good man.'

Lucy took in the room and the pictures on the kitchen wall. One in particular caught her eye: a stick-like man with a smile on his face and the word 'Daddy' with a large kiss beside it.

John turned up again; this time he held up a bottle of pills. 'These yours?'

'No. They're Shaun's. It's his name on the label.'

He read out the name. 'Prozac.'

She sighed and said, 'It's for his depression.'

'I know what it is. It's a selective serotonin reuptake inhibitor, otherwise known as an SSRI, and one of the most popularly pre-scribed drugs for depression. How long has he been taking them?'

Lucy winced at his lack of empathy.

'Since March when our future started to become uncertain.'

'DS Carmichael, could I have a quick word?' said John, moving into the hallway. She joined him, and he spoke in a hushed whisper. 'He's on a strong dosage. I think he's unstable, and if he's got wind we're on to him, he could act again. I found this too.' He passed her a desk diary open on that day.

She stared at the sketch: a set of angry circular scribbles and blotches of red scrawled around a picture of a poorly drawn figure dangling from a noose, and the word 'death' in capital letters repeatedly written in black over it. She flicked back through the diary. There were few entries for meetings and no further drawings. 'He was definitely disturbed,' she said.

'I don't know if that's significant but it looks like it might be,' said John. It was impossible to work out what sex or age the figure was supposed to be, but it seemed to be wearing a dress or robe. 'He's angry, upset and he's taking antidepressants. He's our man and we need to locate him quickly before he acts again.'

Lucy gave a quick nod of acknowledgement and walked back into the kitchen where she showed Kim the diary. 'Does this belong to Shaun?'

'It's his work diary. Why?'

'We need to take it with us.'

'I don't understand.'

'It might be relevant to our enquiries. We'll try the library as you've suggested. In the meantime, if he returns, please ask him to call us immediately.'

Lucy jumped into the passenger seat and told John what Kim had said about Shaun. 'She believes he's mild-mannered,' she said.

'Nah, it's the quiet ones you have to watch. I found all sorts of weird sex toys in their bedroom.'

'What's that got to do with him being in contact with the victims? He didn't molest them.'

'Goes to show appearances are deceiving – a seemingly quiet librarian wears a gimp mask. Can't take anyone at face value,' he said confidently.

Uptown library was quite unlike Samford's and proved to be a fine, late-eighteenth-century, three-storey, red-brick mansion. Each of the five large sash windows was framed in thick grey stone, as was the six-panel front door, over which was a semicircular fanlight with its delicate tracery radiating out like the rays of a setting sun. Stone columns flanked the door and in front of them, two large stone urns filled with flowers which now hung limply, desperate for water. Lucy and John climbed the few steps and rapped on the door. John rested against the cast-iron railings, his head lifted, scouring the windows above for movement.

'Try again,' he said when nobody answered.

She did so. The sign to her left showed the library opening times on a neat blue plaque. The sign on the door stated the place was now closed and the nearest library was Samford.

'He's here somewhere,' said John. The Kia on the driveway bore testament to that fact. A quick number plate check had proved the vehicle belonged to Shaun. 'I'm not waiting about any longer!' He banged on the door and yelled, 'Shaun Castle, open up. It's the police. We know you're here.'

There was no response. He rattled the handle but the door was shut fast and he swore then said, 'That's enough pissing about. I'll try the back. You stay here in case he makes a run for it.'

He bounded away, leaving Lucy in situ. The Kia on the driveway was ten years old and showing signs of its age with dents in its fading silver paintwork. The sticker in the window read 'Baby on Board' and the back seat contained a child seat and various fluffy toys. Everything about Shaun was ordinary yet here they were, chasing after him – a potential killer. Nothing surprised Lucy any more. She'd seen it all, most of it before she'd joined the force, having been in foster care for all her young life. A yell broke her musings and she thundered over the driveway and down a slope to the rear of the building. John had broken open a back door.

'That's not exactly legal,' she said.

'It was like that when I found it,' he retorted, a statement she doubted. If Shaun was here, he had a key to the place and no need to smash his way in. John had gone on ahead and was climbing stone steps to the first floor, the main entrance where she had been standing.

'Shaun!' he yelled. 'It's the police. There's nowhere to hide. Come out. We want to talk to you. Come on, Shaun. We know you weren't at Samford library on Friday.'

Lucy's brow knitted together. She'd have preferred a more softly-softly approach. She followed John, opening doors as they walked around the building, checking each room; most resembled reading rooms in a grand house, with floor-to-ceiling bookcases in dark wood and polished wooden tables, with ornate furniture to sit on. It was more like a museum than a library, a place left in the eighteenth century with wide fireplaces and period fittings and furniture. Posters in frames along the hallway indicated the variety of events planned to bring new readers to the library: a science fair, a 'dress as your favourite character in a book' day, a children's after-school reading club. Shaun had made every attempt to keep the library alive. Lucy comprehended why he'd be devastated to see such a historical place transformed into modern-day housing.

They ascended the carpeted staircase to the second floor with rooms set up for small gatherings, water and notepads in the centre of a large table in one room and chairs with padded seats stacked neatly in another. Another room housed thick reference books that smelt musty and reminded Lucy of her school library – a place she'd avoided. School had held little interest for her. It had been a place she'd been forced to attend until she was old enough to break free.

'Shaun Castle. This is the police. Come out now. You're only making this worse for yourself.'

'Don't keep yelling. You'll scare him off and he might bolt,' she hissed.

'You suddenly in charge, are you?'

'I only voiced an opinion.'

'My opinion is that the bastard's cowering somewhere in here and needs to be convinced to come out and talk to us.'

She bit back a retort. In the end, it didn't matter how they got him as long as they did.

'Castle! You can't get out. Give up now!' John yelled even more loudly. Suddenly there was a scrabbling sound from above. 'Top floor!' he shouted and stormed up the staircase onto a narrow landing with two more rooms. The first was an office – no doubt Shaun's, with a photograph of his family on the desk. John cast about then charged off again. The second room was a kitchen and rest area for staff with chairs and coffee tables filled with books. 'Where the fuck is he?' John was on the move again. He marched towards a smaller door at the end of the corridor and flung it open. Ahead were five steps leading to the rooftop.

John took the steps slowly then froze. Bringing up the rear, Lucy couldn't see what was happening and prodded his back to move him forward. He said quietly, 'Shaun. Don't do this, mate. We can talk it through.' Lucy didn't poke him again. Shaun was clearly about to take his life.

'Go away,' came the reply. 'It's over.'

'There are people who can help you.'

Shaun laughed – a dry, humourless laugh. 'Kids today, they don't want to read. They can't even show any respect.' Angry tears had begun to fall. 'I don't fit in with this world.'

'Sure, you do. You've had some bad luck, that's all. You feel let down by people but this situation can be remedied.'

'You don't get it, do you? I'm a one-man crusader and my mission has failed. There are no other options left open to me. Tell Kim and the girls I'm sorry. I'm so sorry for everything,' said Shaun.

'Whoa! Hang on,' said John and he stepped closer to the man.

Lucy could now make out Shaun, standing on a wall, arms outstretched for balance. He was going to jump. They had no time to waste.

John turned his head slightly so she could hear his urgent whisper, 'We need a professional negotiator – now. Call one up.'

She backed away to do as instructed, heard John say, 'We can talk this through.' She heard Shaun's voice but couldn't make out his reply and no sooner had she brought the communications radio to her lips than she heard John yell, 'No!' He shot forward, Lucy hot on his tails, but it was too late. Shaun Castle had already leapt.

CHAPTER THIRTY-SEVEN

THEN

Pearl is looking anxiously at him.

'But they were doing so well.' The words are mumbled, stifled by lips that refuse to work properly, like he's been drinking alcohol, except he hasn't.

'I'm so sorry,' says the doctor, who goes on to explain why both his babies have suddenly passed away. Her words fade in and out like a badly tuned radio and he picks up 'respiratory distress syndrome'… 'lungs'… 'common in preterms under thirty-four weeks'. He can't concentrate on her words so instead he focuses on the large brown mole on her chin that looks like a squashed fly.

'But they were breathing okay,' he eventually says, his voice raspy with emotion. It doesn't matter what he says. His girls have gone and he is to be allowed to see them, hold them as if they were still alive. He's been told he can dress them or spend as long as he wants with them, even take them home. He's not sure he wants to go through with it.

'It will help with the grieving process,' says the doctor. 'You should make memories and acknowledge their existence. We've taken all the medical equipment away so you can see them properly.'

'I can't face this alone,' he says, fear like iced water running through his veins. He looks at Pearl. 'Help me. Please.'

CHAPTER THIRTY-EIGHT

'The house, the library and his car have been searched from top to bottom and there's no flipping sign of Shaun's laptop,' said John.

'That's a damn nuisance. We need solid evidence,' Natalie replied.

'We have enough to go on. For one thing, we have that diary with the drawing and he confessed. These are his actual words.' He picked up the report on Natalie's desk and read out, '"I'm a one-man crusader and my mission has failed. There are no other options left open to me. Tell Kim and the girls I'm sorry. I'm so sorry for everything," and seconds before he jumped, in response to my plea, "We can talk this through," he said, "Forgive me, Father, for I have sinned."'

'Only you heard him say that. Lucy didn't hear his answer, and from what we can gather, he wasn't big on religion. He never went to church.'

'Are you calling me a liar?'

'I'm saying it won't stand up in court. "Forgive me, Father, for I have sinned" does not necessarily signify a confession to murder.'

'My word isn't good enough for you, is it? My opinion doesn't count. I *know* he was confessing to the murders. I saw it in his eyes. I'm a long-serving copper with a heck of a lot of experience, and I know what I saw,' John insisted. He listed what else they'd discovered, counting off each item on his fingers as he spoke. 'The facts are that Shaun was out somewhere on Friday night but not at a meeting at Samford library like he told his wife. There was no meeting scheduled in his diary. He was supposedly at home Saturday evening but with no proof. We have a drawing of what looks like a girl hanging from a noose, and the word "death" written over and over again.'

Natalie looked at the picture. 'We can't be positive Shaun actually drew this.'

'It's in his diary, for crying out loud!'

'But we don't know for sure he drew it.'

'Who do you suggest drew it, then? One of his daughters?' John's face reddened in anger.

Natalie kept her cool. 'I'm keeping an open mind. Even if he did, it isn't proof he killed the girls. It's simply a vague sketch of what appears to be a person hanging from a noose – a doodle. Even if it is a grim doodle. Shaun was suffering from depression so it's conceivable he drew it when he was feeling low. We can't make out what sex the person is or how old they are so we can't categorically say this is a depiction of an intended victim. We've established he wasn't at the fictitious meeting at Samford library but we don't know for certain he was at Sunmore Hall, nor do we know he left his house on Saturday evening at any time, and we can't prove he was at Samford Shopping Centre in May, trying to encourage girls to sign up to a fictitious competition.'

'His kids were in bed. He could easily have left them alone on Saturday evening. He knew his wife wouldn't be back early. If we had his laptop, I'd bet a month's wages we'd find all of our victims' email addresses on it.'

'It's mere supposition, John.' Natalie shook her head as she spoke. Although everything pointed in Shaun's direction, she was uncomfortable accusing him of the murders until she had physical proof to support their findings.

John continued to drive home his argument. 'We know he used a burner phone to contact Kerry and the twins. The techies found out it transmitted from the library area. It must have been him. He's also the only person who could have been online using Samford library's IP address at the times Kerry received those emails.'

'But he didn't actually confess to murder.'

'Why are you deliberately ignoring what's in front of your eyes?' John's voice increased in volume. 'This is personal, isn't it? You don't trust my judgement.'

'I want concrete evidence to support the fact Shaun Castle is our killer. I'm not going to accuse an innocent man.'

'The man leapt off the top of the bloody library because he was riddled with guilt – how much more fucking proof do you need?'

'He was suffering with depression! Have you not considered the fact he was suicidal for a number of other reasons?'

'He was screwed up. He took medication and told lies about some meeting on Friday night that clearly didn't take place, and he was shut away in an office in the library at the same time as Kerry got emails from this Tom character. Shaun killed them. Face up to it. Don't let your personal feelings about me cloud your judgement.'

Natalie refused to be goaded. John had pushed the DI on the Blossom Twins case and he wasn't doing the same to her. 'I'm not discussing this any further.'

He thumped his fist on the desk and spat, 'That's fucking absurd! Are you getting off on this or something? You've got it in for me, haven't you?'

She returned a steely gaze. 'The case remains open, now go and cool off.'

'You're making a big mistake,' he said, yanking his jacket from the back of the chair. He marched out of the office and past Lucy without saying a word to her.

'Did I just miss something?' she asked.

'I'm not closing the investigation. DS Briggs thinks I'm wrong to leave it open.'

'DS Briggs is a man who likes results and doesn't much care how he gets them,' said Lucy, and she returned to her seat.

Natalie put Shaun's drawing to one side and said, 'Sludge described the man who paid him as six foot, maybe taller. Shaun might have been trying to hide his true identity but how tall was he?'

'Five foot six.'

'He's too short to be our perp. We know the man with the beard passed himself off as a security guard at the Blasted concert. We should run through CCTV footage of Sunmore Hall car park and see if Shaun's car was parked there that night, and talk to his mobile phone provider. He messaged his wife throughout Friday night and they should be able to pinpoint where he was when he did that. There's also something else we need to do – check the surveillance footage at the library. Bradley, the security guard, told you he didn't know who was upstairs using the computers. What if the killer slipped by and was online in secret? A clever killer like this one might not book online time like he was supposed to. He might have simply logged on regardless. All he needed was the library's password. Who was going to check he was online? They're so short-staffed they can't possibly police who is using the library's Wi-Fi. I'll talk to the technical team.'

'I'll make a start with the phone provider.'

'Ian's only nipped out to get a bite to eat. He'll be back shortly and can give you a hand with the car park footage. I won't be long.' She grabbed her mobile and left Lucy to it.

Shaun's suicide was too convenient and she'd make sure Superintendent Tasker was fully aware of her intentions to keep the case open. She wasn't having John go over her head on this. If he blocked her or forced her to step down over it, she'd fight her corner. John Briggs might be getting a promotion but he wasn't running this investigation, and while she was, she was going to do it exactly her way.

*

Leigh and Zoe, sprawled in the garden, were in high spirits.

'I can't believe it,' said Leigh.

'We're actually going to meet *the* Callum Vincetti. I'm going to take hundreds of selfies with him and put them all over Insta, like, "Look at me… I'm with Callum!"' Zoe practised a sexy pout.

'What do you do at a private charity event?'

'Stand around and watch the band like you do normally,' said Zoe, eyes sparkling. 'But they won't actually get to meet them and speak to them like we will. This is fucking ace!'

'I don't know. It's a bit weird. We don't know Tom. Mum says we should be careful online. You don't know who you're talking to.'

'Oh, please! Your mum's a detective. She's bound to say that. Anyway, we do know Tom. I've spoken to him in emails and on the phone, and he sounds lovely. What can go wrong? We'll be together, and it's not like we're going to some house or hotel room in the dead of night. It's happening in the afternoon at the Methodist church hall! And there'll be other people there too. If it looks weird, we'll make a run for it.'

'I guess so,' said Leigh, looking a little hesitant. 'I don't like that it's secret. We should tell our parents where we're going.'

'No, we can't do that. You know what Tom told us. It isn't to get out or the press and Callum's fans will find out and then he won't be able to talk to us. He's only going to sing three songs. We won't be there long.'

'We should at least check out there's actually a secret charity event going on.'

'They won't tell us if there is. Not if it's secret. We'll soon work it out when we get there.' Zoe grabbed her friend's arm. 'We have to go. Come on. Tom said if we get there before the event starts, while they're setting up, we can talk to the band – if we don't go, we'll not get another chance like it to meet Callum and the band. Please, Leigh.'

Leigh bit her bottom lip before saying, 'Yeah. I guess so.'

'Brilliant! Now, ring your dad and ask if you can come over again tomorrow.'

'I could ask him tonight.'

'No way! What if he says no, or he's planned to take you out?'

'I doubt that. He's always working.'

'He might. Go on. Do it now, then we'll know for sure. Come on, Leigh. This is important. I don't want to go alone.'

It was enough to make her agree. She didn't want her best friend to go without her. 'Okay.' She rang David straight away, Zoe watching her all the while, with beseeching eyes.

'Hi, Dad.'

'Hey, you okay?'

'Yeah. Good. Zoe's invited me to come over here again tomorrow. Is that okay?'

'I don't see why not. What time were you thinking of?'

'Lunchtime, half twelve.'

'Sounds fine to me. Sure.'

'Thanks, Dad.'

'Thank you, Mr Ward.'

'That Zoe?'

'Yeah.'

'Hi, Zoe. No problem. I'll see you later.'

'Love you, Dad.'

'Love you too.'

Leigh ended the call and faced Zoe, mouth agape for a moment. 'Wow, that was way easier than I expected,' she said.

Zoe clapped her hands together in glee. 'Your dad's lovely. Anyway, that's sorted and we're going to meet Blasted. Yay!' Leigh grinned at her friend's enthusiasm. 'Now, most important... what are we going to wear?'

*

Unable to locate Dan Tasker, Natalie headed for the Forensics lab, where she shared her thoughts with Mike.

'You spoken to the technical team about this?'

'They're inundated with work and can't start looking at the CCTV files until the weekend. I don't have that much time. If I'm right and Shaun isn't responsible for the deaths of those girls, the real killer is going to be feeling very smug that they still haven't been tracked down. I'm worried they'll strike again just to prove a point. The library doesn't keep CCTV recordings for more than a fortnight so we only have those from Friday the third through to today, and I'm only interested in the first nine days, nothing after the eleventh. By then Isabella was dead.'

'You're asking me to help you?'

'Why else would I be here?' she said.

'Well...' He left it at that. This wasn't the time to be flirtatious.

'The recordings have been sent to our email addresses so you can access them.'

'What are we looking for exactly?'

She handed him a sheet with the email exchange between Kerry and Tom. The times the emails had been sent were highlighted in green. 'Start with people using the library at the times when these emails were sent to Kerry Sharpe, then could you also check out comings and goings around the time Isabella and the twins were in the library?'

'You think the killer was spying on them?'

'Maybe. I just want to make sure I follow up everything. How long will it take you?'

'How long is a piece of string?'

'I need to know today.'

He grunted. 'I'll get the team on it.'

'Thank you. I mean that.'

'I know you do.'

*

He pulsed the hand exerciser repeatedly while staring at his reflection in the mirror. The coke was working its magic as usual as he prepared for his date with his next two victims. Fingers strengthened, he put the gripper down and replaced his signet ring on his pinkie. It was a gift from Jennifer, the day she told him she was expecting – a present to mark the momentous occasion. It bore a crest – the arm of a knight in armour, embowed and pointing upwards, the bow strung with an arrow as if to ward off any enemies who endanger his loved ones. It was, she told him, his family crest. The words echoed in his mind...

'It's your family crest.'

'I don't understand.'

'You've never really had a family before but you do now. You're the head of it and that's your crest to prove it.'

She places a hand on her stomach and he suddenly comprehends the enormity of what she's saying.

'You're expecting a baby?'

She smiles. 'No... I'm expecting two babies. We're going to be a proper family. This is a new start for you, for us all.'

The ring should have been a symbol of pride not sorrow, and shown to the world he was a true family man. That was all he'd ever wanted to be.

He reached for his wallet and pulled out the precious baby scan photo that he'd carried all these years...

*

The midwife rolls the camera over his wife's swollen belly. He can't take his eyes off the screen. His babies are there, facing each other as if casually chatting. It takes his breath away.

'They look like they're holding hands,' says Jennifer in awe.

'They are,' says the midwife.

His throat closes with emotion and his eyes sting. This is the most beautiful thing he has ever seen. He twists the ring on his little finger. He'll protect them from everything. It is his duty. These babies are going to transform his world. From today, he's going to change. The twins will make him a far better person than he's ever been.

He stared at the photo one last time – Rose and Lily. They should have lived. With that thought, he replaced the picture in his wallet and slid it into his inside jacket pocket.

Tomorrow he'd murder one more time and then he'd lie low for a year before striking again, somewhere totally different. A smile spread across his face.

He was one crazy, brilliant fucker and the police would never catch him.

CHAPTER THIRTY-NINE

THURSDAY, 16 AUGUST – EVENING

'What's taking the phone provider so long?' grumbled Natalie. 'They've had more than enough time to pinpoint where Shaun was when he messaged his wife. This is eating into our investigation time. Try them again, Lucy.'

'Can't find his car anywhere on the car park footage at Sunmore Hall,' said Ian, supressing a yawn. 'If he parked there, we can't prove it.'

Natalie pressed the pen top down so it clicked, then repeated the action. She shared her thoughts. 'If Shaun's vehicle wasn't in the car park, does that mean he didn't go there at all, or does it simply mean he didn't park it near the surveillance camera?'

'He might have used another vehicle altogether. The killer's been cunning,' said Ian, stretching his legs out in front of him and grimacing at the discomfort. He'd been in one position for too long.

'The killer's been clever all right, and brazen. He's been in full view of people.'

'Parked somewhere obvious, you mean?' Ian asked.

Natalie flicked the pen again. It made a satisfying *click-click* sound. 'I don't bloody know. I wish I did.'

Lucy got off the phone and said, 'They're on it now. There were some technical difficulties. Their systems crashed.'

'Oh, great! Let's hope they can be quick about it,' said Natalie, aware her patience was wearing thin. 'It'd help if we could find out where Shaun actually was that night. I don't believe he'd drive the family car to Sunmore Hall, hang around a concert in a disguise, abduct Isabella, kill her and then return home. Call it instinct, call it whatever you like, it doesn't sit right with me. And we've found absolutely no proof or evidence to support the fact he's the killer: no laptop, nothing sinister on his mobile.'

Natalie's thoughts fluttered like unsettled butterflies. 'Ian, when you spoke to Tim Dorridge again earlier, he confirmed seeing the security guard just before he spotted Isabella, didn't he? Remind me of his exact words.'

Ian pulled out his notepad and flicking to the correct page read, 'He was a really tall bloke with a ponytail and a beard. I didn't see him for long but I think he headed towards the car park side.'

'See, it couldn't have been Shaun. I've been saying that all along. He was only five foot six. The more I think about this, the more I'm certain Shaun isn't behind the murders, which is why his fucking car isn't in the car park.' She leant back in her chair, her frustration mounting.

'But where did he go on Friday night if he didn't go to Samford library?' Lucy asked.

Natalie threw her hands up in the air. 'I have no frigging idea.'

'Mistress?' suggested Ian.

'That's a possibility,' said Lucy.

Natalie clicked the pen top once more then put it down on her desk. If only she had Shaun's laptop, it would really assist matters. 'I wonder where he put his laptop and why.'

Lucy stretched her legs out in front of her and said, 'I suppose it was to hide evidence – emails between him and the victims, proof he was in contact with them.'

'I thought that at first, but the man hated the Internet with a passion. He limited his ten-year-old daughter's time online and wouldn't let her have a mobile. He blamed the Internet for the failure of libraries yet he supposedly set up an elaborate scheme to entice girls into handing over email addresses and then extracted personal information from them – their hobbies, lives and hopes – using the Internet. I understand we shouldn't overlook him but I'm having huge difficulties in imagining him being behind this. And what's his motive?'

'You have a point,' said Ian.

The computer alerted them to an incoming email. Lucy leapt to her feet. 'Phone provider,' she said, bending over to read the email.

Natalie sat up in an instant. 'At last.'

'The phone company has triangulated the signal, and the messages were all sent from the same place in Samford, in this area.' She pointed out the grey area indicating the location of the phone at the time of transmission.

Natalie groaned. 'It's the area around the sodding library!'

'What on earth was he doing there?' Ian asked.

Lucy shrugged. 'Who knows or even cares what he was up to. What's important is that it proves he wasn't anywhere near Sunmore Hall. We can finally eliminate him as the murderer and concentrate on who really killed the girls.'

Natalie sat back again and lifted the pen once more. Was everything as it seemed to be? She'd feel more certain if she knew exactly what Shaun had been up to that evening. The detective in her knew that the fact his phone was transmitting from that area didn't necessarily mean he was actually sending the text messages. However, he couldn't have been the pretend security guard at Sunmore Hall, and she should be glad she'd found some proof of that fact. She threw the pen down again. She was becoming deeply suspicious of everything – too suspicious and foggy-brained. She needed a break from it all to gain clarity.

'I don't think we can achieve a great deal more today. I'm clearing off,' she said, placing her palms on the desk and preparing to stand up.

'I'm going to take a quick scout around the library area on my way home, see if I can find anybody who might have seen Shaun there on Friday,' said Lucy.

'I'll join you,' Ian said. 'It's on my way home.'

'Thanks. One last thing: has anyone spoken to John?'

'Not seen him.'

Natalie rolled her eyes. The man was a maverick. He was probably out drinking with Dan, telling him she was making a bad call by not closing the investigation. Still, that didn't really bother her. She had other matters to attend to and one of those was collecting the keys to her flat from the letting agency. She'd managed to take time out to speak to the bank and arrange a loan, and the money for the deposit was sitting in her account.

Natalie was halfway down the road when her mobile rang and Dan asked to speak to her in her office immediately. She had an inkling what it was about and wasn't surprised when she was met with a grave face.

'I've received an official complaint regarding your conduct.'

Every muscle in her face tightened. 'John's complained, hasn't he?'

'I specifically requested John join your team. He has expertise and the knowledge you required to bring this investigation to a swift conclusion. I brought him on board because I value him as an officer. However, it appears your personal relationship with John is interfering with the smooth running of the investigation. You have not only questioned his judgement but refused to accept his version of events today, thus discrediting him as an officer.'

'Sir, that is inaccurate. I don't have a *personal relationship* with the man.'

He didn't listen but continued with, 'You allowed your feelings towards him to cloud your judgement.' Those were the exact same words John had used and it annoyed her that he had Dan eating out of his pocket. She wasn't going to be sidelined. She wasn't going to let John poison Dan against her, and she wasn't giving up without a fight.

'Sir, I have treated John no differently to my other officers. I have followed procedure to the letter. I did not discount John's findings, disbelieve him or discredit his statement. I merely pointed out it would not hold up in a court of law, and that we required factual proof before we could categorically establish Shaun Castle was the person responsible for killing Isabella Sharpe and Erin and Ivy Westmore. You know we have little to no evidence to support that accusation, and it is my duty as DI to ensure we have that proof. John was unable to accept that and I had to ask him to cool his heels. He didn't return to the office so I have been unable to speak to him about the incident further.'

Dan allowed her to finish before saying, 'John tells it a different way. He says you have thwarted him at every possible opportunity and refused to accept or act on his findings. He feels you are not the person to lead this investigation.'

Natalie dug her nails into the palms of her hands but kept her voice even. 'You think I should close the case without any actual proof that a man who was clinically depressed and took his own life might have killed three girls?'

'No, I'm not suggesting that at all. I agree the case against Shaun Castle is flimsy without proof. However, you have had accusations levelled at you that worry me. I had you down as a team player, a good leader, and yet it appears you are unable to work with anyone other than your usual officers. You have let petty differences influence your decision-making and that is a cause for concern.'

'Nothing other than good police work ever influences my decisions. Besides, we have new evidence to prove he isn't the killer.'

He silenced her again with a lift of his hand. 'John has requested I remove him from your team for the duration of this investigation.

He feels he is unable to work with someone who harbours grievances towards him and who does not take his opinions seriously. I
have agreed he should take a few days' leave and, on his return, be
transferred to another team here at headquarters. Find the evidence
you require for this case, DI Ward, but you will have to do so
without any further support for the moment. If you are unable to
manage, I'll reassign it to an officer who can.'

'Sir, Shaun Castle was not the killer. He was near the library at
the time Isabella was killed.'

'Then you'd better be able to prove it conclusively and find out
who is responsible before this investigation turns into a farce.'

He gave her one last long look before walking off. As his back
disappeared from view, she thumped the desk hard with the base
of her fist. *Fucking John Briggs!*

Natalie sat in her parked car and shut her eyes for a minute. The
agency was still open. It was now or never. If she got out of the car
and signed the paperwork, there'd be no going back. Her children
would spend their lives toing and froing between her and David.
There'd be tears and tantrums and major upset before things could
even settle into some semblance of normality and they'd all follow
a new routine. She wouldn't be returning each evening to a glass
of chilled wine in the home she'd loved and shared with her family.
She drummed her fingertips against the worn steering wheel. It
wasn't going to be easy but staying put and letting things continue
was going to be even harder.

She breathed in deeply, tugged the door handle and stepped
onto the pavement.

There was no going back.

CHAPTER FORTY

THEN

Pearl throws him a steely look. 'Fuck you,' she says.

'It was a one-off,' he replies.

'You think I was born yesterday?' she retorts, her grey eyes flashing. 'You have a problem and you refuse to acknowledge it. You know what damage drugs do and I'm not having Mikayla exposed to this sort of thing.'

'Don't do this to me. You know how I feel about you and Mikayla. You can't take her away like this.'

'I know exactly how you feel about me. This isn't just about the drugs. You've been really hard on Mikayla recently.'

'She's getting out of hand. She answers back.'

'She's a child and she's scared of you.'

'Crap. I wouldn't hurt her.'

'You threatened her. I heard you and I can't trust you around her.'

'She needs a firm hand, Pearl. You let her get away with all sorts – she dresses like an eighteen-year-old and she's lippy.'

'She is a normal teenager and you have no right to address her the way you do. Let's face it… she isn't even yours!'

The comment is the cruellest Pearl could make and he knows she is fully aware of its impact. She was with him when his own daughters died only minutes apart in the incubators. First Rose, followed swiftly by Lily, as if she'd realised her beloved twin had left the planet. Pearl had held him tightly in the corridor when he'd cried – his heart broken. She saw him through the months of pain and watched him recover little by little. She knows how much he cares about her own child.

'We can fix this,' he offers.

The look she returns says it all. 'No. I'm done. You've broken me. Clean up your act.'

'But I'll change.'

She shakes her head. 'Even if you did, it'd make no difference. I've taken a long, hard look at what we really have and how I feel. There is no true commitment to this relationship.'

'You know I don't want to get married again.'

'I thought you'd change your mind but it's clear now you won't. You live with me because it suits you.'

'No. You're wrong.'

'Am I?'

The fact is she's right. His feelings for her are born out of gratitude rather than love. There's no space in his heart for her. It is filled already with his two dead children. Her words, however, come as a surprise.

'I don't love you any more. I don't want you in my life and I don't trust you to stay out of it, so I'm taking Mikayla away from all of this. I'm returning to Trinidad. I should have gone a long time ago,' she says.

'You planned this?'

'Yes. I did.'

'It's a fucking ocean away. How am I supposed to see Mikayla?'

'You're not.'

He glances at the suitcase in the hallway. Had he not come home unexpectedly, she'd have gone without telling him. The cow has been arranging this for weeks. This is no spur-of-the-moment decision. Mikayla is upstairs in her bedroom, hiding from the arguing pair, waiting for her mother to call her down and take her away.

'Don't try to stop me,' Pearl says. 'My mind's made up. This is the end of the road for us.'

A red-hot poker prods at his heart and flames race through his chest cavity. The anger is almost tangible and he has to restrain his fists that want to pummel her and punch her to the ground. His body vibrates with fury and she sees how close she is to serious trouble. She calls out her daughter's name and Mikayla appears – a large backpack over her shoulders, eyes wide, her dark hair in two bunches that stick up like two furry antennae on her head – and she lowers her gaze as she scurries past him to the door. He wants to reach for her and hug her but Pearl mouths, 'Don't,' and so he clenches his fists even more tightly but says nothing.

She lifts the heavy case and says, 'Open the door, darling.'

Mikayla does as bid and gives him one last look. 'Bye,' is all she says.

Pearl struggles outside towards the waiting taxi and he remains stationary, unable to watch as they clamber inside it and drive off to new beginnings, leaving him with nothing but memories.

CHAPTER FORTY-ONE

The keys to Natalie's flat felt heavier than her usual house keys and she moved them from her skirt pocket to her black handbag, zipping them into a compartment. She'd stop by the flat later to see what essentials she needed to get for it. Whatever happened at work today, she was going to break the news of her departure to her family this evening. There was to be no more putting it off. There was never going to be a right time, and had Josh been at home and not out at the cinema when she'd finally got home last night, she'd have told them then.

'Is John coming in this morning?' asked Lucy, perched on the edge of a desk, a takeaway cup of tea in her hand.

'He's off the team,' said Natalie. She wasn't going to say any more and Lucy didn't press her for more information.

'I thought I might visit Shaun's wife again later today if I get a chance. I feel really sorry for her. She was in bits yesterday after we broke the news about Shaun's death. I want to make sure she's okay.'

'Yes, sure.' Natalie gave her a look. It wasn't like Lucy to get emotionally involved with victims or their families. The liaison officers dealt with the fallout; their job was to find the perpetrators. She didn't press the issue. If Lucy felt she should talk to Kim Castle, then she should.

Ian arrived, grey-faced, and shrugged off a satchel which was slung across his chest.

'What's with the man bag?' said Lucy.

'I'm staying over at Scarlett's tonight. I'm babysitting Ruby. Brought my overnight kit to work.'

'That's great.'

It was the first time Ian's ex-girlfriend had let him look after their child since she'd walked out on him. His lips quivered in a tiny smile of contentment.

'Should be good,' was all he said. He placed his bag under the desk to avoid tripping over it.

Natalie waited for him to settle then spoke up. 'John's left the team, so with a man down, we have to redouble our efforts. How did you get on last night?'

Ian produced a map of the area around Samford and handed it to Natalie. 'This entire area consists of businesses, shops and office blocks that were all shut for the night. We tried every building and there were no staff available to talk to. This street off it is purely shops and takeaways. Again, we tried every single place and spoke to the staff but nobody saw Shaun on Friday evening, or indeed had ever seen him. These two streets, going into the opposite direction and still within the triangulated zone, are housing. We canvassed both streets and again drew blanks. However, this is a church,' he said, pointing to a grey square. 'St Bede's. The place was empty but the lights were on and the door was open. The church warden informed us it is always left open overnight in case any homeless people need shelter. There's a chance Shaun spent the evening there. The warden didn't go in that night so he can't confirm if Shaun was there or not, but he is going to ask the Help the Homeless volunteers who drop by to check the place, to see if any of them spotted Shaun.'

'Good work. That certainly seems logical – the man disappears for the night, doesn't tell his wife where he is because he's trying to seek forgiveness or build himself up to commit suicide. That might also account for his final words, "Forgive me, Father, for I have sinned." I think taking your own life is considered a sin in some religions. I still don't get it though. He wasn't a religious man.' She stopped talking, her eyes suddenly drawn to the corridor, where Mike was striding purposefully towards them. She got up and opened the door for him.

'I need you to come upstairs. We've found something on the CCTV,' he said.

Chairs were pushed back hastily and all three hurried after him into the lab, where a couple of assistants sat in front of terminals. One of the monitors was frozen onto the face of a man with a beard, sunglasses and baseball cap pulled low over his face.

'That's the man,' said Lucy, rushing towards the screen.

'When was that captured?' Natalie asked the assistant in front of the screen.

'This one was taken at ten forty, Wednesday morning, only a few minutes after Erin and Ivy Westmore entered the library.'

'I thought they went to the café that morning,' said Natalie.

Ian responded with, 'They met the boys outside the library and went to the café afterwards.'

The assistant continued, 'We monitored their movements for a few minutes and this guy in the cap appeared.' He pointed to the other screen. 'That picture of him was taken on Monday at eleven fifteen, again, only minutes after Isabella Sharpe went to the library.'

'He followed the girls into the library?' said Ian.

'It seems that way. On both occasions, there were only three to four minutes between the girls' arrival and his appearance.'

'What about the times he used the Internet?' Natalie asked. 'Did you find footage of him then?'

'Other than those two instances, when he appears on CCTV, we haven't been able to locate him.'

'Damn! Then he didn't use the library's Internet,' Natalie said.

Mike held up a finger. 'Hold fire. He might not have gone into the library and used the Wi-Fi there, but Elliot here has come up with a plausible theory as to how else he might have got online, using the library IP. You can actually access the Internet from outside. You don't have to be in the building itself. A strong signal will reach as far as the road or further, so somebody sitting in a car outside the library could log on.' He looked across at a bald-headed assistant, who nodded in agreement.

'That is the most likely explanation. We can check it out to be sure,' said Elliot.

Ian peered again at the frozen image and asked, 'That can't be Shaun – why would he disguise himself in one of his own libraries?'

'Maybe he didn't want to be recognised by the staff,' Mike suggested.

Natalie shook her head. 'We've worked out Shaun was too short to be this man.'

'Shoe lifts?' Mike said.

'They'd have to be massive lifts. He was only five foot six. That bloke's six foot plus. Okay, there's another way to prove it isn't Shaun. Lucy, check his work schedule, see where he was during the times these pictures were taken,' said Natalie.

Lucy raced off.

'Can we get a clearer image of him?' Natalie asked Elliot.

'We can try.'

He put some numbers into a box that appeared on the screen and the picture disappeared only to reappear almost instantly, this time enlarged. It wasn't clear enough. He punched in some more numbers but the image was still too blurred to make out any distinguishing features or identifiers. Natalie squinted hard.

Lucy reappeared slightly out of breath, a file in her hand. 'Shaun was at Uptown on Monday and at the Trove branch on Wednesday. It isn't him.'

Elliot continued to fiddle with the image and gradually it came back into focus. Natalie peered hard. There was nothing to indicate who this person was. She released an angry sigh and her eyes dropped to the man's hand, which was raised. She blinked several times in succession. 'Can you zoom in on his hand?'

The lab assistant worked the keyboard again and the picture faded and rebuilt – a series of pixilated blocks until she could quite clearly see what she'd imagined she had: a signet ring on the killer's little finger.

'I recognise the ring,' she said in a whisper, a conversation from the past swirling in her memory.

Lucy peered at the monogrammed ring, an armour-clad arm with bow and arrow raised, ready to fire.

'It's the Briggs family crest. John Briggs wears one exactly like it on his little finger.'

There wasn't a sound from anyone. They worked in silent horror, fearful of what they had uncovered. John Briggs' service records had been requested and slowly they were piecing together his movements and learning about his life. Natalie rubbed at her forehead, heart thudding as she worked. A killer in their ranks. It was unthinkable yet the evidence was rapidly mounting against John Briggs. She didn't have much time before she would have to bring him in for questioning, and she had to be bloody sure he was her man. The ramifications if she was wrong could be catastrophic. Her conscience questioned if she was pursuing this line of enquiry because of some deep-seated dislike of John. She silenced the voice in her head. There was only one way to ascertain the truth, and that was with facts and evidence.

She'd been in touch with John's previous DCI, who'd sung his praises: exemplary, dedicated – the words had mounted up –

hard-working, decisive. Who was she dealing with? She'd trodden carefully so as not to rouse suspicions and have any information leaked back to John. One piece of vital information had emerged from the conversation: John had requested two weeks' leave not long before his secondment to the team. He'd cited personal circumstances and been granted it without question. Until he told them what he'd been doing for those two weeks, they couldn't account for his whereabouts on the Monday the perp had followed Isabella into the library, or the Wednesday, when the same person had pursued the twins.

Lucy had also uncovered some unsettling information regarding his current abode. 'John's given HQ his address as a B & B here in Samford. I've spoken to his landlady and she said John rented a room but she hasn't clapped eyes on him since Sunday afternoon, when he paid her up front for the room and told her he was working here. She checked it out for me and it's not been used.'

'Where the heck is he living, then? Try the letting agency, friends, anybody. He has to be staying somewhere nearby.'

'You going to bring him in for questioning?' asked Ian.

To do so would cause major ructions if she was wrong about this. She could not only damage his reputation but her own. Her neck was on the line and she ought to gather more proof before she presented her case to Dan Tasker. On the other hand, if John had murdered the three girls, she needed to act. 'Let's find out what the agency has to say.'

The wait was agonising but she checked through the information she had on John again and eventually Lucy had news.

'According to the letting agency, John rented a house in Samford three months ago. That was well before he knew he'd be working here.'

'He was working in Frone. I suppose it's conceivable he rented it so he could commute to Frone but it's twelve miles away and he could have rented somewhere closer or even in Frone. And it doesn't answer the question why he rented a room in a B & B here as well. Where is this house?'

'Harrington Rise.'

'Where exactly is that?' Natalie said as she pulled up a map of the streets in the town. She typed in the address and stared at the marker that appeared. 'Shit! I'd say that's no more than a ten-minute walk from where the Westmores live.'

Natalie grabbed her mobile and rang John, prepared to act casually and ask for his location. It rang out. 'Trace his phone,' she said urgently.

'What car is he driving?' Ian asked.

'I don't know. Find out.'

Natalie grabbed the internal phone to call the superintendent. She didn't care what the consequences were. She had to bring John into the station before he escaped or, worse still, killed again. A sixth sense caused her to replace the receiver without dialling. Dan and John were close, and Dan believed she bore the man a grudge. She couldn't afford for Dan to contact him and alert him to what was going on. This had to remain a covert operation.

*

'By the way, you look very nice today. I like that top on you,' said David as he and Leigh arrived at Zoe's house. She arched one eyebrow and he laughed. 'What? Can't I tell my daughter she looks nice?'

'Yeah, but you don't normally.'

'That's because you don't normally wear that top. It suits you.'

She looked down at the pastel green kimono, teamed with white shorts and sandals. It was the first time she'd worn it since she'd bought it on holiday with her grandfather and his girlfriend. She'd been saving it for a special occasion and that time had arrived. 'Thanks.' She smiled at him.

'Right, here we are. What have you got planned today?' he asked.

'Chilling.'

'Dressed like that?'

'What do you mean?'

'Oh, come on, Leigh. I'm not that old or blind! You and Zoe are meeting up with some boys, aren't you?'

Her cheeks heated up quickly and she was sure her dad would be able to tell if she lied. She had to open up. It wasn't a big deal if he found out that they'd been invited to a special event. He wasn't likely to phone the press and tell them Blasted were in town and performing at a secret venue. Besides, she'd feel better if she fessed up. 'Well—'

He gave another laugh and shook his head. 'No. Don't tell me. It's fine. You can chill out with boys, you know. You're almost fifteen. I know you'll act sensibly. You don't need to tell me every detail of your private life.'

She blew out her cheeks. 'I would if I didn't think you'd get all stuffy and stop me.'

He put a hand on her cheek. 'Like I said, I'm not that old… yet! You're level-headed. You don't need the lecture.'

'Which lecture?'

His eyes crinkled as he spoke. 'Don't do drugs, don't touch alcohol, don't let him give you a love bite and keep your knickers on…' He grinned.

'Dad!'

'Only kidding. Go on, get out of here. I'll pick you up later.'

Leigh opened the old Volvo's door then leant back inside the car to peck him on the cheek.

'What was that for?'

'Cos I love you,' she said.

'Love you too, princess,' he replied. 'Have fun.'

She gave him a cheery wave as she walked down the path. Zoe opened the front door and hugged her friend. He watched until Leigh stepped into the house, then he drew away, whistling contentedly.

'I've got two pieces of information,' said Ian. 'First off, the church warden at St Bede's has spoken to the Help the Homeless volunteers and one of them confirmed speaking to a man matching Shaun's description on Friday evening at nine thirty. They asked him if he needed any food or blankets but he said he was there to make his peace with God and thanked them to leave him alone to pray.'

'That explains that then,' said Natalie with a heavy heart. Shaun should have received proper medical help and never been put in such a position he felt his only option was to take his own life.

'Bloody shame. His poor family,' said Lucy, echoing Natalie's thoughts.

Ian continued, 'Secondly, according to the DVLA, John sold his Lexus only a month ago and there are no other vehicles registered to him.'

'Then he must be renting something. Find out where from and get details so we can track it,' said Natalie.

'His phone isn't showing up. Looks like he switched it off,' said Lucy.

Ian's forehead furrowed as he spoke. 'It's really hard to believe John would do this. I didn't much like the man but this…'

Natalie responded with, 'None of us want to think the worst of a fellow officer, but facts are facts. John has a secret address that he's been using for three months, one that's close to where the Westmore family live. Add to that the fact he was on leave for two weeks, during which time he could well have been here in Samford, hunting for victims and familiarising himself with the location. Whoever killed these girls planned it all meticulously.

They also knew exactly how the Blossom Twins died. We've been looking for somebody who knew Neil Hoskins and was aware of all those details that were kept from the public. John knew that case as well as I did.'

Thoughts collided into each other, rendering her speechless for a few moments. Pieces slotted suddenly into place – John had uncovered the pornographic images on Neil's laptop that had led to his arrest and subsequent confession. It was a confession that, after sentencing, Neil had wished to retract. His last words before he took his own life had been that he hadn't murdered the girls. Now there was Shaun Castle, who, according to John, had confessed to murder and who had thrown himself from the roof. The similarities were startling, and on top of that, there was the convenience of his death – dead men couldn't talk. Her throat went dry. Was John also responsible for the Blossom Twins murders? She pulled herself together and carried on.

'In 2013 John split up from a woman called Pearl. I don't know her surname but she was a nurse at Manchester Infirmary. Track her down. The other person we ought to speak to is PC Harvey Moathouse. He was, to my knowledge, John's closest friend. Remember to keep this as low-key as you can. I don't want John alerted. Lucy, we'll check out Harrington Rise.'

CHAPTER FORTY-TWO

FRIDAY, 17 AUGUST – AFTERNOON

'See you later, Mum,' said Zoe as she shuffled along the back seat and swung her legs out of the SUV.

Her mother twisted around to speak to her before she got out and joined Leigh outside the cinema. 'You remember what I said.'

'We will.'

'And be back no later than five. Your dad's coming home early and lighting the barbecue. We thought we'd eat outside. Okay?'

'Yeah. Sounds good. We'll be back before then.'

'Okay, enjoy yourselves,' said Zoe's mum.

Zoe shut the car door and walked up the cinema steps. 'Phew! That was awks. I thought at one point she was going to come right inside the frikkin' cinema and watch the film with us.'

Zoe had recently begun using lots of teenage slang and transatlantic expressions, and some words sounded at odds with her local Staffordshire accent, but Leigh loved her regardless. Her friend was confident and beautiful with perfect teeth and shining chestnut eyes that drew you in, even more so today, enhanced by the glittering gold eyeshadow and the false eyelashes she had applied. She was in a strappy playsuit bearing a small yellow check pattern that set off her golden skin, and she looked perfect, from the mess of curly dark hair on the top of her head, deliberately styled with shaven sides to show off her boldness and individuality, right down to her toenails painted in bright coral that peeped out from her trendy sandals. Leigh wished she could be more like her, but today she was uneasy about Zoe's cavalier attitude.

'Why didn't you tell her we were going to meet friends or something more truthful?'

'She'd only quiz me to death: Who are they? How old are they? Where do they live? You know what mums are like. It's easier to say we're watching a film and then going shopping; besides, we probably will do after the concert, so it won't be a lie.' She slipped her arm through her friend's. 'I'm so excited.'

Leigh had to admit she had butterflies in her stomach. 'Do I look all right?'

'You look a total babe.'

'Really?' Leigh gave a shy smile.

'Totes. Come on, selfie time!' She lifted her mobile high up and snapped the pair of them, arm in arm, outside the cinema door. 'There, see for yourself.' She showed the picture to Leigh, who had to admit they looked good together. They complemented each other – Zoe with her outgoing personality and trendiness, and Leigh, the shyer of the two, with a paler complexion and a sense of fragility and insecurity. She needed Zoe to bring the best out in her. She was fine at home, but when she was among friends she was always the quiet one, unsure of what to say, especially around boys. She hoped she wouldn't clam up in front of Callum.

Zoe watched as her mum's car disappeared from view then checked the time on her mobile again. She'd looked at it dozens of times already over the last quarter of an hour. Her mum's insistence on driving them to the cinema had slightly messed up their plans, but they still had sufficient time to meet Tom outside the Methodist church hall at half past one as arranged. He and the other roadies would have set up by then and the band was due to arrive around that time to do a sound check before the doors opened at two. They'd get the chance to say hi, take some photos and chat to the guys, then watch them do their warm-up before staying for the actual concert. Zoe squeezed her friend's arm again.

'How long have we got?'

'It's almost quarter past one. We'll be there in time. It only takes fifteen minutes to get to the hall. This is gonna be epic.'

Leigh smiled at her. It was going to be awesome.

*

Harrington Rise was an unremarkable street like so many others in Samford, consisting of rendered detached houses, all in off-cream, set back from the pavement. Number 12, the one John had rented, was a two-storey building with a paved-over front garden and a dull brown door. Curtains were drawn at all the windows. Natalie banged on the front door even though she knew nobody would answer. There was no movement at any of the curtains.

Natalie walked to the gate to the side of the house and rattled it. It was locked.

'Want to break in? He might be lying unconscious or dead,' said Lucy.

Although there was a chance that was the case, they both knew it was unlikely. Natalie's eyes were drawn to an ornament by the front door: a cast-iron tortoise. She recognised its use. Eric, David's father, owned one exactly like it. She bent and lifted its shell. The door keys were lying there.

'No way!' said Lucy.

'I think he's gone,' said Natalie, pulling on gloves and lifting the keys up. She slotted them into the lock, turned them and the door swung open. They pulled on shoe covers and, careful not to touch anything, they entered the plain-carpeted hallway. The staircase rose to their left, and to the right there was a sitting room, a dining room, a downstairs toilet and, at the far end, a kitchen. The place smelt strongly of bleach. Somebody had recently cleaned it.

Lucy headed upstairs and called out, 'There are no clothes, bedding or wash kit up here. It's been cleaned too. There's no sign he was living here at all.'

'He must have left some evidence behind. We'll get Forensics to sweep the place,' Natalie shouted back. She was certain none of what she was looking at belonged to John. The sitting room decor was outdated as was the faded patterned settee, the television set and the bookcase on which stood a mishmash of ornaments: a trio of ceramic vases in pale blue, a porcelain woman in a white dress, a copper-coloured Buddha. Why had he chosen to stay here and yet rent a room in a B & B? She had no answers but she felt she was close to them. Her mobile buzzed. Ian had news for her.

'PC Harvey Moathouse left the force a year ago. Apparently, he bought a boat to go sailing round the world with his family. He's no longer in contact with anyone from Manchester. I have, however, thanks to the hospital in Manchester, located Pearl Toussaint. She's still in nursing and is currently living in Trinidad.'

'Oh, crap!'

'It's okay, I tracked her down on social media and managed to find a contact number for her. I rang her but she wasn't back from her shift yet. Her daughter said she'd be in within the hour.'

'Good. I'll ring her as soon as I get back to the office. Anything else?'

'Still looking into car rental companies.'

'Okay. We won't be long.'

As soon as she ended the call, she rang Mike. 'It looks like he was never here but I think the fucker's scarpered. I'm at 12 Harrington Rise. Could you send somebody around to check it out? He must have left some trace behind.'

'Sure.'

'The front door key will be in the tortoise.'

'Is that a coded message?' She could hear the smile in his voice.

'Funny!'

'Got to get our kicks when we can,' he replied. 'I'll sort it out. Want this kept under wraps still?'

'Yes, although I'm going to have to share this with Dan soon.'

'Good luck with that.'

'Cheers! Catch you later.'

'You will.'

She shoved her phone back into her pocket. Lucy was on her way downstairs.

'Nothing. Not a damn thing. No sheets on the bed – nothing.'

'He must have taken them with him.'

'But where? He must have some endgame plan.'

'He'll probably turn up in a few days and talk his way out of it. We have no actual proof he's behind the murders and he knows it. He's bloody clever, Lucy.'

'He'd need balls of steel to do that. I reckon he's done a runner and will disappear, although where he'd run to is beyond me. He can't stay on the run forever.'

'A man on the run who has nothing left to lose is the most dangerous sort of criminal. We have to find him.'

*

Leigh and Zoe were almost at the Methodist church hall, a low-rise building in plain stone and brick with a slate roof, set back from the street and fronted by a small car park. They glimpsed a van with blacked-out windows and Zoe let out a loud, 'Savage!'

Leigh understood her friend's excitement. This was no doubt the undercover van Tom had described to them on the phone – the one Blasted used when they didn't want fans to know they were on the move.

'You've gotta take a piccy of me beside it,' said Zoe, her pace increasing.

Leigh matched it and lifted her mobile while Zoe posed, hands thrust in the pockets of her jumpsuit, face stern, then smiley with her head thrown back. Leigh clicked away. A cough stopped her in her tracks. A man in a military jacket was standing to one side, in the shadow of the hall.

'And you are?' His voice was unfriendly.

Unfazed and high on the anticipation of what was to come, Zoe responded, 'Tom's friends.'

The man stepped from the shadows. He was dressed in a black Blasted T-shirt and wearing a lanyard from which dangled a pass. He nodded a couple of times. 'Zoe and...' he said, looking at Leigh.

'Leigh,' said Zoe.

The man tapped his head. 'That's it, Leigh. Tom said to look out for you. The band has only just arrived and the lads are about to do a sound check to make sure the equipment's working okay. We're a roadie short so Tom's helping with that. I don't want you to hang about outside in case anybody gets wind of what's going on. You okay coming inside and waiting for them to do that? They'll only be about five minutes. I'm Chris, by the way. I'm one of the security team. He held up his pass that had his photo and name on it along with the word 'Security'.

'We should wait for Tom first,' said Leigh.

'He's busy inside, so if you want to wait for him to come and fetch you, you'll have to go and wait down the road,' said Chris.

Zoe threw Leigh a look and said, 'No, it's fine. We'll come inside.' She urged Leigh on with a series of facial grimaces. When Leigh didn't move, she marched forwards. Leigh's reactions were automatic. She didn't want to be left behind and she didn't want her friend to go inside alone, so she brought up the rear.

'We have to go in the back way. Front door's locked until the event starts.' Chris walked ahead, down the side of the building.

Zoe trotted eagerly after him but Leigh lagged further behind. Some sixth sense held her back.

Zoe stopped, turned and waved her hand. 'Come on!' she said before disappearing around the back of the hall.

Leigh didn't follow her. What was holding her back? The group were inside checking their instruments. She'd miss out on meeting Callum Vincetti if she didn't get a move on.

Zoe called her name. 'Leigh!'

Knowing that her friend wasn't going to return or wait for her spurred Leigh on. She turned the corner, where sunlight burst onto a neatly kept garden. Zoe and Chris weren't in sight; they'd already gone inside. The back door was hidden in a recess in the building and she headed that way, expecting it to be ajar. She was almost upon it when she drew to a halt again. What was troubling her? Then it struck her: she couldn't hear a thing. There was no sound of drums or microphones or electronic guitars. If the group were testing out their instruments, she'd hear something.

She jumped as Chris appeared from the doorway. He looked at her quizzically. 'You okay?'

'Where's Zoe?'

'Inside.'

'Zoe!'

He laughed. 'She won't hear you.'

'Why can't I hear any music?' Leigh asked.

'Soundproofed rooms. You can't hear a thing out here.'

'Zoe!'

He shoved his hands in his pockets. 'You not going in then?'

'No,' she said and began to back away.

'I had a feeling you wouldn't. You're as stubborn as your mother.' He sprang quickly before Leigh could find her feet, and then all she was aware of was blackness.

CHAPTER FORTY-THREE

Having returned to HQ, Natalie had her phone on speaker and Pearl Toussaint's voice could be heard clearly in the office. Lucy sat with elbows resting on her knees as she listened in.

'I really appreciate you talking to us,' said Natalie, who'd explained they were getting some background information on John.

'I don't know how I can really help. We left the UK almost five years ago and my life has changed hugely since those days.'

'Of course, but anything you can tell us might help us now. Whatever we can learn about John could assist us.'

'Has he done something wrong?'

'I can't discuss the nature of our investigation, only that it's imperative we gather as much information as we can about John, and you might be able to provide us with some details. Especially as you lived with him.'

'He's messed up, hasn't he? I knew he would. I warned him he'd need to straighten himself out when I left.'

'Why did you tell him that?'

'He was all over the place – one minute he was high, the next, low, and he was becoming too dependent on drugs.'

This was news to Natalie. She'd never once suspected John was taking anything, not in all the time they'd worked together in Manchester.

'Is that why you left him?'

'That and the fact it wasn't working out between us.'

'Could you be more explicit?'

'I wasn't happy. I'd hoped we'd build a life together, but he couldn't let go of the past and it affected our relationship – badly. You can't live with somebody who doesn't want to move on.'

'Are you talking about the death of his wife?' Natalie flicked through the file, stopping at the relevant information which revealed John had been married to Jennifer Harper, who had died in 2011.

'Yes. I knew at the time he was never really going to get over what had happened, but I'd hoped all the same. It was foolish of me. I fell hard for him and wanted to be the person to bring him back from that horror. I hadn't banked on how deeply he'd be affected by the trauma of it all.'

'Can you tell me what happened? We only have the date of Jennifer's death.'

There was a sigh. 'They were both involved in a car accident. John escaped with minor injuries but we had to put Jennifer on life support. It quickly became apparent she'd never recover. We kept her alive as long as we could, for the sake of the babies, but she suffered a cardiac arrest.'

There was nothing in her files to suggest Jennifer had been carrying a baby.

'Was she pregnant?' Natalie asked.

'Didn't you know? She was expecting twins. They appeared to be uninjured and the specialist decided they'd stand a better chance of survival if they were allowed to continue growing in the womb, but once Jennifer arrested, we had to get them out.'

Lucy let out a gasp of surprise at the news.

'Did they survive?' Natalie asked.

'Thirty-two hours. There were far more complications than we'd suspected.'

'What sex were the twins?'

'Girls. John named them Rose and Lily. They were buried with their mother at a church close to where her parents live. John didn't go to the funeral.'

'Was there a reason for that?'

'We never spoke about it but I think it was down to guilt. He'd been driving at the time they had the accident. I believe he felt responsible for all their deaths.'

It was another vital piece of information, and Natalie was even more convinced that John was responsible for the recent murders and those in Manchester.

'Did he ever discuss the babies?'

'No, and that was one of the reasons we couldn't move forward as a couple.'

'But you lived together for quite a while?'

'Just over two years. Things moved quickly between us, and soon after his wife and children were buried, we moved in together. I thought it was the real deal, but looking back, he was on the rebound and was carrying too much hurt and anger for our relationship to ever succeed. I suppose one of the reasons he was keen to be part of my life was because of my daughter, Mikayla. She became a substitute daughter for him, but I knew it wasn't healthy for either of them.'

'In what way?'

There was another pause and then, 'I don't know if it was the drugs he began taking, or if he really felt he had the right to act like he did, but he became overbearing – telling her what she could and couldn't do, sometimes quite aggressively – and he became very critical of her. She was a typical teenager, experimenting with different hairstyles, clothes, that sort of thing, but it was like he didn't want her to grow up. Mikayla began to resent his interference. He was argumentative and unreasonable: he'd stop her from going out to see friends, make her change her clothes if he didn't approve, and they argued a lot. I had to think of Mikayla's happiness as much as my own, so in the end, I left.'

'Has he been in contact with you or Mikayla since?'

'I told him to stay out of our lives and he has.'

'Did he ever threaten you or Mikayla?'

'No, but he is a man with a temper. You could see it in his eyes some days – the anger and hurt and frustration. Now I'm glad we moved away when we did. So, DI Ward, if you've contacted me, it must be because of something serious. I hope he hasn't hurt anyone.'

Natalie drew the woman away from her suppositions with, 'Does he have any close friends or family you know of?'

'His mother died years ago and he never knew his father. He mostly went out with other police officers. I don't think there was any one in particular. He usually talked about *the lads* rather than individuals.'

'Are there any names you can remember?'

'Harvey somebody-or-other... I can't really think of any others.'

Natalie assumed she meant PC Harvey Moathouse.

'Okay. Well, thank you for your time.'

Pearl didn't respond or ring off and Natalie guessed she wanted to say something else. Eventually she did, 'It was pity, not love, that brought us together. I was a nurse and I saw somebody in acute mental pain and I wanted to help heal that person, but the truth is, nobody can heal John. He lives in a permanent hell.'

Natalie thanked her again before hanging up.

'Shit,' was all Lucy could say.

'John has to be our killer. It's got to be him, on some bonkers vendetta for losing his children. How could this have slipped by everyone?' Natalie was furious.

'He might not have told anyone about it. Doesn't strike me as the sort of person to wear his heart on his sleeve.' Lucy's reply hit home. John had been renowned for being one of the lads and making crass or inappropriate comments, and being what some would describe as a hard nut. He'd never brought his personal life into work. Natalie had only known about Pearl because she'd met the woman one time, when she'd come to pick John up from work. However, John had clearly been through challenging times and his employment records ought to have contained such valuable information. She wondered briefly how much Dan knew about John. Before she could dwell on it, Ian came back into the office.

'I've tried all the car rental companies in this county and had no luck. John hasn't hired a vehicle from any of them.'

Natalie chewed her lip in thought then said, 'Extend the area. Try Derbyshire. I'm going to talk to Superintendent Tasker. It's time we brought our concerns to his attention.'

Dan stood, hands clasped behind his back. 'These are very serious allegations, DI Ward.'

'I'm fully aware of that and I'm also aware that a lot of what we have is only circumstantial, but we have to find John and bring him in for questioning.' She kept her head high and met his gaze.

'I admit some of what he has done sounds like odd behaviour but it is quite a stretch to go from being concerned as to why he has rented a house as well as a room at a B & B in Samford, to accusing him of committing murder.'

'I've told you everything I know. You must be able to see what I see, sir.'

'I see some of it but I also see a man who has suffered a tragedy in his life, who has an unblemished work record and who has earned respect among colleagues.'

Natalie had run out of arguments. She'd presented all the facts. She had nothing left to offer, and if he refused to back her, she didn't know what she'd do. A tap at the door halted proceedings.

'Come in!'

Ian entered. 'I'm sorry to disturb you, sir, but there's been an important development. We've discovered DS Briggs hired a blue Nissan Micra last Sunday, but yesterday afternoon he changed it for a Ford Transit van and expressly requested blacked-out windows. It's one of their higher-priced rentals which has been fitted with a tracking device that activates when the vehicle moves. It's currently travelling northbound on the M6.'

Natalie looked her superior in the eye.

'Okay. Bring him in,' he said.

'Thank you, sir.'

'You'd better be right about this, DI Ward.'

'I'm sure we are, sir.'

CHAPTER FORTY-FOUR

FRIDAY, 17 AUGUST – EVENING

'The Ford Transit van has just passed an ANPR point near Keele services. He's headed towards Knutsford,' said Ian, who was monitoring the vehicle's progress up the M6 motorway.

'Officers have been deployed. They should be able to take him off the motorway at that point,' said Natalie, arms folded as she stared out of the window. She was ready for the bastard. He could wriggle all he liked but she was going to make sure everything she had on him stuck.

Lucy was with Shaun Castle's family, and although Natalie wanted her present when they questioned John, until they captured him, there was little more they could do than wait. Her questions were prepared. Mike's team were still at John's house, searching for evidence that would link him to the murders. She was confident he'd slipped up somewhere along the line. Her confidence flickered for a second – so far John Briggs had outwitted them all and hadn't made any errors other than wear a ring on his pinkie finger. Was he really her man?

Her mobile buzzed and David's name flashed onto the screen. She considered ignoring it but thought better of it. She ought to let him know she probably wouldn't make it home until very late, if at all. 'Call you back,' she said quickly before he could speak, and then hung up. She made for the roof terrace, where she dialled his number. The cool air was a welcome break from the stuffy office and she inhaled deeply.

'Hi. I couldn't speak in the office. What's up?'

David's voice was flat. 'Rowena dropped Zoe and Leigh off at the cinema in Samford at lunchtime with instructions to return at five but neither of them has reappeared and they aren't answering their phones. Rowena's beside herself with worry. We've tried ringing all their friends and I even went to the cinema but no one there recalls seeing them. I don't think they went to the cinema at all. Leigh was wearing her new top and I joked about her meeting a boy. I think that's what they planned to do – meet up with some lads – but none of their friends know anything about it. What do I do, Natalie?'

This was almost a repeat of earlier in the year when they'd believed Leigh had been snatched by a killer Natalie had been pursuing. It had transpired the girl had run away. She swallowed and tried to make sense of what she was hearing. 'Did she not mention any names to you?'

'No, but I'm pretty sure that's what they planned to do. Rowena said Zoe was dressed up too and was even wearing gold eyeshadow, although she didn't suspect anything. She really thought they were going to watch a film.'

'They could have lost track of time.' Even to her own ears it sounded implausible. 'I'll inform missing persons.'

David sounded confused and hurt. She understood why when he said, 'It's probably our fault again. I wouldn't be surprised if she hasn't worked out what's been going on between us. The last time she ran away we patched things up for a while, so she could be trying the same trick again.'

'That's possible, but if that's the case, why has Zoe taken off with her?'

'Maybe Zoe put her up to it.'

'I agree we can't panic over this but I'll get officers onto it. We can't sit back and do nothing.'

'Okay. I've left Josh at home and told him to ring if she comes back. I'm going to wait with Rowena and Patrick in case we hear anything or they come home. I really can't face going through all this again. We should have come clean and told them the situation. This is bloody torture. I've no idea if she's trying to make us pay or if she's in danger.'

'I'll talk to Graham Kilburn. He'll know what's the best action to take.'

'I'm fucking drained, Natalie. We need to do something about this situation when she gets back. She can't keep taking off and scaring us witless.'

He ended the call, leaving her feeling guilty. It was undoubtedly her fault that Leigh had run away yet again. She'd caused this to happen. She rang Graham Kilburn on his private number and told him what she knew. Her daughter had disappeared again and this time with her best friend.

'Are there any reasons she might have run away?'

'We're still having marital difficulties so yes, she might have left because of them.'

'Did the girls take anything with them – clothes, bags, any personal items?'

'Not to my knowledge. David said Leigh was dressed up, possibly to meet up with a boy. They should have come home by five.'

'It's only seven now. They could well be with friends.'

'David and Rowena have tried ringing all their friends and none of them have seen Zoe or Leigh. Neither girl is answering her phone.' A thought, like a fat bubble, rose in her mind and floated there.

'Okay. Well, I don't need to tell you not to get too alarmed at this stage. They could easily come back in an hour or two.'

'I know but… Graham, I'm worried.'

'It's only natural you are. We'll put a high priority on this.'

The thought kept pushing itself to the forefront of her mind – a thought so terrifying it numbed her lips as she tried to convey her fears to Graham. Eventually, it escaped her mouth.

'Graham, I think the girls have been abducted by a murderer.'

'Natalie, you were worried that was the situation last time, too.' His voice was fatherly, soothing, practised in the art of comforting anxious parents.

She could almost hear the unspoken words, *You're overreacting*. She swallowed the lump of fear back down. She was being irrational. John couldn't possibly know her daughter.

'Yes. I'm becoming a little irrational.'

'Leave it with us. I'll send a team across.'

'Thank you.'

She ended the call and stared at the phone screen then rang her son.

'She's not back yet,' said Josh almost immediately.

'Okay. Josh, can you check Leigh's laptop for me?'

'Sure.'

'Check her emails and browsing history. See what websites she's been on recently.'

'Okay…' He sounded uncertain.

'Can you do that and ring me back?'

'Yes.'

'Thanks.'

'Mum, she's probably done what she did last time. We're not deaf and blind. We know you and Dad don't sleep in the same room. You've both been acting really oddly since we came back from holiday. She's probably trying to teach you another lesson.'

Even her seventeen-year-old son thought Leigh had run away because of her and David. 'Yes. That's very likely.'

'She'll be back in a day or two after you've torn your hair out.'

She managed a small laugh for his benefit. 'Let me know what you find.'

She pressed the end call button and rubbed her dry lips together. Everyone seemed to think Leigh had run away because of the problems she and David were having, but she recalled the story about the little boy who cried wolf. Would Leigh really attempt the same trick twice, or could she actually be in danger purely because everyone believed she was hiding out?

While Natalie had been talking to David, Lucy had returned to the office. Both she and Ian were tuned in to the communications unit and observing the M6 motorway via links to the surveillance cameras. The television monitor was divided into four quadrants, each showing sections of the motorway with evening traffic moving freely. Natalie said nothing about Leigh. Everyone here had been party to the last time the girl had gone missing, believing her to have been snatched by a murderer, and they'd pulled out all the stops to trace the girl. She wasn't going to put them through it all again, not until she was sure something awful had happened to her daughter. Facts and evidence… it always came to that. She couldn't afford a knee-jerk reaction, especially given the fact they were closing in on John Briggs.

The communications unit burst into life again with, 'Officers have eyes on the vehicle – eyes on.'

They all watched the monitor, focusing mainly on the section overlooking the exit to Knutsford services. There was a crackle of static and then a disembodied voice. 'Driver alerted, indicating and slowing down. Vehicle halting on slip road to services. Closing in. Closing in.'

Three police cars burst onto the screen, lights flashing, boxing in a black van so the driver had no option other than to pull off at the service station exit. The van's indicator was flashing and the vehicle slowed to a halt just off the motorway. A figure dismounted and marched towards the officers. Although it was impossible to identify the person, Natalie recognised the swaggering gait.

'Apprehend the suspect,' she said and continued observing until John and the police officers disappeared from view.

The unit came alive once more. 'Suspect apprehended and returning to Samford. ETA forty-five minutes.'

'Roger that,' said Natalie. She drew a deep breath then spoke to Ian and Lucy. 'We're going to need our A game. I doubt he'll confess. The van was fitted with a tracking device; find out if the Nissan Micra he hired on Sunday also had a device and ascertain where it went between Sunday and yesterday afternoon, when he exchanged it for the Ford Transit. Ian, ensure Forensics crawl all over that van. We need hard evidence or he'll walk. We can only keep him for so long and he's going to have prepared an answer for most, if not all, of my questions. Grab a quick break first. We need to stay alert.'

Ian said nothing but picked up his mobile and left the room in silence, head lowered. Natalie picked up on his sudden melancholy mood. 'What's up with him?'

'He was supposed to be looking after his daughter this evening. He's already rung Scarlett twice to say he'll be late but that he's definitely coming. I think he was looking forward to it,' said Lucy.

'Oh, crap! I completely forgot about that.'

Lucy gave a shrug. 'Not the first time he's let her down, or the last. It's all part of the job.'

Natalie shuffled some papers and then went outside to find Ian. It was the job but she should have at least spoken to him about it. Dan had believed she was a team player and a good leader, and now she was proving to be the opposite. She was supposed to drive the team and get results but not break them, or their relationships. She'd already done enough damage to her own. She found Ian on the roof, looking over the wall at the traffic below.

'I completely forgot about Ruby,' she said.

'No biggie. Scarlett knows what the job entails. I'll see the little one at the weekend.'

'For what it's worth, I am genuinely sorry.'

'Honestly, it's not a problem. I want to catch this bastard as much as you do.'

'You're a decent officer, Ian, but take a piece of advice from somebody who's been doing this job much longer than you: don't let all this become your world. You have to have a life as well. If you want to leave now and look after your daughter, go. I won't hold it against you. Lucy and I can handle interviewing John.'

'I'd rather be here. You need somebody to handle anything that might happen while you're interviewing him. There could be some last-minute evidence or you might need some information. Besides, if he is the person responsible for the deaths of those children, I want to be around when he gets his comeuppance. The scumbag who killed those girls deserves everything they get.'

She understood and left him to his thoughts, but before she reached the stairs, her phone rang. Seeing it was Josh, she answered.

'Hey.'

'Hey, Mum. I couldn't get into her email cos it's password-protected. Do you know what the password is?'

'It's Z&LBFF2018.' *Zoe and Leigh Best Friends Forever* – it had made her smile when Leigh had come up with the password. Natalie had insisted on being able to get into her children's accounts to ensure they were behaving responsibly.

'I had her old password. Okay, I'll try that one.'

Once more he hung up. Her stomach began to tie itself in knots. Ian left the roof terrace but she was paralysed, waiting to hear back from her son, and the second she felt the phone in her hand vibrate, she pressed the accept button.

'I've got into her account. What am I looking for, Mum?'

'Anything from somebody called Tom?' She waited as he searched. It didn't take long.

'No… nothing. Hardly any emails at all.'

'Anything in the junk or deleted?'

'No.'

Natalie breathed a sigh of relief. 'Check her browsing history. See if it gives a clue as to where she might have gone. Maybe she googled places.'

'She's only been on Teen Vogue, a few girly websites – fashion, make-up. She seems to mostly use it for YouTube.' There was a pause and a faint clicking of keys. 'Music. She's been watching a load of music videos the last couple of days, and she's downloaded lyrics.'

She thought of the lyrics Isabella had copied down and the knot tightened in her stomach. 'Which videos? Is there one group in particular?'

'Yeah. I didn't know she was into them. Blasted. She's watched all their videos.'

She hung up and immediately rang David, and asked him to get Rowena to check Zoe's email account. David told her that she'd already tried but it was password-protected. Graham had told them the team would try and get into it and all of Zoe's social media accounts.

Her flesh was clammy as she made her way to the lab. Mike let her in and sat her down. Her hands were shaking. She explained as best she could and finished with, 'I know it sounds crazy, but I think John's abducted Leigh and her friend, Zoe. I don't know how to prove it and I can't let him know I suspect it. If he's taken them and hidden them somewhere, he'll never let on where they are.'

'We'll handle this.'

'No. I *need* to interview him. I have to see this through to the end and call his bluff. He's behind the original Blossom Twins murders and the deaths of three young girls on my patch, and he's played us for fools. He believes he's above the law, that we can't get to him. I *have* to find something to prove all this or he'll get away.'

'Forensics are examining the van he drove. Unfortunately, they found nothing at the house to even prove he stayed there – not a hair, not a shred of DNA,' said Mike.

'He's so bloody clever. What if there's nothing in the van either?'

'We have to hope there is.'

'He's been several steps ahead of us – all the fucking time.' She ran shaking fingers through her hair.

Mike put his hands on her upper arms and faced her, his words earnest but gentle. 'You're convinced he's responsible, aren't you?'

'Yes.'

'Then we'll find something. What are you hoping for?'

'Some DNA, a link to one or all of the girls – anything.'

'We'll comb the area around the house where he was staying in case he dumped anything.'

Mike and his team would do their job. They'd find something. She needed to pull herself together. She nodded and he removed his hands.

'What about Leigh?' she asked.

'She was only watching videos of a popular group. It's not unusual. You can't jump from Leigh watching videos to assuming she's been in contact with a killer calling himself Tom.'

'You said the killer, not John.'

'You can't call this perp by any name until you can back up your facts. Come on, Natalie. You've been under a shitload of stress both at home and work. Take a step back and be realistic about this.'

The words hit home. For a few frantic minutes, her emotions had taken over, bombarding her with irrational thoughts. She had to take back control. Although she was sure John Briggs was the murderer, she had a really difficult task ahead to prove it. Mike's words had helped calm her. 'Thanks. I feel better.'

The look he gave her was cautious. 'Good. Keep a clear head. Let Graham do his job looking for Leigh and Zoe, and you concentrate on this.'

She headed back to the office feeling more in control. It would soon be time to talk to John and she had to outwit him. He'd had the upper hand until now, but now it was her turn.

CHAPTER FORTY-FIVE

John Briggs folded his arms and glared at Natalie. 'You've really got it in for me, haven't you?' he said. 'Is this all because you flirted with me back in 2014 and I knocked you back?'

Natalie gave the tiniest of smiles and said, 'We both know that isn't the true version of what happened.'

'Yeah, right. You wish!'

'Could you stick to answering the questions, DS Briggs?'

'Okay. No comment.'

'Why did you rent 12 Harrington Rise three months ago?'

'No comment.'

'Why did you subsequently pay for a room at a B & B and tell the landlady you required accommodation while you worked at Samford HQ?'

His lip curled. 'No comment.'

'Did you stay at 12 Harrington Rise?'

'No fucking comment.'

'You've clearly been living somewhere since Sunday and it wasn't at the boarding house, so let's say, for argument's sake, you stayed at 12 Harrington Rise. Why did you give the boarding house as your lodging address to the personnel here?'

'I thought I was going to stay there and then I changed my mind. It's not against the law.'

'I'll ask you again, did you stay in the house in Harrington Rise?'

'No comment.'

'Why are you refusing to cooperate? They're simple enough questions.'

'Because, DI Ward, you are hoping to pin something on me. You've had it in for me since I arrived here. I've already made a complaint regarding your attitude, and here is further proof of victimisation. You have no reason to treat me as a suspect.'

'This photograph we showed you earlier. It is an enlargement of a still taken from Samford library last Monday. It clearly shows a ring bearing a crest identical to the one you are wearing. How can you explain it?'

'Somebody else wears a signet ring like mine,' he retorted, eyes glittering. It was the answer she'd expected him to give. 'You have nothing other than this photograph, have you? This is a complete fit-up.' He turned to his lawyer. 'See that look on her face? They have nothing – absolutely nothing to link me to the deaths of those three girls. They can't charge me but I want it noted that when they actually release me, I am going to sue their fucking arses off!'

Natalie maintained her sangfroid. 'I suggest you calm down, DS Briggs. If you'd like to prove your innocence, you could do so by being cooperative and explaining why you rented a house three months before you actually took up the secondment at Samford.'

He leant across the table, his face puckered in anger. 'I don't have to tell you anything.'

'Then this interview is over for the moment but we shall be requiring you to remain here while we check out a few details.'

He sat back again and sneered. 'Check them out and then you'll have to let me go.'

*

'Did you find out about the Nissan Micra he hired before he swapped it for the Ford Transit van?' Natalie directed her question at Lucy.

'Yes. It's one of the company's cheapest rentals and as such is not considered a theft risk so is not fitted with a tracking device.'

'Shit!'

'I gave all of the car's details to the technical team, who are running the number plate through their systems to try and locate it on CCTV cameras in Samford.'

'Then there's a chance we'll be able to place him at Blithbury Marsh on Saturday night or early Sunday morning?'

'Provided he went along a route that had cameras. Otherwise we're stuffed.'

'Ian, anything?'

Ian was in contact with the forensic team examining John's van. He shook his head at her. 'So far it's clean. They've found an overnight bag, containing clothes and a wash kit belonging to John, and nothing else at all. They've dusted for prints and can only find his.'

'No other prints? Surely one of the rental company's employees, or somebody who previously hired the van, would have left prints on it. That suggests he cleaned it, but if he did, why?' Natalie said. The situation was looking hopeless but she wasn't beaten yet.

Lucy hesitated before speaking. 'This is complete speculation on my part but Kim Castle was sure Shaun didn't leave the house with his laptop. It wasn't in his car or in his office at the library when we got there. Kim thought the laptop was in the spare bedroom. John went upstairs to fetch it while I spoke to her. When I next saw him, he claimed not to have found the laptop. He then went off to check out the rest of the house. Do you think he might have taken the laptop and hidden it to incriminate Shaun? He was hell-bent on trying to persuade us all Shaun had committed suicide because he'd killed the girls, but I was with them both on the roof. John was aggressive and forceful from the moment we arrived at the library and I took him to task over it. He refused to listen to me. Shaun was already in a fragile state and maybe even considering taking his own life, and I think John scared Shaun so much, Shaun jumped. I didn't hear his final words, but he just sounded like an unhappy, frightened man to me.'

It was a consideration and would mean that John would have had to have dumped it somewhere. Natalie digested the facts. 'If he is our killer, he's disposed of anything that could incriminate him, and that includes the disguise he wore. Ian, you said the tracking device on his van was switched on this morning.'

'It activates automatically every time the van moves.'

'And John didn't know this?'

'The girl who gave him the keys to the Nissan Micra was new to the job. She had no idea that the more expensive vehicles have tracking devices on them. When John hired the Nissan, he actually asked her if the cars were fitted with trackers. She checked the system and saw the Nissan hadn't got one; assuming none of the vehicles had them, she told him they didn't have tracking devices fitted to them. When he swapped the Nissan for the Ford Transit, he didn't ask again. The same girl served him and remembers he was in a hurry to hand back the keys and get the van. He told her he had to transport some household goods to his new place and needed a larger vehicle. He had no idea his movements could be traced.'

'Which means this girl's mistake could be his undoing. Find out the exact route he took today.'

Another hour slipped by and tiny invisible needles began to prick the back of Natalie's eyes. John wasn't telling them anything and she had little to keep him at the station. Leigh and Zoe were still missing, and every time she looked at John's smug face, she knew he was laughing at her. Her instinct told her he'd snatched the girls

and hidden them away somewhere to torment her. Her head told
her that wasn't possible. There was no way Leigh or Zoe could have
been in contact with the man; neither girl used the local library,
yet still there was a gnawing in the pit of her stomach.

The tech team were still trying to find out if 'Tom' had contacted
either Zoe or Leigh via email. If John had managed to ensnare her
daughter and her friend the same way he had the other girls, then
they should find some evidence of it. The waiting game was too
long and drawn out for her.

She went to the toilets and doused her face in cold water. She
wasn't going to give up. No matter what Dan Tasker or any of them
thought, she was going to nail this fucker. With renewed determination, she climbed the stairs to the office. It was almost eleven and
she felt wrecked. Her daughter was missing, her marriage was in
tatters but her resolve was still strong. She drew herself to her full
height and walked back into the office.

Ian, holding a printout of a map, scuttled across to Natalie's
desk and with one finger traced a red line along a road. 'John's van
was parked on Harrington Rise. It moved off at nine thirty this
morning and travelled the country roads towards Trove. It came to
a halt at the Grey Goose pub, where it remained stationary for an
hour and a half exactly before continuing towards Trove, where it
stopped for ten minutes, at this location, a recycling facility. The
vehicle left the recycling facility at 12.16 p.m. and returned along
the same route to Samford, where it parked by the Methodist
church hall at 1.10 p.m. and remained in position for fifty-seven
minutes. After that, it headed towards the M6 motorway, taking
this circuitous route that skirts around the town rather than the
most direct one through. It also stopped for a little over an hour
at Keele services before rejoining the motorway, which was when
we started following it.'

Natalie pressed her fingertips to her forehead. 'Right. We need
extra officers to assist us with this. I want every location where

that vehicle stopped checked out, and we need a team sent to the recycling facility pronto. If he was going to dump anything, that's the most obvious place to do it. You mentioned he parked up at the Methodist church hall at ten past one?'

'That's right.'

'Leigh and Zoe were supposed to be at the cinema at that time. It's only a fifteen-minute walk from there. He might, just might, have met them at the hall and abducted them.'

'Shall I inform Graham Kilburn?'

'Yes. I think it needs looking into. Otherwise, I can't imagine why else John would return to Samford and park up outside the church hall.'

'What about Keele services? What are we looking for?'

'Get hold of CCTV footage. He might have dropped the girls off there or disposed of incriminating evidence. Check all the wastepaper bins – he's used them before – and make sure MisPers comb that area.'

Her phone rang and she snatched it from the desk.

'Natalie, it's Mike. He's cleaned out the back of the van with bleach and wiped down all the doors and sides. There's no sign of a struggle or any trace of blood. I can't be sure anyone's been in here other than him.'

The gnawing in her stomach intensified. He'd wiped away any traces left by a person or persons other than himself. Somebody had been in the van with him and that somebody could be her daughter and her friend.

'He's cleaned it for a reason – to hide the fact somebody's been in it.'

'You can't be certain of that and you don't know what time he cleaned it. He might have done it first thing this morning, or after he disposed of evidence.'

While she accepted Mike could be correct, her thoughts boomeranged back to dark thoughts.

They ended the call, both anxious to return to the investigation. Ian was already talking to Graham Kilburn, and Lucy was trying to get the recycling facility opened up so a team could go in. She had no time to waste. Everything depended on her efficiency. They'd lost Avril and Faye Moore because they'd chased after the wrong suspect, and she couldn't make that same mistake. She was sure John was responsible for the murders, and that he had taken Zoe and Leigh. She couldn't be wrong. Too much was riding on it. She rang Dan's direct number. It didn't matter if she woke him. She needed extra officers and quickly.

CHAPTER FORTY-SIX

A new day had begun and at two o'clock, Natalie and Lucy joined the search team at the Trove recycling facility. A night watchman had opened up the facility to them and Natalie was surprised at its size: larger than three football pitches and containing at least fifty huge skips. With signage denoting what could be disposed of in each receptacle – from nappies and garden waste to household chemicals and furniture – they all potentially harboured vital pieces of evidence.

The security guard explained the set-up to Natalie. 'Vehicles come in the marked entrance and then have to follow the one-way route around the facility to the exit point, stopping in one of the offloading bays in front of the skip they require.'

'What happens if somebody is using that skip and the bay is full?' Natalie asked.

'They have to wait on the circuit. It's not ideal and we do get backlogged traffic on a regular basis, but the lads try to assist everyone and help them offload as quickly as possible. The bays hold up to three vehicles each. It gets trickier when there are vanloads of materials that need to go into separate skips. We always check vans and direct them to the extra-large bays on the outside of the circuit, so they can carry or barrow goods to various skips rather than keep stopping and starting.'

'Do you have CCTV footage here?'

'We do but it's automatically wiped at midnight. The cameras are really to make sure we stay on top of the movements and to keep an eye on people putting stuff in the wrong container. Can't have somebody dumping a battery full of acid in a skip for timber or mattresses.'

'Do you have any footage of vehicles that came through earlier today?'

'Sorry, no. That'll have been wiped by now.'

'But the employees here check all the vans that come in?'

'Yes, it's company policy. We have to make sure they're not carrying asbestos or anything else that shouldn't be dropped off here. You'd be surprised at what people try to get away with when they're house-clearing.'

'Can you give us names and contact details of those who were on duty today?' Natalie looked across at Lucy, who'd been party to the conversation, to signal she'd need to contact the individuals concerned and see if they remembered speaking to John.

'I can do that,' he said. The night watchman went into the office to search for details, followed by Lucy. If they could contact someone who might have spoken to John and checked his van, they'd have a better idea of what else they were hunting for.

Officers in protective clothing continued to pick through mounds of general waste in search of anything to indicate the killer had been here. Natalie stood in the cold, clear night; the facility was lit by floodlights, not the stars above her. To the far side was a large storage container in which were old televisions, computers and other electronic equipment. The team had been instructed to hunt for Samsung laptops, and Natalie observed officers carrying two such items to the van to send to the technical team for examination and to establish if either belonged to Shaun Castle. John had travelled out to this facility from Samford for a good reason and that was as good as any.

Her mobile buzzed. Ian was at the Grey Goose pub, which she had passed earlier on her way to the recycling facility. It had been difficult to understand why John had stopped there for so long, given its remote location and the fact it had a for sale notice in the window. 'We've completed a thorough search inside the pub and it's empty,' said Ian. 'We've checked the vicinity and all bins but we've not found anything suspicious.'

'Unless he was there to meet up with somebody, I would hazard a guess that he stayed there to keep out of Samford in case he got spotted. I can't think of any other reason he'd park up for that length of time. Okay, we'll see you back at HQ. We're done here too. I think they've offloaded all the laptops that match the description of Shaun's, and we have some names of employees to contact.'

'I'll see you in a while then.'

Lucy reappeared and lifted her notebook. 'Got the names.'

'Right, let's go try and wake some of them up.'

Natalie had sent Lucy and Ian home for some rest. Even if they only managed a couple of hours' sleep, it would be better than nothing. She couldn't rest and she didn't want to go home. There was nothing she could do about Leigh. She was in DI Graham Kilburn's hands yet again. He and his officers were doing everything they could to track down the two missing girls, and all Natalie could do was wait. She tried the next name on the list the night watchman had given her. No one had picked up her earlier calls so she was surprised when an alert voice answered. She apologised for waking the man at four in the morning and explained who she was.

'It's okay. I don't sleep late in summer. It's these light mornings. I'm always up around this time. Besides, the dog already woke me up,' he said.

She asked about the black Ford Transit van.

'I think I saw it.'

She read out the number plate but he replied, 'Sorry, I don't remember seeing the number plate, or the bloke driving it. I was manoeuvring the on-site crane at the time. I had to replace the oil container for an empty one. I stopped lifting to allow a black Ford Transit to pass by.'

'You didn't see where the van stopped?'

'Nah. I was focused on lifting the container. It's a tricky job. You have to be careful.'

'Any idea who stopped the van at the entrance?'

'Might have been Wilson. He was about at the time.'

'What's his surname?'

'Wilson is his surname. His first name's Herbert but he hates that so we all call him Wilson.'

She scanned the list. They had his contact details. Thanking the man, she tried Wilson's number but it went to answerphone. Outside, the sky was no longer dark. Warm orange and pink heralded the start of another sunny day, and Natalie stared out at the fresh morning. There was no more she could do for now. She had to wait. Not everyone was up at the crack of dawn.

Natalie was dozing, head resting on her arms, body across her desk, when her phone rang. She sat up with a jolt. Her mouth was dry and she could hardly speak.

'We've found Shaun's laptop,' said Mike. 'I've been with the technical team the last hour and they've just this second identified it.'

'You been up all night?'

'Of course.'

She was touched by his evident concern. He could have gone home to bed but instead he'd left Keele services and travelled back to Samford to work with the technical team and check the laptops. The wall clock showed the time to be six fifteen. She'd managed to sleep for a whole hour. She winced as she attempted to move her neck. It had stiffened up but she ignored the discomfort. She was closer still to charging John Briggs and that might also lead her to Leigh and Zoe. 'I just need confirmation from a witness and we've really got him!'

'Any news on Leigh?'

'Nothing.'

He fell silent. There was no need for platitudes. They were both aware that Leigh had run away before, yet mindful that John might have taken the girls. 'Keep me informed when they find her,' he said.

'You'll be the first to know.'

She headed to the staff changing rooms and peeled off her clothes, bundling her underwear and blouse into a plastic bag and pulling out a fresh set she kept in her locker for such emergencies. She took a hot shower, washing away the tiredness and sweat from the long day before, and feeling fresher, she dressed once more. She pulled out her make-up bag and attempted to disguise the heavy bags under her eyes. Every time she looked in the mirror she saw her own mother's face. She was looking increasingly like her by the day, with flecks of grey now prominent in her hair, and lines around her eyes and between her eyebrows that had never been evident before. Stress was taking its toll but that was life. It sucked the energy and enthusiasm from you little by little, leaving you a dried-out husk.

She checked her reflection and decided the pink lipstick brightened her complexion. Determined to put on a professional front, she prepared to do battle with John Briggs. First, she wanted to talk to Wilson.

She was surprised to see Lucy in the office on her return. 'I thought I sent you home?'

'I went home and now I'm back,' Lucy replied. 'With coffee.' She passed a takeaway cup to Natalie.

'Thank you.'

'Figured you'd need it. It might be a long day again.'

The internal phone rang and Lucy answered it. 'You have! Where did you find it?'

It was now seven forty-five in the morning and, once again, Natalie faced John. All parties had identified themselves for the purpose of the recording device.

'You look peaky, Natalie,' he scoffed.

'As do you,' she replied. 'Bed a bit hard for you?'

His eyes grew flinty. Natalie continued, unperturbed. 'Some new evidence has come to light.'

A cloud of doubt passed across his face but he recovered quickly and said, 'That's unlikely, especially as I haven't committed any crime.'

'If you believe that, then this might surprise you.'

Natalie allowed her words to sow seeds of doubt in his mind before pushing forward a photograph.

Lucy said, 'For the recorder, DI Ward is showing DS Briggs photograph IJ109.'

'Do you recognise this, John?'

His face showed no emotion. 'It's a laptop. Looks smashed up.'

'That's correct. It's a Samsung laptop and indeed it has been smashed up. In spite of the damage inflicted on it, the technical department succeeded in rescuing the hard drive and have established that the laptop in question belonged to Shaun Castle. Have you any idea how a laptop that should have been in Mr Castle's spare room ended up in a container in a recycling facility in Trove?'

'No.'

Natalie nodded. 'Do you recognise these?'

Lucy said, 'For the recorder, DI Ward is showing DS Briggs evidence bag IJ67.'

'No.'

'You've never seen these sunglasses before?'

'No.'

'They were picked up from a wastepaper bin in the car park of Keele services.'

He shrugged nonchalantly. 'So what? They're broken. Someone tossed them away.'

'I think you threw them away.'

His lips curled in disgust. 'Fuck off! I didn't throw them away. Test them for fingerprints. You won't find mine on them.'

'We have dusted for prints and indeed there are none. None whatsoever, indicating they have been wiped clean. Don't you think that's unusual? People don't normally wipe clean items that they intend throwing away.'

John shrugged.

'You didn't clean them?'

'No. And you can't prove I did.'

'But you were at Keele services for an hour. What did you do during that time?'

'Had a coffee.'

'For an hour?'

'Yes.'

'What else did you do?'

'Went for a shit.'

Natalie didn't rise to his comment. She lifted another photograph out of her file and slid it across to John. He took a quick look at it then folded his arms and sat back.

'For the recorder, DI Ward is showing DS Briggs photograph IJ110,' said Lucy, her eyes trained on John's face.

'This is a photograph taken from the CCTV camera inside the service station. You can clearly see your face in the picture. Do you deny this is you?'

'No.'

'You are holding a paper takeaway bag bearing the logo of the coffee shop. What was in the bag?'

'A sandwich.'

'You spent an hour in the services and yet you bought a takeaway sandwich. Why didn't you eat it while you were drinking your coffee?'

'I wasn't hungry then. I bought it for later.' John stared hard at her.

'Okay, so you claim you purchased a sandwich to eat later, yet we found no sandwich or wrapper or crumbs in your van after you were stopped at Knutsford service station, only thirty miles away, and there was no sign of this takeaway bag. What happened to them?'

'I ate the sandwich and the bag blew out when I lowered the window.'

'Why did you lower the window.'

'I farted, okay?'

'Then this isn't the bag?' Natalie produced an evidence bag containing a folded paper bag and laid it on the desk in front of him.

'For the recorder, DI Ward is showing DS Briggs evidence bag IJ68,' said Lucy.

'Before you say anything, John, that bag was found in a waste bin at Keele services and has your fingerprints on it, and furthermore, it contained something else.'

She removed a plastic evidence bag from under her folder and pushed it across the table.

Lucy once again spoke up. 'For the recorder, DI Ward is showing DS Briggs evidence bag IJ69.'

'That, John, is a baseball cap. The very same cap that the person who followed Isabella Sharpe and Erin and Ivy Westmore into Samford library was wearing. I'm sure it'll test positive for your DNA.'

John turned his head this way and that. Silence hung in the room. Natalie's cool gaze remained on John's face.

'John Briggs, you have the right to remain silent—' she began.

'I know. I know. But where, DI Ward, is your daughter and her friend, Zoe?' He leant across the table, a cruel smile on his lips.

Natalie's heart jumped in her chest but her face remained immobile. 'We'll find them,' she said.

'I don't think so, not without my help, and that will only come if certain conditions are met.'

Natalie maintained her stare. 'Where's my daughter, you fucker?'

CHAPTER FORTY-SEVEN

SATURDAY, 18 AUGUST – MORNING

By mid-morning Natalie was desperate to find her daughter. The telephone companies confirmed that neither Zoe nor Leigh had received calls from the pay-as-you-go number that make-believe publicist Tom had used to ring Kerry Sharpe and the Westmore twins. The technical team could find no email correspondence to prove that Tom had contacted the girls and yet Natalie still believed John had taken them. Cross-examining John had only served to turn him hostile again, and he flatly refused to tell her anything. However, they continued to amass evidence against him. Herbert Wilson, who worked at the Trove recycling facility, remembered him and even recalled some of what had been in the van, including the laptop, a disco ball and a large cardboard cut-out of a pop star – the front man of boy band Blasted, Callum Vincetti. The Nissan Micra that John had hired had been caught on camera close to Blithbury Marsh at 11.57 Saturday night, the night the Westmore twins had been murdered. John wouldn't be able to talk his way out of this. They were edging closer to a conviction.

The girls were now the centre of her attention. The team and Mike, who'd joined them, examined the printout of the route John had taken. Natalie ran through what was happening.

'MisPers are concentrating on two main areas: the Methodist church hall and Keele services, the two places where the van stopped for some time. They've canvassed the streets between the cinema, where both girls were last seen, and the hall. Leigh's phone last transmitted a signal from that location at 1.34 p.m. yesterday. Zoe's transmitted minutes later at 1.40 p.m. It's logical to assume the hall was the location where John met and presumably abducted the girls.'

Mike examined the red line indicating the route the van had travelled. 'Why didn't he take the main road out of Samford to the motorway? It's by far the most direct route,' he said.

'Presumably because he wanted to avoid being caught on surveillance cameras,' said Lucy.

'Makes no sense. The motorway has ANPR cameras along it. He knows that so he wasn't bothered about the van being spotted. Also, he thought he was safe, that we had no idea what he was driving or where he was. He's shown himself to be really confident throughout. He wouldn't take this route to avoid cameras. He took it for a different reason.'

Natalie's head shot up. Mike was right. John had no way of knowing they were on to him at that point. Even during questioning, he'd been supremely confident he'd got away with it all – that was until they'd revealed the laptop and then he'd clammed up altogether.

'But the van didn't stop,' said Lucy again. 'He can't have thrown the girls out while driving.'

Ian held up a finger. 'No… Mike's right. The tracker stops when the vehicle stops and the engine is switched off. It resumes when the vehicle is restarted. What if John pulled over somewhere but left the engine running?'

'That's possible,' said Mike, looking at Natalie. 'We need to check along this route.'

'Right, Lucy, you and Ian get onto this and identify locations where you think John might have stopped for a few minutes. I'm going to the church hall and then to drive the actual route. Update me as soon as you come up with something.'

'I'll come with you,' said Mike. Natalie didn't stop him. She needed the moral support.

'You do realise John could just be messing with your head,' said Mike in the car.

'He knew Zoe's name. How could he have known that unless he was behind their disappearance? I've never mentioned her name to him.'

'He might have stalked them both and found it out. Who knows what's going on in his mind?'

'You're trying to protect me from feelings of anxiety but you can't. I'm freaking out here. That bastard knows where they are. This is a repeat of the Blossom Twins. Avril and Faye Moore were abducted, and had we not gone after the wrong person, they would be alive today. He's taken Leigh and Zoe somewhere and I'm going to find them. The sole crumb of comfort I have is that while he's in custody, he can't harm them.' She didn't dare acknowledge the voice that whispered it was possibly too late.

They drew into the car park next to the church hall behind a forensic van. Officers were still meticulously searching the grounds, front and back. Mike called out to one of them but received a shake of the head. Nothing had been found as yet.

'John met them here,' she said flatly.

'You can't be sure. Leigh's prudent. She wouldn't meet up with someone she didn't know,' Mike argued.

Natalie turned on him, two fire spots on her cheeks. 'Why are you suddenly determined to convince me John didn't take the girls? What the fuck's wrong with you?'

'Because I can't bear to see you so upset,' he replied. 'It's killing me to see you this way and I'm scared that he did take them.' His forehead creased heavily as he spoke and she could see he was as terrified as she was.

She backed down. 'Sorry. I shouldn't have snapped at you. Maybe John told Leigh he worked with me or knew me, or something to make her drop her guard. I don't know, Mike. I can't think straight any more.'

A cry went up and she darted forwards, ahead of Mike. One of the search party had uncovered something in the grass.

'What is it?' she asked.

'Looks like false eyelashes, ma'am.' He placed it in her gloved hand.

She examined the object and noted small sparkles on the stickiest part where it attached to the eyelid, then she lifted her head up to the sky, focusing on the white clouds above her to prevent her eyes from tearing up. She passed the object to Mike and dialled Graham's number.

'Any news?' he said.

She cleared her throat. 'Rowena gave you a description of what Zoe was wearing, didn't she?'

'That's right.'

'She also mentioned Zoe was wearing gold eyeshadow and false eyelashes.'

'That's correct.'

'I think we've found one of them, here by the Methodist church hall.'

'They were there then?'

'Yes. We're going to follow a route that John took from here to the motorway. We suspect he might have stopped along the way and left the girls somewhere. My team's working on possible locations and I'll have them sent to your phone. Could you arrange for officers to check them?'

'You know I will.'

'I have to go. I have an incoming call.'

The call was from Lucy. 'It was proving an impossible task so we contacted the tracking company again and they've managed to give us information that shows when the car was idling and immobile for several minutes. John stopped at three places: the first is at Wood End, only half a mile from Samford; the second is a small nature reserve, Hopton Mill; and the third is a large layby viewpoint. There's a café there called The View.'

'Good work. He must have left the girls at one of those places. Pass on this information to Graham Kilburn immediately and request he send teams to all three locations. Mike and I will head to Wood End. You and Ian split up and take one of the other spots each.'

'Roger that.'

She relayed the latest information to Mike.

'What are we waiting for? Let's go,' he said, racing off to the car.

Wood End was a fifty-five-acre area of mature woodland that had once been part of a much larger forest, owned by a king Natalie couldn't name and wasn't interested in. Most of the original ancient forest had been removed and replaced by dairy farms and now only this wood remained.

It was almost impossible to know where to start in such a vast area, so they stood on the first of several public footpaths, surfaced with gypsum and easy to navigate, and took in the sight before them.

'They could definitely be lost somewhere in here,' said Natalie, aware she sounded naive. The girls could equally be injured or worse. She breathed deeply to control the palpitations and a waft of wild garlic rose in the warm air. She made herself believe that John hadn't hurt the girls yet. He'd abducted them and she had to find them. Sirens approached, their wails increasing as they climbed the twisting route. More officers were arriving. Graham had been quick to act. A sense of comfort wrapped itself around her heart; her colleagues were here to help her find her daughter.

Mike was searching for any sign that somebody had been dragged against their will into the woods.

'If the van was idling, he wouldn't have had long to deposit them. If they were unconscious,' he said, choosing his words carefully, 'he'd have placed them somewhere near the entrance, so we need to concentrate on that first.'

The first of the search teams appeared and Mike instructed them. All the while, Natalie remained stock-still, willing her daughter and Zoe to appear.

Over an hour later, the dog teams and search parties still had uncovered nothing. Both Natalie and Mike had assisted in the hunt but there was nothing to indicate either of the girls had been dropped off at the woods. It was cooler under the heavy canopy of trees than outside on the road, but even so, both were uncomfortably warm. Natalie was beginning to wish she'd brought some water with her when her phone rang. Lucy had been joined by Graham and was at the viewpoint.

'Nobody at the café has seen the girls. Graham is here with his team and they're searching the area.'

'Are there any obvious places where the girls could have been hidden?'

There was a brief pause. 'The café overlooks Forthington.' Forthington was a village famous for its hillside cemetery, known locally as 'New Cem', which had opened in 1854 after a cholera epidemic had seen the original one fill up. Avril and Faye Moore had been found in a cemetery. Natalie's throat closed. He wouldn't. He couldn't. She caught Mike's eye and began jogging back to the car, him racing after her.

'Are you checking the cemetery?' she asked, although the words almost choked her.

Lucy began to answer but stopped, and Natalie heard background cries.

She drew to a halt by the car. 'Lucy, what's going on? Have you found them?'

'Hang on, Natalie. I'll ring you back.'

She couldn't wait that long. They had to get there quickly. She jumped into the driver's seat and spoke to Mike as they pulled away. 'Graham's found the girls.'

'How do you know?'

'A gut feeling. Lucy was talking to me and I could hear shouting.'

'It might be nothing to do with the girls.'

'No. It's them. John Briggs has been devious from start to finish. He's woven a web of deceit that almost resulted in him getting away. Lucy's at the café that overlooks Forthington cemetery.' She glanced at Mike before speaking again. 'We found Avril and Faye Moore in a cemetery.' He made no reply.

They drove at breakneck speed, hugging the road and rounding the bends to a local beauty spot that overlooked fields and woods that surrounded Samford. In springtime the scent of rapeseed filled the hillside with its rich perfume. The rapeseed had gone, as had the hawthorn blossom that covered the hedgerows between the fields. Now everywhere was green – not one single shade of green, but a hundred different hues that chequered the land. They flashed past them, blurring them into one indistinct colour. Leaving behind the sprawling town, they raced onwards to the café that overlooked Forthington with its hillside cemetery.

Several police vehicles were in the café car park. She drew in parallel to another squad car and jumped out, hunting immediately for Lucy. She couldn't see her but she spotted Graham and the world shifted. He didn't hasten towards Natalie. His head was lowered as if it weighed too much and he plodded towards her, slowly, so slowly, dragging his feet. She realised it wasn't him; it was time. Time was slowing down, like a battery running out of energy, and even the rhythm of her own heart was decreasing, coming gradually to a halt. She tried to walk but couldn't move. Somebody spoke her name, but the noise was distorted, the vowels elongated and eerie. She made out figures squatting on their haunches next to a tarpaulin and she understood. She burst from the dreamlike existence and, screaming Leigh's name, broke free of Mike's hand on her arm. She pushed past Graham and ran and slipped and slid towards the gathered officers. Lucy was among them. She made for Natalie to prevent her from getting any closer.

'Get out of my way! That's a fucking order!' Natalie screamed.

Lucy backed away, her eyes wide and filled with horror. Natalie regained her composure and walked towards the remaining two officers who'd stood to attention on her arrival and now took a step back.

Mike caught up with her and grabbed her arm again. 'No, Natalie, don't.'

'I have to know,' she said.

He released her arm but grabbed her hand and entwined his fingers through hers. 'I'm sticking with you,' he said.

She didn't truly register his words and took the three steps required to see the girls. They'd been positioned facing each other. Transparent plastic bags had been placed over both their heads and they lay immobile, their arms outstretched, hand in hand. Zoe was in a yellow playsuit and her coral toes peeped out of sandals, dirtied by earth and dust. Handfuls of daisies had been strewn over their bodies.

She choked on her own cry. 'No!'

Graham was by her other side. 'I'm so sorry, Natalie.'

Her body anaesthetised her against the shock so although she was fully aware her daughter was dead, she couldn't accept it. Mike held her fingers tightly in his. Her daughter, in her pretty new top that complemented her beautiful complexion, and white shorts that set off her legs, tanned from her holiday with her grandfather. She couldn't be…

'Natalie. You need to move away. We have to let Forensics take over.' Mike's voice was gentle. He tugged again at her hand. She allowed herself to be guided away, away from her daughter, and in spite of the trauma and the knife boring its way into her heart, she didn't cry. She held it together until they reached his car then her legs gave way and she collapsed into a heap, unable to focus on anything other than the fact her beautiful daughter was gone forever, and it was all her fault.

CHAPTER FORTY-EIGHT

Natalie marched into headquarters, back straight, eyes forward. As far as she was concerned, she still had a job to do. The desk sergeants stood up as one, solemn-faced, with their arms crossed in front of them as a mark of respect for her loss.

'So sorry, ma'am,' she heard. She acknowledged them with a small tilt of her head.

Ahead of her in the corridor, officers drew to a halt, unsure of what to say. She stared ahead, aware of the concerned expressions, and took the stairs steadily, one at a time. Her movements exemplified her mental state and her future – one short step at a time. It would be the only way she would be able to cope with the agonising pain that filled her body, her head, her heart. At the top of the stairs, she turned right as always, passing the glass-fronted offices, ignoring heads turning as she passed by. She focused on the multicoloured settee in front of her own office. DS Murray Anderson always joked that nobody sat on it. It was true – in all the time she'd been here, she'd only seen two people sit there: one was Mike and the other, more recently, had been Dan. The office door was open and she walked into silence. Lucy's eyes were damp as she walked towards Natalie and flung her arms around her.

Natalie stiffened at the genuine gesture. She was drained, unable to respond to kindness or love because she'd run out of emotion.

The last few hours had been unmitigated torture like nothing she'd ever experienced before, culminating in the total destruction of everything she'd held dear to her. David had ensured there was nothing left in her shattered world – no pieces to be collected and stuck together, nothing to cling onto.

Josh races from the room, unable to share his feelings with his parents. His face is a mixture of shock and sorrow and sobs rack his body.

Natalie can hardly breathe but she makes after him only to be halted by David, whose voice drips poison.

'Leave him!'

'But he needs me.'

'No, he doesn't. He doesn't need you and neither do I. We needed you but you chose to leave us. We all needed you but you weren't around for us.'

She is aghast. 'I was. You know I was. Admittedly not all the time, but somebody had to—'

He interrupts her with, 'Work. Somebody had to work. Yes, I know. I've had it rammed down my throat ever since I made the mistake of gambling our savings. You never let me forget and you treated me with disdain afterwards. I probably deserved it but the children didn't and they needed you. The truth is that you really went to work because you loved your job more than being around here, around me and all this reality. You took on extra shifts not so much because we needed extra cash but because you wanted to, so you could be at work – closer to Mike.'

'That's not true! I only took them on because we had bills to pay. Mike wasn't the reason.'

He silences her with a look. 'We needed you here. Leigh needed you, especially after what happened earlier this year. Running away was her attempt to get us to fix things between us, but you didn't try.'

Tears tumble as she speaks. 'I did try.'

'Not hard enough!' he bellows. 'This is on your shoulders, Natalie. This is all your fault.'

She starts to speak but again he stops her, this time by raising his hand in the air. 'You wanted to leave, so go on. You've got the keys to your new life. Get out now before I kick you out of the door myself.'

'You're upset…'

'Too true I'm upset. Our daughter is dead and it's because some fucking crackpot had it in for you but chose instead to murder our daughter. I can't look at you. I can't be with you. Just go.'

'What about Josh?'

'I'll look after him.'

'David—'

'We're done. Get out.' He turns his back to her and stumbles out of the room.

Lucy moved away and wiped her eyes. Natalie managed a weak, 'Thank you.'

Ian ran a finger around the collar of his shirt and said, 'I don't know what to say, Natalie.'

'Best if we keep it as it was before. Focus on making sure there is so much evidence against this bastard that he has no loophole, no leg to stand on, and pays for what he's done. Have there been any more developments?' Each word is spoken calmly and numbed by pain. She is able to function as she hoped. The powers that be had tried removing her completely from the case, but she'd stood her ground. She'd explained why she had to see this through. She needed to know the truth. Her sanity depended on it.

Lucy spoke again. 'The team at Keele services discovered a used bottle of bleach and cleaning cloths in the bin in the men's toilet. The bottle had been wiped down, but hastily, and there are partial fingerprints matching John's.'

'He cleaned the van out while he was at Keele.' It was more of a statement than a question.

'It appears that way. We also found the girls' mobile phones wrapped in newspaper in there.'

Natalie couldn't speak for a minute. Her daughter's phone. A part of her burned to see it and hold it – to be close to her child again – but she buried the urge, focused on why she was here. There'd be time enough to crumble.

'The SIM cards had been removed and we haven't found them yet but the technical team found images on both phones proving the girls were standing next to the van only a short time before the phones were disabled,' Ian said.

'And there's this. I think it goes some way to explaining things.' Lucy picked up a plastic wallet in which was a grainy black-and-white photograph – a scan of two unborn babies, facing each other as if holding hands.

Natalie turned over the photograph and read the back: Rose and Lily Briggs. Without a word, she handed it back then noticed both Lucy and Ian look up at someone who had come into the room behind her. She turned to face Dan Tasker, his shoulders slumped, eyes full of sorrow.

'I want to express my sincerest regret and sympathy.'

She could only offer small thanks that she didn't mean.

'Are you sure you want to do this?' he asked.

'Never been more certain about anything.'

'He's been under interrogation for the last two hours and he's cracking. The prospect of what he will probably endure in prison is finally hitting home. He's confessed to most of it, including trying to steer the investigation towards Eddie Ford. We found the fake beard and wig. He certainly went to town on that part of his plan and admitted he even spoke in a Scottish accent to help cover his tracks.' He shook his head in disbelief. 'The barefaced cheek of the man. He even drew that damn drawing in Shaun's diary to point the finger of blame at the man.'

'Did you locate the Westmore twins' mobile phones?'

'We've only retrieved one at the moment. John admitted he threw both mobiles into the water at Blithbury Marsh.'

'What about the Blasted photo competition?'

'He devised the whole contest to get contact details from teenage girls.'

'Has he said why he chose sisters or twins to be his victims?'

'No. He's kept quiet about that.'

'Shall we do this now?' Her voice was quiet but determined.

Dan looked into her eyes one more time. 'I am truly, truly sorry.'

'I'm ready to talk to him,' she replied.

Leaving Lucy and Ian behind, she walked back down the corridor, Dan by her side. 'Has he admitted to any involvement with the Blossom Twins murders?' she asked.

'He categorically denies murdering them and is in no doubt that the right person was brought to justice during that investigation. Neil Hoskins might have denied it later, but John believes Neil killed them. If Neil retracted his statement, it was most likely because of what he was enduring in prison at the time. I've spoken to the prison governor and it appears he was getting a very hard time from fellow prisoners – especially those who had children – so much so they had to put him in solitary for his own protection.'

'With all due respect, sir, I think you're wrong. John Briggs killed all the girls. You need to reopen that investigation.'

'What makes you say that? Briggs was most likely copying Hoskins' MO.'

'The baby scan photo of his children. All the girls killed were positioned the same way... to emulate his own children in that photo. And then their names – Rose and Lily – both names of flowers. It goes some way to explaining why the killer left blossom or petals on every dead girl's body – it was a link to his own dead children. John Briggs is responsible for all the deaths, those in Manchester in 2014 and those here in Samford.'

They reached the interview room and he placed a hand on her shoulder. 'I'd do anything to turn back the clock and change the outcome of this investigation.'

'So would I, sir. So would I.' She opened the door and marched in, stony-faced.

John sat hunched in his chair, his left eye swollen and closed, his upper lip cut.

'What happened to him?' she asked Dan.

'He tripped and fell. Didn't you, John?'

'Yes, sir. That's exactly what happened.'

She didn't pursue it. Somebody at the station had decided to dole out their own private form of justice. John Briggs had suddenly become a hated man. She pulled out a chair and sat down, the superintendent next to her. The recorder was set up and they followed the usual procedure of introductions. She sat up straight, taking in every detail of the broken man opposite her, the copper turned bad.

'Why did you choose my daughter?'

He shuffled his feet and stared down at the desk.

Dan spoke up. 'Tell DI Ward why you chose her daughter.'

'It was bad luck.'

'Bad luck?' said Dan.

'I didn't go hunting for her especially, if that's what you mean. She came to me. I was at the shopping centre searching for potential victims. and she turned up with her friend. It was coincidence she happened to be there that day.'

Natalie couldn't remember Leigh ever mentioning the shopping centre. Had she been there that Saturday in May? A small voice in her head reminded her she'd been involved in an investigation that weekend in May and would have had no idea what her daughter had been up to that day. David would have been looking after the children as he normally did when she was working.

'Why did you choose them? They weren't sisters or related in any way.'

'Zoe was keen to get her picture taken and so was—'

'Don't say her name. Don't you dare speak her name,' Natalie hissed.

'They couldn't wait to sign up.'

'How many other girls handed over their details to you?'

'Twenty-four.'

'Were they all sisters?'

'Yes.'

'So out of twenty-six girls you picked the only two who weren't related in any way.'

'Yes.'

'Why did you choose them?'

'Why do you think?' His eyes glittered coldly.

Seeing the look of horror on Natalie's face, Dan intervened. 'You know you're going to be in for a very uncomfortable stay in prison. Look what happened to Neil Hoskins. It was so unbearable he took his own life. He didn't commit suicide because he felt guilty. It was because he was terrified of what the other inmates would do to him in there. You have all that to come. Even coldhearted killers hate bastards like you who murder children. They'll make you pay.'

John's face scrunched up as if in pain but he didn't respond.

Natalie recovered some of her composure and spoke again. 'Who did you first contact? Was it my daughter, or her friend, or both of them?'

'I only ever spoke to Zoe. I didn't have a phone number for your daughter.'

'Didn't they both fill in one of your questionnaires? I thought all the girls did that.'

'Your daughter only wrote down her first name. Actually, she didn't write much about herself. She provided limited information – hobbies, music and films she liked – but Zoe was far less cautious and mentioned her best friend by name on the questionnaire.'

'I'll ask you again, why did you change your MO and choose to kidnap and murder girls who weren't related?'

'I felt like it. I didn't want to be predictable.'

'That's bullshit and you know it,' said Natalie. 'It was important for you to kill sisters or twins. It all links to Rose and Lily, doesn't it?'

His lips curled back like a wild animal's but Natalie continued.

'You were on some warped crusade to avenge the deaths of your daughters, weren't you?'

He refused to speak.

'We know, John. We know about Rose and Lily and even about Mikayla.'

'Fuck you,' he replied, teeth gritted.

'You knew she was *my* daughter, didn't you?'

He didn't respond.

'Tell me.'

Dan smashed his fist on the table and shouted, 'Answer her, you scumbag!'

'Of course I knew.'

'You killed her to get at me, didn't you?'

He looked her in the eye. 'It was meant to be.'

'No, it wasn't! You made it happen. You didn't have to kill them.'

'Oh yes, I did. Fate sent them my way. I dispatched them as I was meant to. End of.'

'Why? Because you hated me? Because you were angry that I got promotion and you didn't? Why?'

He shrugged a reply. 'Because I could.'

Natalie attempted to control her body, which seemed to be vibrating from within. John had deliberately selected Zoe and Leigh over all the other girls who had given him their details at Samford

Shopping Centre. She might never know if it was due to some deep-seated jealousy, or some other warped reason. All she knew was that it was her fault the girls had been murdered and that was something Natalie wasn't sure she could live with.

She stood up. Dan did likewise. She looked at John's closed bruised eye and bleeding lip, and before she walked out of the room she said, 'I hope you get everything you deserve and more when you're banged up inside. I hope they tear you apart.'

EPILOGUE

Cards of condolence were scattered on the kitchen window sill and every surface but she couldn't draw any comfort from the heartfelt messages contained in them.

John Briggs had confessed to all the murders, including those of Avril and Faye Moore and the two victims, Sharon and Karen Hill, before them. He was responsible for the deaths of nine girls in total. He'd claimed diminished responsibility, brought about by personal tragedy and exacerbated by a drug abuse problem. He was to be assessed by a clinical psychiatrist. She didn't care what happened to him. She couldn't waste any more mental energy on a man who deserved no more of her time. His cruel act had cost her dearly. Her life would never be the same again.

She ran fingers over her mobile screen, rubbing at it and wondering if she should message Josh again. He had responded to her last text, which gave her hope. Maybe he didn't consider her responsible in the same way David did.

She cast about her alien surroundings and fought back the rising anxiety. She'd been through bad times before. She would make it. She still had a job and a team who respected her but she needed time to heal, to repair the damage to her soul.

She stared at the ornament standing on the table: a silver circle frame engraved with Leigh's name, from which dangled a silver heart, inset with a large crystal. It was simple and tasteful and from Mike, and the card that accompanied it simply read, 'Remember, you are not alone.'

She caressed the shining silver heart and traced her daughter's name with her forefinger while silent tears fell onto the table.

A LETTER FROM CAROL

Hello, dear reader,

Thank you for buying and reading *The Blossom Twins*. I very much hope you enjoyed reading it. If you'd like to keep up to date with all my latest releases, just sign up at the following link. Your email address will never be shared and you can unsubscribe at any time.

www.bookouture.com/carol-wyer

This was a tough book to write. It gave me sleepless nights and caused a great deal of sorrow. I found myself on an emotional roller coaster at times and truly feeling for all the characters and sharing their heartache. Over the series, the characters have become very real to me, and to lose one has been hard – really hard. However, this is also a book I have truly loved writing and is one I hold very dear.

What's next for Natalie? Well, her life is going to be very different, but I think both you and I know she is made of stern stuff.

If you enjoyed reading *The Blossom Twins*, please take a few minutes to write a review, no matter how brief. I would truly be most grateful.

I hope you'll join me for the next book in the DI Natalie Ward series, which will be out in March 2020.

Thank you,
Carol

💻 www.carolwyer.co.uk

f AuthorCarolEWyer

🐦 @carolewyer

ACKNOWLEDGEMENTS

Once more I find myself indebted to many people who have made this novel possible. I'd like to start by thanking all of my readers, my street team and all the book bloggers and reviewers. Without all of you, my books would remain under the radar, and without your messages, emails and interaction on social media, I would find writing far less enjoyable.

Book bloggers spend huge amounts of time reading and reviewing, and generously share their recommendations on social media for no reward. I am fortunate to know many of them, and although there are far too many to mention individually, I want to thank them all most sincerely.

Thank you to everyone at Bookouture who helped bring *The Blossom Twins* to publication. There is a dedicated editorial team behind the book, including the eagle-eyed copy editor, DeAndra Lupu, who homes in on every error and also leaves me encouraging comments. I really don't know how they manage to juggle their schedules and make it all work so effortlessly, but they do.

Massive thanks to the marketing team and the dynamic duo Kim Nash and Noelle Holten, who I believe actually manage to survive on even less sleep than I do.

And last but definitely not least, huge thanks go to my editor, Lydia Vassar-Smith, who keeps me on track and who is an incredible support.